LUANNE RICE

THE NEW YORK *TIMES* BESTSELLING AUTHOR OF
DANCE WITH ME

Summer friendships never end....

BEACH GIRLS

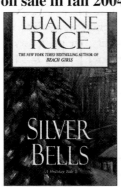

"If you're into stories that explore human emotions, that delve into different psyches and extol those who manage to triumph over some of life's tragedies, then you'll enjoy *The Perfect Summer*." —*Detroit News & Free Press*

THE SECRET HOUR

"Familiar Rice themes of sisterhood, loss and the healing power of love are spotlighted, but Rice's interest in the human psyche has its dark side as well. . . . The shore scenes, including a cinematic climax . . . [are] among the novel's strongest. Rice's heartfelt personal tone and the novel's cunningly deranged villain make this a smooth-flowing and fast-paced effort, with justice served all around at the satisfying . . . conclusion." —*Publishers Weekly*

"Salt-of-the-earth characters form the life-breathing force in this emotionally charged novel. . . . Suspenseful . . . possibly Rice's best work to date." —*Romantic Times*

"Rice's lyrical style humanizes the dilemma of justice by the book versus justice for victims." —*Booklist*

"Luanne Rice is one of the most mesmerizing storytellers. Her books are always deeply emotional, [with] wonderful characters." —*Somerset (PA) Daily American*

"A beautiful book . . . the reader is drawn in from the first word. It's a tense, driven, sometimes harsh and sometimes very gentle love story." —*Old Book Barn Gazette*

"Engrossing . . . captures the reader from the first page. Heartbreaking drama and chilling suspense combine to create an engaging novel of family and new beginnings. Ms. Rice captivates the reader with her detailed and evocative narrative and the multilayered facets of her characters. Beautifully written . . . highly recommended."
—America Online Romance Fiction Forum

"Intense and emotional, *The Secret Hour* has everything [readers] have come to expect and enjoy in novels by Luanne Rice . . . infinitely appealing characters . . . a sense of family that is rich and satisfying. Beyond these familiar elements is the underlying current of the unsolved mystery—the suspense is spine-tingling and well developed. This added dimension in *The Secret Hour* elevates the novel to more than just a deep, meaningful novel of family relationships, and makes it one of Ms. Rice's best yet—A Perfect Ten."
—*Romance Reviews Today*

TRUE BLUE

"With its graceful prose, full-bodied characters and atmospheric setting, this uplifting and enchanting tale is likely to become a beachside staple." —*Publishers Weekly*

"Rice, as always, provides her readers with a delightful love story filled with the subtle nuances of the human heart."
—*Booklist*

SAFE HARBOR

"Luanne Rice has a talent for navigating the emotions that range through familial bonds, from love and respect to anger. . . . A beautiful blend of love and humor, with a little bit of magic thrown in, *Safe Harbor* is Rice's best work to date." —*Denver Post*

"Irresistible . . . fast-paced . . . moving . . . Through Rice's vivid storytelling, readers can almost smell the sea air. Rice has a gift for creating realistic characters, and the pages fly by as those characters explore the bonds of family while unraveling the mystery." —*Orlando Sentinel*

"Heartwarming and convincing . . . a meditation on the importance of family ties . . . buoyed by Rice's evocative prose and her ability to craft intelligent, three-dimensional characters." —*Publishers Weekly*

"Luanne Rice's exploration of the difficult emotional balance between professional success, personal fulfillment and family ties is pure gold. Evocative descriptions add interest to an already compelling tale. Equal parts romance, mystery, and character study . . . Readers beware: don't start this book at bedtime; you may not sleep at all!"
—*Library Journal*

"A story for romantics who have never forgotten their first love." —*Columbia (SC) State*

FIREFLY BEACH

"A beautifully textured summertime read."
—*Publishers Weekly* (starred review)

"Rice does a masterful job of telling this powerful story of love and reconciliation." —*Booklist*

"A story so real it will be deeply etched into the hearts of its readers . . . Rice once again delivers a wonderfully complex and full-bodied romance." —*Booklist*

"Highly readable . . . moving . . . a well-paced plot . . . Rice pulls off some clever surprises." —*Pittsburgh Post-Gazette*

FOLLOW THE STARS HOME

"Addictive . . . irresistible." —*People*

"Involving, moving . . . stays with the reader long after the last page is turned." —*Denver Post*

"Uplifting . . . The novel's theme—love's miraculous ability to heal—has the ingredients to warm readers' hearts."
—*Publishers Weekly*

"A moving romance that also illuminates the tangled resentments, ties and allegiances of family life . . . Rice spins a web of three families intertwined by affection and conflict. . . . [She] is a gifted storyteller with a keen sense of both the possibilities and contingencies of life."
—*Brunswick (ME) Times Record*

"Powerhouse author Luanne Rice returns with a novel guaranteed to wrench your emotional heartstrings. Deeply moving and rich with emotion, *Follow the Stars Home* is another of Ms. Rice's classics." —*Romantic Times*

CLOUD NINE

"A tightly paced story that is hard to put down . . . Rice's message remains a powerful one: the strength of precious family ties can ultimately set things right."
—*Publishers Weekly*

"Eloquent . . . A moving and complete tale of the complicated phenomenon we call family." —*People*

More Critical Acclaim for LUANNE RICE

"What a lovely writer Luanne Rice is." —Dominick Dunne

"Ms. Rice shares Anne Tyler's ability to portray offbeat, fey characters winningly." —*Atlanta Journal-Constitution*

"Luanne Rice handles with marvelous insight and sensitivity the complex chemistry of a family that might be the one next door." —Eileen Goudge

"Miss Rice writes as naturally as she breathes."
—Brendan Gill

"Luanne Rice proves herself a nimble virtuoso."
—*Washington Post Book World*

"Rice has an elegant style, a sharp eye, and a real warmth. In her hands families, and their values . . . seem worth cherishing." —*San Francisco Chronicle*

"Rice's great strength is in creating realistic characters readers care about." —*Denver Post*

"Luanne Rice touches the deepest, most tender corners of the heart." —Tami Hoag, author of *Kill the Messenger*

"Pure gold." —*Library Journal*

Also by Luanne Rice

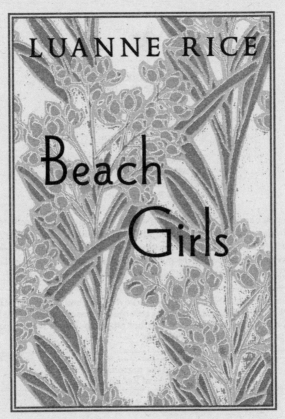

LUANNE RICE

Beach
Girls

BANTAM BOOKS

BEACH GIRLS
A Bantam Book / August 2004

Published by Bantam Dell
A Division of Random House, Inc.
New York, New York

Bantam Books and the rooster colophon are
registered trademarks of Random House, Inc.

ISBN 0-553-58724-2

Manufactured in the United States of America
Published simultaneously in Canada

OPM 10 9 8 7 6 5 4 3 2 1

To Rosemary Goettsche,
Maureen Onorato,
and Suzi Chapman,
with love

Acknowledgments

Sand castles and sea glass to Debbie Buell and Maggie Henry, Karen Covert, Laurette Laramie, Kathleen Stingle, Sue Detombeur, Susan Ravens, Marilyn Gittell, Amy and Molly Gittell-Gallagher, Andrea, Alex, and Jesse Cirillo, Meg Ruley and Alexandra Merrill-Lovett, Sam Whitney and my darling goddaughter, Sadie Whitney-Havlicak.

Love and thanks to Irwyn Applebaum, Nita Taublib, and Tracy Devine—for their encouragement and kindness, and for being such wonderful friends and publishers.

Many thanks to Mark Lonergan and Dore Dedrick for the music, and for introducing me to the real Tilly.

Deep gratitude to Sea Education Association (SEA) of Woods Hole, MA. Many years ago I spent a semester at sea aboard *R/V Westward*, a one-hundred foot staysail schooner. We sailed the Caribbean tracking humpback whales. Navigating by charts, instruments, and the stars, we learned to use sextants and shoot sun lines. We towed hydrophones to listen to and attempt to analyze whale songs; we studied with oceanographers and towed nets and took sediment samples. We spent Christmas on Silver Bank, and visited beaches on Grand Turk, St. Bart's, and Mona Island. Amy Gittell, my shipmate, became a lifelong friend. SEA nurtures students and their love of oceans; it is a wonderful organization.

I am very thankful to Karen, Joshua, and Elijah Stone; Jolaine Johnson; and Pam Paikin and Ed Barker for their friendship and support.

Mia O. and the BDG are great.

Love and beach memories to Bill, Peg, Lindsay, and Katie Decker; Carmen, Stacy, and Stephanie Decker; Rick and Courtney Decker; Laura, Kevin, Stephen, and Jenny Boyle; Rita Decker, Thomas Decker Sisco, and Michael Decker Sisco; Kathy, Michael, and Julie LeDonne; Kevin, Annette, and Christopher Brielmann; Jim and Kathie Brielmann; Tom and Renée Brielmann; Peter, Joanne, Kara, and Alex Brielmann; Harry Jr., Shirley Louise-May, Isabelle, Gabriel, and Rose Brielmann.

Just a few of the beach boys: William Twigg Crawford, Paul James, Gene Reid, Martin Ruf, Tom Murtha, David Ryder, Jeff Woods, Scott Phelps, and the memory of Dennis Shortell.

Beach Girls

Prologue

THE THREE FRIENDS HAD ARRANGED their towels all in a row, on the white sand down by the water's edge, under an azure sky. The beach was hot beneath their backs, but a fresh breeze blew off the Sound to keep them cool. Small waves licked closer, just beyond their feet. The tide was flooding in, and the girls knew they would have to move their towels to avoid getting wet—but this single minute on a late June morning of their sixteenth year was too perfect, too wonderful, to interrupt.

Stevie knew how quickly things could change; when she was very young, she had learned lessons of loss. A natural-born artist, she understood how impossible it was to grab onto a moment—something always happened. The wind shifted, or a shadow moved across the sun, or the light turned the water from dark blue to green. You glanced away, and by the time you looked back, everything could be different. The person you thought would be there forever had disappeared. Drawing was the only way she had discovered to hold on. . . .

Madeleine never had such thoughts. She was the younger sister of the most popular boy in school. Being swept along in his wake had made her feel always safe, always wanted, always part of whatever was going on. He protected her from things she never even thought about—till after it was too late to worry, till the danger or trouble had passed. Maddie savored the hot sun and blue sky, knowing that this was what summer was for— beaching it with her best friends. And when this day passed . . . there'd be another one right behind it.

Emma yawned and stretched, her legs extended, right foot arched as close as she could get to the water. She loved the feeling of the sea spray on her calves, getting more intense with each wave. Sunbathing could be so boring. Knowing the tide was coming up, surging closer with pure force, excited her. The sea was like a great lover—or what she hoped that would turn out to be. Whenever she wanted to dive in, the ocean embraced her. She loved how it was seductive, elusive, constantly changing . . . to Emma, change was like ecstasy—it let her know she was alive.

"So?" Emma asked, lying on her back with her eyes closed. Her friends didn't reply at first—if she didn't know better, she'd think she was alone on the beach.

"I don't want to move," Maddie said, lying between the other two. "This feels too delicious. The sun is perfect."

"Stevie—you're quiet over there," Emma said, calling across Maddie. "Are you ready to swim?"

"Only if we can hold hands," Stevie said. Emma hid a smile. Stevie loved being connected.

Maddie giggled. "People will think we're weird."

"We are—or maybe just I am," Stevie said.

Emma listened for her to laugh, but she didn't. Stevie's absence of laughter always made Emma feel sad, and she didn't like such emotions. Her parents didn't approve of them—they liked everything upbeat and attractive, and so did Emma. She did just about anything she could to avoid introspection, which seemed to be Stevie's lot in life; Emma had found several effective ways of blocking sad or upsetting things, and they involved either boys, shopping, or her best friends. She grabbed onto Maddie's hand and tugged.

They formed a chain—Emma, Madeleine, and Stevie. Holding hands, they faced the sparkling bay. The granite promontories of Hubbard's Point curved out into the Sound, protecting the white crescent beach from ocean waves. The cries of gulls carried from the rock island rookeries; Emma knew Stevie rowed out there at dawn to sketch the baby birds waiting for their mothers to come feed them.

The knowledge made Emma shiver, just slightly. She had been Stevie's best friend from babyhood. Maddie had come along later, but she had fit right in, completed their circle. Emma knew that, in their threesome, she was "the sassy one." Maddie was "the happy one." And Stevie was "the sensitive one."

What Stevie—and definitely Maddie—didn't know was that Emma would just about die for them. She was sassy, funny, bossy, pretty, boy-crazy—all the lighthearted things they loved to tease her about. Although she had created the circle ceremony to bond them together, they thought she was casual about it: that they were just summer friendships that Emma took for granted year after year. The truth was, Stevie and Madeleine were her sun, moon, and stars; who needed celestial navigation when she had the beach girls?

"I thought we were going into the water," Maddie said, tugging on her friends' hands.

"I wish, I wish . . ." Stevie said with her eyes squeezed tight.

Emma held her breath, waiting to hear what Stevie was going to say. Stevie saw the beach in such a different way than anyone else. She was so inspired by it—Emma loved the way she took the light, the breeze, the birdcalls, the stars, right into her being, and sent it all back out into the world, down on paper in her paintings and drawings.

Leaning forward to see around Maddie, Emma felt the waves come up around her ankles. She gazed upon the intensity of Stevie's face—so fine and chiseled, pale from the sunscreen she always wore, framed by sharp black bangs and bobbed hair—and she felt a pang deep inside.

"What, Stevie?" Maddie asked. "What do you wish?"

Emma felt her heart tug. She knew that Stevie was going to say something amazing, unexpected. She always did. She was so odd, the way she'd go rowing out to the bird islands before sunrise, or the way she'd go hiking into the marsh at night, listening for whippoorwills, or the way she would disappear for a whole day, and when Emma and Maddie—her fellow beach girls—would go knocking on her door, her father would tell them that she had gone to sketch the flowers on her mother's grave.

And then Stevie would come back, and she would tell a story about it. She was a true paradox—so solitary, but with intense need for connection with the people she loved most.

So she would tell—in such great detail Emma and Maddie would feel they were right there with her—about riding her bike past the salt-bleached cottages with bright, candy-colored shutters, to the little grave-yard in among the wind-shaped cedars and oaks; about the scarlet trumpet vine growing up the base of the angel overlooking the grave where her dear mother slept. . . .

How the red flowers attracted hummingbirds, tiny one-and-a-half-inch-long birds with emerald feathers, to be with her mother . . . and how Stevie loved the birds beyond all reason, for keeping her mother company.

Stevie would say things like that—just out of the blue! The tale would unfold, with Stevie's words as evocative as her paintings—almost like the beautifully illustrated children's books Emma had grown up loving. And Emma had told her, too. "You're going to be famous, Stevie. Don't forget me and Maddie, after you've written a bunch of books—okay?"

"Never," Stevie promised.

Emma loved Stevie for her talent, but she also felt . . . she hated to say it . . . envious. Because what would it be like—to see the world like that? To love nature and people in such a pure way that it would never occur to her to ask what they could do for her? Emma knew that Stevie was terribly vulnerable—things made her cry so easily.

Emma guessed that that was the trade-off—to be as creative and feel things the way Stevie did, she had to open her heart so wide, to let everything in. Sometimes Emma thought of Stevie as Snow White and herself as Rose Red ... and Madeleine as their nice, normal, happy friend with a really hot brother.

"What *do* you wish?" Emma asked now.

"Just," Stevie said, "that this moment could last forever."

Well—after all that, something so simple. Emma sighed with relief. She had expected Stevie to say something profound about birds and people, summer and love, best friends and life's journey. To her surprise, Madeleine was the one who got philosophical.

"It's the Bicentennial," Maddie said. "We're part of history."

"All I know is, we're sixteen and ready to be kissed, kissed, kissed," Emma said.

"The beach girls of 1976," Stevie said.

"Write a book about our summers," Maddie said. "We'll read it to our children, and it'll become a classic, and people will read it to their kids for the next two hundred years."

Emma shivered to hear that—she didn't like to think of Stevie writing books, becoming famous. It would make her feel second best.

"Come on—what are we waiting for?" Emma said, just to get them off the subject.

Holding hands, the three of them ran into the water, all at once, without stopping or flinching from the cold. They held tight, diving into the curling silver wave. When they came up for breath, they formed a circle—just like the one Emma had drawn in the sand. Their legs kicked underwater, buoying them up.

Once again, the sea had done its mystical work—washed away all unwanted feelings, made everything right again. Emma took the salt water into her mouth, spit it out. Feelings could come and go, but these were her best friends, and she loved them, and she would love them forever.

"What are we doing tonight?" Madeleine asked.

"Watching the moon rise," Stevie said.

"Going to the beach movie to see who's there," Emma said. "Watch out, boys . . ."

"Maybe we can do it all," Maddie said, laughing. "The moon *and* the movie."

"That's what I was thinking," Emma said, watching Stevie gaze up at the sky without replying. The waves beat against the curved beach. Last night's half moon was still there, a white shadow marring the perfect blue. Emma shivered and turned her back on the moon, just taking in the blazing blue sky arching overhead, embracing all the beaches and all the beach girls.

Summer had barely begun.

Part One

Part One

chapter 1

HER MOTHER'S BEST FRIEND LIVED IN A blue house, and that was all Nell Kilvert knew. So, from the minute she and her father had arrived at the beach for their summer vacation, Nell had kept her eyes peeled for a blue house. When she asked her father where it might be, he said that after so many years away, his only strong memory of Hubbard's Point was of falling in love with her mother on the boardwalk.

Beach girls now, beach girls tomorrow, beach girls till the end of time . . . Nell still remembered her mother's stories about Hubbard's Point, where she'd spent her childhood summers. She said that she and Aunt Madeleine and her best friend—what was her name?— were happiest with their feet in salt water. Her mother had said that no matter where they were, no matter where life took them, they would always be united by blue summer skies, high winds and sudden gales, and hot beach sand under their bare feet.

Hot beach sand . . .

Nell felt it now, scalding the soles of her tender feet. "Ouch, ouch," she said out loud.

A girl about nine—her age—looked up from her beach towel. "Stand here," she said, moving over so Nell could get some relief from the hot sand.

"Thanks," Nell said, standing on the very edge of the girl's towel.

"Do you live here?" the girl asked.

"We're renting a cottage," Nell said. "My father and I."

"That's good," the girl said. "What's your name?"

"Nell Kilvert. What's yours?"

"Peggy McCabe. I live here. Year-round."

"Oh," Nell said. She felt funny standing on the corner of the strange red-haired girl's towel, and thought how cool and fun it would be to live at the beach all year. Then, realizing that she had a Hubbard's Point expert on her hands, her eyes widened. "Do you know any blue houses?"

Peggy looked puzzled. "Well—that one," she said, pointing.

Nell looked over. Tall grass grew at the end of the beach, holding the sand in place so that no storm could ever wash it away. A big blue house nestled on the low dune—Nell had thought it had to be a beach club, but her father had told her it belonged to some lucky family. He had told her that it was built on pilings, to keep it above the highest tides, and that when they were young, he and her mother had gone underneath to kiss. *Did it belong to Mom's best friend?* Nell had asked, tingling. *No, we didn't know the owners*, her father had replied.

"A different blue house," Nell said to Peggy.

"Oh," Peggy said, getting a funny look on her face. "The witch's house."

"The witch?"

Peggy nodded, scooting over even farther on her striped towel, inviting Nell to sit down. She pointed across the crescent of white sand and sparkling bay to a house on the Point, hidden in lacy blue shadows of oak and fir trees. Nell peered, shielding her eyes from the sun with visor-hands. "That house looks white to me," she said.

"It is now," Peggy said. "But it used to be blue. When I was really little. I remember, because my sister Annie had a song about it:

> *Heart of stone, house of blue,*
> *If you come in my yard*
> *I'll make you a witch, too. . . ."*

Nell stared up at the house. She was skeptical: her mother's best friend couldn't be a witch. On the other hand, Nell had ruled out just about every other cottage at Hubbard's Point. She had ridden her bike up and down all the roads with her father. And she'd gone back to the only two blue cottages she'd found and asked the people if they remembered her mother, Emma Kilvert. Both times, the answer was no.

"Why do you call her a witch?" Nell asked.

"Because no one ever sees her," Peggy said. "She lives

in New York all winter, and when she's here, she stays in her yard till after dark. She talks to owls. She writes children's books about all different birds. One got made into a movie. People who don't know how weird she is come from outside the beach to look for her—but she doesn't even answer her door! And every morning, before the sun comes up, she walks along the tide line to look for shorebirds and her lost diamond ring."

"Her lost diamond ring?" Nell asked.

"Yes. She's a divorcée. She's been married lots of times. No kids, even though she writes kids' books. She collected the engagement rings, and wears them on all her fingers. But she lost the biggest one while she was swimming in a storm, and she has to find it. It's worth *thousands*. She puts spells on the men who cross her! And on kids who trespass in her yard. They read her books, and she chases them away. You should see the sign she has by her stairs. . . ."

Nell frowned, hugging her knees, making herself small. She didn't like the sound of this woman. Maybe it was a mistake to want to meet her. . . . But then she thought of her father and his new girlfriend, Francesca, and she thought of her mother's soft blue eyes, with the gentle sun lines around the outside corners, and of the way she used to talk about her best friend, and Nell felt a hole in her stomach.

Beach girls now, beach girls tomorrow, beach girls till the end of time . . .

Just thinking of the old saying made the shiver worse, and the hole bigger, and made Nell miss her mother so much she thought the sorrow might crush her right there on the beach. She stared up at the house on the hill, holding her knees tighter.

Could her mother's best friend be a book-writing witch? Nothing seemed impossible anymore. In fact, compared to other things that had happened during Nell's lifetime, that didn't even seem so weird or terrible. She thanked Peggy for the information, and then she set off to find a way up the hill to the House That Used to Be Blue.

THE HUBBARD'S POINT tennis courts had come a long way from when Jack Kilvert was a kid. Back then, they were cracked blacktop, a second thought to the beach and marsh, sloping into the sandy parking lot, underwater during big storms. Now they were green composite, neatly lined, rolled, and maintained—and people had to sign up to use them.

"Thirty-love!" Francesca called from across the net.

Jack concentrated as she prepared to serve. Her hair was honey brown, held back by a wide white band that set off her tan. Willow thin, except for the hourglass factor, she had legs that went on forever, and, in spite of his attempting to focus on the game, Jack was aware that she had stopped some traffic. Two men, smoking cigars and carrying beach chairs and floats, had stopped on their way down Phelps Road to watch her serve. Or stare at her legs.

She served, he returned, she jumped the net into his arms.

"You won, you bum," she said, kissing him on the lips.

"Doesn't that mean *I'm* supposed to jump the net?" he said.

"Don't get technical about everything. Maybe I was just in a big hurry to hold your big sweaty body—did you ever think of that?"

Jack laughed as she kissed him again. She felt thin and hard in his arms. He had a memory that bypassed his mind entirely, existing solely in his heart: of holding Emma twenty-five years ago, right in this same spot. Francesca was the spitting image of his wife as a young woman. Jack did the age math, and his head hurt.

"Come on, let's jump in the ocean," Francesca said.

"I want to go home and check on Nell."

"She told me she was going to the beach," Francesca said. "In fact, she saw me pull up in front of the house, and she met me before I even got out of the car. I think she wanted to go through my trunk, to make sure I hadn't brought an overnight bag. Honestly, she's like the border patrol."

"No, she was just welcoming you."

Francesca snorted through her pretty, perfect nose. "You are so not right about that. My parents were divorced, and when my father brought women home, I gave them hell. This is my payback—and believe me, I deserve it. Don't worry, though. I don't scare easy, and I totally respect her need to stake out her territory. I'll win her over—you'll see."

Jack didn't say anything, not wanting to give her the wrong idea about where things were going.

"Look . . . if she's at the beach, that means your house is empty," Francesca said, squeezing his hand. "I already know you have to be proper on the chance she'll walk in on us, but can we at least hold hands on the couch?"

"While going over our British North Sea plans . . ." Jack said. They both laughed, Jack pulling back his hand as they set off, thinking, *Real romantic, you jerk.* He was forty-eight, overwhelmed, overworked, and totally confused about life's twists and turns. She was twenty-nine, dangerously beautiful.

For the last six months, Jack had been in the Boston office of an Atlanta engineering firm. Francesca worked in his department now, and they had been colleagues for several years before that. They played mixed doubles together with people from work. He admired her serve, the precision of her mind, the excellence of her engineering skills, her great sense of humor.

Did she notice that he was keeping distance between them, not wanting people to think he was part of a couple? And just who would care? Who would even remember him? Emma had spent about fifteen childhood summers here, before her family had moved to Chicago. Jack's family had rented here for three years in a row; Emma was four years younger—his sister's age. He had met her on the boardwalk one clear July night, and their fates were sealed. This year, needing a place to take Nell on vacation, he had chosen Hubbard's Point over the Vineyard, Nantucket, the Cape, islands in

Maine . . . not so much because he wanted her to see the place where her parents had met, but because he'd been pulled here by forces he couldn't understand.

"If your daughter's not home," Francesca whispered, closing the gap as they walked, "I can't promise that I'll behave myself. . . ."

Jack felt the grin on his face, in the muscles around his mouth, but it didn't register anywhere else. He could show a smile, but he couldn't feel one. That had been the biggest curse of losing Emma. He was numb to the bone, as if winter had come to stay for the rest of his life. He was six foot three, had been an athlete since he could throw a ball, and he couldn't feel anything. Guys in his basketball league didn't know, his tennis partners had no clue, the women he dated wouldn't guess, his own sister, Madeleine, was in the dark.

Only Nell knew, and he hated that she did.

THE ROAD to the Point looped up from the beach, right past the tennis courts. Nell glanced over, just in time to see her father and Francesca kissing at the net, too busy to look up and witness her passing by. Seeing her father kiss Francesca was like a dagger in Nell's heart and made her in a greater rush to get to the House That Used to Be Blue. She began to trot, turning right at the top of the hill.

The shadows were soft and dark here on the Point. Nell slowed down, looking at all the houses, trying to figure where she was in relation to the beach. Her parents had talked about this place, but never brought her here. Their family lived in Atlanta and vacationed on the beautiful Georgia barrier islands.

Nell was used to southern white sand beaches and soft green grasses and warm water . . . nothing like this jagged coast, the chilly Long Island Sound. A craggy bay showed through the trees of the yards on the left. Some of the gardens were beautiful, overflowing with roses and lilies. A few had flagpoles. The breeze was blowing, and the flags stood out. Some of the flag houses had lovely window boxes cascading with petunias and ivy.

Suddenly, looking up the hill that rose to the right, Nell saw a different kind of yard. It was mostly rock, with patches of wild-looking grass filling in between bushes and trees. Lilies bloomed in the shade, scraps of yellow and orange, like birds hiding in the woods. Pine needles and oak leaves rustled overhead, and stonecrop thatched in the crevices of stone steps curving up the rocky hill. Nell's heart began to beat very hard when she saw the sign:

PLEASE GO AWAY

It was hand-lettered, white paint on gray driftwood, nailed to a stake and driven into the ground beside the steps. Nell raised her eyes from the sign to the house. It was painted white, but the white looked almost blue in the shade of two tall oak trees.

Nell looked back at the sign. Then at the house. She heard Peggy's words about the lady being a witch, and felt a tug-of-war inside. What if she was mean and scary and put a spell on her? The possibility gave Nell a cold shiver.

But some feelings are stronger than fear: love, longing, desire. She had a lump in her throat and couldn't shake it loose. Her feet began to walk up the hill, and then she started to run. Staring upward, she saw a face in the window. She felt afraid, but she couldn't stop now. Barefoot, she caught her toe on a rock in the yard, tumbled head over heels, skinned both her knees.

STEVIE MOORE had been at her kitchen table, watercolor brush poised as she stared out the window at hummingbirds darting in and out of the trumpet vine. Her seventeen-year-old cat, Tilly, sat on the table beside her, no less intent. Stevie wanted to capture the hummingbird's essence, which she thought was its amazing ability to be purely still yet in constant motion, all at the same time. Tilly just wanted to capture the hummingbird.

Stevie really didn't know how she would survive without Tilly. The cat had been Stevie's constant companion through everything. Tilly had gotten her through more lonely nights than she could ever count. Sighing with love for her cat, she saw the hummingbirds suddenly dart away. Looking toward the stairs, she saw a child running up the hill.

"Tilly, don't schools teach kids to read anymore?" Stevie asked, wondering whether maybe her nemeses, the young boys next door, had stolen her sign again.

The cat, spying the approaching stranger, sprang up

on top of the refrigerator to hide in a wicker bread basket. Stevie stood up. She brushed cat hair off her black T-shirt and slacks. This child seemed hell-bent on something, so Stevie grabbed her panama hat and put it on, preparing to look stern and imposing, a split second before she saw the child fall on the rocks.

Stevie ran outside. The girl was crumpled up on the ground, trying to pick herself up. Her knees and big toe were bleeding. Stevie hesitated for just a moment, just long enough for the girl to look up at her. Her green eyes were cavernous, flooded with pain, and the sight of them sent a current of unexpected, unfamiliar emotion through Stevie.

"Are you okay?" she asked, but before she could even crouch down, the girl nodded her head vigorously, and tears flew out of her eyes.

"It's you, it's you," the girl said, her voice thin and reedy.

"You're a reader," Stevie said, assuming the child had made a pilgrimage to meet the person who'd written *Owl Night* or *Summer of the Swans* or *Seahawk;* but just then, the girl looked past her and through her, as if she was seeing a ghost.

"My mother knew you," the girl said, in a southern accent.

"Your mother?"

"Emma Lincoln," the girl said. "That was her name before she married my father."

"Oh, my," Stevie said softly. The name came from the distant past. Memories swept in, clear and bright as sunshine, all the way back to earliest childhood, girls who had learned to swim together. "How is Emma?" she asked.

"She died," the girl said.

Oh, the sky changed color. It really did. It lost several shades of blue as the words sunk in. How could such a thing have happened, and Stevie not have known? A breeze moved the leaves overhead with a rush; Stevie stared into the little girl's eyes, and she swore she saw Emma right there.

Stevie reached out her hand, and the girl took it with a scraped, sweaty palm. "You'd better come inside," Stevie said. And they went into the house.

chapter 2

AFTER STEVIE CLEANED OFF THE GIRL'S hands and knees and gave her Band-Aids, she made tea, because that's what her mother would have done. She set out Blue Willow china cups and saucers, the sugar bowl with tiny brown sugar cubes, and a plate of lemon drop cookies. Then she and the girl—whose name was Nell—went to sit at the table in front of the stone fireplace.

"Your mother and I used to have tea parties right here," Stevie said.

"When your house was blue?" Nell asked.

"Yes."

The child's gaze was avid, taking everything in: the wicker chairs, faded green loveseat—arms and back clawed by Tilly and her sisters—bird illustrations from some of Stevie's books, her collections of feathers, shells, birds' nests, and bones. Stevie watched Nell's face and knew the child was wondering where her mother had sat, what objects her eyes had seen. Stevie had done the same at Nell's age, visiting places where her mother had once been.

The two sipped their tea for a while. Stevie wanted to find the right words, to comfort the child. She wanted to ask what had happened to Emma. But she felt constrained, afraid she would say something wrong. Her own mother had died when she was young, and she remembered a world of adults who meant well but just seemed to make everything worse.

Besides, Stevie was a hermit. She wrote and painted, mostly in silence. It hadn't always been that way; there had been much love, and men, and the men's children. But now it was her and Tilly, and for a long time, that had been enough. So, she held her teacup and waited for Nell to speak. It took a few minutes, during which time they listened to sounds of early summer coming through the open windows: small waves breaking on the beach, finches singing in the privet, a squirrel chattering in the hollow oak.

Nell finished her cookie, politely wiped her fingers and mouth on the pink linen napkin, and looked up. She was about nine, very thin, with shoulder-length brown hair held back from her face by flower barrettes, and enormous green eyes.

"My mother said you were her best friend."

"Oh, yes. We were best, best friends."

"With Madeleine?"

"Maddie Kilvert!" Stevie said, laughing. "Yes, the three of us were inseparable. Emma—your mother—and I knew each other first. Her family had a cottage here as long as my family—since we were very young.

But then Maddie came along . . . that's when we really got close. The three of us, for three summers . . ." As she said it, the words came flooding back: " 'Three summers, with the length of three long winters . . .' " Seeing Nell's expression of peace as she closed her eyes to listen, Stevie knew she had heard the words before. "Did your mother tell you we borrowed that line from Wordsworth?"

"From a famous poet, she told me. To describe how long the winters were without her best friends, the beach girls."

"Beach girls!" Stevie said, delighted as another great old memory tumbled out of cold storage. "That's what we called ourselves. Because we were always happiest with our tootsies in salt water . . . we could hardly stand the winters, apart from each other. Our phone bills were massive. I used to intercept the mail, before my father could see the bills I'd run up talking to Emma and Maddie. One month I had to sell my clothes!"

"What?"

"I did! I sold two brand-new sweaters and a pair of boots to the lady I babysat for, to give my father money to pay my share of the phone bill. Thank God there wasn't three-way calling back then, or it would have been total financial ruin."

"You all lived far apart from each other?"

Stevie nodded. "Well, it seemed that way at the time. During the winters I lived in New Britain, Maddie lived in Hartford, and your mom lived in New Haven. But then summer would finally get here, and we'd all be in our rightful place—right here, at Hubbard's Point."

"Aunt Maddie lives in Rhode Island now," Nell said.

"Your aunt . . ." Stevie paused, putting it together. "Your mother married Jack!"

Nell nodded. "You didn't know?"

Stevie held back a sigh. How to explain a crazy chiaroscuro life, all its layers and lapses and messiness and separations—the losing-touchness of it all—to this sweet nine-year-old child? "No," she said. "Once the beach girls got to college, we sort of went our separate ways. And lost touch with each other."

"Mom didn't lose touch with Aunt Maddie," Nell said. "They saw each other a lot, because she married Aunt Maddie's brother. Was he like the beach girls' brother? The 'beach boy'?"

Stevie laughed. "It didn't work that way, Nell. It was just us—we were closed to the rest of the world. Besides, he was four years older, which, back then, made him ancient. I do remember, though, the summer before we all went to college, your mother started going out with him."

"They fell in love here," Nell said.

Stevie nodded, although her face remained inscrutable. "Hubbard's Point has always been the place to fall in love."

"Dad said they used to kiss under the boardwalk, and at Little Beach, and behind that blue house." Nell pointed out the front window, at Stevens' Hideaway, the sprawling place at the end of the beach.

Stevie smiled, remembering several key kisses of her

own in that exact spot. But not wanting to burst the parents'-singular-romance bubble of a young girl, she kept them to herself.

"Blue houses," Nell said. "That's how I found you, you know. My mother always said you lived in a blue house."

"She didn't tell you my name?"

"I think she did," Nell said. "But Stevie is a boy's name. I guess I couldn't keep it straight. Why'd your parents call you that?"

"It reminded them of where I came from," Stevie said after a long moment, deciding that Emma's daughter didn't need to hear the story of how she was conceived in a hotel on St. Stephen's Green in Dublin.

"What made you paint your house not-blue?" Nell asked.

"Let me see your knees. . . ." Stevie said suddenly. "You really skinned them."

"They're fine," Nell said, staring. Her accent made *fine* come out "fahn."

"Where do you live now?" Stevie asked, happier when she was the one asking the questions.

"Atlanta's our real home, but my father transferred to the Boston office, so we're there temporarily. And he's taking the summer off, sort of. I mean, he's working, but he doesn't have to go to the office so much."

A silence rose, and Stevie felt Nell's steady gaze on her. It wasn't so bad. But then Stevie noticed Nell wasn't looking away, and she began to feel enclosed.

"The reason I painted my house," Stevie said, just so the child would stop staring, "was that it had always been blue. Always, from the time I was born. And I started to think . . . maybe if I changed my house color, I would change . . . some things I didn't like. About . . . life. Does that make any sense at all?"

Nell nodded gravely, and Stevie saw her gaze shift down, to Stevie's left hand.

"You're looking for the engagement rings," Stevie said. "I know. All the kids do."

"Did you lose them all in the water?"

Stevie tried to smile. "Just one," she said. "And I didn't lose it."

"Didn't lose it?"

"I threw it in," Stevie said.

"But you look for it every morning!"

Stevie shook her head. "No," she said. "I walk the beach every morning looking for sandpipers to draw. And because I like to swim before the sun comes up. And walk with my feet in the water."

"Your tootsies," Nell said with a grin.

Stevie nodded. The child's smile gave her a lump in her throat and sent a powerful sting right into her eyes.

"Why do you go down to the beach before the sun's all the way up?"

"Because there's no one else there," Stevie said. "I'm a hermit."

"Is that a special kind of witch?"

Stevie smiled. "Sort of," she said.

A quiet breeze blew, and in the distance a motorboat started up. Stevie saw Tilly slink into the room, making herself invisible. The old cat sat statue-still in the corner, beside a Gothic-style birdhouse, watching her mistress and the stranger.

"Well," Nell said, folding her napkin. "I'm very glad I met you."

"And I'm very glad I met you," Stevie said.

They stood up, facing each other. Stevie had many more questions she wanted to ask about Emma, about what had happened, but she remembered from her own experience the value of delicacy in such matters. Together they walked through the house, to the kitchen door. Tilly followed.

"Oh, a cat!" Nell said, spotting her. She made a move to pet Tilly and was met with a hiss and the whisk of a tail. "Oooh—sorry!"

"She's a bit crotchety," Stevie said. "She's old."

"I understand," Nell said. She gazed around the kitchen, noticing all the sketches and watercolors of birds, squirrels, rabbits, field mice. "Are those from your books?"

"Some from books I haven't written yet." Stevie paused. "Did your mom ever read my books to you?"

"No. I don't know why she didn't," Nell said, apologetically. "Your pictures are really nice."

"Thank you," Stevie said, wondering herself why her old friend hadn't shown her daughter her work. She opened the door to let Nell out, but suddenly the child turned with a fierce expression on her face.

"The reason we went to Boston is a lot like the reason you painted your house not-blue," Nell said.

"It is?"

Nell nodded. "It's because everything in Atlanta is so

the-same. The same as it was when Mom was alive. The kitchen smells like her cooking; the yard looks like her planting. She sat in the chairs. Her shoes are in the closet. The . . . the hairbrush she brushed my hair with is there."

Nell squeezed her eyes shut tight. Stevie knew she was feeling the touch of her mother's hand on her head. The pain on her face was wild and alive. It passed over to Stevie, who wished she could take it away, but knew she could not. Nell said with a whisper, "She died one year ago."

"I'm so sorry, Nell."

"It's too hard to live where she lived. So we had to leave."

"Sometimes that helps," Stevie said, gazing steadily at the child, her heart pierced with memories of losing her own mother, of the winter her father had taken a sabbatical in Paris, and the summer they couldn't bear Hubbard's Point and went to Newport instead. They had always, eventually, returned.

"Will we ever go back?" Nell asked suddenly. She lurched forward, as if she wanted to grasp Stevie's hand. She gazed into Stevie's eyes, as if wanting her to be an oracle, to have the answers.

Stevie wanted to say the right thing—for Emma. She wanted to grab this moment, be wise and kind, help her dear friend's child through this terrible moment. A film of tears separated them, and when Stevie blinked, they went rolling down her cheeks. Awash in grief for the loss of a friend she hadn't seen in over twenty-five years, she could barely speak.

"Leaving a place doesn't have to be forever," she said finally. "Sometimes it's the best thing you can do, and then, all of a sudden, you'll find it's time to go home."

"Time to go home," Nell said, grabbing onto the words.

"Meanwhile," Stevie said, "your aunt can come to visit with you and your father while you're here. Hubbard's Point isn't far from Rhode Island—"

"She can't come," Nell said so sharply that Stevie was taken aback. She cast around for something comfortable to say.

"Well, I think you're a very smart girl, leaving Atlanta for a while. Sometimes it's a very good idea to go away," Stevie said. "I find that when I stay in the same place too long, I forget where I put myself." They both smiled at the strange turn of phrase.

"Like now?" Nell asked.

"Now?"

Nell's brown head remained cocked as a great smile came to her lips. She stood right there in Stevie's kitchen door, looking as pleased with herself as a small brown wren.

"You've forgotten that you need to go to the beach more," Nell said. "Not just before the sun comes up! My goodness, it's dark then! You need sun and waves and hot sand under your feet!"

"I do, do I?"

Nell nodded vigorously, earnestly, with such heart that Stevie was more reminded of a small brown wren than ever, and Nell said, "You do! Hot sand!"

Then Nell thanked her, and they said goodbye,

shook hands, and Nell started down the hill. Watching her go, Stevie felt a series of pangs that could not immediately be identified. All she knew was that "goodbye" felt like a very precarious word to end on.

"And just why do I need hot sand?" she called.

"Because you're a beach girl!" Nell called, shooting Stevie a wicked, wonderful grin that instantly put Stevie in mind of Emma—the image sent a shiver through her body, down to her knees. Stevie watched the girl make her way down the hill. Tilly came to stand with her by the open door.

Nell waved once. And then she was gone.

"WHERE WERE YOU?" Jack asked the minute Nell walked into the cottage. It was small and functional, set up for rentals. Standard-issue duck-covered sofa, two armchairs facing a big TV, Formica table and four chairs, framed generic seascapes.

"We were about to call out the National Guard," Francesca said.

"That would be a big waste of the taxpayers' money," Nell said.

"Nell . . ." Jack said warningly. "Be polite."

"I'm sorry. 'Ma'am,' I should've said."

Francesca, to her credit, looked amused. "I just adore being called 'ma'am,'" she said. "How did you know?"

Nell shrugged. Jack noticed that her knees were all skinned, with two small Band-Aids trying to cover them up. "What happened?" he asked.

"I took a spill," Nell said.

"Who gave you the Band-Aids?"

"A nice lady."

Jack stared at his daughter. When she was mad, she could seethe with the best of them. The news that Francesca was driving down from Boston for tennis and a swim had set something off, and it was still in motion. Jack saw the darkness in his daughter's eyes and wished he could chase it away.

"Nell. You told Francesca you were going to the beach. We went down to look for you, and you weren't there. Francesca was only half kidding when she said we were going to call out the forces. I was going to give you five more minutes, and then I was dialing 911. You could have drowned, you could have been kidnapped— that's what goes through your old man's mind. So— take it from the top. What nice lady?"

"A friend of Mom's."

Jack stared. He thought he heard Francesca clear her throat: a very polite, quiet "ahem."

"How did you happen to run into a friend of Mom's? Mom's family stopped coming here a long time ago."

"Some things don't change over time," Nell said, casting a sidelong glance at Francesca. "Some friend-ships last forever. The important ones."

"What's the friend's name?"

"Stevie Moore."

"Oh my God!" Francesca said. "The one who writes children's books?"

Nell nodded. "She was my mother's best friend when they were young."

Jack tried to remember Emma's beach friends, but they all blurred together. He had only had eyes for Emma. But Stevie Moore was a familiar name; Emma had had some issue with her books, hadn't wanted Nell to read them.

"That is just so, so cool," Francesca said. "I used to *love* her books when I was little. In fact, the one she wrote about birds' nests inspired me to become an engineer, I swear. All those amazing drawings—she made them look like blueprints! Sticks, twigs, scraps of paper, ribbon—when you clean your hairbrush and put the hair on your windowsill, birds take it and weave it into their nests."

Jack watched Nell for her reaction, and it came.

"My mother used to do that," Nell said. "Brushed my hair and shared with the mama birds, to help them build their nests . . ."

She was right: Emma had done that very thing. After brushing Nell's hair . . . it had been part of the ritual, and Jack had loved to see her do it; it had seemed part of who Emma was, how much she had loved being Nell's mother.

Jack stared at Nell. How had she tracked down her mother's friend? She hadn't asked him for help—or had she? What were those questions about the blue house at the end of the beach? Was she keeping secrets again? He remembered those terrible nights last winter, when she had woken herself up screaming for her mother. Six months with a therapist had helped—they were experimenting by taking the summer off. Dr. Galford was two hours away, in Boston. Nell still had trouble sleeping, but at least the screams were no longer blood-curdling.

"Back to the Band-Aids, Nell. What happened?"

"Well, like I said, Dad. I took a fall, and Stevie fixed me up."

Stevie. Jack narrowed his eyes, giving Nell his sternest look, but she just looked back with that implacable green gaze. "Would you like to tell me how you found her?"

"All the kids around here know her. They flock to her house."

"Like the birds she paints!" Francesca said.

"You know, you're almost like a kid yourself," Nell said so radiantly that Francesca missed the barb and beamed.

Jack was tired. He had planned to take everyone out for a shore dinner, but right now he just wanted to lie down and stop thinking. Since Emma's death a year ago, anything could wear him down. He wanted her here, back with him, right now. He wanted it so badly, he knew that was why he had returned to the beach where he'd first met her, and he knew—thinking of Nell seeking out Emma's best friend and seeing the glitter the meeting had put in her eyes—that coming to this beach was a huge mistake.

"Just don't bother her again," Jack said. "That's an order."

"I won't," Nell promised.

"I want you to make best friends of your own," Jack said. "Kids your own age, to play with at the beach."

Nell giggled.

"What's so funny?"

"Nothing. 'Cept that when you say 'kids my own age' you remind me of something she said. Stevie mentioned you," Nell said.

"What did she say?"

"That you were ancient!" Nell laughed teasingly, but the look she shot Francesca was all business. And by the time she looked back at her father, her eyes were once again wide-open, waiting, devoid of the joke. Jack tried to take her hand now, but she ran out of the room, up the stairs. He heard her footsteps on the bare boards overhead. Francesca walked over to hug him, whisper something in his ear, but he couldn't feel her or hear her.

chapter 3

STEVIE'S NEXT BOOK WAS PROVISION-
ally titled *Red Nectar*, about hummingbirds
and their penchant for red flowers. Although she was under a tight deadline to finish, that
evening she set it aside and began a series of watercolor
sketches of a small brown wren.

Tilly looked on with total disapproval. She knew,
somehow—Stevie had long since stopped trying to understand the mystical connection between her and the
cat, had ceased trying to look through the veil between
humans and felines—that her mistress was shirking her
work duty in favor of inspiration *not likely* to bring
money and *likely* to bring a certain amount of pain.

Generally Stevie preferred to paint—or at least draw—
from life. Every one of her books had come from real-
life stories, birds that had entered her sphere, if only for
a very short time. She liked to set up her paints in the
backyard, behind the hedge, and draw the birds that
landed at her feeders, pecked in her yard, perched on

her roof. But right now it was dark, and there were no wrens awake—and besides, this particular wren was not really a wren.

Tilly grumbled. When Stevie glanced over, the cat showed her teeth—the front four missing. "Till—let me finish, okay? Then I'll go mousing with you."

She used a block of watercolor paper and paints from Sennelier on the Quai Voltaire in Paris, her favorite art supply store. A soft green wash, fine brush-strokes suggesting obsidian leaves—the color a close match for Nell's eyes. The bird, nut brown, chestnut-smooth, eyes alert and curious. Stevie knew the criticism she always received—imbuing birds with human characteristics. Could she help it if that was how she saw the world? One big anthropomorphic and wrong-headed story about creatures and humans and their ever sad-ending quest for love?

She sketched a baby wren in the nest overhead. Learning to fly. Perched on the branch. Spread your wings. . . . You can do it. . . . The mother looking up, giving encouragement.

Then, the next frame: baby alone, mother gone. A flood of emotion swamped her, but she rechanneled it: "Oh, Emma," she said. And, *Nell.*

Stevie held her brush, out of breath as if she had just learned to fly herself. The sable brush dripped on the picture. Tears, she thought. Crying for the lost mother, the lonely child.

Children abandoned by the universe—and that was how it felt to those whose mothers went away or died young—always spent their lives seeking perfect, intense union. Anything less felt like a failure. Stevie thought about all the pain that quest had caused herself and others. Discouraged by it all, she had just devoted herself to writing and painting. But she had had that closeness with the beach girls.

How had she let those friendships slip away? Great friends who had known her, and each other, so well. Stevie closed her eyes tight, and a snapshot of Emma flashed: pixie-cut brown hair, blue-and-white-striped bathing suit, pierced earrings, laughing so hard she was holding her sides. She could make Stevie and Maddie crack up with a word or a look.

Stevie hadn't realized till just now how much she missed her friends. Maybe they could have kept her from self-destructing in love. Her quest for intensity of connection, passion in all things, had led her to this spot: sitting alone in her quiet beach house. She had become such a recluse; she couldn't remember the last visitor she'd had before Nell. She found herself wondering about Jack, hoping he was a good father.

Too bad wrens—humans, for that matter—couldn't learn something from the emperor penguin. She remembered a trip—a research expedition—to Antarctica, with Linus Mars, her second husband. She remembered the fragile light, the quilt of darkness, the closeness of stars—the way they had hung, low in the sky, like lanterns just waiting to be picked up and carried. She recalled the fur blankets, and how they had made her cry, because life was hard enough for creatures on the tundra without humans slaughtering them for their skins.

Linus had held her, in love but amused. How funny it was, to love a woman with such a soft heart that she would mourn for dead animals with such fervor that she'd rather be cold than wrapped in their pelts. Even then—and it was their honeymoon, as well as a research trip—Stevie had known she had made a mistake in marrying him. The passion she'd felt for Linus was as strong as ever, but it gave way to the dawning realization that there was a fold between them—a wrinkle in their relationship, in their universe—and it was big, and came between them.

Linus could always step back from her and see her from the distance of humor, amusement, judgment. But Stevie's fatal flaw was her longing to be *as one* with the man she loved, to merge her heart and soul with his completely. He was a scientist; she was an artist. His sketches were analytical, seeking greater understanding of the penguins' amazing adaptations to a brutally harsh environment. Hers, although also analytical, steered for the emotional, the miraculous, the outstandingly warm heart of a wickedly cold climate bird.

Stevie had met Dr. Linus Mars in Woods Hole, at the Marine Biological Laboratory, where he was presenting a paper on *Aptenodytes foresteri*—emperor penguins. She was there to gain background for her next book, *The Good Father,* based on the birds.

She had sat, rapt, as Linus lectured on the largest species of penguin. Unable to fly, they spent their entire lives on pack ice in Antarctica, kept warm by their blubber and seventy-five feathers per square inch, more than any other bird.

"They huddle together en masse," Linus said, standing at the front of the dark auditorium as photographs he had taken on his last expedition flashed on the screen. Light from the screen behind illuminated craggy features: honey brown hair that needed cutting, high cheekbones, a long straight nose, a strong chin. Sitting in the front row, Stevie thought he looked like an Oxford don.

Which he was.

"They move in a sort of dance, choreographed by the cold. Constantly moving, circulating, they take turns standing at the center of the circle. March is the onset of winter—when nearly all other life has left the continent—but *Aptenodytes foresteri* stays to breed."

Stevie had shivered in her seat, in the air-conditioned hush of the small theater, thinking of the romance of penguins, their ice dance and mating ritual. Dr. Mars looked right at her—he really did, she was convinced to this day—and said, "They have quite a courtship. It lasts several weeks, which seems to be enough."

Could he see her blush in the dark? Impossible, Stevie thought, but he didn't look away. She was holding a notebook in her left hand, and she saw him look straight at her ring finger. She was married at the time—it must be admitted, there was no getting around it—to a man she had met in art school. Kevin Lassiter. Artist, musician, chef, alcoholic. Dr. Mars stared at her wedding band—designed by Kevin himself—and Stevie thought, *Good; let there be no mistake that I am a married woman.*

"After the courtship," Dr. Mars said in his beautiful

English accent, "the female lays an egg—one single egg. And then . . . she leaves. She is quite a feminist, to use the vernacular, and in that same spirit, although I normally fail my students for making any such humanistic equation, he, the father, is quite a liberated man.

"While she traverses up to seventy kilometers to reach the open sea to feed, he stays with his fellows to tend the egg. Balanced on his feet—which shuffle constantly as the penguins take turns in the center of the crowd—the egg stays safe in his brood pouch. Liberated man indeed!"

The scientists laughed. Stevie slouched down in her seat. Now that she had established her marital status—to the doctor, but more importantly, to herself—she felt a wave of emotion washing over her. This part of the lecture was why she had chosen the emperor penguin as her next project: because of the intense, protective love of a father for his only child.

Stevie and her dad, Johnny Moore. Oh, she could hardly stand this next part, as Dr. Mars continued to lecture in his soft, cultured voice, to point out the pictures with his strong, tweed-clad arm. Stevie's father had been a professor, too—at Trinity College, in Hartford. He was Irish-born and -raised, a lover of the English language, a professor of Irish literature. He was best known for his papers on James Joyce and his schizophrenic daughter, Lucia. The helpless love a man could feel for the damaged girl he'd brought into this world . . .

As Dr. Mars continued, Stevie sank lower in her seat. "There the father stands, in cruel weather, for seventy-two days. The storms are vicious, with winds blowing one hundred and fifty kilometers an hour, driving snow and ice. The father eats nothing during this time, while feeding the chick with liquid—of milklike consistency—produced by a gland in his esophagus."

Thinking of the sacrifices her father had made raising her, Stevie stopped taking notes and just stared at the slides. The professor continued: "Finally the females return from two months of fishing. They find their mates and chicks, among hundreds of others, by matching calls. You see, no two birds make the same precise call. And once a pair has mated, the exact sound of each other's cry is imprinted upon their—"

"Hearts," Stevie heard herself say out loud.

"I was going to say 'brains,' " Linus Mars said.

The crowd of scientists laughed.

"But of course, nothing is so clear-cut. The world is harsh for animals of all kinds, and it is natural for us—man—that is, *Homo sapiens*—to imagine an emotional connection as well as a biological one. Especially when, as is all too often the case, the mother does not return from the sea. As heroic as it might seem for the father to care for the egg, during those seventy-two days, he does not face the same southern ocean conditions, the same predators. Sometimes she doesn't return." Stevie's eyes filled.

"I therefore defer to the woman in the front row. 'Heart' is also correct. In that, the body of any creature is a road map for all of its experiences, and therefore the sound of *Aptenodytes foresteri*'s call is imprinted upon its mate's heart. And when the call is not answered, it creates a disaster that, as humans, we can imagine all too well." He paused, staring down at her.

When the lecture was over, the professor approached Stevie. Although she had by then dried her tears, he handed her a perfectly starched, folded linen handkerchief—just like the kind her father used to carry.

"I'm fine," she said. "But thank you."

"You seemed very engaged with the lecture."

"I'm writing a children's book about emperor penguins, and you gave me some wonderful material."

"I would have said . . . you were engaged with the love story."

"The love story?"

The professor was very tall. His tweed jacket was heathery tan, of stiff, thorny yarn the color of a briar patch, and made Stevie think of trips she had taken with her father to Sligo, Galway, and the Aran Isles. He had hazel eyes with soft brown lashes. A pair of gold spectacles was about to fall out of his breast pocket; she gently pushed them back in.

"The love of the father for his mate. And their offspring."

"I thought scientists didn't think that birds have love stories," she said.

"We don't. And they don't. But I thought perhaps you believed otherwise."

"I do," she said.

"That is honest of you to admit here in the bastion of biology—what you're saying is sacrilege to an ornithologist like myself."

"I'm sorry," she said. "Artists don't always think in straight lines."

A troubled look crossed his brow. It lasted for a full ten seconds, and then he looked up at the ceiling and exhaled with abject regret. She wondered whether perhaps he had been too linear for too long.

"I wish I could unlearn . . . certain things," he said. "Rigidity of thought is a trap too many of us fall into. . . ."

"Rigidity isn't all bad," she whispered as she looked straight at his bare ring finger, as she thought of Kevin, at home at that minute, lying on the sofa with a beer and some bourbon, flipping channels on the TV in a miasmic puddle of despair.

"Defend your thesis," the professor said.

"My husband was the most talented artist in our class," Stevie said. "But then he stopped painting, because he said he wasn't inspired. I told him that discipline was more important than inspiration—any day. Go to your studio, and pictures will flow from your brush. That's how it happens—it's the alchemy of being an artist. The gift, you know? But it's getting to the easel that's the hard part."

"Did he listen to you?"

She shook his head. "Now he never paints at all." She felt swamped by the loneliness of being married to a man drinking himself into the distance.

"I'm sorry."

Stevie nodded.

"Do you really believe what you're saying? That discipline is more important than inspiration?"

"Yes. I know it is. My father told me. . . ."

"And how did your father know?"

Stevie swallowed hard. "My father was a professor—like you. Dr. John Moore. He was also a poet. He had it all—a Ph.D., tenure, and the soul of Ireland. And then my mother . . . went away, like a mother penguin. She went to France on a painting tour that my father gave her for her thirty-fifth birthday, and she never came home."

"What happened to her?"

"She died in a plane crash."

"I'm very sorry," he said, and seeing that she now did require his handkerchief, offered it again.

She blew her nose.

"A lovely call," he said. "It's quite imprinted upon my heart."

She laughed, returning the refolded linen square.

"And the discipline segment of your story?" he asked, then shook his head. "What a fool I am. Breaking into your tender narrative, for the sole purpose of driving you back on course. See what I mean by the curse of linear thought?"

"It's okay. What I was going to say is, my father took care of me from then on. Nothing ever got in the way of it. Not his teaching, not his poetry. He stopped publishing after she died—I think I took up too much of his time. He was passed over as department head—because he had to drive me to riding lessons and take me drawing in fields along the Farmington River."

"He sounds like a wonderful man."

"He was," Stevie said. "And father."

"You make the distinction? They're not one and the same?" he asked, with hunger in his eyes. "Is it possible to be one without the other? Wonderful man, wonderful father?"

"I think they're the same," she said.

"Bloody hell, I was afraid you'd say that," he said. "I've been the most appalling father to my son. Would I have stood seventy-two minutes on the pack ice with him, never mind seventy-two days? I would not."

"I'm sure he'd forgive you."

"Forgive me? He bloody worships me. The ground I've walked since the day I left his mother is molten gold to William. Is there any fairness to that?"

"Your boy loves his father. Sounds fair to me."

The professor smiled. "Well, aren't you dear to say that? Very, very dear. Come now—I'll buy you a drink at the Landfall, and you can teach me the fine points of not thinking straight. What's your name?"

"Stevie Moore."

"I'm Linus Mars. Please, come? I think you know things that I need to hear."

"About your son?"

"About my heart."

"Oh . . ."

She thought of Kevin, back in New York, four and a half hours away. He wouldn't eat until she got home and either fed him or bodily forced him to pick up the phone and order Chinese. On the other hand, he would probably have passed out long before she arrived. Her own heart had been pummeled by a marriage she had once desired with all her soul. Staring up at Linus's handsome, angular face, hooded hazel eyes, she felt the first stirrings of long-buried feeling.

Now, in the dark quiet of her house at Hubbard's Point, she let her brush move across the paper's rough surface. The baby wren stood alone.

Stevie wiped her brow. Nell's visit had stirred her up. Again she thought of Emma. Stevie, Madeleine, and Emma.

Hubbard's Point was cut off from the rest of Connecticut by a railroad trestle, passing over the road. Driving though the gate was like entering an enchanted realm where friends were as close as sisters. For three years, as they changed from girls to young women, they had lain on towels in the sun, soaking up warmth and promise, believing that life, and their friendship, would survive forever. They had promised to grow old together, to become just like the leathery old ladies who arranged their beach chairs in a sewing circle and wore their grandmotherly necklaces into the water.

How easily people give up on things, Stevie thought, painting. *Why didn't I work harder to stay in touch?* As she feathered the small wren's wings, she thought of all the things she had done in life that the beach girls hadn't known about. She remembered how they had healed her first broken heart—a trip to Paradise Ice Cream for sundaes, a ritual burying of the maraschino cherries in the sand.

She could have used that ceremony many times since. Laying down her brush, she put the wren sketches aside for the night. Then, because she had promised Tilly she'd take her mousing, she opened the kitchen door and let the cat run into the night. Barefoot, she walked through the yard, to stand on the rock that faced the beach. She heard the waves and saw their sharp white edges rippling through the inky blackness.

One after another, the small waves of Long Island Sound touched the beach in steady rhythm. Stevie tried to catch her breath, get her heartbeat in synch with the waves. Tilly rustled through the underbrush. A nearly toothless cat, in search of prey. It made Stevie smile—it really did—to think of such hope in the face of dental reality.

"Go, Tilly," Stevie said, still gazing down at the beach, at the place where she and her friends had spent so many happy days so long ago. She looked up at the stars and found one for Madeleine and one for Emma. "And one for Nell," Stevie said, staring at one bright star, twinkling white-blue in night's endless black.

A WARM BREEZE blew through the screens, and the sound of crickets and night birds was a lullaby. Nell lay in her bed, her stomach aching from eating too much lobster, and tried to be soothed by the sounds of nature. It didn't work.

"Ohhh!" she said.

"Go to sleep, Nell," came her father's voice.

"I'm trying!" she said.

"Try harder."

She stuck out her tongue. What kind of answer was that? *Try harder!* God, fathers didn't get it. Didn't they know that the harder you tried to sleep, the faster it slipped away? Nell's mother would have said. . . . Nell squinched her eyes extra tight, trying to remember what her mother would have said.

The memory wouldn't come. Nell used to be able to fill in the blanks with her mother's words, but suddenly there were none. None! She tried to conjure up her mother's voice, and that wouldn't come, either!

"Ohhh!" she cried out louder. Suddenly her stomachache was much worse. "Daddy!"

He came into the small room. She saw his tall silhouette in the doorway. Then he sat down on the edge of her bed. The house was small, and it smelled musty. The curtains were ugly. Nell hated it here. Her stomach ached. She missed her mother. Seeing Stevie was both too little and too much. All of these feelings swirled through her mind, cutting her with tiny knives, making her cry and cry.

"It's okay, Nell," her father said, putting his arms around her.

It's not, it's never going to be okay again, she wanted to say, but she was sobbing too hard to get the words out.

"Maybe you shouldn't have finished your lobster," he said. "It was pretty big."

Nell remembered the scene at the restaurant: her father and Francesca talking about some bridge they were building, the table so festive and covered with lobsters and clams and corn on the cob, and Nell just rolling up her sleeves and dipping the pink lobster meat into melted butter, feeling fuller and fuller, and

Francesca smiling and stifling a laugh as she said, "Someone's eyes are bigger than her stomach."

"She's gone," her father said now.

"I know," Nell cried. She closed her eyes, drawing her knees up to her chest and wrapping her arms around them. She had heard Francesca saying goodbye a short while ago. She had to drive all the way back to Boston, and Nell could just tell she wanted to be invited to stay over.

"Don't worry about her, Nell," he said.

"Mary Donovan's father married his girlfriend," Nell wept.

"I'm not Mary Donovan's father."

"Mommy loved lobster."

"I know."

"She told me the beach girls used to go lobstering together."

"Maybe they did. I don't know."

"Can we ask Aunt Maddie?"

Silence. Her father's hand felt heavy on her head. Nell waited for him to say something, even though she knew he never would. Every time she asked him about Aunt Maddie, he just stopped talking till her question went away. Thinking of how her mother and aunt used to laugh together made Nell's stomach shrink and hurt so much that she just held herself with her own arms, rolling toward the wall so her father wouldn't see her face.

chapter 4

IT TOOK THREE DAYS TO CONVINCE Nell that she should sign up for beach recreation: it would be fun, she'd improve her swimming, and Jack would be waiting for her on the boardwalk every single day when she was finished. Maybe physical exercise would tire her out, help her to sleep. Jack had Dr. Galford on speed dial, but he didn't want to call. He wanted his daughter to have a quiet, fun, psychiatrist-free summer vacation.

So they trooped down to the end of the beach, Nell doing an excellent imitation of a sullen prisoner. She stood behind Jack as he introduced her to Laurel Thompson, the enthusiastic recreation teacher. Bright, blonde, seventeen, she leaned around Jack to smile at Nell. Nell obliged by retreating around Jack's other leg.

"Hi, Nell."

"She's not sure about this," Jack said.

"Oh, that's okay," the teacher said. Tall and thin, she

flashed a smile straight at Nell. "Lots of kids aren't too sure at first. But you can be my helper today, Nell."

"Hear that, Nell?" Jack asked, hoping Nell would be swayed. He didn't hold out much hope, watching her dig her bare feet into the wet sand. "Nell?"

"Nnnnn," she said.

"We'll have fun!" Laurel said.

"I'll meet you at twelve noon," Jack said, placing his hand on his daughter's head. Her brown hair felt warm in the sun. "On the boardwalk."

"Dad," Nell said as other kids her age began to gather round, "I'm not staying."

"Hi, Nell!" said a freckled girl with red hair and a huge smile. "Remember me? You stood on my towel a few days ago! I'm Peggy."

Nell nodded. "I remember."

Jack's heart was beating fast, waiting for a smile or a frown or some sign from his daughter that this was going to be okay, that he could leave her here with a new friend.

Peggy grabbed her hand. "You're going to be my partner in the relay race. We're together, okay, Laurel?"

"Excellent, Peggy, Nell. Come on, everyone—line up on the hard sand, right here."

Still holding Peggy's hand, Nell gave her father one last look. It wasn't quite a smile, but almost. He saw her mother in her eyes. When Emma had been dying, unconscious in her hospital bed, Jack had held her face between his hands and begged her to haunt him. She did just that, every day, in the body of their daughter.

Leaving Nell to the Hubbard's Point Recreation

Program, Jack walked back along the beach, vaguely aiming toward the house where his wife's best friend had lived. He stared up at the cottages along the rock ledge, half hidden by pine trees. He tried to remember which one it was. Nell had found it.

Leave it to Nell: she was a magnet for any little detail about her mother. Back before Emma's death, Nell would hound her aunt for stories, memories, secrets, favorite songs. Madeleine had even taught Nell the harmony Emma used to sing for "Lemon Tree." Nell sang the song every chance she got—in the bathtub, in the car, just waiting for an adult woman's voice to pitch in out of nowhere.

Maybe that was her motive for stopping in on Stevie Moore. Jack had certainly never mentioned her to Nell before—he probably wouldn't even have remembered her name. She was one of his kid sister's friends—none of whom he'd paid any attention to except Emma.

Jack's chest was tight; he turned around to make sure he didn't have a shadow—Nell wasn't following him. Good. He'd needed to find something for her to do for a few hours every day. He had plans to make, and with Nell constantly around, he couldn't get anything done.

He checked his watch: nine-twenty. That gave him nearly three hours of free time. He had plenty of time to take a walk first, before getting down to business. He crossed the footbridge over the creek, headed up the stone steps into the woods.

"HEY—don't drop it!"

"I'm not dropping it—you're the one with butterfingers."

"Will you two shut up and carry the ladder? Jeez—do I have to tell you how to do everything?"

"What if she puts a spell on us?"

"You're an idiot—she's not a real witch."

"She's a good witch, like that one in a bubble on *The Wizard of Oz*."

"Why, 'cause she likes birds? Well, birds have gross scaly claws, and beaks that peck out your eyes. Hear that, Billy? We're gonna call you Bird Boy. Just like the witch is Bird Woman. She's weird. My mom says she never hangs out with normal people."

"She never hangs out with anyone. She sleeps all day and does spells all night."

"Nah," said Billy McCabe, whose mother had read Stevie's books to him and his sisters when he was little. He carried the doughnut box, with the young bird bumping around inside. "She's good."

"Bull crap! She's like that witch in the stupid jerky movie where the camera kids got chomped."

"Chomped? Witches don't chomp. Sharks chomp."

"The Jaws Witch Project."

"You're fucked up."

"Oh—big cool Jeremy, saying 'fucked.' "

"You say it."

"I'm twelve."

"Yeah, well, I'm eleven."

The boys tromped through the backyards, carrying the tools of their trade: a ladder, a camera, and a candle.

They had named their summer club WHA: Witch
Hunters Anonymous. Billy carried a box that was *not*
part of the expedition: a baby crow they'd found under
a bush. The mother must have been teaching it to fly,
and it fell out of the nest. Billy had rescued it, which de-
layed the whole expedition. When they finished spying,
he'd drop the bird off at the veterinarian's house—
Rumer Larkin lived just two houses away from Stevie
Moore.

They cut through the property of the old hunting
lodge, looked both ways, and ran over to the side of the
white shingled house. The land sloped steeply down
toward the beach—getting the ladder steady was tricky.
Jeremy Spring propped one leg on the earth, Rafe
Morgan evened it out with flat rocks under the other,
and the ladder's top crashed against the house with a
rude thump. The other boys scrambled into bushes.
They all held their breaths, waiting for an angry face in
the window—Billy crouched under a shaggy yew, holding the box. This had to be a mistake—their mothers
would kill them if they got caught. And what did they
even hope to see going on inside?

"Let's forget it," he said, watching the windows.

"We've come too far," Rafe said.

"What are we even going to see?"

"She does her magic in the nude," Jeremy said.

"Yeah."

"That's what I heard!"

Two boys held the ladder's base, while Jeremy and
Eugene Tyrone jostled for first up. Eugene won. He
scrambled up. Because the house was built into the rock

ledge, this side of the house had quite a drop-off. The boys had no idea what the windows looked into—her living room, bedroom, magic room, or torture chamber. They all stared up at Eugene for a clue to what he was seeing.

"Hey! What's she doing?"

"Report in!"

Jeremy gave the ladder's base a slight shake. Eugene slashed his left hand through the air, telling them to be quiet. Everyone stood still, heads back. It wasn't fair that Eugene was taking so much time. A scrawny oak, stunted by storm winds, grew alongside the house, and Rafe and Jeremy began trying to climb up for a look at what Eugene was viewing.

"Can you see her?" Rafe asked.

Eugene nodded. He didn't speak. He was frowning. Now he shook his head, as if he was seeing something he didn't like, and started to climb down.

"Is she el-nude-o?"

"Is she chopping the tails off salamanders?"

"Can you see her collection of shrunken heads? That's what she does to kids who look in her windows," Billy said. Everyone else had been whispering, but he spoke in a normal voice. Rafe grabbed a handful of green acorns off a branch to pelt him with—his windup was fierce, and the nuts felt like gunfire. Billy dropped the doughnut box, the bird fell out, and as Billy lunged to catch him, he bumped into the ladder. It weaved slightly, and then fell with a crash to the ground.

STEVIE DIDN'T KNOW what had gotten into her. She sat at her easel, staring at her paper, unable to paint. She was wearing what an old lover had called her "Welcome to the Black Hole of the Universe" garment: an old cream satin dressing gown imprinted with dark blue Chinese characters reputed to have been worn backstage by Joan Morgana, a rising young Metropolitan Opera star, suffering through a disastrous affair with a famous tenor, who had committed suicide shortly after a performance of *Madame Butterfly*. Moved by the dark love story, shortly after her split from Linus, Stevie had bought the gown at the Opera Thrift Store on East Twenty-third Street.

Sitting at her easel, she was trying to concentrate on her painting when she heard a thump. She ignored it. Several days had passed since Nell's visit. She had spent two of them drawing wrens, and now she was back to hummingbirds. The trumpet vine on the house's north side was a magnet for them. She had been watching a pair for weeks—the female a subdued green, the male blazing emerald with a ruby throat.

But all she could think about was Emma—and Nell. She sipped from her teacup—chipped, with blue roses, one of her grandmother's mismatched bone-china collection—and remembered how she and the beach girls would have "tea parties" with them. They would make lemonade and drink it from the cups. This one had been Emma's favorite. The thought made her eyes brim with tears.

Suddenly she heard a scraping noise that sent Tilly flying off the back of the sofa, running for cover. A voice: "Whooooooaaaaa, *stop!*" And then metal clattering against rock. Stevie had heard that sound before. She sighed and hoped that no one was badly hurt. Drying her eyes, she tugged her robe around her and ran to the window.

The ladder lay on its side. The boys had scattered—she saw them peering out of bushes and from behind rocks. One was still shinnying down the oak tree. Yet another was chasing a young crow on the ground.

Out of the corner of her eye, she saw a man running through her yard. He jumped over the low boxwood hedge, displaying truly impressive college-football form. Alarmed by the chaos, she ran barefoot downstairs, out the kitchen door, and toward the group.

"Are you okay?" the man asked, leaning over a boy who was holding his wrist.

"I'm fine," the boy said. "I kind of jammed it."

"You'd better get it checked out," the man said.

"You shouldn't put ladders against people's houses," she said darkly. "You never know what might happen." Her tone was dark, and two of the boys ran away. One stayed where he was, on all fours, trying to lure something out from under a thatch of honeysuckle vines.

"What have you got there?" she asked.

"Back up, Billy," one of his friends called. "She's going to turn you into a snake!"

Stevie tried not to react. Sometimes the kids' teasing made her laugh, but today it made her feel apart, different, and spurned, and it forced tears back into her eyes.

The freckled boy didn't move; he just concentrated on trying to reach the bird.

"A baby crow. He fell out of the nest or something. He was squawking like crazy before, but now he's just so quiet . . . I tried to feed him, but he wouldn't eat. So I decided to take him to the vet. . . ."

"Come on, Billy—leave the bird," his friends said.

"I can't!"

"Go, all of you," Stevie said. "Go home now, and I won't turn you into reptiles. I'll take care of the bird."

The boy looked up at her, concern in his brown eyes. Then he nodded, taking off with his friends. Stevie got down on her knees, studying the small crow hidden in shadow. He cringed against the stone foundation, his neck feathers ruffed like a collar.

"Do you need some help?" the man asked.

"I don't think so," Stevie said coolly. "Are you the father of one of those boys?"

"No—I was just walking by, and I saw a ladder fall over, and I figured someone might be hurt."

Stevie peered at him. He looked somewhat familiar—like a beach kid from the past. Tall, dark, longish almost-black hair, wearing sunglasses, a white dress shirt, and khaki shorts with too many pockets. One of her complaints about Hubbard's Point was how people seemed concerned with everyone else's business. The community was small and insular. Nothing like the wide-open anonymity of New York City . . . Whoever he was, he'd be spreading the news about kids peeking into her windows, spying on "the witch."

Stevie lay down on her side, reaching into the vegetation, to try to get the bird. Her fingers brushed feathers.

"Let me," the man said. "My arms are longer." Without waiting for a response, he knelt down, closed his hand around the bird, and held it out for Stevie.

"Thank you," she said.

"You're welcome."

Stevie's hands enclosed the small crow; she wanted to get inside. She was already thinking of how she could nurse it back to health, keep it safe from Tilly. But the man didn't move. Maybe she *was* a witch: he stared down at her, and suddenly she knew that she knew him. The shape of his face, the curve of his mouth—he had to be Nell's father.

"Jack?" she asked.

"Yes—hi, Stevie."

"I hear you met my daughter."

"I did," she said. "She's wonderful. Jack—I'm so sorry—"

"Emma. I know. Thank you."

He seemed so uncomfortable, and Stevie felt so awkward. Wearing a robe, feeling disheveled, holding a lost bird, the very picture of a crazy artist. She tried to smile. "Listen, can you come inside? I'd like to talk to you—"

He seemed to hesitate, as if trying to think of an excuse. He checked his watch—a huge chronometer—and then shook his head. "I have an appointment," he said. "I'm sorry, but I've got to go."

chapter 5

JACK RETURNED HOME TO AN EMPTY house. He walked inside, closed the door behind him, looked around. There was almost nothing more depressing than a rented vacation place when you weren't really sure why you'd come there in the first place. Other people's strange taste in art, furniture, rugs. Was it possible that that orange macramé wall hanging had been seriously chosen? Jack scowled—he was well on his way to becoming a permanent, intractable curmudgeon.

He pulled out his briefcase, portfolio, and cell phone. Checked the time: just before four in Inverness. The North Sea, his next frontier. Francesca had paved the way, unintentionally, during her Scotland trip in April. Romanov had liked her, been impressed by the firm's credentials. Bids were being taken, but Jack wanted this chance to talk one-on-one with the guy who would make the ultimate decision.

Waiting for his phone to ring, he tried to settle

down. What had him so keyed up? Was it the idea of Nell down at the beach with a bunch of people he didn't know? No—it wasn't that. Laurel seemed steady and responsible, the Hubbard's Point Recreation Program had been in full force since Jack was a kid, and Nell was fine going to school by herself—at home in Atlanta, in Boston. Once she adjusted, she'd be fine.

The phone rang—five minutes early.

"Jack Kilvert," he said, exactly as if he was sitting in his office overlooking Boston Harbor.

"Hi there," came Francesca's throaty voice. "Are you on the beach?"

"Not exactly," he said, feeling a pang of guilt. No one at the firm—including Francesca—had any idea of what he was about to do.

"At the tennis court, on a sailboat, getting ready to tee off? Just tell me you're out in the sun, and not sitting in that house."

"I'm getting ready to go out," he said, forcing a laugh, wanting to defuse the call, get her off the line.

"You'd better be. I'm making you my number one project," she said. "I am going to get you to have fun by the end of the summer. As a matter of fact, I'm calling because I have some documents. Now, I *could* fax them to you—that *is* an option. But I was thinking, wouldn't it be much more fun if I drove them down? Say, tonight?"

"Francesca, that's too far to come," he began, looking at his watch again. Three minutes till the call . . .

"Oh, you're hopeless! Is it your daughter? Come on, Jack—that beach must be loaded with babysitters. Find a nice kid who needs the money, and take the night off!"

"Look, Francesca," Jack said. "That won't work for tonight. Fax the papers, if you don't mind—okay? I have to run now."

She was silent. He knew he'd sounded rude. But the time was ticking by—and wasn't it better for her to get the message now rather than later? She said, "Yes, sure, have fun," and hung up the phone. Jack's heart was in a vise. The pain was great—in his body, and in his soul. He thought of how Emma had told him to pray. The memory made him shudder. He was like a dead man these days—somehow the imminent phone call was a form of redemption. He sat there in a cold sweat, waiting for the ring.

He bowed his head. He needed respite, a break from his universe. He closed his eyes—and what he saw surprised him.

Stevie Moore. She had looked like he felt: a ghost stuck in this life. What had she been doing, just half-dressed on a bright morning? Those streaks on her cheeks were tears. He knew. He was an expert on tears.

He'd been struck by her firm handshake and warm smile. Also by her size: she was small. About five-three, very slight. Her robe had been about four sizes too big for her, the sash tied tight. She had sleek, chin-length black hair and bangs that parted over wide, violet eyes. Her skin was pale and flawless. Except for those tear marks.

He pictured her cupping that pathetic little lost bird in her hands. What chance did it have? No mother, no father. At least Nell had *him*. . . . He shook his head. What good was he, anyway? He held tight to the vision of Stevie holding that bird. Holding on, holding on . . .

The phone rang. It jangled, making him jump. His pulse leapt, and he felt his heart crashing. *This had to work.* . . .

"Hello," he said. "Jack Kilvert . . ."

NELL AND PEGGY won the relay race. They beat all the girls *and* all the boys. They looked like teammates in their navy blue bathing suits—as if they had planned it that morning, as if they were already best friends.

Peggy had bright red hair and lots of freckles, and she wore a cool sunhat to keep the sun off her face except for when she went swimming. She kept hold of Nell's hand practically the whole time—they even did the floating contest, on their backs in the calm bay, holding hands.

"It's like having a sister!" Nell said when the contests were over and the whole rec class took a rest break on their towels.

"*Better*, I'm telling you," Peggy said. "My sister Annie's a teenager, and she can't be bothered with me! All she wants to do is hang out with her boyfriend. My mother always says about her best friend, Tara, 'You can't choose your family, but you can choose your friends.' "

Nell felt her shoulders collapse a little. "I'd choose my family, just the way it was," she said.

"Well, me too," Peggy said. "But best friends are

second best. A *close* second best—you should see my mom and Tara. They do everything together."

"My mom had friends like that," Nell said. "They grew up here, at Hubbard's Point. That's why my dad and I came here. Because there were so many happy times."

"You and your dad?" Peggy asked, blinking slowly; the unasked question: *what about your mom?*

"Yes," Nell said, her shoulders caving in a little more. She could never say the words: *my mom died.*

"You miss your mom," Peggy said.

Nell glanced up. How could she possibly know?

"I miss my dad," Peggy explained. "I could tell about you . . . at least, I thought I could. And when you said it was just you and your dad here, I knew for sure. . . . It rots, doesn't it?"

"Big time," Nell said.

The girls were sitting on the edge of their towels, their heads so close together that Nell's face was in the shade of Peggy's hat. The sand was so warm; they burrowed their feet down as far as possible, till they got to the cool, damp layer. Nell wished they could just sit there for the rest of the day. But just then a long shadow fell across their towels, and she looked up— into the freckled face of a boy who looked a lot like Peggy.

"Hey, squirt," he said.

"Billy—where's the bird?" she asked.

"I left it up there." He gestured up at the cottages on the stone hill—at the House That Used to Be Blue. Nell felt a shiver, remembering Stevie.

"Not with the witch!" Peggy said. "Are you crazy? She'll pluck its feathers to make a hat, or a cape, or something! Crows are black, *hello*!"

Nell felt the first instant of doubt regarding her new best friend. She wanted to defend Stevie, but the boy—the way he looked and acted meant he had to be Peggy's brother—beat her to it.

"I don't think so," he said. "She's not the bird-plucking type. She seems, like, depressed or something. Eugene was spying on her, like, looking in her windows? And he saw her crying. All alone, in the middle of the morning. It was weird."

"Depressed?" Nell asked. She knew she had found a family of kindred spirits: that word was part of their language, too.

"Yeah," the boy said. "And who might you be?"

"Nell Kilvert," she said.

"Nell, this is Billy, my brother," Peggy said. "It sounds *just* like something a witch would do—crying on a summer day. Excuse me, but that's strange."

"Maybe someone she loved died," Nell said.

Peggy and her brother Billy just stared and stared as if she'd just said the most unspeakable thing in the world. Billy shrugged and walked down the beach.

Peggy decided to laugh it off. "Hah! Like her black cat, or her pet newt. Or maybe she's getting divorced again, for the fifteenth time. Or maybe she lost another huge diamond ring . . ."

"She's special," Nell said.

"She wants you to think that," Peggy said. "To lure you in!"

"I don't think she wants to lure anyone in," Nell said. "She has that 'Please Go Away' sign in her yard."

Peggy frowned—Nell had her there.

"She and my mom and my aunt were really close. They even had a name for themselves," Nell said. "I was thinking . . . we could call ourselves the same thing!"

"What is it?" Peggy asked.

"Beach girls," Nell said.

Peggy's nose wrinkled, and she squinted into the sun. Her gaze swept up the rocky point, toward the House That Used to Be Blue. Nell could almost read her mind: she'd been seeing dark magic and crystal balls and pointy black hats, but those images were being replaced by beach balls, bright towels, and blue bathing suits. Nell smiled.

"Witches aren't beach girls," Peggy said doubtfully.

"Beach girls aren't witches," Nell countered, and Peggy cocked her eyebrows in a thoughtful way.

Just then Laurel came running over from the lifeguard chair, where she'd been talking to a bunch of her friends, and clapped her hands.

"Okay, everyone into the water for one last thing— we're going to tread water for ten minutes! Find your partners!"

Peggy grabbed Nell's hand, and together they ran into the water, diving under the first wave. Their bodies, hot from the sun, felt the saltwater shock, and they came up squealing. Nell thought of her mother holding Stevie's hand. Or Aunt Madeleine's . . . Peggy's gaze was directed over Nell's head, to the cottage on the hill—as if she, like Nell, was wondering what could be making a beach girl cry on such a beautiful day.

AS BABIES, crows, blue jays, and starlings were insectivores. Their parents would catch mosquitoes and gnats, eat them, and regurgitate them. Their offspring would grow, eventually turning into omnivores, the goats of the avian world: birds that would eat anything. Stevie credited her editor for that bit of knowledge: Ariel Stone was a stickler for scientific details, and she loved emotional love stories. The combination made her a great editor—and had led her to push Stevie into writing *Crow Totem*.

"Crows are intensely loyal," she said to the baby, quoting from her own book, trying to get the bird to eat a crushed fly. "Did you know that?"

The bird refused to budge, or open its beak. Tilly hovered outside the bedroom, scratching at the door. Stevie wondered how refined the bird's responses were, whether he registered the noises as direct threats upon his young life. She kept trying, until finally—perhaps trying to squawk—the bird opened his beak, and she shoved the fly in.

"There you go," she said. "Wasn't that good?"

It must have been, because the baby opened wider, and she dropped in a pair of mosquitoes and another fly, snagged in a spiderweb by the back door. Country life, she thought . . . Trumpet vines, hummingbirds, spiderwebs, a motherless crow: nature at her back door, inspiration to do her work.

"This is for you, Emma," she said, giving the baby crow another dead fly.

Emma would have laughed at that. "Thanks, Stevie," she'd have said. "A dead fly." She'd had a strange, dark sense of humor. Stevie spun back in time . . . the warm breeze brought it all to the fore.

The air on their skin, driving in Stevie's convertible Hillman, on their way to pick up Maddie at the New London train station, coming back from visiting her aunt in Providence. Two sixteen-year-old girls, wearing wet bathing suits under T-shirts, damp hair blowing in the wind—nothing could have torn them away from the beach, except the arrival of their friend.

Downtown New London had been different back then. Crumbling beauty and abject poverty had defined the old whaling town. Driving along Bank Street, they'd seen a homeless woman curled up in a doorway across from the Custom House.

"We have to help her," Stevie had said, pulling over. The woman had cracked skin and dirty clothes. Her hair was matted, unwashed. A shopping cart from Two Guys held her belongings.

"And do what?" Emma had asked. "Pick her up and take her back to the beach?"

"Yes, and feed her," Stevie had said.

The two friends had stared at each other, Emma realizing that Stevie was serious. Their families were very different. Stevie's father taught Stevie that all human beings were connected, and that art and poetry held them together. Emma's parents taught her that life was one big case of keeping up with the Joneses: you looked at your neighbors not to help them, but to judge how well you were doing in relation to them. Emma gently took Stevie's hand.

"I love you," she said. "But you are a crackpot."

"No, Em—we have to . . ."

"Don't you know that there are ways . . . and there are ways? That's what *charity* is for. My mother taught me that . . ." Emma trailed off, the unspoken, unfinished, mournful part of the thought being that Stevie didn't have a mother to teach *her*. "Suburbia isn't built for people like her, not even passing through. Can't you imagine the beach ladies flipping out? No—we have to help her here, on her own turf."

"So we can just go back to the beach and forget her?"

"Yes—and that's not mean, Stevie. We'll buy her some food, and she'll be better off. And then we'll go back home."

Stevie remembered feeling sick. *People like her:* had Emma really said that? Yet Emma's desire to help seemed real. She patted her pockets for money. Stevie looked through her purse. They had six-fifty between them.

So when they'd gotten to the graceful brick train station, sixteen-year-old Emma had picked out a pair of Coast Guard Academy cadets. The young men were standing on the siding, dressed in their white uniforms, waiting for the train. Their trousers were so clean, so sharply pressed; their shoes shined to a high polish. Overhead, pigeons cooed in the eaves. Ferry whistles sounded, and seagulls screeched from the dock pilings.

Across the Thames River, just-built nuclear submarines lurked in the open bays of Electric Boat.

Emma's hair was messed up from driving in the open car. Her skin was tan, gleaming. She wore a gold necklace and bracelet. Her damp T-shirt clung to her body, and Stevie saw the men notice her even before she approached them.

"Hello," she said to the cadets.

"Hi," they both said at once.

"We're raising money," she said. "My friend and I."

The young men looked at the two girls, fresh from the beach, and tried not to laugh.

"For a really good cause," Emma said. "There's a hungry lady, and we want to buy her some food. My friend will cry if you don't help. She honestly will."

It took the cadets exactly thirty seconds to open their wallets. Stevie watched in amazement. She saw how Emma smiled with the strangest combination of flirtation and humility, how she had kissed them both on the cheek when they'd handed her the money, how she thanked them for keeping the coast safe for everyone.

"Easiest thing I ever did," Emma said, walking back to Stevie.

The men had given her ten dollars each.

After Madeleine arrived, Stevie drove back to Bank Street. They went to the granite Custom House, and looked for the woman. Her cart was still there, parked in the alley, but she was gone. They drove down the street slowly, looking for her.

"We have to find her," Stevie said.

"She's all right," Emma said. "She probably got hot from lying in the sun and went to find some shade."

"We have to give her the money," Stevie said.

"She's survived without our help all these years," Emma said. The words were harsh, but her voice was gentle. Stevie knew that Emma was trying to make her feel better, even when Emma turned toward the back-seat and told Maddie how Stevie wanted to save the world by bringing street people back to Hubbard's Point.

They had waited for fifteen or twenty minutes. Emma was impatient; Stevie could tell by the way she kept flipping around the radio dial, trying to find good songs. The woman didn't come back. Stevie folded up the two tens and stuck them into a tattered blanket on the top of the loaded shopping cart.

Emma got out of the car and took one back.

"This is to feed us," she said. "You can't take care of others and forget about yourself."

"Emma—"

"I begged for that woman's food," she said. "I'm a beggar now—my mother would totally kill me if she knew. So you have to let me treat you and Maddie to an ice cream."

"You've never been hungry in your life. You wear gold jewelry to the *beach*."

"Stevie, you need someone to tell you it's okay to be happy. It really is. We love you, Maddie and I. You want to save every person, every lost bird. Well, your friends are here to save you—how about that? Come on—let's get back to the beach, okay?"

The top was down, the sun was shining; Maddie was so glad to be back from seeing her aunt, and she wanted to hear everything that had happened at the beach in her absence. They had stopped at Paradise for sundaes, and when they'd buried their cherries in the sand, they'd done it in honor of the homeless woman. Stevie had felt guilty for wasting food. Her sundae tasted like sawdust. When Emma saw her put the dish down, she leaned over and fed Stevie with her own spoon.

"There, little birdy," she said, gazing into Stevie's eyes, making sure she included a big taste of whipped cream as she put the plastic spoon into her mouth. "Enjoy the summer day."

"But . . ."

"Enjoy the summer day," Emma had repeated, with something dark in her eyes that Stevie had taken to mean that this was a lesson she had to learn. Why should happiness be so hard? Did girls who still had their mothers feel it much easier? Yet she couldn't block out the picture of Emma taking that ten-dollar bill from the shopping cart. . . .

Those memories were in Stevie's mind as she fed the baby crow.

Her thoughts of Emma turned to Nell and Jack. The man's eyes looked bruised—as if he had been beaten up. She stroked the bird's ruffled black back. If she could save its life, help it to live, somehow she'd be honoring Emma and the daughter she'd left behind.

Or maybe there was another, better way.

chapter 6

WHEN NELL AND HER FATHER WALKED home from their noontime meeting at the boardwalk, they found a note stuck in their screen door. Nell saw the drawing of two birds and cried out, "It's from Stevie!"

Her father read the message: "You are cordially invited to dinner with me and Tilly, tonight, six o'clock." It was signed "SM," with a cat sitting on top of the letters.

"Can we go, can we go?" Nell asked.

"I have a lot of work," her father said.

"Work, work, *work!*" she said, her hands on her hips, feeling a tidal wave of frustration. "What kind of vacation is this? I know—I'll bet Francesca is bringing papers down, and you have to have dinner with her."

"No. As a matter of fact, I told her to fax them." He gave a slow smile that meant Nell was going to get her way.

"Well?" Nell grinned. "Then we really have no excuse! We're goin' to Stevie's!"

AND THEY DID. At six o'clock sharp they walked up Stevie's hill. Nell wore her best yellow sundress with white daisies embroidered around the hem. Her father was wearing chinos and a blue shirt, and Nell had seen him smoothing his too-long hair behind his ears the way he did when he wanted to look nice and realized he should have gotten a haircut. Nell held a bouquet of wildflowers she had picked at the end of the beach. Her father carried a bottle of wine.

They knocked on the screen door. Tilly was sitting right inside, and she gave an evil, toothless hiss. Nell jumped, then giggled.

"You must be Tilly," her father said.

"Right you are," Stevie said, letting them in. She looked really pretty, with her dark hair combed and shiny, one smooth bird's-wing curl on each cheek. Her eyes were made up, and she wore a white shirt over blue jeans. Nell beamed, wishing Peggy could see Stevie now: she looked so beautiful and bright.

"We brought you flowers!" Nell said, handing her the bouquet. "We picked them at the end of the beach! Did you used to go there with Mom and Aunt Maddie? Did you pick flowers there, too?"

"Nell, slow down!" her dad said.

But Stevie was wonderful. She knew that Nell was giving her much more than a few stalks of aster, beach heather, and Queen Anne's lace: she knew that Nell was giving her the chance to remember her two best friends. She crouched down, looked Nell right in the eyes, and nodded. "That's exactly where we used to go to pick flowers," she said.

Nell shot her father a smile and a look of triumph.

Stevie stood up, looking at the bottle in Nell's father's hand. "Would you mind opening that while I put these in water?" she asked. "You look like maybe you could use a glass."

JACK WAS GLAD for something to do. Stevie handed him a corkscrew and pointed at a shelf filled with glasses. He couldn't find two alike. They were all different heights and sizes—some with stems, some short and round, some clear crystal, others colored glass. Engineers and architects tended to like things in order, matched, symmetrical. Stevie, her house, and her glasses threw him off balance. He wound up choosing two, with different length stems. She asked him to pour her a ginger ale.

Nell also had ginger ale. Jack watched her face as Stevie garnished all three drinks with slices of fresh peach: his daughter smiled so wide, you'd think it was her birthday. They all went into the living room, with a great view of the beach. Stevie put out cheese and crackers; she sat in a wicker rocker, while Jack and Nell squeezed together in a faded-chintz loveseat. The old cat curled up on the arm beside Stevie.

"How's the bird?" Jack asked.

"Oh, he's great," Stevie said. "Eating every bug in the place."

"I heard about the bird," Nell said. "From my best friend's brother."

"You have a best friend already?" Stevie asked. Jack watched her smile. She had a great, warm smile that lit up her whole face.

"I do!" Nell said, so eager to talk that she bounced on the loveseat and nearly upset the cheese and crackers. Jack touched her arm to steady her, struck by her enthusiasm. "Her name is Peggy McCabe!"

"Oh, Bay's daughter," Stevie said. "Her brother Billy paid me a visit this morning."

"One of the hooligans?" Jack asked.

"The what?" Nell asked.

Stevie laughed. "They do it every year—a whole different age group. The story got started, so long ago now, that I'm a witch. I guess it's a rite of passage for Hubbard's Point boys to look in my windows and try to catch me—I don't know—stirring a cauldron, I guess."

"They're just dumb," Nell said. "They don't know you."

"Thank you, Nell," she said.

"Can we see the bird?"

"Nell—" Jack warned.

"Sure," Stevie said. "Do you want to come, Jack?"

Her smile was radiant. He did want to go. But even more, he wanted Nell to have a minute with her—that was obviously what Nell wanted. "That's okay," he said. "I'll keep Tilly company."

Nell gave him an approving look and tore up the

stairs after Stevie. Jack sipped his wine and tried to figure out why he felt so uncomfortable. This wasn't a date or anything. It was dinner with an old friend of his wife's. That's all. He didn't even know Stevie—he was doing this for Nell.

Jack didn't want Nell getting hurt. He was sure Stevie wouldn't intentionally do anything, but he felt protective anyway. Nell was one way with company, another way when she went to bed at night. Her mother's death had left her totally traumatized, and Jack knew that she was latching onto Stevie because she was a link to Emma. But he had to admit, it felt good to see her so happy.

Their voices drifted down from upstairs—he loved hearing Nell laughing. He heard the bird chirping, Nell's voice trying to imitate the sound. After a few minutes, they came back down—Nell holding Stevie's hand.

"Dad! You should see her studio! She has an easel in her bedroom! There are paints all over, and paintings and drawings of all these birds, and Dad—there's one of me! I'm a baby wren in it."

"Wow," Jack said, watching his daughter's face glowing. He felt a knife edge—worrying that she was counting on too much from a woman they barely knew.

"I inspired her," Nell said. "Mommy and I did. . . ."

"Really?" Jack said. He raised his eyes to meet Stevie's. Behind her smile, he saw the sadness he'd spotted that morning, looking like a lost soul in her too-big bathrobe. He had a distant almost-forgotten memory of Emma reading one of her books—about swans, he thought. She had disapproved of the way Stevie depicted violence in the bird world.

"Yes," she said.

"Her mother died when she was little, too," Nell said.

"Oh," Jack said, and sipped his wine because he was momentarily tongue-tied. How was it that women and girls could get so much said so quickly? Had Stevie managed to tell Nell that upstairs, just now? How had she done it without anyone crying? Both Stevie and Nell were gleaming—he hadn't seen Nell happier in . . . he couldn't remember how long.

"I'm sorry," Jack said, finally.

"She was okay," Nell said. "She had a great dad, too. He was like you."

"He was," Stevie said, nodding.

"She's going to give me a book about emperor penguins," Nell said. "She wrote it! It was about her father and her, but it could also be about you and me!"

"Wow," Jack said, for the second time in two minutes. They had really gotten a lot said on that visit upstairs. He looked up at Stevie and saw her violet eyes looking incredibly dramatic in the light coming through the west-facing windows. Again, he recalled Emma's disapproval of her books.

He reached for his wine, knocking it over.

WITHOUT KIDS of her own, Stevie was never too sure what to serve for dinner. She had a beloved aunt, her father's sister Aida, who had married a man with a very young son. Raising Henry, Aida had learned that she could never go wrong with steak, salad, mashed potatoes, and chocolate cake for dessert. So, hoping for the best, Stevie served Aunt Aida's menu.

"I love mashed potatoes," Nell said. "Dad, how come we never have them except on Thanksgiving?"

"I don't know," Jack said. "I guess because I thought you liked frozen fries."

"Is the steak done enough?" Stevie asked.

"It's good," Nell said.

"Great," Jack said.

The sun was setting, casting a golden glow throughout the room. Stevie loved this time of day, and often used this last hour of light to do her best work. Having friends for dinner felt unfamiliar. It had been so long . . .

She wanted everything to be right for Emma's family. She had caught the way he'd looked taken aback when Nell had mentioned the wren pictures. Should Stevie have kept them to herself? Motherless children seemed to be everywhere, reminding Stevie of her own life, of Emma and Nell.

"Cake, anyone?" she asked, clearing the table.

"Sure," Jack said, helping her.

"Can I visit the bird again?" Nell asked.

"If it's okay with your dad," Stevie said, and Jack nodded. Nell clapped her hands and went running upstairs.

Stevie put coffee on, and she and Jack went into the living room to wait for it to perk. The worry lines in his brow reminded her of her father. She wanted to ask about Emma, but she didn't want to upset him. It all seemed so difficult to navigate. He cleared his throat and, as if he'd read her mind, spoke in a voice too low for Nell to hear.

"It was a car crash," he said. "In Georgia, on her way home from a weekend away."

"Oh, Emma," Stevie said, her hand going to her mouth.

"Nell was eight. Last year. It was Emma's first time away, without us, since Nell was born."

"Was she alone?"

Jack shook his head. He started to speak, then closed his mouth. In that space—in whatever lay between Stevie's question and the answer he'd been about to give—there was great anger. She could see it in the set of his eyes and mouth. He looked at the beach, at the flowers he and Nell had brought, and then at Stevie. "She was with my sister," he said.

"Madeleine?"

Jack nodded.

"Maddie—was she—?" Stevie asked, barely able to ask.

"She was hurt," Jack said. "But she's fine now."

"I'm sorry, Jack," Stevie said.

He nodded, as if there was nothing more to say. Stevie tried to imagine what it might be like, to lose a wife and have a sister hurt in the same accident. They were silent for a minute, listening to Nell talk to the bird upstairs.

"How about you, Stevie?" he asked. "Do you have kids? You're great with Nell."

"No," she said, feeling strangely hollow as she told what felt like a partial truth. "I don't."

"Were you ever married?"

She hesitated. This was not fun. "Three times," she said.

"Oh." He smiled—was it her imagination, or did he already know? She was embarrassed about some of the press she'd gotten: "Some birds mate for life, but not beloved children's book author Stevie Moore."

"Guess I'm not the married type," she said, trying to make a joke, just as at other times she'd called herself "the Elizabeth Taylor of southeastern New England."

"Hmm," he said, not laughing, as if he couldn't even pretend it was funny. His reaction, oddly, made her feel good.

The sun dipped lower, throwing butterscotch light over the beach and bay. Jack stared at her, and she saw kindness in his eyes. He didn't find her situation funny, as other people sometimes did. Stevie had friends in New York who introduced her as "the much-married Stevie Moore." She had once jokingly, drunkenly, back when drinking still worked, referred to herself as a "serial marry-er."

"Why do you think . . ." he began after another minute.

"That I got married three times?"

He nodded. The coffee had finished perking, but neither of them moved. Stevie found herself staring at the empty wine bottle, wishing there was a little more left. She remembered her Aunt Aida telling her that her old Irish grandmother had warned her to never drink the "last drops," or she'd die an old maid. *If only*, Stevie thought now.

"Well," Stevie said, "the first time, it was a boy I'd met in art school. The second time, it was a man who took me to Antarctica to see the emperor penguins. And the last time, I married a man who . . ." She paused, trying to think of a way to describe what Sven had meant to her. "Took my breath away," was the only way she could possibly put it.

"And why didn't they work?"

"I wish I knew," Stevie said.

Jack was polite and didn't tease, but he also seemed to know that she wasn't giving a straight answer. He waited.

"Have you ever heard of 'geographics'?" she asked, using a word she'd heard in recovery. "When a person is really uncomfortable with herself, and she decides that moving would solve everything? So she picks up and transplants herself to another city, or another state, or another country, hoping that everything will be different and better there? She leaves what's familiar and pulls a 'geographic.' "

Was it Stevie's imagination, or the sunset, or was Jack turning red?

"I've heard of that," he said quietly.

"Well, I pulled 'matrimonials.' Left one unhappy marriage, or relationship, hoping the next one would be better." She clasped her hands, feeling the shame she always felt about it. The sound of waves hitting the shore came through the open window. Why was she telling this to Jack? She supposed it was because they went back so far—beach acquaintances, if not actual friends.

"I wish they'd been happier for you," Jack said.

"Well, I needed connection. Emma used to tease me about it. Even here at the beach, when we were kids."

"Don't blame yourself," he said.

"It's so unfair," she said, staring at him. "You had Emma—and she was taken away so soon. And I just threw my marriages away. . . ."

"Losing Emma was unfair," he said. "That doesn't even begin to cover it. But don't be so hard on yourself. Maybe those guys didn't deserve you."

She glanced up. His eyes were fierce, and for a second she felt the protection she remembered from her father. The sensation shocked her—it was completely unexpected. She smiled, relaxing in spite of herself. She hadn't had a friend in so long. Opening the door to Nell the other day had been such a gift: she stared at Jack, surprised to feel tension spinning out of her shoulders.

"Thank you," she said.

"You're welcome." They stood up, ready to walk into the kitchen. Her heart was beating hard. She felt something in the way Jack was looking at her that made her gaze back at the beach. The sun was all the way down now; the bay was tarnished silver, nearly black. The sky was growing darker, and Stevie's pulse raced faster.

A look passed between her and Jack with a ferocity of emotion that shook Stevie inside. It embarrassed and confused her. She cast around, trying to think of something innocuous to say. Tilly lay on the windowsill, growling at mice in the underbrush. Stevie touched Tilly's head with her fingertips, and the cat bolted.

"I'd love to see Madeleine," Stevie said.

Jack didn't reply—she saw his mood change in that instant.

"Could you give me her number? Maybe I could call her—if she comes to see you and Nell, I'd love to have her over."

"She won't be coming," he said quietly.

Stevie glanced up at his face and was shocked by the expression. He looked troubled, upset.

"No?"

"It's better that she and Nell don't see each other right now. If it's okay with you, I'd just as soon not talk about it."

Stevie was stunned. She had no idea what to say and felt completely confused by the shift. The pain quickly left Jack's eyes, but so did all expression. He looked numb, and he couldn't meet Stevie's gaze.

"I think the coffee's ready," she said after a moment.

"That's good," he said, seeming relieved. Just then she thought of Nell upstairs. She excused herself, and went up to get her.

NELL WAS TALKING to the crow, prowling around Stevie's room, feeling so happy. Her dad and Stevie were downstairs—she could hear their voices. It made her feel safe and happy, to think they were talking about her, about her mother. Stevie was almost like another aunt!

To think that Stevie knew what Nell was feeling; that she had lost her mother when she was young. Just like the little crow . . .

Nell stood by the cage, staring at the bird's bright black eyes. She went to the mirror. She had brown hair and green eyes, like her mom. Had her mother ever been in this room? Maybe she and Aunt Madeleine had had sleepovers with Stevie!

Maybe Stevie could get her father to forgive . . . oh, she could hardly let herself hope. With the sun just set behind her, Nell stared into the mirror at her own, her mother's, green eyes and made a huge wish.

Just then, she noticed a picture on the bureau. It was in a silver frame, and it showed a woman and a little girl. They stood beside an easel, both holding paintbrushes, looking solemnly into the camera. Could it be Stevie and her mother?

Hearing footsteps, Nell wheeled around. Stevie stood framed in the doorway.

"Is that you?" Nell asked, pointing.

"It is," Stevie said.

"With your mother?"

"No," Stevie said. "With my father's sister. Aunt Aida. She's the reason I became an artist."

"Is she an artist?"

"A painter, yes," Stevie said. "A very well known one. She does huge paintings that . . . look like wide-open spaces."

"What do you mean? Modern art like that picture there?" Nell asked, pointing at a painting that had only two colors in it. It hung on the wall behind Stevie's bed, and it was a very large square made up of two rectangles: one white and one light blue. That was the whole painting.

Stevie laughed, as if Nell had just said the best thing. "Exactly," she said. "That's from Aunt Aida's *Beach Series*."

Nell squinted at the picture. The room was dark, so Stevie turned on a lamp. The blue was on top. "Blue sky, white sand?" she asked.

"Aunt Aida would love you," Stevie told her, chuckling.

Nell grinned. Then she stopped. A bad thought had come over her. "Is she . . . alive or not?"

"Oh, she's alive," Stevie said. "Very much so."

"Like my aunt," Nell said.

"Yes," Stevie said, but the smile wavered on her face.

Nell's heart seized up. Oh, she had something she had to ask, she'd been getting her courage up. "Stevie," she began.

"How about some chocolate cake?" Stevie said carefully. "And let me find that book on penguins I want to give you. . . ." She began looking through a bookshelf, peering at every title.

"Stevie!" Nell said again.

As if she knew what Nell was about to ask, Stevie began searching even more diligently. She reached for a pair of half-spectacles, like Nell's father sometimes wore, and put them on.

"Nell!" her father called from downstairs. "Come on, now. It's getting late, and I think we'd better be getting home."

"Where's that book?" Stevie asked.

"Come on, Nell," her father called louder.

"She's your dear friend," Nell said suddenly, quickly.

Stevie paused, but immediately resumed looking.

"A best friend, from the beach," Nell said. "Friends like that never stop being friends. . . ."

"Here it is," Stevie said, pulling a thin volume from the shelf. She looked so steady and wise with her dark hair and bangs and half-glasses, and Nell had a swift, urgent longing to throw herself into her arms. But she held herself back, even as the tears came flooding out.

"My aunt Madeleine," Nell said, unable to keep herself from weeping. "I miss her so much, so much! You have to call her! She's your friend! Madeleine Kilvert, just like before, the same name as ours! My father hates her, but I love her! Just like you love Aunt Aida!" Her voice rose to a cry, and Nell felt herself enveloped by Stevie's arms. Stevie lifted her up, holding her so tightly, kissing her neck the way Nell's mother used to, the way Aunt Madeleine used to.

Her tears felt hot on the skin between them, and her sobs shook the air. She heard her father's footsteps and felt him take her away from Stevie. Nell lost track of whether she was just tired or too full or overcome with the grief of missing the women in her life, but she heard herself wailing as if the world was ending, and she heard her father whispering, "That's okay, Nell. Don't cry, honey, don't cry . . ."

"I'm so sorry," she heard Stevie say.

"It's okay," she heard her father say in his cross voice that said, *No, it's not okay.*

"I want Aunt Madeleine!" Nell wept.

"I shouldn't have let her upstairs," Stevie said. "Showed her the picture . . ."

"She's very emotional," her father said.

Then Stevie said something about understanding, not wanting to intrude again. Nell felt Stevie's lips brush her tear-soaked cheek, then felt the hard edge of a book pressed into her hand. One arm slung around her father's neck, Nell sobbed the whole way back to their rented cottage, clinging tightly to Stevie's book about penguin babies and the fathers who loved them.

chapter 7

A JULY HEAT SPELL DESCENDED ON
the beach, with long hot days and barely a
breeze. Jack grabbed the morning hours—
when Nell was at recreation—to do his work. Sitting on
the screen porch, he talked to Ivan Romanov at IR in
Inverness, typed out pages of ideas for that project,
drew up plans for his Boston office, wished he was
in an air-conditioned office somewhere, anywhere but
here.

He wished he could walk up the hill and talk to
Stevie.

Nell had recovered from the scene at Stevie's house.
She had eventually cried herself to sleep that night, and
woken up the next morning quiet and withdrawn. But
she had gone to recreation—Jack had been afraid she
wouldn't—and seemed happy the minute she saw
Peggy. She had a friend, and they played together all
day long.

Jack wanted to apologize to Stevie, but he wasn't

sure what to say. He didn't want to open a door that was better left closed. Stevie, for her part, left them alone. Jack knew it was better that way. But the strange thing was, he found himself thinking of her anyway. He wished that he and Nell could go back there for dinner again, drink from the mismatched glasses, watch the sunset from her window. He wanted to see that beautiful smile again.

What was he thinking?

Dealing with Ivan Romanov, he thought of what Stevie had said about geographics. It was human nature to think a change of scene could solve everything, when the real problem was inside—he'd learned that when he was just a kid. He and Madeleine had run away together when she was eight and he was twelve. Their grandfather had come to visit from Providence—he took over Jack's room, smoked a pipe, and watched TV programs that no one else liked. He had hair in his ears and nose. He was deaf and refused to use his hearing aid. Maddie was afraid of him, because he talked in a really loud voice and had a wart on the top of his bald head.

Running away seemed like a good solution; Jack and Maddie hopped a bus to Elizabeth Park, checked out the rose garden, and scouted out places to build a tree house where no one would find them. Jack began to look for branches to lash together for the tree house floor, and Maddie started to cry—thinking of how much their mother would miss them. Jack pretended to be exasperated, but he was secretly glad for the chance to return home.

It killed him to think that this time he'd be running away *from* Maddie—not with her. He frowned, turning back to his work and his plans, putting his sister out of his mind.

Coming to Hubbard's Point had, in some ways, been a good plan—Nell was like her mother. She loved the beach, had salt water in her veins. She dragged Jack down for a swim every afternoon. It was elixir to him, the cool water, swimming to the raft with Nell. He found himself glancing up the hill at Stevie's house, wondering what she was doing.

Every evening, things were just the way they'd been since the accident. Not even salt air could change the fact that Nell could never fall asleep right away. She began getting panicky an hour or so after dinner. Now that she had Stevie's book, she wanted to hear it every night. Jack read the story of the penguin father tending the egg, over and over, till he knew it by heart.

He'd kiss Nell goodnight, and then the drama would begin. She'd toss and turn, call Jack in to read to her some more, talk to her, rub her back. They had a pattern where he'd go in six, seven times before dawn. Some nights Nell would start to cry with frustration and exhaustion, and she couldn't stop—she missed her mother with every cell in her body.

One night a huge thunderstorm roared down the Connecticut River valley. Murderous thunder shook the trees. Jagged bolts flashed. The storm accelerated, dread and immediate. The crashes terrified Nell. She clung to her father like a koala bear, shrieking and trembling.

Jack held her, unable to comfort her. Somehow Stevie's book had highlighted the emptiness he felt—defined his life in a new way, put it into words and pictures. How could he deliver, be both mother and father to Nell? Yet seeing Stevie, talking to her that one time, made him feel as if he was on the right track.

He was incredibly selfish, to be keeping Nell away from Madeleine—and to be making plans for Scotland. He tried to tell himself that the move made sense career-wise. That it was a step up, to work directly for such an important client. But he knew, deep down, that he was running—and taking Nell with him.

Suddenly, rage at Emma boiled through him. Not Madeleine—*Emma*. He rocked Nell, trying to remember a lullaby—any lullaby—overcome with hatred for his dead wife.

Whom he had loved more than his own life. He had fallen in love with Emma right here, at Hubbard's Point. She had been so pretty and funny, with such a sharp edge. They had met on the boardwalk. He was just standing there after a basketball game, covered with sweat and grime, trying to cool off in the breeze. She came walking along, took the towel off from around her waist and handed it to him.

"You need this," she said drolly.

"Excuse me?" Taken aback, he stared at her standing there in a pink-checked bikini, a gold chain around her neck and others around her wrist and ankle. She had cleavage. Serious cleavage. He'd never paid attention before—she was one of his younger sister's friends. She'd been over at the house the weekend before, when a bunch of Jack's friends came down from Hartford. Jack's girlfriend, Ruth Ann O'Malley, was there, and he'd noticed Emma talking to her about colleges.

They were both beautiful girls. He had certainly been aware of that about Emma since the first time Maddie brought her home. Ruth Ann wasn't a serious student—and she didn't pretend to be. She had gotten into Pine Manor, a junior college not far from Jack at MIT. Jack had pegged Emma as having the same sort of college path, but he was wrong—he'd heard her telling Ruth Ann that her first two choices were Wellesley and Smith.

"You're sweating," she said.

"No kidding. I just played one-on-one."

"Who won?"

He laughed in spite of himself. She seemed completely sure of herself—she had more confidence than most girls his own age—she was, in fact, in the same league as Ruth Ann.

"I did," he said.

"Hmm," she said. "I didn't know math majors could play ball."

Was that as double-entendre as it sounded? Jack's head spun; he didn't want to let on that he had made wrong assumptions about her, too: he'd noticed her looks, not her brains, and he'd been surprised to hear she was aiming for the Seven Sisters. He'd finished using her towel. She took it from him, then stood on her tiptoes and wiped his brow.

"You missed a spot," she said.

His knees had practically given out when she'd

passed the towel across his skin, pressing her breasts against his chest. She was Madeleine's friend, he already had a girlfriend . . . the reasons he shouldn't be feeling what he felt were legion and severe.

Ruth Ann was gorgeous, athletic. She had been the head cheerleader at South, Jack's old high school. Jack could see her now: the way she always did her hair, put on lipstick, wore a sarong to match her bathing suit. All his friends thought she was hot and he was lucky. He told himself that as he stood on the boardwalk. Young Emma must not know the effect she had on men. It couldn't be intentional.

A few mornings later Jack was at the cottage, sitting at the kitchen table drinking OJ and reading the *Hartford Courant*'s sports page. A knock sounded at the door, and it was Emma—coming to pick up Maddie. She wore a yellow alligator shirt, tight cutoffs, and huge movie-star sunglasses, and she grinned when she saw him.

"Played basketball lately?" she asked.

"Every day."

"And you didn't come to me, to dry off?" she asked.

"Nope. I used my girlfriend's towel," he said, trying to ignore the shaking in his bones.

"How *is* little 'Pith' Ann?" Emma asked, the invisible quotation marks around the name both wicked and seductive.

"*Ruth* Ann," he corrected.

"Oh, right."

"Watch what you say, little girl."

"I'm not a little girl, and you know it."

"You're my sister's friend. Let's leave it at that, okay?"

"Okay with me if it's okay with you," she said, giving him a smile that set his skin on fire. What was she—a professional Lolita?

"How old are you, anyway?"

"Same age as your sister. Half a year older, actually."

"Seventeen?"

"Nearly eighteen."

"Why'd you call Ruth Ann that?"

"Because she's a little fluff—exquisite to look at, but dumb as the day is long."

Jack's mouth dropped—okay, so she was nearly eighteen. Somewhere along the line he'd forgotten to notice that Maddie—and her friends—were growing up. But what was she doing, putting down Ruth Ann—his girlfriend and the most popular girl at South Catholic?

"She doesn't seem your type at all," Emma said, taking a step closer, pulling her sunglasses down her nose, looking right into his eyes. "I would have thought you were too smart to fall for a girl like her. *Pine Manor?* Really!"

"Just because you're going to Wellesley . . ."

"A-ha! You *were* paying attention!"

"Why do you want to go there?"

"Because I want a brilliant career and because I want to date boys at MIT," she said, smiling wickedly. "What are you doing going out with a girl who's going to *finishing* school, better known as 'Pine *Mattress*'? That's not enough for a smart, smart boy like you."

"What would you know about it?"

"I've grown up watching you, Jack Kilvert," Emma whispered. "I know more about it than you do. . . ."

Jack had wanted to kiss Emma right there. He had fallen in love with her three days before—the minute she'd handed him her towel. He'd fought the feelings for seventy-two hours, and he'd continue to battle them for another few days. He and Ruth Ann had been going steady. But Emma was right—Ruth Ann wasn't enough for him. He'd felt guilty by how bored he felt talking to her. He tried to tell himself that her beauty would be enough to make any man happy—and that what he had with her would be enough for just about anyone. Why not for him?

And then, along came Emma . . .

She had the most brilliant way of twisting his heart by flattering and putting him down, all at the same time. The practice had never failed. She'd won him over by making him want, more than anything in the world, to make her believe the best about him.

The crazy thing was, Emma had more in common with Ruth Ann than he was sharp enough to see. So much, in those early days, had to do with the outsides of things. They looked like such a good couple, they forgot to actually become one. Their hearts were completely alien to each other. Jack had never guessed what Emma really wanted, the importance of what—eventually—would steal her from him and Nell.

Had she ever really loved him? Or had she just wanted to prove to herself that she could get him?

Now, alone in the night with their daughter, he was racked by the storm inside him, a storm that put the lightning bolts and thunder cracks outside to shame: to make up for it, he rocked his little girl as gently as he could. "It's okay, Nell," he said. "Everything's fine. . . ."

The words sounded so feeble. Could Nell feel his heart crashing against his ribs? If she had any idea of the thoughts in his head, the words he'd like to scream at her mother for leaving them like this, she'd never rest again.

The storm trailed away across Long Island Sound, leaving peace and cool, clean air behind it. The humidity had broken. More amazing, Nell was sound asleep. Her breath was as steady as it used to be when she was tiny and Emma was there. She didn't even flinch when Jack lay her down in her bed.

"Nell?" he said out loud, to test her. She snored quietly and didn't stir.

Jack knew exhaustion when he saw it. She had tired herself out. Outside, the sky was clear. He checked his watch: five-thirty. He was wrapped so tight, he thought he might explode. Although the heat was gone, he was burning up. If he hurried, he could run down for a quick swim. The beach was less than a minute away.

Tying on his running shoes, he checked on Nell once more: out cold. He slipped out silently, closing the door behind him. He began to jog down the winding road, but it turned into a sprint. He raced against the feelings inside. His feet pounded, loud in his ears. The beach was asleep. Overhead, the stars blazed in the dark blue sky. He wanted to shout and wail, wake up the world. Wake up Emma.

When he got to the boardwalk—the place he had

first met his wife—he slowed down. His chest hurt, and he slapped his hand over his heart. What if he died right now? It would be so easy, the pain would stop, the confusion of hating Emma, resenting her for leaving him with Nell and no idea how to do it all. But the idea of abandoning Nell made him straighten up, shake his head to clear the bad thoughts.

A layer of gray hung in the east, lightening the sky with approaching dawn. The stars were white globes, with the morning star shining brightest of all. Jack sat on the boardwalk bench to take off his shoes. Then he saw Stevie.

Twenty yards off, she crossed the footbridge in silence. She looked barely human coming through the dark, more like an apparition. He saw her leap onto the sand, and then run down the hard part of the beach, below the tide line. She stopped, just even with where he was sitting, and looked up and down the beach. For a moment, he thought she had seen him. He held his breath.

But she turned toward the Sound. She seemed to gaze out, out, toward the east, greeting the day. She opened her arms wide, as if she wanted to embrace every single thing. The sight moved Jack in a way he hadn't felt in too long to remember. He strained to see through the darkness, and he saw her drop her robe on the sand.

Her bare skin was pale in the starlight. He saw the curve of her breasts and hips, and he drew in a slow breath. He sat on the edge of his seat, as if something was about to happen, something almost unbearable. She dove into the water—straight in, without having to stop and get used to the cold.

He watched her head, her strong strokes, as she swam straight out. Venus hung in the west, illuminating her wake. Jack craned his neck, to keep her in his sight. He felt incredibly guilty and disloyal, thinking this way. But he was rocked by a surge of passion, and he wanted only to run down to the water's edge, dive in, swim out fast, meet Stevie in the waves.

He momentarily lost sight of her—panic came up— where was she? Had she gone under? He scanned the water around the raft, about fifty yards offshore, and the big rock just beyond.

She didn't need saving: she had bypassed the raft, swum straight to the huge rock. Jack remembered going out there as a boy. It was massive, granite, a great place to pretend to be shipwrecked. Mussels and barnacles covered its surface; lobster pots washed up in storms, their lines snagged on its jagged outcroppings.

Jack watched as she hauled herself out of the sea, climbed to the top of the rock. She was nude and beautiful, and black water turned silver streaming off her body. Again, she opened her arms, as if to hold an invisible lover, and then she dove back in. She came steadily toward shore. Could she see him? Jack's pulse raced. He was torn in half—knowing he had to stay hidden, wanting to stand up so she'd see him.

But he didn't move. She swam before dawn for privacy. This was her beach. He knew that right down to his bones. She owned the white sand, the deep blue sea, the granite, quartz, moonstones, and sea glass, the mystical seaweed: she possessed this place. All those people who came during sunny daylight hours and set up their blankets and chairs and umbrellas were missing the secret magic.

Stevie had it. Backing silently away, Jack could almost believe she had called down the thunderstorm, cooled off the night. He wanted to wait, to see her body again, closer this time, silvered with sea water. He was in a trance. Part of him wanted to taste the salt on her skin—he knew it was wrong, didn't know where it was coming from. Still, the desire to watch her was so strong, he felt it pulling him down, down—to the tide's edge.

He turned instead, to give her back the beach.

Quickly, hoping she hadn't seen him, he grabbed his shoes and ran back up the sandy road to the house where his daughter lay sleeping.

STEVIE SAW JACK on the boardwalk just as she was finishing her swim. Her heart caught and lurched—was he waiting for her? Had he seen her undress? How could she get out of the water if he was standing there? She watched him hesitate, as if deciding whether to walk toward her. Instead he backed away, grabbed his shoes from the boardwalk, trotted up the road.

The beach was hers again, as it was every day at this time. She wanted to feel the serenity, a connection with the earth's rhythms and mystery, that she always felt—but instead she felt almost wild.

Seeing him there, that split second before he'd turned away, she had sensed his yearning. She could read it in his posture. She knew it by heart, because she felt it herself. Since childhood, since her mother had gone, Stevie had felt a sense of helpless longing; she satisfied it in all sorts of ways. She had fallen in love too hard and too wrong, traveled far and wide to escape herself, reached for stars that were really just cheap lights.

Stevie's longing was deep and eternal; she knew she'd be searching for love until she found it. And on good days, she knew she had found it already: in nature, her early morning swims, Tilly, her birds, the secrets and intimacy of New York City. She hoped that the man would find it in something he already had and could never lose: the love of his daughter.

She wondered who had been staying with Nell while he'd come down to the beach. Maybe he had a girlfriend. Or maybe he didn't. . . .

In any case, nothing quite explained the stirring she felt as she wrapped the robe around her bare shoulders, ran barefoot through the sand and across the wooden bridge, up the stone stairs. Every sensation was a bolt to her heart. She took a quick outside shower, making sure to grab a few bugs from the early morning cobwebs in the dew-laden grass: "fairy tablecloths," she had called them as a child.

She thought of what her father had once told her: "Stevie, there are two ways to look at the world. You can either believe that there's no magic anywhere on earth, or you can believe that there's magic in every little thing."

Going inside to feed her thriving crow, thinking of how she had felt to know Jack was watching her swim, she really had no choice but to believe in the second.

"WANT TO SING 'Lemon Tree'?" Nell asked during recreation break two days later. "My aunt taught it to me."

Peggy chuckled. "My mother and Tara sing that song. They take turns playing the guitar. It's really pretty."

"I'll bet Stevie sings it, too," Nell said. She liked saying her name: *Stevie.* "Stevie gave me a book she wrote. She has an aunt who inspired her to be an artist!"

"A weird, witchy artist!"

"Would a witch sing 'Lemon Tree'?" Nell teased.

"Maybe she likes to turn kids into lemons!" Peggy teased back. They had just come out of the water, and they sat on Nell's towel with Peggy's wrapped around their shoulders.

The group sat in a circle, so Laurel could tell them a real-life story about how some of the cottages were almost a hundred years old, and how, long before they were built, the Eastern Woodland Indians used to hunt and fish on these rocky points, and how, later, the Black Hall artists used to come here to paint. "Use your imaginations," she told the kids. "Think about the beach in a new way."

Nell loved the assignment. She and Peggy decided to

explore the beach—and in doing so, Nell knew she was visiting places her mother, her aunt, and Stevie had gone before. They stopped at Foley's Store, to look in the drawer for love notes, and they went to the Point, where they sat on the rocks watching someone fish from a rowboat, and they cut through more backyards than Nell could count to look at secret gardens and hidden birdbaths.

A few days later they lay in the sand—no towels—at Little Beach, another secret place they'd reached through a path in the woods. They had collected the best sea glass Nell had ever found anywhere, including two rare blue pieces. Staring at the sky, Nell thought of Aunt Aida's painting in Stevie's room. Peggy told her about school in Black Hall, and Nell told Peggy about moving up to Boston from Atlanta.

"That's why you have that pretty accent?" Peggy asked.

"Yes. I'm a Southerner."

"I'm a New Englander."

"I like the way you talk," Nell said. "You sound like my mother. She was from the North. My father, too."

"Um, you don't have to tell me, but how . . . well, what happened to her?"

The question made Nell sit up. Her chest deflated fast, fast, and her shoulders caved around her heart. She shook her head—she could never talk about it.

"I'll tell you," Peggy said, hiking up to sit beside her. "What happened to my dad. It was bad. I'm only telling you 'cause I want you to know it isn't just your mom . . . other parents die, too."

"I dream about it at night," Nell whispered. "My mother being gone. I miss her all the time. And I think, if she's gone, then I could be gone too. As if I were never here. And I get afraid to fall asleep. I make my father hold me till I get so tired I can't keep my eyes open. I think if he holds tight enough, I won't go away." A feeling of her mother's touch came over her—the light way her fingers trailed down the back of Nell's head when she brushed her hair. It was so gentle, almost like the summer breeze. Her father tried, but his hand was so heavy. . . .

"I used to make my mother take me to the bridge where my father's car . . ."

Nell's eyes flew open. "Car accident?"

"Um, sort of," Peggy said, turning red. "He, well, he was killed. And his car went into a creek."

"My mother had a car accident too," Nell said.

"Really?" Peggy asked, her mouth dropping open.

"She lived after it. She did . . . I thought she was going to be okay. I wanted her to be. . . ."

"How did hers happen?"

Nell huddled up, arms around her knees, making herself very small. She didn't like to talk about it. But something in Peggy made her want to tell the story, find words for how her mother had died. Yet the sudden change of feelings confused her so much, she couldn't speak. Peggy just sat there, no expression on her face at all, waiting. Finally, Nell was ready.

"She and my aunt were driving home," Nell said. "It was my aunt's birthday. She and my mom went away for the weekend." She swallowed. The words seemed to scratch her throat coming out, as if each one had claws. "It was my mom's first time away from me."

"Ever?"

Nell nodded. "My aunt flew down, and she rented a special birthday car. A sports car. Pretty and red . . . They drove to St. Simons Island. I used to love St. Simons Island . . . it was our favorite Georgia beach. . . ."

"And they had an accident?"

"Uh-huh."

"Are you mad at your aunt when you see her?" Peggy asked.

"I don't see her," Nell said.

"Because you hate her for what happened?"

"No . . ." Nell grabbed a handful of sand and let it run out through her fingers onto her knee. The grains stuck in the fine blonde hairs, trickled down her skin. She did it again and again. The funny thing was, her throat felt as if the sand was in *there*. As if she had swallowed a whole lot of sand, and it was making it very hard to swallow. "I love my aunt," she said.

"Then why don't you see her?"

"My father will never forgive her," Nell said. "For what happened." The two friends were silent then. Nell held the pieces of sea glass she had collected, feeling them with her thumb.

Her mother had once told her that sea glass took a long time to make. You had to throw back the pieces that weren't ready—that were too sharp or shiny, not yet tumbled smooth by the sea. Closing her eyes once more, she thought of her mother, her aunt, and Stevie. She wondered whether they had ever sat in this spot.

She wondered whether her sea glass had been here then, whether maybe one of them had picked it up, thrown it back into the waves because it wasn't ready.

It would be nice to think that she had, Nell thought. Oh, it would be so nice. . . .

chapter 8

THE NEXT THREE MORNINGS WERE dark and clear, and each time Stevie crossed the footbridge on her way to swim, she glanced at the boardwalk and saw Jack waiting. Daylight began to infuse the sky before actual sunrise. While Stevie swam—in a bathing suit now—she saw the stars fade so that only the brightest planets were left. They cast a passionate spell, somewhere between romance and Eros. Stevie felt crazy and confused. As if knowing, and not wanting to leave her alone in that state, Jack would wait until she'd safely emerge from the sea, and then he'd turn to go home.

On the fourth morning, she woke up earlier than usual. The air was muggy again, hazy and thick. She heard the Wickland Shoal foghorn, off in the distance. She imagined Jack hearing it, too. They were connected by strange mysteries—they'd barely had a conversation, but she could hardly wait to see him. The sheets felt sensuous on her body, reminded her of the brush of the sea. Her thighs ached, and her nipples stung. The sensations were wild, made her think of making love with a man she barely knew.

That day she skipped her swim.

Tilly lay on top of the bureau, already awake, green eyes glowing. The gaze seemed to accuse Stevie of cowardice. "I know," Stevie said. She got out of bed, pulled on some clothes, refrained from looking out the window to see whether Jack was on the boardwalk. She fed her cat and the bird, and instead of going down to the beach, she climbed into her car and drove out of Hubbard's Point.

She sped along the Shore Road, through the marshes and past the Lovecraft Wildlife Preserve. The air was heavy, thick and white. Egrets fishing the shallow coves, pale sentries, raised their heads as she passed. Stevie imagined the birds telegraphing her approach to the castle, its ivy-covered stone tower and ruined crenellated parapet just visible above the tree line. She pulled through the stone gates, touched the horn as she passed the fieldstone gatehouse where Henry lived, then turned up the steep driveway—smooth pavement giving way to a dirt-and-gravel track. When she reached the top, she smelled coffee.

It was only six A.M., and fog hung in wisps in the pine trees. Stevie took a deep breath, listening to the low foghorn—Wickland Shoal. Although the castle compound was high on Lovecraft Hill, it overlooked the mouth of the Connecticut River and Long Island Sound, and water sounds carried as if they were just feet, and not half a mile, away.

Stevie's aunt and mentor, Aida Moore Von Lichen, lived and painted here. She was seventy-nine, going on thirty, with more life and verve than most people a quarter her age. Born in Ireland, just like her beloved brother Johnny, Aida was an abstract expressionist of great repute. She had come of age in New York with the Cedar Tavern crowd, as artistic as her brother was literary.

Aunt Aida owned the castle—a folly built in the 1920s by her much-older second husband, Van Von Lichen, the heir to a ball-bearing fortune and, more famously, a Shakespearian actor known for playing Iago and Falstaff. Uncle Van had died twenty years ago, having run through the bulk of his once considerable inheritance. Lacking a desire for grandeur, and, in any case, the money to sustain it, Aunt Aida had let the castle fall to bat-and-mouse-infested ruin, and she lived instead in a small wooden outbuilding with no inside plumbing. She drew her water from an old white pump with wrought-iron curlicues. An ardent environmentalist, she loved her simple life. Summers in Black Hall, winters in the Everglades. Her stepson, Henry, recently retired from the Navy, was spending the summer in the castle gatehouse.

"Hey, Lulu," Henry called to Stevie as he hiked up the hill. Fifty and movie-star handsome, he *looked* like he belonged on the grounds of a ruined castle.

"Hey, Commander," she called back.

He had nicknamed her Lulu for her dark-haired and messy-love-lifed resemblance to the Hollywood silent-screen femme fatale Louise Brooks. She called him

Commander because that was his rank at the time of his retirement.

"You're out early," he said.

"I've got a lot on my mind," she said.

Henry raised his eyebrows. "Oh no," he said. Very tall and powerfully built, he had silver hair, sun-struck blue eyes, and wind-weathered ruddy skin from nearly thirty years of standing on the bridge of various naval vessels.

"What?" she asked.

"Who's the lucky man?"

"I'm not in love."

"Lulu, you're always in love. That's your blessing and curse."

"More curse," she said, giving a small laugh. She turned away to hide the blush in her cheeks.

They walked over to a rounded boulder at the edge of what Aunt Aida called "the pine barrens"—a forest of white pines and cedars stretching all the way to Mount Lamentation. Developers were always offering her tons of money to sell the land, but she swore she'd die penniless before giving in.

Henry lit a cigarette and handed it to Stevie. She blew three perfect smoke rings, and then gave it back to him.

"You bring out the bad habits in me," she said.

"Someone has to, and you have so few left. Now that you're sober, I've lost my drinking buddy," he said. They laughed and shared the cigarette, watching fog clear from the mouth of the river. The foghorn continued, even though the Sound was now visible, flat-calm and silver-blue, already dotted with boats trailing the scratched lines of white wakes. Across the Sound, Orient Point was a thick pencil smudge.

"You're not going to tell me?" he asked.

She shook her head.

"You've had it rough, kid," he said. "You've given so much and gotten so little."

Cocking her head, she looked up at him. "Really? I feel as if I've hurt everyone I've ever loved."

"That, too," he said. Although Henry had never married, he had had a long relationship with a woman in Newport. She had broken up with him last year, and although he did his best to act like a stoic sailor, he was really heartbroken. "Love's a bitch for all concerned."

"Except when it isn't," she said. She closed her eyes, wondering what that even meant. She had never stopped hoping. In spite of all her missed connections and thwarted starts, she had always expected to find lasting, thriving, nurturing love. The desire for it was so strong, it still brought tears to her eyes, and again she thought of her friend on the boardwalk.

"Press on regardless," he said, falling back into Navy-speak as he so often did. It was oddly comforting, and Stevie smiled.

"Really?" she asked.

He nodded. "I admire you," he said.

"For getting divorced three times?"

"For getting *married* three times," he said. "You are the bravest girl in the world. I should have had the balls you have. All Doreen ever wanted was a ring, and I was too chickenshit to give it to her."

"Oh, Commander," she said. "Marriage isn't any guarantee. . . . I'm living proof."

"You're a force of nature, is what you are," he said. "I've sailed frigates and aircraft carriers through hurricanes that didn't have half the power you have."

"Get out," she said, watching boat traffic in the water below, listening to birds in the trees all around.

"All those years aboard *Cushing*," he said, "I used to read two things. Shakespeare, because . . . well, you can imagine. And the *Odyssey*."

"Makes sense for a man on a voyage."

"You know what you are, Lulu? You're a new character in the *Odyssey*." He searched for the name. "Luocious," he said, pronouncing it *Lu-oh-shus*. "You're a siren who lures men onto the rocks . . . but it's always your boat that gets wrecked."

She looked away, because it felt so true. "Is Aida up?" she asked, kissing his cheek and then pressing herself up from the rock.

"Of course," he said. "Sometimes I think she never sleeps."

"See you later, Henry."

He saluted, watching her go.

Stevie let herself into the house. Aida was already painting. She stretched her own canvases, and this one was a six-by-six-foot square, almost as big as the north-facing picture window. Stevie stood back and assessed the work, the latest in her *Beach Series*: the top half was pale gray, the bottom half dark blue. The line where they met resembled a horizon.

"How are you, dear?" Aida asked without turning around.

"In need of a wise aunt," Stevie said.

Aida laughed. "And you came here?"

Stevie gave her a hug. Her aunt was tall, like her father. She wore a red bandana over short curly white hair, and a smock on top of denim overalls. Her nails were short and chipped, caked with oil paint.

"There's coffee on the stove," Aida said.

"Thanks." Stevie refilled her aunt's *Cushing* mug—a tribute to her stepson's last vessel. Then she filled one for herself. The two women sat down at the old pine table, sipping their coffee. The cottage windows were wide open, and the salt-and-pine-scented breeze blew through.

"What brings you here so early?" Aida asked.

"I'm trying to figure some things out," Stevie said. "I had two visitors last week. They've both . . . gotten under my skin."

"Hmm," her aunt said, staring at her painting.

"One is a little girl, Nell. She's the daughter of an old, dear friend of mine . . . Emma. She told me that Emma died."

"Oh dear," Aida said, looking directly at Stevie.

"I know. I can hardly believe it—it seems like we were just swimming together, lying on the sand, planning to have wonderful lives . . ."

"So young . . . too soon," Aida murmured.

"It's awful. She died in a car crash—and our other friend, Emma's sister-in-law Madeleine, was driving."

"How terrible for Madeleine!"

"I know," Stevie said. "I can't even imagine."

She and her aunt just sat in silence for a minute. Stevie stared over at the new painting, at the pale rectangles. Were they sea and sky or sand and sea? She didn't know, and it didn't really matter: the feeling of beach washed over her, calming her.

"Emma did have a wonderful life, it seems," Stevie said. "Her daughter is just like her—so smart and sweet, curious about life. She wanted to meet me, because I was her mother's friend, and she just marched up the hill and introduced herself."

"*That* took courage," Aunt Aida said, deadpan.

"What do you mean?"

"Well, that *sign*, for one thing. It puts the fear of God into all who approach. But, of course, that's the point, isn't it?"

Stevie didn't reply at first. She knew she pushed people away—and it worked. Kept her safe, free from making any more mistakes, from getting hurt, from hurting others. "Well," she said finally, "Nell made it past the sign. And I invited her and her father over for dinner last week."

"That was good of you."

"It went well—except toward the end, I mentioned getting together with Madeleine, and that didn't go over at all. Jack—Nell's father—wants nothing to do with her. And she's his sister!"

Aunt Aida tilted her head, as if that made sense. Stevie stared at her.

"She's his sister—how can he just write her off like that?"

"You're an only child, dear."

"What does that have to do with anything?"

Aunt Aida took a deep breath, stared at her seascape as if for strength, then looked directly into Stevie's eyes. "I always wished that your parents had had another child. Always thought that you needed a sibling. I wanted you to have what Johnny and I had. And what your mother had. Then you would understand about Madeleine and . . . what was his name? Jack. That's it."

"Well, I don't have a sibling, so you have to tell me, Aunt Aida."

She sighed. "Siblings are each other's world—when they're young. For me, it was The World According to Johnny. The sun rose and set on him. We had the same family, same house, same music . . . we walked each other to school."

"Jack was four years older than Maddie."

"Johnny was three years older than I . . ."

Stevie listened.

"Age isn't so important. It's the *feeling* that is. You grow up counting on each other. You never want to let each other down. So when something big happens, it's cataclysmic. It might be easier to write each other off than actually ever talk about it. Or *deal* with it."

Stevie pictured how angry Jack had gotten when Stevie had started talking about Madeleine. He had looked so upset—not just furious, now that she thought about it, but hurt. As if the breach had taken something away from him.

"Did that ever happen with you and Dad?" Stevie asked.

Her aunt didn't reply. Instead, she stood up, got the coffeepot, and refilled their mugs. Then she sat down again. "You could call Madeleine yourself," she said.

"I know," Stevie said. Having this talk with Aida solidified the thought she'd already had. "I plan to."

"Good," Aunt Aida said.

Again they fell silent, sipping the hot coffee. Stevie couldn't stop looking at her aunt's painting. It seemed so open and free—with a feel of the bigness of sea, sky, and beach. The series captured the beach's changing colors and moods. Stevie felt disturbed about her morning swims, about how much she looked forward to the silent connection with her old friend's husband. She had made so many mistakes in love—and in the last few years, barricaded herself off from the world. She pictured the sign in her yard, and she thought of Henry's words, about boats being wrecked on the rocks of love.

"What's that?" her aunt asked, watching Stevie's face.

"Oh, I was just thinking of Henry," she said. "He was just cautioning me about falling in love."

"He's a fine one to talk," her aunt snorted.

"Won't Doreen give him a second chance?"

"How about a *hundred*-and-second chance? Henry sailed the seven seas, always expecting that she would be there waiting for him. Then he left the Navy, expecting to just move in and expect her to welcome him with open arms. She wanted a commitment; Henry, as much as I love and adore him, wanted a roommate."

"He loves her," Stevie said.

"Does he?" Aunt Aida asked. "Or does he just want

her to be there when he wants her? I'm unconventional in plenty of ways, but I think he should have married her. It upsets me to see him so sad. Just as it upsets me to see *you* so sad. . . ."

Stevie blinked, looked away. "I'm fine," she said.

"Sweetheart," Aunt Aida said. "You are not. I can see it. It's a beautiful summer day, and you are troubled. Meeting Nell and her father has stirred you up, and it's not just about Madeleine, is it?"

Stevie shook her head. Sometimes she and her aunt didn't even need words. Aunt Aida had been there for her after her mother's death; no one could ever take her mother's place, but her aunt had loved her so steadily, and knew her so well.

"We think love's supposed to solve everything," her aunt said quietly. "But so often, it's just the opposite. It creates difficulties we never even dreamed of."

"Love?" Stevie asked. "I barely know them. . . ."

"You loved your friend Emma," her aunt said. "And they are her family. I have the feeling that meeting them, seeing them together, has set you thinking about your own life. About family . . ."

"You're my family."

"I love you, Stevie, but I'm not enough. You deserve to find someone to really share a life with. Have children with . . . I had my years with Van—and the happiness of watching Henry grow up. I wish Van and I could have had kids of our own, but it wasn't to be. Henry's like a son to me." Her gaze became very somber. "I don't want you to be lonely."

"I'm not lonely. I'm just being careful—I'm not going to make the same mistakes again. I have you . . . Tilly . . . my work. You know what a balm it is, our painting, our art . . ."

"Tell yourself that, my love," Aunt Aida said, "when your whole life has passed you by, and you have nothing but canvases to show for it."

Stevie felt herself blush. She stared at the wood grain in the pine table, shocked by the feeling in her heart.

"When do you think you might call Madeleine?" her aunt asked, gently changing the subject.

"I'm not sure," Stevie said. "Maybe after Jack and Nell leave the beach."

"Too bad you have to wait that long," Aunt Aida said. "I have the feeling that she's in great need of a friend. And so are you. . . . Perhaps more to the point, Nell's in need of an aunt."

The words hung in the air. Stevie waited, but Aunt Aida said nothing more. The only sounds were birds singing in the trees outside, and her own heart pounding in her ears.

Driving home, Stevie remembered one sunny day— the afternoon of the July full moon. She and her friends had walked through the path to Little Beach. They were teenagers, wanting to escape the prying eyes of adults. Boys were on their minds. Everyone liked someone— the details were delicious and absorbing. Falling in love was one summer-long fever.

"They want us," Emma said.

"And we want them," Madeleine said.

"I told Jon I'd meet him on the Point," Stevie said.

Desire was new to her. Already she was experiencing the loveliness of obsession, the crazy heat of getting lost in wanting someone, thinking about him all the time.

"What time did you say you'd be there?" Madeleine asked.

"Two," Stevie said, and Madeleine nodded, as if to say she'd better go.

But Emma had a different take on it. She grabbed both her friends by the hand and pulled them down the hard sand, just below the dry seaweed of the tide line.

"Nighttime is for them," she said. "Daytime is for *us*."

"But . . ." Stevie began.

"Listen," Emma said. "After dark is boy time. When the sun goes down, and the air is cool, and we get chilly, so they put their arms around us . . . And our bare feet get so cold, and their kisses are so hot . . ."

"And driving around in their cars," Maddie said, "listening to the radio, where every song reminds you of what you're going to do later."

"And makes you want to marry them," Stevie said.

Maddie chuckled, but Emma shrieked with laughter. Stevie stood there, turning red and trying to keep her expression steady—to look as if they hadn't just cut her to the quick. They thought she was joking. How could she explain to her two best friends that she was completely serious. She knew it was crazy, but that was how she felt.

"Good one, Stevie," Emma said. "You're going to marry *Jon*?"

"I didn't say that," Stevie said, knowing that her

friends thought he was too shy, too serious, and not tall enough.

"Let me just tell you something about the reality of the situation," Emma said. "My mother's younger cousin is visiting us. She's only twenty-two—just graduated from Wellesley—so for me, it's like spending the summer in a sex seminar. I know things you don't. You have to be very careful about finding the *right one*. You have to choose someone who'll be your friend for life. He has to be cute enough to want to kiss forever. That's a tall order, in itself. When you find that person, then you go on the twenty-four-hour plan, all day and all night long, around the clock . . . but till then . . ."

"We get your days," said Madeleine, who, with an older brother, seemed to know the same thing. "And full-moon nights."

"Not nights," Emma said.

Stevie smiled, but she felt rattled inside. Was something wrong with her? Her friends seemed better equipped for the uncertainties of dating. She hadn't been kidding when she'd said songs on the radio made her dream of getting married. She wanted to feel safe forever; she wanted to know that the person she loved would never leave her, never hurt her. She wanted to get it all nailed down.

Emma ran up to the tall grass that grew between the beach and the marsh. She looked around, came back with a long white driftwood stick, bleached by the salt and sun.

"What are you doing?" Stevie asked.

"Drawing a magic circle," Emma said. "With us inside."

Stevie and Maddie gathered together, holding hands. Emma joined them, reaching her arm out and tracing a big "O" in the sand. She spun around and around, scoring the circle deep and sure.

"It's like the sun and the moon," Stevie said.

"Heavenly bodies," Maddie said.

"Exactly," Emma said. "Boys are one thing, but true friends are another. Let's never forget that, okay? No matter what happens? We can't lose each other. . . ."

Stevie's throat tightened. Already she had felt herself being pulled away: wanting to be with Jon, instead of her best friends. She wanted summers to continue forever, with the beach girls by her side.

There was nothing like being held in the night, by a boy whispering her name. But why couldn't Emma and Maddie fill the void instead? If she willed it, tried hard enough, she could make it so. . . . As the girls turned round and round, Emma's stick tracing the hot sand, it seemed as if a spell was being cast.

"We can't lose each other, we won't lose each other," Maddie chanted, getting into the spirit of the magic.

"By the power vested in me," Emma said, "by the power of . . ."

"The noonday sun," Madeleine supplied.

"The full moon and the Pleiades," Stevie added.

"I now pronounce us . . . bonded for life," Emma finished.

Dizzy, they all collapsed on the sand. It occurred to Stevie that Emma was stating the obvious: bonded for life. Hadn't that always been so? They lay on their backs, laughing till they cried. For Stevie, lying on her back in the sun, the tears streaming down her cheeks were pure emotion, and only half laughter.

When they got up, they ran to the most private part of the beach, behind the big rock that looked like a great white shark. Emma was the first to peel off her bathing suit. The others followed, and ran into the water after her. They formed a new circle, just offshore.

"We should do this tonight—skinny-dip in the moonlight," Madeleine said, treading water.

"She doesn't listen," Emma said with pretend sadness.

Stevie waited—she was thinking the same thing as Maddie.

"Daytime is for us," Emma said. "Nighttime is for *them*."

"Boys," Maddie said.

"Jon," Stevie said.

"It's how we keep them," Emma said. "We already know we have each other . . . but even though we're not together, looking up at night, we have to just know that the girl in the moon is winking down at us. . . ."

"The girl in the moon?" Stevie asked, delighted.

"Yep," Emma said. "That old man in the moon got tired, and the future was clear."

"It's a job for a woman," Stevie said.

"That's clear, all right," Maddie said.

"You know it," Emma said, and they all dove laughing into the next wave.

STEVIE DROVE home from her aunt's house that July day intending to call Madeleine that afternoon. But in the end, she didn't phone at all. She called information and got an address for Madeleine Kilvert on Benefit Street in Providence, and wrote out an invitation. Driving to the post office, to mail it, she held it in her hand. She might be making things worse; she hadn't been completely forthcoming in the note. . . .

But the sound of Nell crying for her aunt, and the memory of three best friends on the beach, were too much for her, and Stevie did the only thing she could: dropped the envelope into the box and hoped for the best.

ONE MORNING, while Nell was at recreation, Jack took a walk up the hill. He told himself this was all business—it had nothing to do with the dreams he'd been having, passionate, sweat-drenched dreams, during the few hours of sleep he'd had this last week. This visit was strictly because Stevie had had a childhood similar to Nell's—she'd lost her mother young. Maybe she could help him know what to do.

He knocked at the door, feeling like one of those young boys climbing the tree outside her window— afraid of intruding, yet wanting to know what happened inside her world. His heart was beating in his throat. She walked barefoot into the kitchen, dressed in jeans and a halter top.

"Hi," she said through the screen door.

"I don't want to bother you," he said. "Are you painting?"

"That's okay—come in." She held the door open, and as he walked past he waited for her to say something about seeing him at the beach, at dawn, but she didn't. They were both pretending it hadn't happened. Even though he had been here before, this felt all new. He wanted to seem serious, to cover up the strong attraction he felt toward her. And this *was* serious—he needed help with Nell. He stood in the kitchen.

"Is everything okay?" she asked.

"It's fine," he began. "Well, it's not really fine. Nell . . ."

"I'm sorry about what happened, when you were here," she said. "I didn't mean to get her so upset."

He nodded. The memories of how Nell had been the last few nights surged up. He was exhausted from not sleeping. "She's really having a tough time," he said.

"What do you mean?"

"Not falling asleep, crying a lot. We—she—has a therapist in Boston. Dr. Galford. He's a nice guy; he was recommended by the psychiatrist she saw in Atlanta after her mother's death."

"That's good," Stevie said. Her eyes were so bright. The smile was there, as warm as ever, but just not as big. It made Jack want to embrace her. He wanted to be held. *That's it*, he thought. He just wanted someone to put her arms around him and tell him he was doing a good job. That he wasn't screwing up too badly. That's what Stevie's smile made him feel like. But he'd been drawn in by smiles before—and he didn't quite trust himself to know what was happening.

"Good that she sees Dr. Galford? Or good that she saw the one in Atlanta? See, I don't know . . . about any of it. I never went to a therapist when I was a kid. Neither did my sister. We never had anything—any reason to go. We thought that only troubled kids saw shrinks."

"I saw one," Stevie said.

"You did?"

She nodded. The smile was gone from her lips, but it was still there in her eyes. Jack leaned toward her. He wanted to lean right into her. He wanted her to know how much he wanted her to catch him. He felt so tired . . . he'd made a mess of his life with Emma. He couldn't do it again—not to Nell. He made himself stand straighter.

"After my mother died," she said. "I saw someone every week. I don't think I'd have survived without her."

"Really?"

"Really," she said, with complete resolve.

"What did you do with her? How did she help?"

"We played," Stevie said. "She had a dollhouse, toys, dolls. I would sit at her table and draw. I didn't know it then, but I was learning how to be an artist, and how to make sense of my world by telling stories about it . . . they were always about birds. Bird mommies and babies . . ."

"Like your books," he said.

"Yes. It was easier to write about robins falling out of the nest, blue jays flying away and not coming back, than people. Does Dr. Galford draw with Nell?"

"I don't know," Jack said. "Our deal is that what goes on between them stays there."

"That's good," Stevie said, the smile coming back. "My father did that. Let it be between me and Susan. That was her name—Susan."

"I wanted Nell to have a summer off," Jack said. "I just wanted her to have some time to be normal . . . to not have to spend these beautiful beach days seeing a doctor."

"Maybe that's how she'll be able to enjoy the beach days," Stevie said. "By seeing her doctor."

Jack moved his hand on the counter; his finger brushed against Stevie's. She moved her hand away—but when he looked into her eyes, he saw such emotion, again he wanted to hold her. She was rocked—maybe remembering her own painful childhood. He had to let her know how much talking to her helped. But before he could come up with the words, she spoke.

"I sensed that being here upset Nell the other night," she said. "Maybe it's because I remind her of Emma. Knowing that her mother and I were friends . . . or that she spent time in this house. And I think she wants to see Madeleine so badly, and she sees me as a way to make that happen."

"You're right about that," Jack said, hearing Nell's weeping, ringing in his ears.

"I've decided to stay away from her," Stevie said. "And not invite her—or you—back. It's not that I don't want to—"

"Stevie," Jack began.

But she stepped back. He could see her trembling,

and now her smile was completely gone. This conversation had shaken her to the core—but what part of it? About Nell? Or Emma? Or was she looking at the circles under his eyes, the two days' growth that he needed to shave—and thinking that her father had done a much better job of holding it together?

"I really just came to get your advice," he said. "I shouldn't have bothered you."

She stepped forward, took his hand. The touch seared his heart.

"You're not bothering me," she whispered. "I just . . . I'm afraid I'm hurting more than I'm helping. For right now, anyway. Something about meeting me seems to have stirred Nell up. Especially since I've invited Madeleine here."

"You have?" Jack asked. His first reaction was joy—followed, and overridden, by panic.

"Yes. Don't worry—I'm not going to push anything."

"Even though you don't agree with my decision?"

"Even so. You seem like a wonderful father. I don't want to get in the way of that. I'll try not to, I really will. But since you seem to be leaning toward it, why don't you take Nell back to Dr. Galford?"

"And then?"

"See if she feels better. If she does . . ."

We can come back, Jack thought. *We can be friends.* . . . He looked around: Madeleine was going to visit Stevie here. What if he just backed down—let Nell and Maddie see each other? It would make them both so happy. But the thought of seeing his sister, looking into those eyes, bringing her back into their lives . . . It was too much.

"What Nell is going through is so terrible," Stevie said, her voice stronger now. "It's the worst thing in a child's world. Losing a parent . . . But Nell is strong, and she has you. You're doing a great job."

"Even in keeping Maddie away?"

Stevie stared at him, as if deciding how much to say. "I don't understand your reasons for that," she said. She couldn't give him her blessing on that—wasn't even going to pretend to. She just stared into his eyes, as if she could will him to back down and change his mind.

Jack couldn't do that.

He hated to let go of Stevie's hand, but he knew that he had to. They were standing so close. He was so exhausted, he hardly remembered backing away, saying goodbye. But he held on to that smile. . . .

As soon as he got home, he arranged for an emergency session with Dr. Galford. A quick drive up to the office outside Boston, after normal hours, so the doctor could fit Nell in. Jack sat in the waiting room while his child was inside, seeing her psychiatrist. Was she drawing? he wondered. Was she weaving a story about losing her mother and aunt all in the same year?

Jack didn't know. He tried not to think about his sister, how much Nell missed her. Was Maddie on her way to Hubbard's Point? Was she already there? He hung on to the picture of Stevie's smile, and to the words she had said to him: *you seem like a wonderful father*.

Part Two

chapter 9

MADELEINE KILVERT PACKED AN OVER-
night bag, made sure Amanda had the office
covered, and kissed her husband goodbye.
She drove out the driveway of their old house, down
Benefit Street, onto the highway. Chris had been fine
about her leaving—he was a great husband and all for
anything that would cheer her up.

Receiving Stevie's invitation had, initially, buoyed
Madeleine up like nothing in recent memory. She had
gotten the mail, gone through all the bills and cata-
logues. There was a white envelope with elusively familiar handwriting; where had Madeleine seen it before?

The postmark—Black Hall, Connecticut—unleashed
tides of memory. Summers at Hubbard's Point, a series
of rented cottages—one of which had required that she
share a room with her brother—the crescent beach nestled between two rocky points, the lazy days with her
two best friends . . .

Stevie—it was from Stevie Moore.

The card had been seductively short and to the point:

> *Your presence*
> *Is requested*
> *To celebrate*
> *The July full moon*
> *Regrets only . . .*

At the bottom, a pencil drawing of the backs of three young girls sitting on a jetty, holding hands, watching a full moon rise out of the sea. Moonlight shimmered, a path on the water.

A banner overhead said, BEACH GIRLS SWOON BY THE LIGHT OF THE MOON. Along the bottom of the picture, Stevie had written the date, an address, and the words "Plan to stay over!"

Madeleine had rushed to show Chris.

"An original Stevie Moore," she said.

"Your famous friend," he said. "I've heard so much about her over the years . . . great drawing."

"It's of the three of us. She doesn't know about Emma."

"How did she find your address?"

"I have no idea," Madeleine said, staring at the invitation.

Stevie was her wonderful "friend who got away." Along with Emma, they had been so close at one time. But then Emma had moved to Chicago, and the Kilverts had stopped renting at Hubbard's Point. Emma had become part of the family, falling in love with Jack. But once everyone headed off to college, they lost track of

Stevie. She had written for a while—Madeleine recognized Stevie's handwriting and remembered being at Georgetown, getting mail from RISD.

At one point, Stevie had shocked Madeleine by announcing that she was married. It was sudden—elopement, justice of the peace, a done deal. Madeleine had called Emma, and she remembered that they'd both felt strange—that it had happened so fast, and that Stevie hadn't considered inviting them. They'd remembered how intensely she'd gotten involved with boys at the beach—Emma would always give her a hard time about it, but Maddie had somehow realized that it had to do with the huge loneliness left by her mother's death.

Then . . . what had happened? Madeleine had gotten engaged to Chris, Jack had married Emma . . . weddings, family holidays.

They began to see Stevie's books at bookstores. Her career took off. Madeleine always read the "author's note" in the back of the books. In that way, she tracked Stevie's life. Some books mentioned a husband, others didn't. In light of how intensely Stevie had always fallen in love, it made Madeleine sad. "Living the life of an artist—unconventional and unstable," Emma had said.

Madeleine once bought one of Stevie's books—a Christmas present for Nell, when she was five. Driving down I-95, Madeleine tried to remember the story; something about swans . . . about two males fighting for the female. Emma had taken one look at the book and said, "This is obviously Stevie's life. All that drama . . ."

"Well, swans do fight to the death," Madeleine had

said. "Remember at Hubbard's Point, seeing them go at it?"

"Not really," Emma had said, holding Nell on her lap. "I don't remember it, and I don't really like the idea of you-know-who reading about violence—even in the world of swans! Poor Stevie—I hope she gets it together and finds happiness."

"She had it tough," Madeleine said. "Losing her mother. I always figured that that's what made her get married so quickly, in college. I wish we hadn't lost touch with her. We were all so close! How can life take people so far away from each other?"

"She'd probably be bored with us," Emma had said. "Two happily married ladies, no turmoil or torment . . ."

"Looks like an interesting story," Jack had said, flipping through. "And the pictures are great."

"Maybe so, but not for our daughter. Nice thought, buying her the book, Maddie—but I think I'll donate it to the library."

"Okay," Madeleine had said. She remembered shooting Jack a little look—Emma had signed on to her mother's way of romanticizing life, wanting everything to look and, if possible, *be* perfect.

Back then, Madeleine and Jack and their families took turns having Christmas at each other's house. That year they were in Atlanta, enjoying Emma's evergreen-and-white-lighted fantasy of the season. Gorgeous decorations, a never-ending loop of carols, cookies for the whole neighborhood, the fattest goose from the best butcher on Peachtree Road.

Leaning forward, in that one swift glance, Madeleine

and her brother had a private chuckle—they loved Emma enough to indulge her in banning Nell from reading Stevie Moore's too-true book about swans, and in so many other things.

Madeleine had avoided really looking at the reality of her brother's marriage—he kept it from her. And Emma had just held her unhappiness inside, trying out new ways of finding comfort.

The irony was, within a couple of years, Emma's search for perfection had led her to get very involved in her church. She joined committees, got swept up in a group of lay volunteers. Madeleine had watched with amazement as Emma seemed to decide her life was frivolous and changed direction in midstream. When Nell was seven, Emma decided not to decorate at all: to save the money she would have spent on a tree and wreaths and lights, donate it to charity instead. Jack was upset because Nell was so disappointed. Madeleine secretly remembered Emma, Stevie, and the homeless woman in New London; she wondered whether somehow Emma was doing penance for taking that ten dollars.

Or had Emma really wanted to do good works—to volunteer somewhere that mattered, change the world a little? She couldn't possibly have known that her last choice would destroy her family.

All of that, and more, had been present in Madeleine's initial reaction to Stevie's invitation: trepidation, happy memories, excitement, curiosity, and a need to tell someone the whole story. But now, driving south, crossing the Rhode Island–Connecticut border, getting closer to Hubbard's Point, she wasn't feeling so positive.

Stevie's drawing of three girls . . . Stevie, Madeleine, and Emma. *Beach girls swoon by the light of the moon.* Maddie couldn't help thinking of Emma's proclamation of long ago: *the days are for us, the nights are for them.* . . .

Emma. Driving along, Madeleine couldn't help glancing into the empty seat beside her. She missed her sister-in-law terribly. After the accident, in the hospital for rehab on her injured shoulder and arm, Madeleine had met other patients who had survived bad wrecks. One woman who had lost her right arm told Maddie about "phantom limb."

"Sometimes I'll be sitting there, and I feel my right arm itching, and I'll go to scratch it. The itch is so real! Or I'll go to pick up a pen—I'm so used to writing with that hand—and be amazed when I can't do it. It's exactly as if I have a phantom arm."

Now, driving past Mystic Seaport, Madeleine knew she was suffering from "phantom Emma syndrome." It seemed impossible that she wasn't here—riding alongside, talking away, changing the radio station from Madeleine's favorite oldies rock to Emma's ever-elegant classical music.

And one syndrome begot others. Madeleine now experienced phantom-Jack syndrome, phantom-Nell syndrome. She missed her brother and niece so terribly. It got harder, not easier.

What was she doing, going back to Hubbard's Point, the place where she and Jack had first met Emma? Stevie might have happy thoughts of the three teenage girls, but to Madeleine, the strongest Hubbard's Point memories had to do with how her family came there together.

It was going to be very difficult, trying to explain that to a woman who, apparently, got married the way some people changed shoes. Stevie was probably great in her own way, but Madeleine couldn't expect her to understand what she was going through. She glanced at her face in the rearview mirror: this last nightmare year really showed. She'd put on weight, and she'd gotten into the habit of drinking a little more than she should—to forget the things she couldn't stand to remember.

Madeleine hoped that Stevie's free-spiritedness extended to liking to drink. She had brought along two bottles of champagne—Mumm Cordon Rouge. They had to toast the July full moon in style!

Numbness was really the only way to go.

PEGGY'S AUNT TARA had a bicycle-built-for-two. After recreation and lunch, Nell and Peggy went over to ride it. Peggy's mother was looking after Nell while her father went to Boston on business; she was there, too. Nell watched the two older women showing the girls how it was done, riding the long blue bike up and down the quiet street behind the seawall.

"One of you gets to steer," Tara called. "The one in front. The other rides in back, and has to completely give up control."

"Which is the hardest thing in the world to do," said

Peggy's mother, riding behind, laughing. "Giving up control . . ."

"What?" Peggy asked. "Will you two speak English?"

Nell watched the two women and thought of her mother and aunt. They had acted the same way: laughing, joking, saying things that made sense to no one but them. Grown-up women with young-girl secrets. The funny thing was, instead of feeling left out, Nell had felt safe and secure seeing and hearing them together. She felt that way now, watching the women laugh and have fun.

They were wearing matching straw hats with daisies in the headbands. Mrs. McCabe had on a Black Hall High School T-shirt, and cutoff shorts, and Tara wore a black shirt with FBI in yellow letters over her bathing suit. Tara rode the bike down the middle of the road, weaving in and out, as if it was an invisible obstacle course. Peggy's mother took her bare feet off the pedals and held them up in the air, saying, "Wheeeeee!"

"Mom, you're being totally embarrassing," Peggy said.

"She can't help herself," Tara said, stopping the bright blue bike in front of the girls. "It's completely hopeless."

"You're just jealous because I have such a great voice," Mrs. McCabe said.

"Wheeee!" Tara said, even louder, even though they had stopped. *"Wheeeeeeee!"*

"My God, you are both demented," Peggy said, but she laughed. Nell tried to, but she was too busy remembering her aunt teasing her mother for having such a perfect house: always clean, never any dust, nothing out of place, garden like something out of a magazine. Something else that reminded her of home: the way Tara's and Peggy's mother's gardens were so beautiful and cared for.

"Nell's not embarrassed by us, are you, Nell?" Mrs. McCabe asked.

Nell shook her head. "No," she said.

"Thank you. Now," Tara said, "who wants to drive?"

"That'd be me," Peggy said.

"Okay with you, Nell?" Mrs. McCabe asked. "You think it's easy to sit in back, but I'm telling you, it's not. You have handlebars, but you can't steer."

"That's okay," Nell said.

Tara showed Peggy the handbrake and made sure her seat was the right height, and Mrs. McCabe adjusted Nell's seat and helped her climb on. Her arm felt so strong and sure, and for a few seconds Nell remembered what it was to have a mother.

The girls went up and down Tara's road a couple of times, then biked along the seawall and boardwalk, around the boat basin, up the road that bordered the marsh. They passed Foley's Store and cut through the old cemetery, past Nell's cottage, up toward the Point. It was as if Peggy could read Nell's mind. . . .

Peggy had to half stand, riding the bike up the small hill to Stevie's dead-end street; Nell pedaled with all her might, to help. Tall trees shaded the pavement, and a fresh breeze blew off the water. Peggy was pointing to the left, saying something about how there'd be a full moon that night, that maybe they could watch it rise.

But Nell was staring up to the right: at Stevie's

house. It sat in the shadow of oak and pine trees; in this light, the white shingles looked blue. She wondered if that's how it had looked when her mother and Aunt Madeleine used to visit, when it used to really *be* blue.

She thought of the baby crow, wondered whether it had learned to fly yet. She wondered whether Stevie ever thought about her. Whether she wondered why Nell hadn't come back to visit.

Nell knew that the reason her father didn't want her going over to Stevie's wasn't because of her writing schedule. It was because Nell had had a meltdown, let the cat out of the bag about missing Aunt Madeleine. Nell knew that her father was definite about not wanting her to see her aunt, and he didn't want Stevie stirring things up and making them worse.

The knowledge brought tears to Nell's eyes. If Peggy happened to turn around, Nell would say that it was the wind, that she'd gotten dust in her eyes. They rode the bike to the end of the road, turned around, and came back.

On the second pass, Nell saw that the sign was still there:

PLEASE GO AWAY

The sight of it made her bite her lip. She didn't want to go away. She wanted to climb the hill, knock on Stevie's door, have ginger ale with a slice of peach in the glass, and look at Stevie's and Aunt Aida's paintings and talk about her mother, Aunt Maddie, everything.

Just then, a beige car pulled slowly down the road.

The driver must have been looking for an address, because he didn't see the bike—Peggy had to swerve to avoid the car. The move gave Nell butterflies in her stomach.

"Crazy Rhode Island driver!" Peggy said.

"Rhode Island?"

"Yep. With a sailboat 'Ocean State' license plate."

Nell didn't reply, thinking of how strange it was that a Rhode Island car would drive up Stevie's street just as she'd been daydreaming about her aunt. Aunt Madeleine and Uncle Chris had moved to Rhode Island. Providence. Nell knew, because her aunt still sent her cards. She wasn't to respond, but Aunt Maddie never stopped trying.

Peggy rode them toward the hill down to the beach.

"Get ready," she called back to Nell. "Think we can handle the hill?"

"Hope so."

"Hold on tight!"

"I'm holding on," Nell said.

They started picking up speed. Nell gave a half-turn over her shoulder, for one last look at Stevie's shadow-blue house. She tried to see the car from Rhode Island, but Peggy was going too fast.

If only things were different, Nell thought. If only we could all be together.

She held on to the handlebars that couldn't steer, closed her eyes because Peggy was driving and it didn't matter anyway. She felt the wind rushing through her hair, and she wished and wished.

chapter 10

STEVIE HAD TAKEN A WALK IN THE dark last night. Barefoot, she had gone up the road to Jack's house. Standing behind the privet hedge, she'd listened to crickets and smelled the salt wind. It stirred the leaves overhead.

The cottage windows were open. Stevie wanted to call through them: to ask Jack to come to the door, let her in. She wanted to ask him how Nell's visit to Dr. Galford had gone. Taking a step through the hedge, she paused.

They were sitting on the sofa. Golden light from a table light illuminated Nell's brown hair; Jack's head was bent close to hers, and the steady sound of his voice came through the open window.

" 'The field mouse ran for the fallen tree, scrambling into the hollow, as the owl dove through the darkness, talons open . . .' "

Stevie watched as Nell nestled under his arm, heard the expression in Jack's voice as he read from her book

Owl Night. She saw Nell delight in being so close to her father, and she watched the way Jack looked down, to make sure she wasn't too scared. Stevie felt frozen, standing in the yard. She wanted to go inside more than she could remember wanting anything in a long, long time. Instead, she had just turned, walking home through the warm night.

Now, again, Stevie stood back and watched a different drama unfold, also involving Nell—standing at her kitchen window, waiting for Madeleine to arrive, she saw the bicycle-built-for-two go riding past. Just then she saw a beige car drive slowly down the street, saw the bicycle turn around in the cul-de-sac and come back, recognized Nell and her friend, and then held her breath as Madeleine climbed out of the beige car.

Her heart racing, she waited for Madeleine and Nell to see each other. They didn't, and Stevie didn't know whether to feel relieved or disappointed. She opened the door and hurried down the hill.

"You made it!" she called.

"I can't believe this!" Madeleine said.

They hugged and hugged. Stevie grabbed Madeleine's bag, and they walked arm-in-arm up the stairs.

"This place is exactly the same," Madeleine said, looking around. "As soon as I drove under the train trestle, I felt I'd entered Brigadoon or something!"

"The land time forgot," Stevie said.

"The houses are still so small and quaint, the gardens are straight out of the Irish countryside, kids still ride their bikes down the middle of the street, as if they own it—just like we did! I practically mowed down a bicycle-built-for-two!"

Stevie held her breath, but Madeleine said nothing more on that subject. They went into the house, and Madeleine walked through, exclaiming with delight. "Oh my God! It's just the same! I can just see your father sitting at his desk over there"—she pointed at the mahogany keyhole desk in a corner of the living room. "We'd have to be so quiet when he was working . . . and I remember thinking how cool it was to have a father whose work was writing poetry!"

Stevie smiled. "I felt the same way," she said.

"I used to wonder why, with this incredible view"— she pointed at the windows, overlooking the rock hillside, beach, and sapphire blue cove below—"he arranged his desk so it was facing the wall. And I asked him, and he said, 'Because poetry requires a different kind of view, one where you look *inside*.' "

"I remember."

"Is that true for you, too?" Madeleine asked. "You've done so well, Stevie. I'm always so proud to see your books. Do you need an interior view, too?"

"The opposite!" Stevie laughed. "Come on up-stairs—I'll show you your room and my studio!"

Up they went. Stevie gave Madeleine the guest room, where her mother's mother used to sleep. It faced east, and because the house was on a point jutting out into the Sound, blue water was visible through the trees on that side of the house, too. Next, they went into Stevie's room.

"This is incredible," Madeleine said, looking around

at the bedroom/studio. It extended the width of the house, with big picture windows overlooking the beach. Because it was up so high, the aerie had an incredible view looking southwest over the Sound. A stark picture, very modern and striking, hung on one wall. A black bird perched in a cage. Bookcases lined the interior wall. "I don't remember your room being so big, when we were young."

"It wasn't," Stevie said. "After my father died, and I decided to keep the house, I knocked out a wall and made one long room out of two."

"You paint here. . . ." Madeleine said, standing before Stevie's easel, looking at the paintings.

"Yes," Stevie said. "I like to fall out of bed, directly into work. I guess . . . I use my dreams for inspiration." She blushed. Watching Madeleine gaze at the painting of two ruby-throated hummingbirds, mates drawing nectar from red flowers, Stevie wondered what her friend would think if she knew that Stevie's recent dreams had all been of Jack?

"These are beautiful," Madeleine said. "Is this your next book?"

"It is," Stevie said. She stared at her own work: the brilliant green birds, symbolic to her of hope and perseverance. She thought of how the story had changed since its inception at the beginning of the summer. It had once been about two birds and their long migration from New England to Costa Rica; now it was about one summer in the life of a pair nesting and raising a chick—inspired by Stevie's dreams, and by meeting Nell. The constant, in both stories, was the flowering red trumpet vine that attracted and fed the tiny birds.

"I feel so honored to see it in progress," Madeleine said. "To think that my old friend would turn out to be such a well-known artist!"

"It's nice of you to say that," Stevie said, smiling.

"Everyone at Hubbard's Point must be so proud."

"The local kids all call me a witch."

"You're kidding!"

"I've become this generation's resident eccentric— just like old Hecate. Remember her?"

"Yes, of course. Is she still here? And Mrs. Lightfoot, and Mrs. Mayhew—do they still have their cottages? And does your aunt still live in that bizarre castle? Oh, and all the cute boys that we all liked. I need the rundown on everyone. That was really our raison d'être back then—the beach and boys."

"Let's go outside and have some iced tea—I'll fill you in on the whole story," Stevie said. She walked downstairs ahead of Madeleine, feeling slightly guilty. She had a secret agenda that her friend knew nothing about. Seeing Madeleine felt unspeakably poignant— she seemed so vulnerable. She wore a flowing black jacket, even though it was eighty degrees out, to hide the weight she'd gained. Madeleine's eyes were bruised with sadness—she didn't know that Stevie already knew why.

Stevie opened the side door, settled Madeleine in a teak chair beneath the white market umbrella, and went into the kitchen to assemble a tray. When she returned to the terrace, Madeleine put a finger to her lips, pointed at the trumpet vine. The resident humming-birds—four of them—were darting in and out of the tubular flowers.

Stevie served the iced tea and sugar cookies, and the old friends sat there in silence, watching the birds. Their green feathers were iridescent in the sunlight, their wings a blur. Finally, when they left, Madeleine spoke.

"Emma would love this," she said.

Stevie clutched her glass, wondering what to say.

"She died," Madeleine said. "In a car accident, a year ago."

"I'm so sorry," Stevie said. If Madeleine wondered why she didn't sound surprised, she didn't show it.

"She married my brother, Jack. You know they met right here, at the beach." Madeleine gazed down the hill.

"Yes," Stevie said, trying to breathe, picturing Jack and Nell sitting alone on the sofa last night.

"They met right there, on the boardwalk," Madeleine said. She pointed at the blue pavilion, a roof built over the boardwalk just for shade. "They went out all through her college and his grad school. Jack went to MIT, became an engineer. Emma went to Wellesley. When she graduated, they got married and moved to Atlanta. She never really worked, but she became a crackerjack volunteer. If you needed something done, and had no money, Emma was the one you called."

"Really?" Stevie asked, trying to see Emma in that role.

"I used to tease her, saying she'd developed a social

conscience in order to pay back that woman with the shopping cart in New London . . . she turned out to be very good at raising money."

"That shouldn't surprise me at all," Stevie said, thinking back. "I remember that day, when she got the money in the first place—all she had to do was smile at those young Coasties! She came toward me, holding the two tens . . . that devilish smile on her face. She said 'easiest thing I ever did,' and we laughed so hard."

They both smiled, thinking of Emma's smile and the way she could get boys to do what she wanted.

"I lost track of you both," Stevie said. "We were inseparable for those summers, and I never imagined we wouldn't stay in touch forever. But life got crazy. . . ."

"We all watched you," Madeleine said. "You were our famous friend. I remember when Disney did a movie of your book on robins in the orchard."

"It was supposed to be set here in Connecticut, but they filmed it on Bainbridge Island, in Washington State."

"We watched it, hoping to see you."

"I was an extra," Stevie said. "I was a beekeeper, with netting over my face. If you blinked, you'd miss me. Did you and Emma watch it?"

"Not Emma," Madeleine said, and something about the way she said it made Stevie's stomach flip. "My husband, Chris, and I."

"I wish Emma were here," Stevie said.

Madeleine nodded. "I miss her every day. Driving down from Providence, it seemed unbelievable to me that she wasn't with me. Two of us . . . just doesn't seem right. We were always three."

"Down there," Stevie said, staring down at the beach. It seemed a million miles away, all the happy people, families with kids, girlfriends with towels close together, blankets and umbrellas covering the sand. Stevie looked at Madeleine's pale skin, and her own, and thought of how far away the beach seemed to two girls who once had practically lived on it.

"Emma would have none of this," Madeleine said. "Sitting up here in street clothes. She'd be in her bathing suit already, slathering our shoulders with sunscreen."

"Maybe we should follow her lead—?"

"No way," Madeleine said. "I'm perfectly happy on your terrace, watching all those skinny people having fun."

"The calorically challenged," Stevie said.

"You should talk. Look, let's get down to business. Is the sun above the yardarm? Well, it is somewhere. I brought champagne—I stuck it in the fridge as I walked by. Let's pop the cork and toast to the good old days."

Stevie went into the kitchen and took one of Madeleine's bottles from the refrigerator. She filled a glass of ginger ale for herself, grabbed a champagne flute from the back of the shelf, and returned to the terrace.

"These were wedding presents, and the first time I used them," Stevie said, placing the flute on the teak table, "was after my second wedding. It was here, on this very terrace. You are sitting in the exact spot where I said 'I do.' "

"You were married at your childhood home—how romantic!"

"That's one way to put it," Stevie said darkly. She undid the foil, took the wire cage from the cork, and expertly opened the bottle without causing a pop—just a gentle cascading hiss, the way Linus had taught her. She poured.

"What's this? You're not joining me?" Madeleine asked.

"I'm joining you," Stevie said. "It's just that I've had my lifetime quota of champagne. Ginger ale works better for me now."

"Well, that's no fun," Madeleine said, frowning. But she lifted her glass anyway. "Here's to you, Emma—wherever you are!"

"To the beach girls!" Stevie said. They sipped their drinks. Madeleine downed half of hers at once. Stevie remembered drinking that way; she could almost feel the sudden, yet fleeting, relief Madeleine would be feeling right now.

"Beach girls," Madeleine said, delighted by the phrase. "Remember, it was like a sorority. Just the three of us."

" 'Beach girls now, beach girls tomorrow, beach girls till the end of time,' " Stevie said. She looked down the hill. The sands were so white, and the Sound was so blue—as if the calm bay between the headlands was a mirror held to the sky. She watched as Madeleine filled her glass again.

"Here's to," Madeleine began, then stopped. She gazed into the distance, as if trying to come up with a suitable next toast. "Here's to . . . what?"

Stevie's spine tingled as she sat very still, the next toast right there on the tip of her tongue. *It's not time*, she told herself. *You have to wait.* As hard as it was, she did. And Madeleine made the next toast herself: "Here's to being together again!"

"Together again," Stevie murmured.

They clinked glasses. Madeleine happily sipped her drink and didn't even seem to notice that Stevie's gaze was trained down toward the beach, on a cottage behind the seawall at the edge of the silver-green marsh. A house with a beautiful garden, and with two women in straw hats standing out in the middle of the road—Bay McCabe and Tara O'Toole, greeting two girls on a bicycle-built-for-two.

IN BOSTON, Jack sat in his office at Structural Associates, on the thirtieth floor, watching planes land at Logan Airport across the glittering blue harbor. Francesca walked in, closed the door behind her. She looked beautiful, stylish in a perfectly tailored Prada suit and black slingback heels. Her tan glowed, from the last two weekends visiting friends on Nantucket. She leaned against his desk.

"Hello, stranger," she said.

"Hi, Francesca."

"Let's see. I sent you postcards from Siasconset, and extremely tantalizing—if I do say so myself—photos of me aboard my friend's boyfriend's hundred-foot yacht, and invitations for you—and Nell—to hop a ferry and come see me, and you *ignore* me."

"I'm not ignoring you . . ."

"All summer, you've made yourself scarce. You came to Boston from Atlanta months ago, and you've barely showed your face here since June. The boss doesn't mind that you're hardly in the office," Francesca said. "I'm wondering whether he's figured it out."

"Figured what out?"

"That you're leaving the firm."

Jack stared down at the blueprints on his desk. They were for his most recent project, a new highway bridge in New Hampshire. Francesca had worked on it with him. He remembered how she had surprised him, kissing him on site, their first visit after construction began. He felt bad. Not because he was leaving the firm, and her, but because he didn't have any feelings about it at all.

"How did you hear?" he asked.

"I haven't heard—I've seen. Seen how you're never around. How the boss gives all the big stuff to Taylor. How I'm alone every weekend. When I thought we'd have lots of fun this summer."

"It's not you, Francesca," he said. Now his eyes fell on the Faneuil Hall Bookstore bag. Inside were more books he'd bought for Nell, both by Stevie Moore: *The Red Robin and the North Wind* and *Gull Island*. He didn't think anything could beat *Owl Night*, but he wanted to buy them all. He raised his gaze from the bag.

"No? Well, it feels as if it is. I spoke with Ivan

Romanov, and he asked me whether I'd be coming to visit you in Inverness. You couldn't even tell me yourself!"

Jack stared at her. He had no excuse, no justification. She was a wonderful woman, a fine engineer, a great colleague. He had gone behind her back, taken a job with a client of their company. "I'm sorry if you think I've undercut you."

"Undercut me? Excuse me, but you're an idiot. I didn't want the job—I knew Ivan was planning to put it out to headhunters—he floated it out there to me at the same time he did you. I just feel—betrayed. We're friends, Jack. I thought we might even be more than that."

"I'm sorry." Jack wanted to take her hand, because he had thought they might be more than that, too. When had his feelings changed? *When Nell met her*, he knew. . . .

"What was it?" she asked. "Trying to have a relationship while we worked together? Did I push too hard?"

"You were, you are, wonderful," he said. "I told you—it's not you."

"Then, what?"

"It's us—me and Nell," he said. "We've been in a hurricane. That's what it feels like. A big storm that knocked our house out from around us. Nothing feels safe or right anymore. It's not fair for me to invite anyone else into the storm."

She rolled her eyes. "Beautiful metaphor."

"It's the best I can do."

"Your child is so traumatized you can't date, so you

uproot her from America and take her to Scotland? That makes sense."

Jack thought of Stevie and what she had said about "geographics." His gaze went back to the bag.

"My parents were divorced," Francesca said. "Nell's a big girl now. She'll get over you dating. She really will. You don't have to protect—"

Jack felt ice in his veins. Francesca's words went straight through him. He thought of Emma in her hospital bed, Madeleine in hers, the huge hole in his and Nell's family. "Divorce?" he said. "Nell's parents aren't divorced. Her mother is dead. She was killed, suddenly, one beautiful Georgia day, driving home from the beach with my sister."

"I don't mean to be insensitive. I get what you're saying. My point is, you're off base. A father starting to see other women is the same as far as a girl is concerned—it's going to suck no matter what."

Jack shook his head hard. He knew that the exchange was just making it very easy for him—much easier than he deserved.

"No, *you* don't get it," he said. "Nell comes first. Period. She's having a problem with us. She's not ready for this—for me seeing other people. Seeing you. I'm sorry, Francesca."

She put her hand on the door and stared at Jack. "You should be," she said.

Plenty of comments ran through his head, but he stayed silent and let her have the last word. He was relieved when she walked out and closed the door behind her.

He leaned back in his chair. Looking around, he realized that this place had never felt right. He had come to Boston hoping to escape the grief and loneliness of Atlanta. Francesca had tried to be a good friend, but it wasn't enough. He opened his desk drawer, took out his and Nell's passports.

What would she think of Scotland? Suddenly he couldn't even imagine what he'd been thinking, making these plans. He pictured standing in Stevie's kitchen, talking about Dr. Galford. Nell had had two sessions since then. Suddenly she was sleeping a little better. Would they have to find a new doctor in Inverness? And who would Jack have to talk to, when he felt overwhelmed by everything Nell was going through?

At the beginning, Scotland had seemed like a good place to take a little girl. Jack's parents had traveled there with him and Madeleine when they were young. He remembered that they had bought Maddie a tartan kilt. Muted red-and-green plaid, it had a big silver thistle pin in front.

They had gone to the northwest highlands, seen the ancient, rounded mountains at the edge of the sea, taken a ferry out to the Isle of Harris to buy tweed. They'd returned to the mainland, staying in a hotel overlooking a sea loch. Their father had hired a gillie to take them salmon fishing on the river. He remembered the low mist, the green hills, the river winding its way into the loch.

"I'm not catching anything. I never catch anything," Maddie said.

"Be patient," their father said. Maddie caught her brother's eye, and he made a face and shrugged.

"Jack, if you catch a fish, I'll kill you," she said.

"You'll get one before me," he said. "I'll bet you."

"Does the Loch Ness Monster live in there?" Maddie had asked, tugging Jack's hand. She was ten, and he was fourteen, wishing he was back in Hartford with his friends.

"No," he'd told her, just to keep himself amused. "A worse monster lives in there. The River Creature."

"What's that?"

"Trust me, Maddie—you don't want to know."

"No, I do! I do want to know!"

Their father and Murdoch, the gillie, fished in earnest while Jack and Maddie held their rods and talked. Jack described the River Creature: long and slimy, like a snake, a white snake that lived in the deepest hole in the river. It liked to eat salmon, so when the fish were biting, the River Creature was right behind them—to spring out of the water and catch the fish *and* the fisherman.

"See?" Jack said. "We're lucky we're not catching anything."

Madeleine had laughed—seeing right through him, knowing he was just trying to make her feel better. Now, holding his and Nell's passports, Jack hoped he could do the same thing for Nell.

He hoped he could take her to Scotland, chase her sorrow and worries away. He'd never forget how happy Madeleine had seemed on that trip. She had loved the heather, the bagpipes, even the streams of clear brown water tumbling over the peat. If Scotland could do that for his little sister, it might weave the same magic for Nell.

It had to.

He rolled up the blueprints, put them into the tube. Then he packed up his briefcase with a few travel documents and Stevie's books, and he left the office. He hoped he wouldn't run into Francesca on the way out, and he didn't. Saying goodbye to the receptionist, he got into the elevator and headed down to his car. Nell was safe at the beach with her friend Peggy and her family. He knew she'd be anxiously awaiting his return—she didn't like him gone for too long.

Most of all, he was glad to have new Stevie Moore books to read to her. He really loved *Owl Night*, but he couldn't bring himself to pick up the one about emperor penguins again. That book had come to remind him of the talk he and Stevie had had in her kitchen. When he'd had to hold himself back . . .

He had been reading the penguin book to Nell over and over, the nights just before those three incredible mornings, when he would go down to the beach to watch Stevie swim.

He missed those mornings, more than he could believe. The memory of seeing her silhouetted against the rising sun gave him goosebumps, even now. Watching her dive into the dark water, come up for air, swim all the way out to the rock. Why hadn't he just gone for it—swum out to meet her?

She had to have seen him there, yet she hadn't mentioned it when he'd dropped by her house. How did she feel about it? If she'd been upset or mad, wouldn't she have mentioned it to him?

The memory was like a hidden vice—something no one had to know about, the fact that he pined for those mornings, spying on Stevie. He felt it in his skin, his groin, every inch of his body. He told himself that he wasn't looking for a relationship—he and Nell were nowhere near ready for that. The fact that Nell liked her had nothing to do with anything. The fact that she understood losing a mother didn't really mean much; or that she'd reassured him about Nell needing help, needing to go back to see Dr. Galford. She had helped him through a hard time, but it didn't really count.

Or did it?

No, desire seemed safer than anything that might lead to a real relationship. This thing he felt for Stevie was pure desire.

It was, in spite of the fact that his daughter loved her.

If only Stevie hadn't been so insistent about Madeleine—to the point of inviting her to visit Hubbard's Point. Jack's stomach flipped, wondering when that would happen. He just wanted to be left out of it. That was one subject closed to Jack forever. As far as he was concerned, he used to have a sister. The little girl he loved so much—in Scotland, at school in Hartford, playing tennis at the beach—was gone.

Nell couldn't understand why he wouldn't see or talk to Madeleine—and Jack prayed she never would. If that moment ever arrived, she'd be grateful to him for keeping them apart.

He got into the car, pulled into Boston traffic for the long ride back to the beach.

The great thing about longing, about fantasy, about the picture in his mind of Stevie climbing out of the water, silver drops streaming from her lean, lithe body, was that reason had nothing to do with it.

chapter 11

THE FIRST BOTTLE OF CHAMPAGNE
tasted so good going down, Madeleine could
hardly wait to open the second one. It wasn't
much fun to drink alone—especially while Stevie just
nursed her ginger ale. Madeleine pretended not to notice.

"Tell me all about you," Madeleine said. "Do you live
here all year round?"

"No," Stevie said. "I spend the winters in New York
City, come out here at the end of May."

"I guess that's the beauty of being an artist—flexibility.
I work in the Brown development office, raising money."

"Providence is a great city. I went to school there,
RISD. It's where I met my first husband."

Madeleine hadn't wanted to ask about the husband
situation, but she was glad Stevie had brought it up.
She sipped her champagne.

"Kevin was so bright and talented," Stevie said. "We
fell in love the first week of freshman year. He had such

raw talent . . . no one could do with a line what he could. Just so simple, and spare . . . he cut away all the bullshit. RISD can be so progressive, avant-garde . . ."

"The graduate show is certainly eye-opening," Madeleine said.

Stevie nodded. "It is. It's wild and wonderful. But Kevin did work that was almost classical. He loved the figure; he worked in charcoal and paper. His best work reminded me of Picasso. Not cubism, but line . . ."

"And you got married?"

"Yes. While we were still in college. We eloped . . ."

"I remember you wrote to tell me. I think that was the last I heard from you."

Stevie sighed. "That's probably true. I was on such a quest—"

"What kind of quest?"

"To find art and love."

Madeleine laughed. "I thought you'd found both."

Stevie shook her head. "I was born with both. Most people are, I think. But then we spend our lives complicating things. My parents loved me so much. I was—I don't want to say spoiled by it—affected, I guess. I had such high expectations. To think that life could always, *would* always, be that way. Even after my mother died, my father was—"

"Everything to you. I remember."

"He was. He loved me so much. Always put me first, made me feel as if I could do anything. He raised me to be really independent, to believe in myself, but to question everything. He'd tell me, 'Stevie, artists look at what *is*, what they can see, and they draw it. Poets never trust the surface. They learn to look beneath, and to trust what they *can't* see.' "

"What they can't see . . ." Madeleine said.

"I looked at Kevin and saw a handsome, brilliant artist. It wasn't until years later, married to him, that I looked beneath . . . I saw a troubled man who envied everyone. He was so bitter. Any time one of our classmates had a show, he'd make comments about selling out, pandering to collectors. He hated them. And then I started doing children's books. . . ."

"And became very successful," Madeleine added.

"And that made him start to hate me, too. It was so hard to live with," Stevie said, looking out over the sea, tension in her eyes. "I found Tilly—she was a kitten, a little New York street cat born in the alley behind our building. She was such a comfort to me—my husband was so closed off, he barely talked to me. We never slept together. But I had Tilly."

"Unconditional love."

"Yes. That's it. I kept thinking of my father's words . . . I still wasn't looking inward—below the surface. I knew how happy love had made me when I was young, and I knew that loving a cat wasn't enough, so I became almost frantic about finding it. I went to a lecture in Woods Hole, and that's when I met Linus."

"Linus?"

"My second husband. I left Kevin for him. By then, Kevin was lost in the bottle. I'm not sure he even noticed."

Madeleine sipped her champagne. *Lost in the bottle* did not refer to her. She sipped again.

"Linus was an ornithologist. He was English, so bright and interesting. He had a son from his first marriage—I loved being a stepmother. I really thought I had found it all. He was used to carrying different species of birds in and out of England, knew all the inspectors—somehow we beat the quarantine they had for pets. He told me not to worry about Tilly, that the inspectors would look the other way. And they did."

"Grounds enough to love the man!"

Stevie laughed. "Exactly. We lived in Oxford, in a stone house across from a medieval church. His son lived in London, but would come to us on weekends and holidays. My painting flowed—it was during that time that I sold the movie rights to *Red Robin* . . . I wanted to have a baby. . . ."

"You did?" Madeleine asked. "I wanted to, too. . . ."

"But you didn't?"

Madeleine shook her head. "No. I couldn't get pregnant. We tried for years, and even did two rounds of in vitro. But it didn't happen. It was okay, because I had . . ." She trailed off, unable to say "Nell." Stevie waited for her to finish her thought, but Madeleine just shrugged and smiled. "I had Chris."

"I did get pregnant," Stevie said. Her voice sounded calm, but her cheeks turned bright pink.

"You have a child?"

"No. I miscarried. . . ."

"Oh, Stevie. I'm sorry."

Stevie closed her eyes. "I never knew how terrible that could be. Before, when I'd heard about women it happened to, I'd think, 'They can try again.' 'It's not like losing a real baby.' But it is like that. It *is* a real baby."

"How far along were you?"

"Three months. I had just told my father and aunt. It was a girl."

"A girl . . ." Like Nell. "What happened?"

"I was very upset. I wanted us to name her, have a funeral. Linus refused. He thought I was being ridiculous. He was so scientific, clinical about it. He talked about how 'it' must have been sick, probably wouldn't have lived on 'its' own, and he started explaining Darwin to me, natural selection and survival of the fittest. I told him that *she* deserved better than that. I named her Clare, after my mother. I had a private funeral for her. And then I left Linus."

"How sad," Madeleine said. "That he couldn't understand what you needed."

"It was," Stevie said.

They sat quietly for a few minutes. Madeleine thought about the pain of losing a little girl. She thought about Nell and knew that Stevie was thinking about Clare.

"And it was sad that I couldn't understand what I needed. I really didn't know myself at all," Stevie said.

"What do you mean?"

"Emma used to tease me—saying that I always needed to be connected. She was right. I was convinced that I needed a man to make me okay. I looked at Kevin, at Linus, and saw what I needed to see. I married them expecting—needing—them to give me things they weren't capable of. I had seen my parents' marriage, and I wanted life to be like that. Wonderful couple who were really, *really* soul mates, a child to love . . . The old clock thing, you know?"

"Oh, all too well."

"I moved back to New York—by freighter. Tilly and I in our own cabin. We sailed out of Southampton. By the time we reached the Azores—"

"You jumped ship?"

"Nope. Fell in love with the captain."

Madeleine laughed, and so did Stevie. "Don't tell me . . ."

"It was a long voyage. Freighters aren't like cruise ships. They don't go directly from one port to the next. It's more like one port to another, by way of a long circle, halfway around the world. Months go by. I had signed on wanting time at sea, to think and figure things out."

"Maybe a little too much time at sea?"

"Yes. With a lot too much aquavit. It was a Swedish vessel, and they were very big on broiled salmon, smoked salmon, cured salmon, and salmon roe . . . all served with large quantities of aquavit. Also, champagne was served every time we left port—and we made a lot of ports."

"Is that when you gave up drinking?"

"Yes, but not quite soon enough," Stevie said. "I was out at sea, steaming to the Azores, Tenerife, Cape Town, Rio, Miami, with a lot of water in between, and a lot of time for thinking. I was a two-time divorcée, I was looking down the barrel at thirty-seven—"

"You wanted a baby."

"Yep."

"So you married the captain."

"At least he didn't perform his own ceremony," Stevie said, and laughed lightly. "The first mate did."

"How resourceful."

"Well, sort of. It was also, luckily, illegal. By the time we docked in Manhattan, I knew I was in trouble, and in deep. My father met the ship, and he got me a lawyer who would have gotten me an annulment—if the marriage had been lawful."

"What did the captain do?"

Stevie stared down at the beach. "He was angry. But in the short time I spent with him, after our 'I do's,' I saw that he was always angry. Through the aquavit, I had mistaken it for passionate intensity. I realized what it was when he kicked Tilly."

"He kicked your cat?"

"Tried to. But I dove to protect her, and he caught my chin instead."

"Bastard."

Stevie nodded and sighed. Madeleine reached over to squeeze her hand. They sat there for a few minutes, and Madeleine felt grateful for her life with Chris. A seagull flew past the terrace, coasting on an updraft from the beach. The women watched it fly by so effortlessly, not even flapping its wings. Tilly sat inside the screen door, tracking it with fierce eyes.

"It's the last time."

"The last time what?"

"That I'm getting married."

"You don't know that. Someone wonderful might come along. Someone like Chris."

"Tell me about him."

"Well, he's smart, funny, a great friend . . . he has his own insurance agency, and he's very good at it. He really cares about his clients—he sees them through all life's passages. Getting married, buying houses, having kids, taking care of sick parents, dying. . . . He really gets involved."

"How did you meet?"

"Jack bought insurance from him. Way back, when he and Emma were first together. They liked him so much, they set us up."

"That's a good way—introduced by people who know and love you."

"Yes," Madeleine said. "It was." She sat still, amazed how comfortable she felt, slipping into the old friendship. Stevie had always been so easy to talk to. She remembered how, sometimes, Emma would be busy with her mother, or doing errands, and Madeleine would savor the chance to have Stevie to herself.

"What are you thinking?"

"Oh, of Emma," Madeleine said.

"It's as if she's here," Stevie said. "I can feel her with us now."

"I was just remembering," Maddie said, her voice shaking, "of how she tended to take things over. When she wanted something, she got it."

"She really stood up for herself," Stevie said.

Emma had had a possessive streak—of friends, and later, of Jack and Nell. How could she have decided to throw them away? The thought made Madeleine want to refill her glass, but after Stevie's words about her own drinking, she held back.

"What do you say we take a walk?" Stevie said after a while.

"I'd love to look around, see what's changed and what's the same," Madeleine said, relieved to move, to hopefully get away from her own dark thoughts.

The day was clear, the sky bright blue. Madeleine was glad to stretch her legs. It kept her from thinking about the champagne. As they wandered slowly up and down the winding roads of Hubbard's Point, Stevie seemed very vigilant, as if she was hoping—or fearing— to see someone. They strolled down past the tennis court, into the beach parking lot.

"I remember playing here," Madeleine said.

"Really?" Stevie said. "I don't remember that we played much tennis—we were always on the beach."

"Not with you and Emma," Madeleine said. "With my brother. Jack was always so patient with me—I was four years younger, but he'd stand right there and hit to me . . ."

Maddie stared at the baseline, and she swore she could see her brother right there—six-three, with that long dark hair he always forgot to cut, now turning gray. How would he look today? It had been a full year. Would he still wear those dark-rimmed sunglasses? Would his hair be much grayer? Would grief have etched his face with lines, as it had hers?

The two friends walked all the way through the sandy parking lot to the boardwalk. Stevie kicked off her sandals, and Madeleine followed suit. They walked across the sand—and it was so hot, they had to run down to the water's edge just to cool off the soles of their feet.

"I look at children that age and think of me and Emma," Stevie said, glancing at two toddlers at the water's edge. "We met the very first summer of our lives."

"Way before I came along."

"Yes, but we were never as close as we were when you joined in."

"Remember when we went to Little Beach, and Emma found that stick and drew the circle?"

"And we swore we'd be bonded for life . . ."

"By the power vested by the full moon . . ."

They looked at each other and knew what they had to do: they didn't even speak, but set off for Little Beach. The walk was long and hot. Madeleine's dress stuck to her body, but she didn't care. She felt like a girl again, traveling back through time. Stevie held her hand, pulling her up the steep part of the hidden path.

They ran through the trees—Madeleine remembered every inch of the way. She recognized the old oaks and black gum trees, grown huge since she'd last been here. Their branches interlaced overhead; sunlight and shadows dappled the narrow dirt path. Suddenly they emerged on a secret beach, the sands blazing white with sun.

The two friends rushed across the beach, behind the enormous great-white-shark boulder, to the even more secret sands . . . where Emma had drawn the circle.

"She's here with us now," Stevie said. "Can't you feel it?"

"I can," Madeleine said. Driftwood littered the tide line, smooth and gleaming like bones. Stevie bent down, picked up a long stick, handed it to Madeleine. They didn't speak, brushed hands. Turning slowly, Madeleine tried to trace a ring.

"By the power vested by tonight's full moon . . ." Stevie said.

"The girl in the moon," Madeleine said—the words coming out of the past, making her feel dizzy.

Madeleine dropped the stick and closed her eyes. She longed for the magic to be there. She felt her blood crackle and her hair tingle. But it was just the heat and the wind. The beach girl magic was gone. . . . Emma was gone. . . .

"I can't," Madeleine whispered.

Stevie's grip tightened on her hands. "I'm sorry," Stevie said. "I shouldn't have brought you here."

"I'm thinking of Emma," Madeleine said, her eyes filling. "Of how much she loved the beach. How she should be here."

"She *is* here," Stevie said. "In our love for her."

Madeleine shook her head, and the tears spilled out. She couldn't tell Stevie what she was really feeling— that what she felt for Emma was no longer lifelong love, but a sort of warped, twisted hate. For what she had been about to do to Jack and Nell . . .

"She's not here," Madeleine said, trying to maintain control of her voice. She wanted to run and scream. If she didn't hold on tight, she'd tell Stevie everything: every last detail of what Emma had told her, the look on Jack's face when Madeleine had divulged it to him—all of it.

"Maddie—" Stevie said, her eyes wild with concern.

Madeleine squeezed her eyes tight. *Emma's not here,* she told herself. Yet she was. The phantom-limb–sister-in-law syndrome was kicking in again. Being with Stevie had activated it like mad. Her right side itched. Her right arm longed to encircle Emma's shoulders, hold her tight, draw her back into the fold, into the family, back to *life*—where she belonged.

"Let's go back to the main beach," Stevie said gently.

Madeleine nodded. As they walked away, she glanced back over her shoulder: the circle was right there in the sand, where she had drawn it. The waves licked up the beach, the tide encroaching. Soon the ring would be washed away—just like the original one that Emma had drawn so many years ago.

Did she still believe in the magic?

She thought about the crazy longing, the need to believe in something, the yearning that all young girls had. They—Emma, Stevie, and Maddie, the beach girls—had needed to surround themselves with the symbols of sun and moon, sand and sea—to convince themselves that it would all go on forever. They had convinced themselves in the magic of the beach.

How foolish.

By the time Stevie and Madeleine had climbed back down the path and emerged on the main beach, Madeleine had chased all tears and vestiges of the "magic" circle away. She desperately craved champagne. The quicker she could get Stevie back to her house, the happier she would be.

But as they walked along, barefoot in the water, every sight chipped away at her a little more.

"I look at children that age and think of . . ." Madeleine began, gazing at a little girl, about four years old, carefully patting a sand castle to make it strong and beautiful. Her mother helped her by adding several shells for decoration. Madeleine's mind filled with Nell, and she had to look away.

"Think of what, Maddie?"

Madeleine couldn't speak, so she pretended not to hear. They continued walking along the wet sand, feeling the waves lick their ankles. Again, the water washed away her feelings, replaced them with the peace of a summer day. The tide was coming in, and Madeleine nearly tripped on a boy scurrying out of the way of a wave. She caught Stevie's arm, nearly dragging her down.

Laughing, Stevie splashed Madeleine, who kicked up water in a quick silver arc. The drops felt so salty and cool, and they kept at it, playing and giggling as if they were teenagers again. Bit by bit, they waded in deeper—Stevie in shorts and a sleeveless shirt, and Madeleine holding up the hem of her long dress.

"Let's go swimming," Stevie said suddenly, eyes shining, peeking out from under her bangs.

"We're dressed!"

"Who cares? Let's just do it!"

"That's something your wild aunt would do! Or a woman who'd go halfway around the world on a freighter—go swimming in clothes in Portofino or Positano or . . . I don't know, somewhere glamorous! But I can't go in front of all these proper suburban people."

"It's the beach!"

"And, darling, we are wearing *clothes*."

"We're Zelda, and life is a fountain!" Stevie said, diving into the water and coming up looking the way Madeleine had always remembered her—edgy and creative and crazy in a way that seemed sexy and in love with life. She watched as Stevie swam to the jetty and back, her black head as sleek as a seal.

"Did you bring a bathing suit? Want to go up and change into it?" Stevie asked, treading water.

"Please—I don't even own one anymore."

The champagne and joy of seeing Stevie had made Madeleine forget to feel self-conscious about her weight. But now she noticed her friend's trim, muscular legs and arms, her narrow face and high cheekbones, and she took two steps back, out of the shallow water.

"You go ahead," she said to Stevie. "Keep swimming."

"Not without you," Stevie said, her eyes twinkling as she jumped out of the water and shook her head like a wet Labrador retriever. She stood beside Madeleine and took her arm. "But I promise you this—by the end of the summer, I'll get you back here to see me *and* go swimming."

"You *must* be a witch," Madeleine murmured, laughing. "Because I'll tell you right now: no way, no how. Not without some very powerful juju or black magic." She shivered in the heat, uncomfortable in her body and in her soul. Being on the beach reminded her of her last time with Emma. Suddenly it seemed that this walk—this trip—was a big mistake.

Stevie, sopping wet, began walking along the shore, past all the people going in and getting out of the water, past the women in beach chairs, the children building sand castles. Madeleine grabbed her arm. "Would you mind if we went back up to your house? It's so lovely up there. . . ."

"Of course—let's go," Stevie said, turning around. They picked up their sandals and took the shortcut— across the wooden footbridge over the creek, up the stairs into thick trees. They turned left onto a path that Madeleine had forgotten—a secret stone path through the brush that led straight to Stevie's cottage. She glanced up into the tree branches spreading overhead, greening the brilliant sky with bright leaves, and felt a severe lump in her throat.

On the way, Stevie rinsed herself off in the outside shower. Madeleine saw her bend down to pick some bugs off a hydrangea bush. She grinned at Madeleine and said, "For the bird."

"Ah," Madeleine said.

Madeleine rinsed the sand off her feet with a hose in the yard, and then Stevie went upstairs to change, and to feed her bird. Madeleine's head ached, and her stomach was churning. Being on the beach had taken a lot out of her. She took the opportunity of solitude to open the refrigerator and pull out her little friend: bottle number two.

Stevie came into the kitchen just as Madeleine was popping the cork.

"I hope you don't mind," Madeleine said. "I just feel like celebrating. It's so incredible to be together again."

"It *is* incredible," Stevie said. Her face was bright, as if she had a secret she couldn't wait to tell. Madeleine had noticed her alertness, as they'd walked up and down the roads through the beach. Perhaps that had something to do with it. Stevie poured herself a glass of iced tea, and they raised their glasses.

"Let's see," Madeleine said. "We drank to beach girls, and to being together . . . now what?"

"How about, here's to the newest beach girl . . ." Stevie said solemnly, staring straight into Madeleine's eyes. "I wanted to tell you about her when we were over at Little Beach. After you'd drawn the circle . . ."

"The newest . . . ?"

"Nell," Stevie said.

Madeleine blinked, hardly believing she'd heard the name. Stevie just stared at her. "What are you talking about?" Madeleine asked, confused.

"I've met her, Maddie. She's here—at Hubbard's Point, right now. She and your brother came to the beach. They're renting a house near the tennis court."

chapter 12

STEVIE SHOULDN'T HAVE SPRUNG IT on Madeleine—she saw the wounded look in her eyes the moment the words were out. Madeleine put down her glass, covered her eyes with her hands, and sobbed. She was shaking, so Stevie put her arm around her. After a few moments, they eased apart.

"I'm sorry to shock you," Stevie said.

"I'm not sure it's *you* who shocked me—it's my brother and niece, coming to this place. What are they *doing* here, at Hubbard's Point, of all places?"

"Jack transferred to his company's Boston office—"

Madeleine shook her head. "God, it hurts to hear this from you. Instead of from him. He's here in New England, and he couldn't even call me in Providence? To tell me?"

"He seems as if . . ." Stevie hesitated. "As if he has his hands full."

"Because of Nell?" Madeleine asked, drawing a sharp

breath. "Tell me about her, Stevie. I haven't seen her in nearly a year."

"She's extraordinary," Stevie said. She led Maddie into the living room, to the loveseat where Jack and Nell had sat the night of their visit. They sat together, knees touching, and Stevie told Madeleine the whole story, beginning with Nell's expedition to find a blue house. Stevie described her short brown hair and bright green eyes, her quick mind, her easy smile.

She watched Madeleine react to each detail so eagerly, yet with obvious hurt. So much had happened since she had last seen the niece she loved so much; Stevie wished she could take the pain away, wished that she didn't have to tell her friend about the child she obviously knew and adored.

"She goes to school in Boston?"

"Yes," Stevie said.

Madeleine squeezed her eyes shut. "She loved her Atlanta school and teacher very much. . . . I hate to think of her leaving it. Emma chose the house because the neighborhood kids went to such a great school. Nell loved to learn from the very beginning."

"She seems so smart."

"She is. She picks up everything, right off the bat. She's got Emma's curiosity and drive, her father's ability to figure anything out. She had a best friend down in Georgia. Tristan, I think . . . Nell must miss her terribly."

Stevie had seen the depths of loss that Nell was capable of feeling, but instead she said, "She made a summer friend, Maddie. At least she's not lonely up here. I saw her and Peggy riding around the beach earlier." She left out *on a bicycle-built-for-two,* in case Madeleine remembered seeing it. Her friend seemed so fragile right now, her hands shaking as she clasped them together.

"What else did she say, Stevie?" she asked. "Did she—" Madeleine bit her lip, seeming afraid to finish the question. "Did she mention me?"

Stevie nodded. "She did, Maddie."

"Tell me," Madeleine said. "What did she say?"

"She misses you."

Madeleine drew a sharp breath.

"She had gone upstairs to visit the bird," Stevie said. "And when I went up to check on her, she begged me . . . to find you."

"Me?"

Stevie nodded. "She saw the painting my aunt did. And she knew all the stories about the beach girls, how close we were. And she cried for me to call you. Because she misses you so much."

Madeleine took it in, wide-eyed, with tears streaming down her cheeks. She looked around the room, as if she was looking for Nell. Stevie wanted to show her all the places Nell had been—sitting in this seat, looking at that painting, examining this conch shell.

"There's a saying my father always used to use," Madeleine said. " 'So near, and yet so far.' That's how I feel right now. As if the people I love most are right here, practically within sight, but I can't reach them."

"You can reach them," Stevie said.

Madeleine shook her head. "You don't know Jack.

When he makes up his mind, that's it. He's written me off."

"You're his sister, Maddie," Stevie said, even while remembering Aunt Aida's words.

"I know. That makes it worse. It makes him feel more justified. He's really stubborn, Stevie. He gets an idea in his head, and nothing turns him away from it."

"He can't keep Nell away from you. If only you could have heard her. She wants to see you so badly. . . . I think that's the real reason she came to see me."

"I think she wanted to meet her mother's oldest friend," Madeleine said.

"That's partly it," Stevie said. "But you didn't hear the way she was sobbing for you. Jack had to carry her out of here."

Madeleine looked pale. She stared at the glass of champagne she held in her hand, but didn't drink. The windows were open, and a cool breeze blew through the house, but her face and throat were coated with a sheen of sweat.

"Are you okay?" Stevie asked.

Madeleine nodded. Then she shook her head. "Not really," she said. "This is just all a little too much for me to take. Stevie, I hate to do this, but I think I'd better go home."

"You can't leave!"

"I have to. It's too painful to be here, knowing my brother and Nell are just down the road—and I'm not allowed to see them."

"You can just go over there—I'll go with you!"

Madeleine shook her head. "That wouldn't be good

for Nell. I don't know what Jack would say, or do, and I wouldn't want to put her through an upsetting scene."

"But it wouldn't be! They'd see you, and know how much you love them."

"Don't you think I've told Jack that already?"

"But for him to actually see you . . ."

Stevie held her breath, waiting for her friend to respond.

MADELEINE FELT anger building. "You don't know, Stevie. I can't believe you brought me here—we shared so much, you talked about such deep things, but you left out this little thing."

"No, I—"

Madeleine shook her head. "I don't want to hear it. You had dinner with Jack and Nell one night, and you think you know what it's like for them, for us. But you really don't. You don't know the whole story. And you shouldn't have done this."

"Nell wanted me to!"

Madeleine was so upset, she couldn't stand to hear Nell's name. She went upstairs and got her bag. Her hands were shaking, but she knew it wasn't from the champagne. That had worn off on their walk to the beach.

When she returned to the kitchen, Stevie was standing by the door. Her hair was almost dry, so dark and perfectly smooth. Her violet eyes looked worried, and she reached out her hands. Madeleine was still angry, but she took them anyway. The two old friends stood looking into each other's eyes.

"I hope you'll come back," Stevie said.

"It's not the same without Emma," Madeleine said.

"No, it's not the same, but it can still be good."

Madeleine just shook her head. "If you see Nell, tell her I love her."

"Maddie—please, go tell her yourself."

Madeleine couldn't respond to that. She just hugged Stevie, murmured something about taking care, staying in touch, and walked out the door. When she got down to the road, she looked up at the house. Stevie and Tilly were in the window. Birds called from the trees. Madeleine waved goodbye. She felt a pain in her throat, sharp as the driftwood stick.

Leaving the beach. Saying goodbye to her old friend. It reminded her, so deeply, of how it had felt, when they were teenagers, leaving each other for another whole, long winter.

> *Five years have passed; five summers,*
>   *with the length*
> *Of five long winters! And again I hear*
> *These waters . . .*

Wordsworth's "Lines Composed a Few Miles Above Tintern Abbey"—adopted when she and her friends were teenagers—came back to Madeleine as she headed north, away from the beach, her old friend, her brother and niece. It was a beautiful, hot summer day, tonight the July full moon would be rising, but as she sped along, Madeleine felt the grip of winter.

NOT THE SAME WITHOUT EMMA, Madeleine had said.

Stevie was so churned up by Madeleine's departure, and those words, that she took another walk along the beach. What had happened over at Little Beach, when Stevie had handed Maddie the silvery driftwood stick? Maddie had looked as if she might faint. Stevie had so much energy inside, she had to get it out. Walking along, she wished she'd meet up with Jack. She wanted to shake him, tell him what a great sister he had. What didn't Stevie understand?

She wanted to see Nell, tell her that her aunt loved her.

Not the same without Emma.

From the beach, the cottages on the rocky point looked like dollhouses, each tidy and perfect and filled with happiness. Gardens and window boxes spilled over with petunias and English ivy. Stevie's own house looked like a stage set for contentment. Seagulls soared against the azure sky. Children played in the small waves while their mothers sat in beach chairs and shared the secrets of life.

Stevie and Emma had been two of those children. Their mothers spent the summer of 1959 pregnant together on the beach at Hubbard's Point, talking about how different the next summer would be—and how happy they were that their kids would grow up together.

Stevie was born in October. Emma was born in December.

The following July, the girls met for the first time. Bathing-suited—nine-month-old Stevie in a little blue and white tank, seven-month-old Emma in a pink-checked sunsuit—they were gently placed together, balanced by their mother's hands, in a wave-washed sandy hollow freshly dug below the tide line.

Stevie swore she could remember the meeting: the soft *brush, brush* of the waves' forward edge, the cool curl of sea foam, the steadiness of her mother's hand between her shoulder blades, Emma's long lashes framing her huge green eyes as she stared back at her new—and first—best friend.

"It was like an arranged marriage, Emma," she'd once said. "Our mothers had it all mapped out for us, that whole long winter after we were born. We were destined to love each other even before we met. Really, if you think about it, we had no choice."

"But what if we hadn't loved—or even liked—each other? What if we'd taken one look at each other and started crying? What if one of us hated being in the water and started throwing sand? What if only one of us loved the beach?"

"That could never have happened," Stevie said confidently.

"Why not?" Emma pressed.

"Because we're beach girls," Stevie said. "And our mothers were before us. . . ." Was that the first time they'd used the name?

Regardless, Emma had had no option but to agree;

life itself had convinced her—she and Stevie had spent every summer of their childhood together at Hubbard's Point, on the Connecticut shoreline. Running barefoot along the beach, crabbing in the marsh behind the big blue house, taking the path to Little Beach, riding their bikes to Foley's Store for penny candy, racing each other out to the raft—climbing onto the wooden slats warmed by the sun, catching their breath as they looked back at the gentle curve of beach between two rocky points, the slice of heaven here on earth that they called their home.

By night, Hubbard's Point was no less magical. The Milky Way blazed a white trail through the sky overhead. Oak leaves rustled in the sea breeze, and late in August owls would roost in the branches, their mysterious calls hooting through the night. Stevie used to draw them, the birds at the Point.

She did cartoons about them, with messages to Emma about the boys they liked. Emma tried to draw, but she always gave up. She'd throw the crumpled paper down and say she didn't care about art because she was going to be famous someday—as a model. Stevie believed it. Emma was beautiful and flirtatious, and all the boys liked her.

Madeleine's family came to the beach. Stevie and Emma met her in line at the Good Humor truck. Emma didn't have enough change to buy a chocolate chip crunch, and Madeleine made up the difference. That was Maddie: instantly friendly, generous, and crazy for ice cream. Stevie and Emma adopted her instantly.

On Sunday nights, the girls would trek down the

stone steps from Stevie's house on the Point for movies on the beach. The films were mostly old—sometimes black and white. Sometimes they were light and funny, like *The Love Bug* or *Pollyanna*, and sometimes they were dark and hard to understand—more for the parents, Stevie thought—like *The Postman Always Rings Twice*.

But what was on the screen didn't actually matter to the girls. They would dig their pit in the sand, spread out their blanket and spray bug stuff on each other's feet, eat ice creams, and wait for dark so the show could begin.

Those movies were where summers became more complex, where beach girls grew up a little. Stevie still remembered the summer when they were fifteen, when boys seriously entered the picture.

The show that night was one of the dark parental ones, with grown-ups kissing hard. Stevie sat with Creighton Reid, Maddie with his brother Hunter, and Emma huddled with James Martell. Their blankets were side-by-side. Stevie remembered her and Maddie being at least as interested in what was happening on Emma's blanket as they were in their own experience. Stevie was very afraid that Creighton would want to kiss her the way John Garfield was kissing Lana Turner, when suddenly she saw James doing just that to Emma.

She caught Madeleine's eye and threw a pebble at Emma. Stevie gestured sharply toward the boardwalk, and the three friends met there five minutes later.

"What are you *doing*?" Stevie asked.

"Hey—I saw you holding hands," Emma said.

"Holding hands! That's nothing—you're making out!"

Maddie said. "Just like my brother and his girlfriend—look at them going at it." Jack and his girlfriend—were on a blanket so far from the screen it couldn't actually be said that they were at the movie at all.

Emma just smiled—a little slyly, as if she'd just gotten caught at something she'd been doing all summer.

"Is he forcing you? I'll come over and kick sand in his eyes so you can escape," Stevie said.

"Don't you dare!"

"You're kidding—you want him to do it?"

"Um, we're missing the movie," Maddie said matter-of-factly. "Think I'll go back to the blanket now." She ran off.

"You *like* it?" Stevie asked Emma. She felt bereft, as if she were losing her two best friends to boys. She wanted to hold on to the beach girls forever—a trio of girls who loved life and each other.

"Don't be a baby," Emma said.

Stevie's mouth dropped open, as if she'd been slapped. Emma took Stevie by the shoulders, looked her straight on. Her green eyes looked hard in the shadowy light, and impatient—as if she were much older than Stevie. Soft brown curls framed her tan face, tossed by the night wind blowing off the water. The movie voices were low and urgent. James called out, "Emma!" Stevie wanted to grab her hand and pull her fast across the sand, into the water to wash this moment away.

"I'm sorry," Emma said holding her gaze. "You're not a baby."

"I know."

"We might as well want to kiss them," Emma said.

"Because they're going to do it anyway. Just do what they want, and it's much more fun."

"What about what we want?"

"We want *them*," Emma said. "Right?"

"I'm not sure." Stevie's lips quivered in an almost-smile, wanting to hold on to the childhood she loved so much, feeling it slip away.

"Yes, you are," Emma said. "You just don't know it yet."

"But how do *you* know it?"

"Because it's what happens," Emma said. "And it makes us appreciate *us* even more. The beach girls."

She was only fifteen. Stevie had no idea of what she meant, or where such a definite statement had come from, or why Emma's eyes looked so electric as she said the words. Sometimes it seemed she had never looked back. The next year she had a different boyfriend, and after that, Jack, and life had gone on from there.

It's what happens. Walking along, Stevie heard Emma's words. The waves licked her feet as the sun began to set. It made her feel sad, the end of day. She wished that Madeleine had stayed, to watch the full moon rise.

Because even though Emma wasn't here to see the moonrise anymore, Stevie and Madeleine still were. And so were Jack and Nell. Stevie had hoped that they'd all be able to watch it together.

Emma would have been with them in spirit.

chapter 13

FULL-MOON NIGHTS WERE ALWAYS celebrated at Hubbard's Point. Families would gather at the beach, or on the rocks, talking quietly while they waited. People with houses on the water had parties. Some people bet on the exact time the moon would start to rise, straight out of the sea.

If the night was hazy, the mist over the sea would obscure the moon's actual emergence, and it would magically appear up in the sky, bright yellow, after it had cleared the mist.

But on very clear nights like this, the moon would crown the surface—a copper-colored orb slipping out of one element into another. It would shimmer, then clarify, turn glowing white, and grow smaller as it rose high in the sky, its light trickling onto the surface of the Sound. People would watch it, speechless. The Hubbard's Point full moon was always worth the wait.

Nell planned to see it with her dad, but then Peggy's

mom invited them both to join their group for a picnic first. Nell was so happy when her dad said yes. At six o'clock, way before dark, they walked through the beach roads to Peggy's house. It was an old farmhouse, bigger than most of the beach cottages, across the marsh from the rest of Hubbard's Point.

"Who's going to be there?" her father asked as they started across the narrow trail through the tall reeds.

"Peggy, of course. And her brother Billy and sister Annie and stepsister Eliza. They're teenagers. And her mom, who's really nice, and her stepfather, who builds boats. He's nice, too. And her aunt, who's not really her aunt, Tara, and her fiancé, Joe. He's in the FBI!"

"Wow," her dad said.

Nell smiled, happy that she knew so many people here. They got to the old wooden planks, laid across the swampy ground, and Nell held her father's hand to cross. He thought he was helping her, but she was actually helping *him*. She and Peggy came this way every day.

"Is anyone else going to be here?" he asked as the house came into sight.

"Like who?"

"I don't know," he said. "Your friend Stevie, maybe?"

"You told me I couldn't see her!" Nell said, wheeling around. She stared at her father, who seemed to be scanning the crowd of McCabes and O'Tooles gathered around the picnic table in the garden.

"I didn't want us interrupting her life," her father said. "But I'm sure she goes out with friends—I just thought she might be here to see the moonrise. That's all."

"She's a hermit, Dad," Nell said, darkly. "She doesn't go out."

"Okay, then. Calm down, Nell."

Nell glowered at him. They stood just outside the picket fence. Peggy saw them and waved. Nell's father opened the gate, and Nell stared up at him. She loved him so much, but he got everything wrong. Didn't he know how special it was that Stevie had invited them for dinner? She never saw people at all. She had invited them because they were magically connected to her—through Nell's mother and Aunt Madeleine.

"Hi, Nell, hi, Mr. Kilvert!" Peggy said, running over to meet them.

"Hi, Peggy," Nell's father said, walking through the gate.

Nell just stood staring, unable to move her feet. She watched as Peggy's mother and stepfather started over to greet them. Her father shook their hands, but he kept glancing over at Nell. She felt that aura she sometimes got—anger, frustration, that her mother had died and her aunt was gone and her father didn't get it. She pictured a big black cloud over her head.

But, because she didn't want to ruin the evening, she shook it off. She smiled stiffly at Peggy and her parents—ignoring her father. Peggy grabbed her hand, pulled her toward the table. Nell no longer felt like being at a party, but she went along anyway.

JACK KNEW he'd done it again—said the wrong thing to Nell. He thought she'd *like* being asked about Stevie. Instead, she'd shriveled up before his eyes, looking as if he'd just said the worst thing in the world. More to the point, being honest with himself, Jack knew that his question had relatively little to do with Nell's feelings. It had to do with wanting to know whether Stevie would be at the party.

Peggy's family was wonderful and welcoming. Her mother, Bay, swept Jack right into the crowd. Bay was about his age, red-haired and freckled, just like Peggy. She was newly married to Dan Connolly, and they were both glowing. Jack met Bay's best friend, Tara O'Toole, and her fiancé, Joe Holmes. The kids came over to say hi—Annie, Eliza, and Billy. Jack recognized Billy from the ladder incident outside Stevie's house. Billy looked scared, but Jack didn't mention anything.

"Nice to meet you all," Jack said.

"You, too," Tara said. "We love your daughter."

"She's something special, that's for sure."

"Nell tells us you're an old Hubbard's Point kid," Bay said.

"Yes. Our family rented here when I was a teenager. But my life was up home, in Hartford, and I had my license. I didn't really hang around the beach too much."

"That explains why we don't know you from back then," Tara said. "Bay and I are lifers."

"My wife was," Jack said. "I finally left Hartford long enough to meet her here, on the boardwalk."

"Nell told us about her. I'm sorry," Bay said. The others nodded, and Dan said, "We know it's hard."

"Thank you." Jack looked over at Nell, saw her engrossed in conversation with Peggy.

"What'll you have to drink?" Bay asked, leading Jack to a bar under the trees. He took a beer, and so did Bay.

"Thanks," he said. He glanced around the garden, at all the roses and lilies. "You have a beautiful place here."

"Thank you. It's been a great place to raise the kids. Tara lives over there"—she pointed at a white house just across the marsh. "I don't know what I'd have done without her. I really am sorry about your wife. . . . I lost my first husband a few years ago."

"I'm sorry about that," Jack said.

"How is Nell doing?"

Jack looked over. Nell was doing cartwheels across the yard with Peggy right behind her. As usual, the way she was in public was at total odds with how she seemed alone, at home.

"Right now, she seems to be having the time of her life," he said.

"Sure, in a crowd . . ."

"When it's just the two of us, it's another story," Jack said. "She can't sleep—has bad dreams when she gets to sleep at all. I read to her, rub her back, but . . ."

"But you can't bring back her mother."

"Sounds as if you know the deal."

Bay nodded. "When Sean died, everyone fell apart. Some more than others—including me. We all went a little crazy."

"With grief?"

"And everything that comes with it. You must know the lovely five stages. . . ."

"Ah, yes," Jack said, remembering the bereavement group his boss had convinced him to try. The other widowers and widows, the adults who had recently lost parents, and worst of all, the parents who had lost children. *Denial, anger, bargaining, depression, acceptance.* "I know them well."

"I know that it sounds trite, but time does heal all things."

" 'This too shall pass,' " Jack said. "That's my personal favorite."

He and Bay clinked beer bottles, smiled at each other.

"I'm sure you know the importance of having support," she said. When Jack didn't reply, she smiled. "Oh, you're a guy."

"Um, yes?"

"Well, for better or worse, women are programmed to reach out. Our survival instincts include knowing how to pick up the telephone and call each other for help. I did that with Tara—like you wouldn't believe. My husband, Danny, was a widower, and from what I can gather, he never talked to a soul. He could offer me a shoulder, and did . . . but when it came to his own inner demons . . . forget it. He was like the Tin Man when I met him—so frozen and rusty." Jack watched her eyes fill with tears, and he couldn't help feeling touched. He could see how much she loved him.

"Did he say 'Oil can'?" Jack asked.

Bay laughed, wiping her eyes. "No way. That would

have been asking for help! And I was completely wrecked by Sean's death, and none too swift about knowing how to be around him. But eventually we figured it out. We got each other through. . . ."

"I'm glad."

"Do you have friends? Siblings?"

"A sister," he said.

"Really? Was she here with you, way back when?"

"She was. Madeleine Kilvert." Saying her name tugged hard at Jack's heart. He watched for recognition in Bay's eyes.

"I can't remember anyone with that name," she said.

"Maddie was really close with my wife, Emma. And they had another friend. Stevie Moore." If Madeleine's name was a tug, Stevie's name was a downright yank. Jack felt shocked by it.

"Oh, Stevie. She's amazing," Bay said. "She's a few years younger than Tara and I, but we always knew of her. And then, when she grew up and began writing those beautiful books . . . all the kids love them."

"They love her books, but they give her a bad rap," Tara said, coming over to join them.

"Calling her a witch?"

"Exactly. We're in suburban fantasyland here," Tara said. "The moms—Bay notwithstanding—tend to be a wee bit suspicious of the perpetually single. I think the whole witch-drama started with someone who can't understand why a wonderful woman like Stevie can't stay married."

"Can't?" Bay asked, raising her eyebrows. "That sounds a little judgmental, especially coming from you."

Tara chuckled. "From another brazen hussy, she means. Well, those days are over—Joe's making an honest woman out of me, come Christmastime. Anyway, what I meant was, the married beach set looks askance at Stevie for getting divorced and keeping to herself. And the kids pick up on that. When the real truth is, she just hasn't found someone good enough for her, who'll make her happy!"

"She deserves that," Jack said.

"You know her?"

"Well, a little. She seems great. I just know she likes her privacy."

Both women smiled. Was it his imagination, or had they just homed in on him like ospreys on a fish? "She doesn't like it *that* much," Tara said.

"Well, anyway," Jack said, remembering the last visit, trying to keep his expression neutral. He didn't feel like getting into it with Bay and Tara, but he could almost see the matchmaking wheels turning. "Really," he said, just so they wouldn't get any ideas, "I think it's better left alone."

"You *are* a guy," Bay said, sounding fond and indulgent.

"Isn't he, though?" Tara asked.

Just then, Dan called over to ask how he liked his burger done. Jack was glad for the chance to get away, join the men at the grill. He went over to find Joe and Dan talking about the Red Sox, and he slipped in easily. The panacea of baseball: balm to his troubled soul.

The rush was on to feed everyone and make it to the beach before the moon rose. Jack thought of watching the moonrise with these two great couples and all their kids. He'd have Nell, of course, but he'd be missing someone else.

Emma, of course.

He'd be missing his wife. He told himself that, and even believed it. He had blocked out any feelings to the contrary. Sometimes he told himself he hadn't been good enough to her. She had become so selfless, those last two years. Her volunteer work at church had transformed her. The priest had touched the deepest part of her soul, turned her into a woman who wanted only to give, never take. What other woman from their comfortable neighborhood would spend time working at Dixon Correctional Institute? Her time at the prison just showed what a fine woman she was. To want to help people through their struggle.

Don't think about it, Jack told himself. Look at the moon—tell yourself that you miss your wife, your daughter's mother. Remember how you fell in love with her on this beach. That's what you came to Hubbard's Point to remember! Think about *that* Emma. How much you loved each other . . .

He told himself those five stages of grief were more than just talk. They were the real thing. He had looked at them as steps in an engineering project to work through: on schedule, in time, and under budget. But they hadn't happened that way. They hadn't gone according to any manageable plan at all. He had crashed through them all, and although he had stopped believing it possible, he seemed to be coming out the other side.

He knew he was, because he found himself staring east over the marsh, past the beach, to the rocky point. The houses were so far off from here, but he could make out Stevie's above the tree line. Peggy called out that everyone had better hurry—they didn't want to miss the full moon.

Full moons had always seemed mysterious to Jack. He was an engineer, used to dealing with absolutes. He drew very precise, detailed plans, and bridges, buildings, oil rigs were built to his exact specifications. He liked—and expected—results. He knew that rules of physics were immutable, and he liked them that way.

As Dan and Bay set out plates of burgers, potato salad, and cole slaw, Jack thought that dinners fell into the category of results. You cooked, you invited people over, you fed them. That worked.

The moon and the five stages of grief fell into another category entirely: Father Kearsage would have called them "luminous mysteries." That had been the priest's phrase for what had happened with Emma. Although Jack had been blind with rage at the time, the words had stuck in his mind. Once he found out that Kearsage hadn't made it up but taken it from the writings of a monk in Kentucky, Jack actually liked it. To him, "luminous mysteries" included ocean tides, heartbreak, prison walls, spiritual release, lies and truths, falling in love, moving to Scotland.

Stevie was in there, somehow. Her painting, the way she'd looked in that white robe, the black bird she was raising with bugs from her garden, the kindness she had shown Nell—and him, the feeling he'd had, those early mornings two weeks back when he'd watched her swim. Picturing her with clear, dark water pouring off her naked body, he had a shining thought: I don't want to move to Scotland.

How could he get out of it?

Luminous mysteries, he thought. A poetic name for a real struggle. He had signed a contract, made his plans. But he could change them—he knew he could. As he ate dinner with his daughter and new friends, he listened and talked, laughed at a few jokes, eventually joined the procession through the marsh and across the sea-wall to the beach.

They assembled, friends and family, along the tide line. They gazed east at the placid Sound, waiting with an abundance of faith. That's what it took, Jack thought. Nothing less than faith, to get through the day, the summer, the moonrise. Faith that he'd made the right decision about Scotland. Doubtfully, he glanced down at Nell.

Mysteries of life. Nell snuggled beside him on the sand, and he put his arm around her. His daughter made his top-three list of luminous mysteries, right up there with the full moon.

And Stevie Moore.

chapter 14

THE CASTLE WAS INCREDIBLE AT THE most ordinary of times: on a sunny April morning, say, or on one of November's dull gray afternoons. But on nights of celestial doings, when the midsummer moon was set to rise and anticipation was running high, the castle was nothing less than enchanted.

Stevie drove up the hill. The night was warm, scented with honeysuckle and pine. Parking her car, she started toward her aunt's cottage, but turned when she heard her name called from the castle. Her aunt was in the tower, waving. Stevie grabbed a flashlight from her glove compartment and started up.

The castle had fallen upon hard times, but its grandeur was unmistakable. Oak beams, heavy leaded windows, stone floors. Stevie had come here as a child, when Aunt Aida had first married Van. She remembered feeling so lucky to be able to play in an actual castle. She felt

that same way tonight, and wished she could bring Nell
here to see it.

The tower stairs wound around and around; the
stone passageway was oppressively dark and musty,
and she startled bats as she passed. When she reached
the top, she walked out onto a carved balustrade to
meet her aunt. The fresh air felt good, and the view
across treetops to the river mouth and Sound was mag-
nificent.

"Where's Henry?" she asked.

"He went to Newport, hoping to see Doreen," Aunt
Aida said.

"Didn't he call first?"

"I think he's given up on that. He's just planning to
present himself at her door and see what happens."

"Brave man."

"With all the action he's seen at sea and in battle, I
don't think he's ever been as afraid as he is right now, at
the idea of losing Doreen. The worst of it is, he brought
it on himself, and he knows it."

Stevie nodded. She knew that feeling. Driven by her
own needs and fears, she'd been the architect of plenty
of unhappiness—for herself and for others. She had felt
torn earlier. On the one hand, she had wanted to stay at
the Point, hoping that she'd run into Nell and Jack. On
the other, she was afraid of making things worse.

They gazed east, in the direction the moon would
rise. The sun had completely set now, and the forest
was coming alive with night sounds: crickets, animals
hunting through the underbrush, whippoorwills calling from the Lovecraft marshes.

Aunt Aida had changed from her painting clothes into Mandarin black silk pajamas, but she still smelled of turpentine and oil paint. Stevie loved that smell, and felt comforted by it.

"And you?" Aunt Aida asked after a few minutes. "Why are you here with me instead of with your friends?"

"Friends?"

Her aunt cast a patient smile that informed Stevie she knew she was being deliberately obtuse. "The man and his young daughter. What were their names?"

"Jack and Nell."

"Ah, yes. And his sister?"

"Madeleine. I saw her. After our last visit, I invited her down to the beach."

"That was the right thing to do."

"Well, I wish it was, but I have my doubts. She came, and we had a great visit. Until I told her that Jack and Nell were just down the road, and she got upset and left in a hurry."

"She was in a bit of shock, that's all. She'll give it some thought and be back. You'll see."

Stevie pictured Madeleine driving out of Hubbard's Point, not looking back, and thought her aunt was wrong on this one.

"In less than three weeks, I've managed to alienate a whole family," Stevie said. "I should stick to being a hermit."

"I doubt that Nell feels that way," Aida said.

"Nell?"

Aida nodded. "She's the one who started this ball rolling."

"By coming to my house," Stevie said.

"And speaking her mind, letting you and her father know she needs her aunt." The older woman smiled. "I put great stock in a niece's love for her aunt. And vice versa."

"So do I," Stevie said, squeezing her hand, wondering what to do about Nell and her family.

Now they leaned forward, elbows on the stone parapet, gazing east. A fresh breeze ruffled the leaves all around them, cooled their faces. The hill sloped steadily down to the Sound. The town was hidden in the trees. Stevie heard her aunt sigh, and glanced over.

"What is it?" she asked.

"Oh, another developer contacted me this week," Aida said. "He wants to build a hotel and spa here, put condos on the hill, and turn the castle into a conference center."

"I hope you told him to go jump in the river."

Her aunt hesitated, and Stevie saw her bite her lip. "I haven't . . . yet."

"But you're going to?"

"My taxes are so high now, and the assessor is sending someone around for a reassessment. I've heard that Augusta Renwick's taxes doubled in one year! I can't afford to keep the castle up as it is. . . . I worry that some kids will sneak up here and fall through my crumbling stonework."

Stevie was stunned. For the first time, her aunt seemed to be seriously considering a developer's offer.

An owl called from deep in the trees. They heard its wing beats, saw it pass overhead.

"If you let them put condos in," Stevie said, "where will the owls go?"

Her aunt tried to smile. "That sounds like a Stevie Moore Caldecott winner. *Where Will the Owls Go?*"

"I mean it seriously," Stevie said. "You can't develop the hillside. Aunt Aida?"

"It's a conundrum," her aunt replied after a moment. "Because I can't afford not to."

"There must be a way to raise money," Stevie said. "Maybe open the castle to the public for one or two days a week."

Aunt Aida smiled sadly. "Why would they come? To see my darling husband's romantic but useless folly?"

"Since when have you believed that anything romantic was useless?" Stevie hugged her. "You are the last of the great romantics, Aunt Aida. It's why you've held on to this land as long as you have. Henry and I both know that it would be easier for you to stay in Florida every year, but you can't let this place go . . . because it reminds you of Uncle Van."

"It does," her aunt whispered, wiping away tears. "I feel him here with me right now. If his ghost is anywhere, it's here."

Stevie's heart hurt; she thought of getting to her aunt's age, having loved someone so much that she would sacrifice so much just to be near his spirit. "You must never feel alone," she said.

"I don't."

Stevie nodded, gazing over the trees.

"You'll find someone," her aunt said. "And you'll stop feeling so alone."

Stevie shook her head. "I had my chances," she said.

"*Smiles of a Summer Night*," her aunt said.

Stevie looked over, curious.

"It was a film by Ingmar Bergman, and it inspired Sondheim's *A Little Night Music*."

" 'Send in the Clowns' was in that musical," Stevie said. "The story of my love life."

Her aunt laughed. "It is about human foibles and missteps in love. All but the most fearful of us make them, dear Stevie. It's how we know we're alive! You are far from alone."

"I've made more and worse than most people."

Her aunt shook her head, laughing no longer. "You've reached for love body and soul," she said. "You've believed in it, needed it, so very much, that you've taken *three* chances. . . . In the play, the grand duchess says that of a summer night, the moon smiles three times. . . . Well, tonight, I'd like for you to think of me as the grand duchess."

"I've had my three times," Stevie said.

"No, dear. I'm not referring to that. Think *now*, tonight, and think *deep*. Time and experience are measured differently during summer, and especially on full-moon nights."

At that moment, the moon came out of the sea, far to the east. It emerged slowly, a huge burnt-orange disc hovering over the horizon, upside down, as if spilling gold into the water. "The first smile . . . see?" Aunt Aida asked as the moon shone huge and bright, grinning like the Cheshire Cat.

The amazing thing was, Stevie could.

As they watched in silence, the moon rose slowly, turning smaller and paler, until it was pure white, glowing, high in the sky. The face appeared in the craters, and Stevie laughed out loud.

"What is it?"

"I just remembered," Stevie said. "When we were young, my friends Emma and Madeleine and I used to call her 'the girl in the moon.' See her, laughing?"

"The second smile," her aunt said.

Stevie herself was beaming. She remembered being fifteen with her friends, happy and sassy, claiming the moon as their own.

"When will we see the third smile?" Stevie asked. "Since you're grand duchess for the night, you must know!"

"You will see it when you are brave enough to knock on the right door," her aunt said.

Stevie glanced over, ready to tease her aunt, but she could see that Aunt Aida was purely serious. She regarded Stevie with grave eyes. Stevie's stomach fluttered. Her aunt was contemplating serious matters: the sale of her hillside, her woods, the birds' habitat. An owl called from deep in the forest, and another replied from very close by.

Looking up, Stevie saw the silhouette of a great horned owl, perched on the top of the tower. Its face was ferocious in moonlight, its eyes and beak glinting yellow. A shiver went down Stevie's spine as it flew away, into the trees.

Now, gazing back at the moon, she saw that it had spun a net across the water. Filaments of moonlight shimmered and danced on the waves. Stevie imagined it connecting everyone she had ever loved. She saw Aunt Aida staring, and knew she was thinking of Uncle Van.

Stevie's heart pounded. *Knock on the right door . . .* She thought of Nell standing outside, on the top step, with her skinned knees. And she thought of herself, leaving the invitation in the screen door at Jack and Nell's house. And she remembered Madeleine coming up the hill with her two bottles of champagne. The moon brought the memories together, and Stevie suddenly knew.

She knew what she had to do, where she had to go, to knock on the door.

NELL WAS so tired, she could hardly keep her eyes open. The moon had come charging out of the water, rising into the sky, while everyone watched. She had liked snuggling into her dad's side, feeling his warmth as the night grew cooler. Then, later, Peggy had pulled her to her feet, to "dance by the light of the moon" with Annie and Eliza. The waves had provided music, and the girls had danced barefoot in the sand until their parents all said it was time to head home.

The families walked together as far as the seawall. The wall was really thick, made of huge rocks, to keep the sea off the road. Peggy and her family said goodbye and headed through the marsh with flashlights.

Nell and her father walked through the sandy parking lot, behind the boat basin. Nell heard the boat hardware groaning and creaking gently in the darkness as the water rose and fell. Walking along, she yawned and stumbled, and her father caught her and kept her going straight.

"That was fun," she said.

"It was," he said.

Nell felt exhausted from the fresh air, running around, and general excitement of watching the great big moon come up out of the sea. She had loved being with so many people, all gathered together on the sand.

"It was like having a big family," she said, holding her father's hand.

He didn't reply. She felt the tar beneath her feet, still warm from the day's sun.

"I liked it. I like when it's just us, you and me," she said. "But I also like it when it's other people, too."

"Well, it's mostly just us," he said. "We'll be leaving the beach soon, in a couple of weeks. But then you can write to Peggy."

"From Boston?" she asked, unsure of whether they were going back to Massachusetts or home to Georgia.

"Not Boston," he said, sounding funny—*hesitant*, she thought. Which was a very unusual way for her father to sound.

"We're going to Atlanta?"

"Nell, do you know how to dance the Highland fling?"

"The what?"

"It's a Scottish dance."

"Scottish? Like, with bagpipes?"

"Yes."

"Ohhh," Nell said, shivering. "Aunt Madeleine told me about going to Scotland when she was little, and hearing bagpipes everywhere she went. She liked it, but I wouldn't."

"Why not?"

"Because I hate bagpipes," Nell said. "Because of that one that played at church for Mom's . . ." she refused to say *funeral*. She remembered that some man her mother had met at Dixon, the prison where she had volunteered, a guard or a police officer or something, knew how to play the bagpipes, and he'd stood by the altar playing "Amazing Grace."

"Well, Scotland has a lot more going on than bagpipes."

"True, but if I heard even one it would ruin my time. They're awful. I hate them. Don't talk about them anymore, okay? Because I'll have nightmares."

"But, Nell—"

"Shh! Shhhh!" Nell said, covering her ears.

Her father stopped talking. Nell reached for his hand, yawning again. She was very tired, but she wanted to make sure her mind didn't get all upset and filled with funeral music and the prison just before going to sleep. To push it away, she hummed "Lemon Tree" and tried to decide which book she wanted him to read her that night.

Should it be *Owl Night* or *Summer of the Swans*? Or, maybe, *Seahawk*? When they got to their cottage, her father unlocked the back door, and they went inside. Nell changed right into her pajamas. She knew she should wash her face and feet and brush her teeth, but she wanted to get right into bed and hear the story.

She had already decided on the book—*Summer of the Swans*—and was just hanging her toothbrush back in the rack, when she heard a knock at the door. Her stomach clenched up.

A knock at the door, especially after dark, was not good. She remembered the police officers who had come to her house that night, to tell them about her mother—she had gotten all confused and thought they were guards from the prison, warning them that that awful prisoner who had called her mom had somehow escaped. And she remembered the times she'd hear *tap-tap-tap*, after they thought she'd gone to sleep, when Francesca would come to their door with some papers her father just "had to see that night." Or what? London Bridge would come falling down?

Hearing the light hand at the door, Nell knew it had to be Francesca.

"*Go away,*" she said into her pillow.

A few moments passed, and then she heard a second knock—her father tapping at her bedroom door. "Nell?" he asked.

"Dad," she said, feeling tired and close to tears. "Please tell Francesca to go away, and tell her we're not going back to Boston! Then come in here, because I need my Stevie story!"

"Francesca's not here. And tonight you're the luckiest

girl around. You're going to get a story straight from Stevie herself."

And with that, Nell sat up straight and peered into the light flooding in from the hall lamp, and she saw Stevie smiling down at her, coming to sit on the edge of her bed, without even a book in her hands to read from.

chapter 15

NELL SCOOTED OVER IN THE BED, TO make room for Stevie to sit on the edge. Jack hovered in the doorway, as if he wasn't sure whether to stay or go. Stevie smiled at him, waiting. He was tall, and his broad shoulders completely blocked the hall light. Her heart was in her throat, wanting more than anything for him to sit beside her.

"Sit down, Dad . . . come listen to Stevie's story," Nell said.

"Oh, I think she came to tell it to you," he said. "I'll go out in the other room. . . ."

"It's for both of you," Stevie said.

He moved toward her, then stopped himself—as if maybe he thought better of sitting beside her on the bed. Instead, he pulled a straight-backed chair in from the other room. The bedside lamp had a ship's wheel on its parchment shade, and it threw warm orange light on Stevie's hands and sketchpad.

"This is a story about Lovecraft Hill," she said. "A

magical stone castle sits in the midst of fields and woodlands, overlooking the mouth of a majestic river, just where it empties into the sea. Ivy and vines grow up the castle walls. . . ." As she spoke, she drew, passing the pictures to Nell.

"Does a princess live there?" Nell asked.

"No," Stevie said. "The castle and its grounds belong to nature. But it's watched over, tended, by a wise old aunt."

"An aunt," Nell whispered. Stevie sketched a woman who looked like a cross between Stevie's Aunt Aida and Madeleine. Stevie heard Nell draw a sharp breath; she glanced up for Jack's reaction. His eyes were sparkling, gazing at Stevie, not even looking at her drawing.

"The castle is old, and crumbling," Stevie said, hardly able to look away from him. "High winds topple stones from the tower. The steps threaten to give way. Bats live in the rafters, and vines twist up the copper drainpipes." Swiftly she drew the enchanted ruin.

"Acres of pine trees grow on the hillside, providing shade and cover for every kind of bird and animal. Finches, thrushes, warblers, robins nest in the pine barrens, building nests of twigs and needles. They lay their eggs, raise their broods. Deer, raccoons, and rabbits live there, too. The deep forest gives them shelter and food. They survive in their habitat so they won't have to stray into ours. . . ."

Stevie drew a quick series of pictures showing deer crossing the busy shore road, eating the flowers and shrubs around a house; raccoons toppling over a garbage can; and rabbits overtaking a lettuce patch. Nell giggled.

"Opposite the castle from the pine barrens are the Old Oaks. These are the oldest woods in Connecticut. They are thick and tall. There are trees in the deepest part called 'dawn redwoods' that date back to a time when the land was new. Owls live in this part of the forest. They call through the night, and only the bravest people dare stray into their woods, answer their call."

"What do they say?" Nell whispered, and Stevie answered with the call Aunt Aida had taught her when she was Nell's age.

"Who-hoo-who-hoo-hoo-hoo . . ."

Nell tried it, got it right the first time. Stevie drew a picture of three people standing in the thick forest: Stevie herself, the wise aunt, and Nell. Nell beamed.

Stevie kept talking, making it up as she went along, drawing quick sketches. She had never done this before—written a story for an actual, real child. If felt incredible—not least of all because Jack was leaning forward, seemingly as interested as Nell. Their knees touched, and Stevie felt voltage shoot all through her body.

Nell was getting sleepy, her eyes starting to close.

"Should I stop?" Stevie asked.

"No," the Kilverts both said at once.

"The castle grounds belong to nature, but others want it, too," Stevie said. "Men with bulldozers want to come and clear the trees. They want to own the beautiful view and sell it for gold. They want to turn the deers' nests into houses, and they want to turn the wild castle into a tame conference hall."

"But the wise aunt . . ." Nell murmured, struggling to keep her eyes open.

"Yes, the wild aunt will protect the hillside," Stevie said, drawing.

"I knew she would," Nell whispered.

"How did you know that?" Jack asked.

"Because she's good. She's like Aunt Maddie," Nell said. "And like Stevie's Aunt Aida. Right, Stevie?"

"Very much so."

"When the sun rises, the owls go to sleep, and the other creatures come out of their nests and burrows. The warblers sing in the bushes, and the rabbits hop through the wet grass. The hummingbirds come to the red flowers that grow on vines attached to the castle. They feed on the nectar, their wings such a blur you can't even see them moving. Summer days pass by, turn into nights. The moon starts off as a thin crescent, and grows larger all through the month, till it is full and rises, like tonight, right out of the sea. . . ."

When she drew the last picture, of the full moon shining down on the castle and hillside, Nell was asleep. Stevie left the sketchbook by the side of her bed, followed Jack out into the living room. Being so close to him made her shiver. She felt whispers of air across her skin; she couldn't quite look at him.

"She never does that," he said, turning to face Stevie. "Falls right asleep. There usually have to be three or four books, and a back rub, and checking to make sure no one's hiding in the closet. How did you do it?"

"I didn't do anything," Stevie said. "It's the full moon. It has magical powers, it really does. It entices even the most wound-up children to sleep."

"No, it was your wonderful story," Jack said. "It soothed her . . . that, and the sound of your voice."

"I've been thinking about her—about both of you," Stevie said. "So much. Ever since . . . did you wind up taking her to see Dr. Galford again?"

"I did. It was good to talk to you about that—it helped."

"I'm so glad."

"About your story—is there really a place like that? What did you call it—Lovecraft Hill?"

"Yes. There is," Stevie said.

"Where is it?"

"Just a few miles from here. My aunt lives there."

Jack's eyes widened. He pushed the dark hair back from his face, watching Stevie and waiting for her to say more. She was entranced by him. The shape of his face, the way his long hair fell into his eyes. When she didn't speak, he asked, "Is it a true story?"

Stevie nodded, shaken from her trance. The full moon had a hold over her—that's what it had to be. The girl in the moon was playing games with her heart. She stared into Jack's emerald green eyes and wondered whether she had ever felt anything quite like this. . . .

"She lives in a castle?"

"No, she moved out of it years ago," Stevie said. Thinking of Aunt Aida, and the truth of her situation, chased the magic away. "The upkeep was too much. She lives in a cottage on the property. But she loves the castle, and goes inside often. She says it's where her husband's ghost lives. She's an artist too, and I swear she needs the place for her inspiration. She comes up from the Florida Keys in May or June and paints all through the summer. She knows every bird species, every owl call. . . . I can't bear to think of something happening to the hillside."

"The bulldozers are real?"

"Realer than they've ever been before," Stevie said, her heart sinking. "Developers have offered her a lot of money for the property, but she's always sent them packing. This summer . . . she's worried about the taxes, and that the castle is really falling apart. She's afraid someone will sneak in and get hurt. Another developer has come along. . . ."

"And she's considering the offer?"

"Seems so. It would break her heart, though. It really would."

"Why doesn't she donate the land to a nonprofit? Or form her own land trust?"

Stevie had never thought of such a thing, and she bet Aunt Aida never had, either. They were artists through and through, without much care or concern for how the financial or real estate world worked.

"She could do that?"

"Absolutely. I worked on a project up on Mount Desert Island, in Maine, where the property owners donated their land to the national park. I had to go up and rebuild the stone bridges on all the carriage trails, and plan others consistent with the original architecture."

"That sounds wonderful. I guess . . . we could get someone to do that with the castle."

"I'd be happy to take a look."

"Are you serious? Thank you!" Stevie had a sudden vision of Jack rebuilding the castle, of a nature center opening for all the people of Black Hall to enjoy.

"Aunt Aida and I could give art classes," she said out loud.

"What?"

"Oh, my thoughts are racing," she said. "I just had a wild picture of turning the castle into a nature center . . . with exhibits on birds, trees, the animals . . . and I imagined my aunt and I teaching a couple of classes . . . about feeling 'what is,' and using nature as our inspiration. Giving back, you know?"

"That sounds wonderful. So, you really have a wise aunt?" Jack took a step closer.

"I do," Stevie said. She felt her face flush as she gazed up at him. She couldn't hold the next part back; she had to say it—she cared too much not to. "And so does Nell."

He blinked, looked away.

"I took your suggestion," Stevie said. "And called Madeleine on my own."

"I was wondering," he said, his expression hardening, "if you'd done that." He closed his eyes, and Stevie had the idea it wasn't so much to shut her out but to better face something deep inside himself.

"Jack, you came here because you have history here. Even though you left Atlanta because it's so painful and reminds you of Emma, you came *here*, to a place where you couldn't help spinning back into the past every time you turn around."

"That's what it's like, you're right. . . ."

"Your family spent summers here. You and Maddie. That's why I think you came. Because you can't bear the distance between you and your sister."

Jack didn't respond to that. He was so silent, Stevie heard only crickets chirping and wind blowing through the trees outside.

"How is she?" he asked after a long time.

"She's . . . sad," Stevie said gently.

"Because of me?"

"Because of life. Losing Emma, losing you and Nell. It was hard for her to be here, knowing you were up the road. She got mad at me for tricking her, and she left." Stevie looked into Jack's face. He looked so troubled and somehow locked in, with something that went excruciatingly far beyond this conversation. "You're probably mad at me now, too," Stevie said.

"What do you want me to do, Stevie?"

"Forgive her."

"You don't understand—you really don't. It's not just a matter of forgiveness."

"Then what is it? Why can't you talk to her?" His words, and the look on his face, tore her heart. He was suffering terribly, and it brought tears to her eyes. "Can't you do it for Nell?" she said. "And Maddie . . . and mostly, Jack, for yourself ?"

She thought she had gone too far. She was pushing him, and he was right—she didn't have the whole story. She reached up to touch the side of his face. She wanted to apologize, but mostly she wanted to soothe the agony away. He caught her hand—the motion was so sharp, she gasped.

Jack took her in his arms and kissed her. His body felt hard, and his mouth was so hot. She stood on her tiptoes to reach up, and she felt his arms holding her, pulling her closer and tighter. Her head was tipped back, her heart beating in her throat, her blood on fire.

He led her to the sofa. They sat down together, holding hands. Jack reached over, to brush the bangs away from her eyes. She felt the earth go out from under her. She hadn't been touched in so long.

She tried to get control of her breath. She had butterflies in her stomach, and she felt a wave of shyness wash over her. Looking into Jack's eyes, she held his gaze. It was so direct and filled with desire that she turned to liquid, hot and melting. Her thoughts were racing: *Don't do it, Stevie. Don't let this go any farther.*

She could almost hear Henry teasing her, calling her Lulu, Luocious . . . the newest character in the *Odyssey*, the one whose song lured men to crash their boats on the rocks. He'd tell her to warn Jack to block his ears and sail on. Weren't three marriages enough? Her head was telling her one thing, her heart was pushing her toward another. She told herself, *It's not marriage, for heaven's sake—it's just sitting here holding hands; it's just a few kisses.* . . .

But those few kisses . . . they were so sweet. Stevie tilted her head back, felt Jack kissing her lips, the side of her neck. She shivered and wanted him to keep going. She also wanted him to stop. Her thoughts got crazy again, all jumbled up: she always wanted so much, never knew how to hold back, was a bottomless pit for affection. She curved over slightly, protecting her heart.

"I'm sorry," he said. "I shouldn't have."

"No, I'm sorry. I shouldn't have," she said.

The apologies brought them up short. Stevie bowed her head. What was she doing?

"What do you think is going on with us?" he asked, their arms still around each other.

"I think," she began, but stopped herself, because suddenly all she could see was a picture of them at dawn, alone on the deserted beach, meeting to kiss by the water's edge. It was the culmination of all her dreams of this entire summer. . . .

Their eyes locked. Jack was hanging on her answer. She wanted to warn him, tell him that she was no good for him—fantasy was one thing, this was something else. She had made big mistakes before, and she didn't want anyone to be hurt. She thought of Nell sleeping in the other room, and remembered what it had been like to lose her mother. The loss had created an abyss of longing, and Stevie felt it even now.

In fact, gazing into Jack's dark eyes, she felt it in a whole new way. Although she had pulled away, he kept one arm around her shoulders. His touch was wildly romantic and somehow erotic, the feel of his fingertips against the bare skin of her left arm. She found it hard to sit still.

"I should go," she said.

"You're saying that, but I don't believe you want to."

"Why?"

"Because I know how I feel . . . and I think you feel the same way."

He leaned down, brushed his lips against hers, found the kiss. Stevie's arms went around his neck again. He smelled of salt and sweat and citrus. She wanted to swim with him. Her body yearned for it, and she pressed her chest against his, feeling wild and wordless, for once the thoughts stopping and the sensations taking over.

Nell turned over, made a small sound.

And that was it. Stevie was on her feet. Swaying, none too steady, she backed away. Jack reached out, tried to pull her back. But Stevie didn't want Nell to wake up and find her new friend kissing her father.

"I have to go," she whispered.

"No—Stevie . . . I want to talk to you."

"Not tonight," she said. She felt dizzy. "Okay? I really do have to go."

"When can we see the castle?"

"Tomorrow? The next day? Anytime you're ready."

"The sooner the better," he said. "We'll be leaving in three weeks."

"Three weeks?" she asked.

"That's one of the things I wanted to talk to you about." He stood, walked over, touched her arm.

She nodded. Her face felt hot, and the dizziness felt more intense. She knew she had to get out of there right then, or she never would. She pulled back her arm, smiled into his eyes.

"I'm taking a job in Scotland," he said, and she felt the smile leave her face.

"When?"

"In three weeks," he repeated.

Stevie thought of Nell, going so far away. She thought of Madeleine, losing the chance to reconcile. And she thought of Jack, of how very little she could hope to sort out her feelings for him during three short weeks. Her heart caved in, and she made herself stand tall.

"What are you thinking?" he asked.

"I'm sorry you have to leave," she said. "With so much left to do . . ."

"Your aunt's castle?"

Stevie smiled sadly. "That's what you think?" she asked.

He squinted, not replying. Then he shook his head. "It's just the easiest," he said finally.

"Wow," she said, thinking of the ivy-covered walls, the vines snaking through mortar, the tumbling-down rocks, the overgrown paths . . . He was right, really, that the physical work was so much easier than the emotional. "I wish, I wish," she began.

"What do you wish, Stevie?"

"I wish that Nell could have her aunt in her life, the way I have mine."

He looked away, cleared his throat, ignoring her words. "We'd better go see the castle soon," he said. "Tomorrow—how's noon?"

"Noon is fine."

"I'm just curious," he said after a moment, touching the side of her face.

"What?" she said, her skin tingling.

"Is that the only reaction you have to my saying we're moving to Scotland?"

"The only one I'm prepared to say out loud," she said softly. And then she turned and walked out the door into the bright, moonlit night.

JACK WATCHED her go. He had to hold himself back, to keep from following her. His heart was racing, and he felt strange. Stevie was gone, but some kind of . . . of aura, or spirit, was left behind. The room crackled. Jack didn't understand, had never felt anything like this before. He felt overloaded with energy—as if he could run twenty miles. He stretched, trying to discharge it.

He wanted everything to be different, he wanted to undo so much. He knew that Stevie was right about Nell. But she didn't know the whole story. There was more to it than she thought.

Still, he felt the strange energy left by their talk, and he found himself picking up the telephone. He dialed information, got a number.

His fingers were trembling as he held the receiver to his ear.

The phone rang and rang. He looked at his watch: maybe they were out.

But then a woman answered, and he heard her voice.

"Hello?" his sister said.

Jack didn't speak. He just held on, wanting to say the

one thing that would make everything okay, wipe away all the hurt and suspicion. He didn't want to leave with this between them.

"Hello?" she said again.

Jack's mind spun out with their last meeting, the truth of what Madeleine had told him, the fury with which he'd fought her story. If he talked to her now, it would be letting her version of the events back into his life, and he knew he couldn't do that to Nell.

"Who is this?" Madeleine asked.

Jack wanted to tell her, but he couldn't. So he just hung up.

chapter 16

STEVIE PICKED THEM UP AT NOON, after Nell's morning at recreation, and they drove under the train trestle and onto Shore Road. Nell was beside herself with excitement—she squirmed in the backseat, pointing out landmarks and talking nonstop. Jack's excitement surpassed his daughter's. For once, Nell had slept through the night while he lay awake staring at the ceiling, trying to figure out what was happening.

They stopped at Paradise Ice Cream for lunch, with Stevie ordering an extra lobster roll for her aunt. They carried their trays over to picnic tables behind the white shack, overlooking the marsh. Seagulls circled around, watching for someone to drop a scrap.

Bright sunlight turned the streams and coves to mirrors. It highlighted Stevie's ebony hair, close-cropped to expose the beautiful neck that Jack recalled kissing the night before. He wanted to reach across, push the bangs from her violet eyes, touch her porcelain cheek.

He restrained himself, and it wasn't easy. Especially when she looked directly into his eyes with a look that said she was having the same difficulty.

When they finished, they climbed back into Stevie's car and drove a little farther along the main road. Then they turned off onto a lane that took them back under the train line, and then onto a side road that led them up a steep hill. Soon the pavement gave way to a gravel track, and the ride got bumpy. Nell jumped and cried out—her nightmares all had to do with what she imagined about her mother's last ride on that godforsaken country road—so Jack just reached into the backseat to hold her hand and tell her they were safe.

"We're almost there," Stevie said, glancing into the rearview mirror. She could see that Nell was pure white, gripping her father's hand. "Look, Nell—see? There's the gatehouse!"

She slowed the car down, and tooted the horn. A man and a red-haired woman leaned out the door to wave. The man was beaming, and he raised the woman's left hand in the air and pointed at it as the car drove by.

"Who's that? Is that Aunt Aida?" Nell asked.

"No," Stevie said, smiling broadly. "I can hardly believe it, but that's Aida's stepson, Henry, and his friend Doreen."

Suddenly the castle came into view, and Nell gasped. Even Jack was stunned—it was spectacular and strange, completely unexpected in the staid Connecticut countryside—it looked like it belonged in the Alps, in the Black Forest, some half-mad baron's fantasy of fairytale grandeur.

"There it is," Stevie said proudly as they climbed out of the car. "And there's my aunt!"

A tall, elegant woman, dressed in a painting smock and jeans with the knees torn out, velvet slippers, and a gold lamé headband, strode from the small cottage beside the castle. She had a high, intelligent forehead and violet eyes made up with kohl and blue shadow. Although she was much taller than Stevie, the resemblance was striking. It was there in her eyes, her bearing, and her beauty.

"This is my aunt Aida Von Lichen," Stevie said.

"You must be Jack," she said. "And you must be Nell. Please, call me Aida. Will you join me for lunch?"

"We stopped at Paradise and ate already," Stevie said, handing her the brown bag.

"Stevie brought you a lobster roll!" Nell said.

"She is the most darling, thoughtful niece an aunt could have," Aida said. "Let me just put this in the refrigerator, for later."

"Aunt Aida—what was that sparkling on Doreen's ring finger?" Stevie asked when the older woman emerged from her door.

"It's a miracle—that's what it was! Henry asked her to marry him, and she accepted. They're affianced!" Aida said in an imperious but affectionate way as her eyes filled with tears. She spoke in exactly the tones Jack would expect of a woman who owned a castle, but he was taken by her obvious emotion and love.

"I saw him pointing at her hand," Stevie said.

"Yes . . . I gave him my engagement ring to give her."

"Oh, Aunt Aida," Stevie said, hugging her. Jack watched the private moment between aunt and niece; he remembered what Stevie had said about her uncle's ghost haunting this castle, and had a sense that Aida's ring was precious beyond its mortal worth.

Aida steadied herself against Stevie, and then pushed back. Her eye makeup had smudged. Stevie wiped it from her cheek. Jack felt a stab, thinking about their lifelong relationship, thinking of Maddie and Nell. Aida nodded that she was fine, and she laughed lightly.

"Jack and Nell, you must think I'm a crazy old lady. Let me explain to you . . . Henry is my stepson, just retired from the U.S. Navy. I adore him, beyond all reason, exactly as if he were my own son. He is a brilliant officer and gentleman, but, sadly, has been a tad moronic in the ways of love. He had this wonderful relationship with a dear, dear woman—Doreen—and he let it go . . ."

"How?" Nell asked.

"Well, by always sailing away. That's what sailors do. They make port, stay as long as they stay, and then sail away. Henry expected Doreen to always be there, waiting for him. And she was . . . until he retired. And he expected to just waltz right into Newport and be taken in. He wasn't planning to marry her, mind you. He just wanted to come and go as he pleased."

Jack listened. Aida's words were hitting him in a completely unexpected way. Suddenly he saw his passport and the air tickets and the brochures about the corporate rooms-to-let in Inverness, the plaids and bagpipes of Scotland. He was running away, of course. From the pain of the past, but also from what he'd started to feel about Stevie. He was exactly like Henry.

"She gave him the boot," Aida continued. "And I completely applauded her for it. Now, marriage isn't the be-all and end-all for everyone. It is far from a panacea. But once you know . . . as I believe Henry knew about Doreen a good ten port-calls ago . . . you owe it to yourself and your beloved to make it legal."

"It's the knowing when, and when not, that can trip a person up," Stevie said in a low voice, and when Jack looked over, he could see that her lively, beautiful eyes had turned faraway and tragic.

"Lulu!" Henry called, lumbering up the hill holding hands with Doreen. There were hugs and congratulations all around, and Stevie admired the ring, and then Jack and Nell introduced themselves.

"The famous Nell," Henry said.

"I'm famous?" she asked, beaming.

"Absolutely. Stevie holds you in the highest esteem. You and your father." He met Jack's eyes, and Jack saw a flash there—a challenge, as if some sort of gauntlet had just been thrown down.

"She told you about me?" Nell asked, delighted.

"Oh, my," Aida said. "She talked and talked about you. She loved that you were brave enough to climb her hill and walk right past that *awful* sign she has. . . ."

"Please Go Away!" Nell giggled.

"Precisely," Henry said. "That's a sign that needs to find a home in a nice trash heap."

Jack watched his daughter interact with these people

she had never met before—she was so open and happy, thirsty for their affection. It was all because of Stevie. Somehow Nell had adopted her as her own—like a stand-in aunt, her mother's former best friend. He felt a lump in his throat. He'd forgotten what it felt like to have extended family. His own parents and aunts and uncles were dead; all he had left was Madeleine.

Henry and Doreen had errands to run—they were going to see the priest at St. Mary's in Newport about a date for their wedding. Aida started toward the castle, leading Stevie and her visitors. Stevie and Nell were holding hands, and Jack was just behind them, when suddenly Henry called out.

"Hey, Stevie," he said.

She turned around.

"Luocious is no more."

"Why do you say that?"

"Because the *Odyssey* doesn't need another character. And because Stevie knows what she's doing. I can tell. Press on regardless, okay?"

Stevie stood rooted to the ground. Something about her bearing and posture made Jack want to wrap her in a hug—she looked as if she needed shoring up. But then a wide smile overtook her face, and she nodded and waved at her stepcousin, who waved back.

Jack didn't know what it meant, that exchange that had just passed between them, but he knew one thing— Stevie and Henry were each other's family, however attenuated, and they cared about each other's next step in life. He thought of Maddie and felt a little more hollow than before.

They stood at the door to the castle. A blast of cool, musty air greeted them. Jack's heart was pounding as he peered into the darkness. As an engineer, he was excited about the possibilities. Nell shivered, grabbed his hand and Stevie's. They all walked in together, Jack's pulse going a mile a minute.

All he could think was, *I've got to get out of going to Scotland.*

NELL HELD her father's and Stevie's hands, thrilled by the castle. She noticed all sorts of magical things. The walls were made of dark oak, carved with heads and faces. The floor was made of slate squares, and shields and words were etched in them. Aunt Aida pointed them out, saying they were the names of theaters where her husband had acted in plays.

"He made his name at the Royal Shakespeare Company," she said. "Very early on, he was mentioned alongside Gielgud. He played at Covent Garden, and his notices as Iago were brilliant. I'm talking rare air, Olivier territory. He played Prince Hal, and same thing. Then . . . well, life took hold and interested him more than theater. He was a bon vivant of the highest order, my Van. As he aged, he settled into Falstaff. It suited him, the darling."

Nell didn't understand all the words, or what they meant, but she could tell from Aunt Aida's voice that she had loved Van a lot. And she could tell from the way Stevie leaned over to hug her that she knew that something about this visit was hard for her aunt.

They walked through the downstairs, their footsteps echoing. There was a great hall, with cobwebs hanging from a huge black chandelier and scary mildew on a big wooden table. Nell held tight to her father and Stevie. Her father was talking, in his steady business voice.

It was the one she heard him use on the phone, and when she visited him at the office. One of the ways she knew he didn't *really* like Francesca was the fact that he used it with her. He never really dropped it when she was around.

Her father never used that voice with Nell. He had used it with her mother only once, just before she'd gone away. And he didn't use it with Stevie. Even when he was mad that day Nell had gotten so upset about Aunt Maddie at Stevie's house, her father hadn't used his business voice. He had used his upset Daddy voice, which he usually only used with family—Aunt Maddie, for example.

He was saying something about donating the land and castle, a directed gift, a tax shelter . . . whole bunches of stuff Nell didn't get. But she could tell from looking at Stevie and Aunt Aida that they were interested, even happy. Her father took out a notepad and measuring tape, began making notations. He measured the thickness of walls, the height of ceilings.

Aunt Aida began pointing out things like dry rot and termite holes, and her father took out his penknife and dug into the wood along the floor a little. He said something about having an inspection to make sure, but not seeing any insects or eggs. Aunt Aida seemed relieved.

They entered a small door in the wall and found themselves in a darkened circular stairway. It reminded Nell of a prison. The only light came from small stained-glass windows, so Aunt Aida pulled a flashlight from her smock pocket to illuminate their way. Nell felt afraid because she had to let go of the adults' hands, but she was right between them as they climbed, so she knew it would be okay.

Stevie was saying something about a "nature center," and Aunt Aida said, "One hundred and sixty-four acres would make a wonderful wildlife refuge," and her dad said, "This castle is incredible, and it should be preserved just as it is," and Aunt Aida actually let out a cry and said, "Thank you for seeing it that way! The developers all want to gussy it up with media centers and hot tubs!"

When they had climbed four tall stories to the very top, it was like stepping out of jail into a garden of sunshine. The tower overlooked the entire valley, straight down to the silver sea. Moss and weeds grew from the cracks in the stones. Wildflower seeds must have blown up here, because flowers were growing out of the mortar, waving in the summer wind.

Nell blinked into the bright sunlight, staring over the treetops. Birds hopped from branch to branch. She thought of Stevie's story about the pine barrens and Old Oaks, about the deer and rabbits and songbirds and owls. She felt the mysterious blessing of having stepped straight into a real-life fairy tale. She could almost believe that a white stag, or unicorn, would come bounding out of the forest before her very eyes.

The woods went on forever. Her father was talking calmly, but excitedly, about preserving them and the castle. Aunt Aida was asking questions a mile a minute: what should she do, who should she talk to, what papers should she sign?

Stevie stepped away from the adults, to crouch down beside Nell. Together they looked at the thick pine woods, at the tall and ancient oaks. They looked at the vine of red flowers that grew out of the castle stones, trailing all the way up to the parapet above. As they watched, two tiny emerald green hummingbirds hovered in midair, drinking nectar from the tubular blossoms.

"How did they fly all the way up here?" Nell whispered. Just watching them—no larger than dragonflies—made her knees feel strange. She wobbled a little, thinking of how hard it could be for little things, how much they had to go through to get to the red nectar.

"They fly halfway around the world," Stevie said. "They are strong and determined."

"They look so small," Nell said. The wind was blowing, and she felt afraid it would dash them into the castle's rock walls. "What if the wind kills them?"

"It won't," Stevie said, taking her hand. "Their wings are powerful, and they resist strong winds."

"How come only one has a red throat?" Nell asked, watching the pair dart in and out, noticing their iridescent green feathers, wings a blur, long beaks reaching into the flowers.

"That's the male," Stevie said. "They're ruby-throated hummingbirds. Nature gave the male brighter markings, but I think the female is just as beautiful—maybe even more. She's subtle and mysterious."

"How come nature did it that way?"

"So she would be attracted to him. And so she would be protected from predators."

Nell's eyes filled with tears. She didn't know what "predators" meant. Was it a rough and bumpy country road? Was it a wrong turn taken by a loving aunt, who had lost her way in the dark? Was it the monsters that came out of the night, any night, to remind a girl her mother was dead?

"What is it, Nell?" Stevie asked, her voice steady but her eyes sad.

"I miss them," Nell whispered.

Stevie hugged Nell close, and held her there without letting go, and Nell felt her thinking of the beach girls, of Nell's mother and aunt, and Nell heard her whisper back, "I know. So do I."

THAT NIGHT, after Nell was asleep, Jack picked up the phone and dialed a now-almost-familiar number. His heart was racing, but not quite as bad as the first time he'd called. This time he was ready—this time he'd speak, say hello, ask how she and Chris were doing. He would tell her he'd heard she had been to visit Stevie. He'd tell her that Nell missed her.

She answered on the third ring.

"Hello?" she said.

Jack closed his eyes.

His heart picked up the pace. This wasn't a flatlands

sprint, it was an uphill climb, too steep for him to handle. If he talked to her, really talked, he'd have to drop the charade and the story, the steel that had gotten him through this last year. He'd have to acknowledge that he believed what she'd told him about Kearsage. And Nell might find out the truth. . . . His hands were sweating so hard, the phone slipped.

"I'm glad you called," she said, her voice breaking.

How could she know? Or could she? Even if she had caller ID, how would she recognize the number of this rental cottage?

"I miss you, I do," she said, her voice full of tears. "I wish I could turn back time and do everything differently. . . . I miss my big brother."

Jack's throat was too closed to speak. He heard her sobbing softly, and he didn't want to make it worse. Quietly, without a word, he hung up.

chapter 17

MADELEINE KNEW IT WAS JACK. SHE had caller ID, and the number was from Hubbard's Point, Connecticut, and she checked her phone book and saw it wasn't Stevie's, so she knew it had to be his. She sat in the study of her Federal house, wiping her eyes, feeling cold in spite of the warm summer air coming through the open window.

Chris poked his head into the room. She looked at his bright blue eyes and graying blond hair and forced a smile, nodding to let him know she was okay. He'd been checking on her more than usual since she'd come home from seeing Stevie. In fact, his attentiveness reminded her of how he had been in the months immediately after the accident, when she'd been in such bad shape.

"Who was that?" he asked.

"Wrong number," she said.

"I thought I heard you talking . . ."

At least he hadn't said "crying." Madeleine smiled and said, "I was just being polite."

Chris believed her and went back to watching the baseball game on TV. Madeleine shivered. She hated lying to her husband. But she knew if she told him that her brother had called, he'd hit *69 and give Jack a piece of his mind. A part of Madeleine wanted to do the very same thing.

She couldn't believe that he still wouldn't, or couldn't, talk to her. She took responsibility for driving, for taking Emma away. But the rest—Jack had been unable to handle hearing the truth. Madeleine remembered how—through the Demerol haze that first day in the hospital, when she came to and found Jack at her bedside—she had told him, and only him, what had really happened. He had broken down—shaking his head, wailing like a madman, smashing his fist against the wall.

The nurse had run in—whisked Jack away, to bandage his hand—and Madeleine had slipped back into a shocked and tormented sleep. Chris had stayed with her day and night; doctors came and went. They had her see a psychiatrist. The police showed up, but Chris convinced them to come back when Madeleine was more alert.

She couldn't remember much about the accident. The psychiatrist told her she was having a "trauma reaction." The words pricked her—they brought her too close to the trauma itself. The screams, the crash, the blood.

Other things came to her easily, from the days and

hours before. She recalled picking Emma up at their house at the start of the trip; she could see the white fence and the peach tree in their front yard. She could feel Nell's hand in hers, hear her niece chatting brightly about school and the story she was writing about a pony named Stars. She remembered kissing Jack goodbye, thanking him for letting her take Emma away for the weekend.

And the weekend . . . lazy mornings over coffee and fresh-squeezed orange juice, power-walking on the beach for exercise, finding the right spot for their blanket and chairs, settling into the hot sand with nothing but hours for talking to Emma. Maddie remembered looking into Emma's eyes that very first day, smiling at her, saying, "Oh, the beaches we've been on together."

"We've come a long way from Hubbard's Point," Emma had said.

"That's where we first came together. I remember the day I first met you and Stevie Moore. We thought we'd be together forever . . . remember how inseparable we were?"

Emma hadn't seemed interested in remembering, but Madeleine couldn't stop. "Remember how her father got her that little English car . . . what was it? A Hillman! That's right. It was so cute, just perfect for the beach. And she'd put the top down and take us to Paradise Ice Cream?"

"We'd all be squeezed into the front seat in our bikinis," Emma said, unable to resist smiling. "Eating ice cream cones as we drove along . . . all the boys beeping at us. Remember how Jimmy Peterson nearly drove off the road?"

They'd laughed, remembering rides in the sea green Hillman, the mysterious powers they'd had at seventeen. Madeleine had glanced over at Emma, remembering buying *Summer of the Swans* for Nell. How negatively Emma had reacted to Stevie's work . . .

"Stevie was so shy about boys at first," Madeleine said. "I guess she was so sheltered, living alone with her father."

"The professor," Emma said. "I remember his English accent . . . I had a little crush on him."

"Me, too," Maddie said.

"Stevie had it lucky," Emma said with surprising harshness. "She found a career to take care of herself, so she didn't have to rely on any one man to support her. She made up for being shy with boys by marrying and divorcing anyone she pleased."

"Emma . . ."

"I'm sorry, Maddie. You're not going to want to hear any of this. But it's why I came away with you. I need to talk. . . ."

They had tilted their sunscreened faces toward the sun, reveling in the warmth even as Maddie felt the chill of what Emma was saying. She had known of her sister-in-law's unhappiness; she just hadn't realized the extent. She had known about her drifting away from Jack, but she hadn't known there was someone else. She hadn't had any idea at all.

The beach, the island, the cottage, the long, wrenching talks—all were indelibly recorded in Madeleine's memory. She remembered feeling completely shocked—no, those words weren't too dramatic—by what Emma told her. How would she keep it a secret? From her own brother? As the hours passed, the sun kissing their skin and the waves gently lapping the island's white sands, Madeleine listened and listened. And her skin began to crawl. . . .

She was Emma's best friend. But she was also Jack's sister. It was that statement that had, finally, sent Emma off in the car. When Madeleine had finally spoken up, told Emma she couldn't hold back any longer, that as much as she loved Emma and was trying to understand her choices, her behavior, she was, after all, Jack's sister.

And Nell's aunt.

It was the mention of Nell that had made Emma slap Madeleine. At the end of the weekend, they were hours into the ride home. There had been a buildup of tension between them; Madeleine had had to stop herself more than once from sounding sanctimonious. Emma must have sensed Madeleine's growing anger and disapproval, her disgust with what she'd been hearing. And her worry over how it would affect Jack and, especially, Nell.

"You ought to think about your daughter," Madeleine said finally, very softly, as they drove through the Georgia countryside, east of Atlanta—so Emma could show Madeleine where Richard Kearsage had come from.

"How dare you say that? She's all I think of!"

"It doesn't sound that way."

"You think you care about her more than I do? She's

my daughter!" Emma had said, her right hand flying through the air—striking Madeleine's cheek as she drove, shocking her more than she could ever recall—till that moment—being shocked.

So, when Jack had stood by Madeleine's bedside, and she, weeping, had told him the whole truth of what had happened, she had expected him to thank her. To see how she had stood up for him and Nell—at the risk of angering Emma, of losing Emma's friendship.

But he hadn't seen it that way. To Madeleine's shock, he had seemed to blame her for what Emma had done. Or maybe it was just the shock and shame of having his sister know. He was wild with grief over losing his wife. If he believed what Maddie was telling him, he'd be forced to see her in a whole new way.

Sitting in her Providence home, Madeleine stared at the phone and wished it would ring again. She had heard of estrangements in other people's families. They had always seemed so unnecessary, so petty. She, secretly, had always believed that the family members involved had to be awfully unreasonable or selfish, to keep such feuds going. She had assumed that they were always, or mostly, about money—the inheritance or the family home. The siblings must not have been very close in the first place. They probably just wrote each other off with no great sense of loss—just moving on with their lives.

How very little she had known.

The greatest shock she'd had to face was that it only took one person to bring about an estrangement. Just one person had to decide to close the door, to stop talk-

ing; just one person had to determine that life was easier without the other. The other had nothing to say
about it. Or, at least, no opportunity to say it . . .

The minutes ticked on, and Madeleine had to face
that the phone wasn't going to ring again that night.
She leaned her head toward the window and saw the
big moon—just past full—shining in the sky. Her eyes
filled with tears, to think of how beautiful it must look,
on the bay at Hubbard's Point.

She thought of the view from Stevie's house; somehow she knew that her old friend had prompted Jack's
phone calls. She wasn't sure how or why, she couldn't
imagine what Stevie had said, but she felt that somehow her fellow beach girl was touching her brother's
heart, putting in a good word for her.

Gazing up at the moon, she imagined its light form-
ing a path all the way from Providence to Hubbard's
Point. The girl in the moon . . . Maddie saw the face
and prayed she could reunite her with her brother . . .
Nell. Stevie.

A cheer burst out in the other room—the Red Sox
must have scored, she thought as Chris called her in to
watch the replay. She wiped her eyes, took one last look
at the moon. It was glowing white in the dark blue sky;
it looked like something Stevie would paint.

If only Stevie could paint a picture and bring them
all back together, she thought with a catch in her
throat; if only it could be that simple. Her throat
burned, but instead of going to the kitchen for some
wine, she sipped her Diet Coke. Day four without a
drink . . . she thought of the words Stevie had used to

describe her first husband: *lost in the bottle*. They had stayed with her.

Calling to Chris that she'd be there in a moment, she paged through her address book. Finding the number, she dialed it.

The answering machine picked up, so she left a message.

"Stevie, it's Madeleine. I just wanted to thank you. That's all . . . just, thank you. Give them my love, okay? You know who I mean. Talk to you soon."

Hanging up, she felt better. And then she went in to sit on the arm of her husband's chair, and give thanks for what she had under her own roof.

MADELEINE'S MESSAGE had meant so much to Stevie, somehow giving her permission to open her heart more. She felt the closeness of her fellow beach girl, urging her along. She got up really early the next morning, made coffee, and took it in a thermos to Jack's house. Nell was still asleep.

The birds were busy, singing in the trees. She and Jack sat outside, side by side on a picnic bench. He leaned against her side, pouring the coffee. The feeling sent pins and needles through her skin.

"This was so nice of you to do," he said.

"I just . . ." she began. "I can't stop thinking—you're leaving so soon."

"I know. I don't want to rush it, by thinking about it. But you're right."

"What will you do about someone for Nell to see

over there? Can Dr. Galford recommend another doctor?"

"He's looking into it," Jack said. "The strange thing is, she's been sleeping fine lately."

"Since going back to Dr. Galford?"

"I think," Jack said quietly, "since spending more time with you."

Stevie leaned over, pressed her face into his neck. She couldn't believe he had said that. She wanted to believe it was true.

"Would you mind if I took Nell swimming early tomorrow?" she asked. "I have to turn a painting in today, and I'm meeting my aunt tonight."

"I know she'd love that," Jack said, touching the back of Stevie's hand, in spite of the fact that the sun was all the way up and that Nell could very well be awake, looking out the window. . . .

Stevie waited for Nell by the tide line early the next day, before recreation class began. She had the beach to herself—the rest of Hubbard's Point was just waking up. The air was fresh and clean, the sky brilliant, cloudless. The Sound was blue glass, and the only sounds came from seagulls wheeling and crying, and from a lone fishing boat putting out to sea.

Nell came running down in a red bathing suit, flying off the boardwalk with a towel fluttering behind like Supergirl's cape. She did a broad jump, landing with a grin in the sand at Stevie's feet.

"My dad told me you wanted to meet me! I've never seen you on the beach before," Nell said.

"I'm making a rare daylight appearance," Stevie said.

Don't let the other kids know, or my reputation as a witch will be ruined."

Nell laughed. "I like your bathing suit," she said.

"Thank you," Stevie said, smiling. Her suit was one in a long line of black tank suits—sleek, no frills. "I like yours, too."

The tide was out, and they walked barefoot along the dry seaweed left behind by last night's high tide. Their feet made soft impressions in the hard sand, up above the waves' reach. Sunlight warmed their heads and shoulders, but the day was too early for any real heat. They picked up moonstones, jingle shells, and sea glass, holding their treasures in cupped hands.

"Tell me how the beach girls started," Nell said.

"Well, it began right here," Stevie said. "Your mother and I. When we were young, even younger than you."

"How did you meet?"

"Our mothers were friends. . . ."

"Like Bay and Tara?"

"Yes," Stevie said. "Just like that. Our mothers loved summer, and the beach, and when they had daughters at the same time, they couldn't wait to introduce us."

Nell smiled, seeming happy with that thought. "And what did you do together?" she asked.

"When we were *really* little, like one or two, our mothers would dig holes in the sand, right here where we're walking. They'd build little seawalls of sand to protect us from the biggest waves, and let the holes fill with water, and make us our own private wading pools."

"She did that with me," Nell said wistfully. "I remember her holding me in the waves."

"She must have loved you so much," Stevie said.

"Yes, she did," Nell said. As they walked along, Stevie felt the tug of the waves and tide, and her heart felt the endless connection of having strolled these sands with this child's mother.

When they got to the end of the beach, they dropped their towels and ran into the water. Stevie dove right in and swam underwater for a few yards. Looking over, she saw Nell swimming beside her, bubbles escaping from a wide grin.

They came up for air, laughing and gasping.

"How far can you swim?" Nell asked.

"To France!" Stevie said.

"Really—how far? To the raft? Or the big rock?"

"The big rock," Stevie said.

"Let's go then!"

"It's over your head," Stevie said. "I think we'd better wait for your father to take you."

"He trusts you!" Nell said. "Come on! I've done it with Peggy and her mom. I'll race you."

They set off, across the cove, diagonally from the end of the beach. Stevie took care to go slow, but she was amazed by Nell's strength as a swimmer. She had a steady, even stroke, a graceful scissor kick that barely broke the surface. The beach itself was still quiet but coming to life, with just a few people sitting on the boardwalk, gazing out. Stevie loved these early morning hours, when she had the place to herself. But it was even better to share it with Nell.

They swam fifty yards, to the big rock—rounded like a whale's back, a little higher in front, sloping down to the tail in back. Climbing out, they scrambled over sea-weed and barnacles to rest on the sun-warmed surface. Colonies of blue-black mussels glistened in the sun.

Crouching, Stevie and Nell watched as a ribbon of minnows wove past, followed by a swift school of snapper blues. The birds came, seagulls and terns, circling and crying overhead, then dive-bombing the school.

Nell squealed with excitement. Stevie loved that she wasn't afraid, that her curiosity kept her from ducking from the birds, or being afraid of the blues. They watched the fish zigzag, flashing silver, then dive and disappear.

"That was so cool!" Nell said.

"The food chain in action."

"What's the food chain?"

"Well, the minnows are eaten by the snapper blues, who are eaten by bigger blues . . ."

"Who are eaten by blues as big as this rock, with seagulls chasing them all!"

Stevie laughed, thinking of a book she could write about it. "You are something, Nell Kilvert," she said. "I might have to keep you around, just to give me great ideas. I'd never run out of books if I had you nearby."

"Really?" she asked, beaming.

"Really."

They sat there for a few minutes, till their bathing suits dried in the sun. Stevie glanced at Nell's feet. They were the exact same shape as Emma's—slender, with a high arch. Raising her gaze to Nell's face, she saw Jack's eyes, his straight nose, his high cheekbones. The observation made her swoon slightly. How amazing it must be, to have a child who had your feet, and looked just like the man you loved.

Her thoughts turned to Madeleine's message, how she had asked Stevie to give "them" her love. She didn't want to upset Nell by stirring up emotions about her aunt. So, sitting there on the rock, she stared at Nell's feet as hard as she could, filling her gaze with Madeleine's love, hoping Nell could somehow feel it.

"Ready to go back in?" Nell asked.

"If you are."

Nell shook her head. She shielded her eyes from the sun and looked directly into Stevie's. "I never want to leave," she said.

"The sun feels so good, doesn't it?" Stevie said.

Nell shrugged and said, "Hmm." She probably thought Stevie had missed the point, although she hadn't.

Stevie knew that Nell had been talking about Hubbard's Point, this summer in general. She never wanted to leave the beach . . . Stevie remembered that feeling so well.

They eased into the water, pushing off from a submerged shelf, and began to swim back to shore. The bay glittered ahead of them, as if it were covered with diamonds and silver. When they got to shore, Stevie looked along the beach where they had walked.

She saw their footprints, two by two, still in the sand. But the tide was coming in, and the first silky waves were starting to erase them.

The sand was firm and smooth, but as each wave

licked over the surface, tiny holes appeared, bubbling with froth. Nell knelt down, staring at them.

"What are they?" she asked.

"Clams," Stevie said.

"Can we dig them?"

"Not here," Stevie said. "The sand's too hard, and people will be coming down to spread their blankets any time now. But I know a place . . ."

"Will you take us? Me and my dad?"

"I could do that," Stevie said slowly. "If he wanted to."

"He will," Nell said.

"Okay, then," Stevie said. "How about late this afternoon? I think the tide will be right. If your father is free . . . and if he's not, maybe you and I can go alone."

"He'll be free," Nell said confidently. "He'll want to come. He likes you."

"He does?" Stevie asked, blushing.

Nell nodded and gave a devilish smile.

They gave each other a hug, and then Nell ran off to meet Peggy for recreation class. Stevie started back along the beach. As she walked the tide line, she kept her eyes on the last of hers and Nell's footprints. The waves covered them a little more each time. Every day came with a little loss, Stevie thought. But right now it didn't matter so much—because this afternoon they were all going clamming.

chapter 18

THEY TROOPED DOWN THE ROAD, looking like adventurers on an expedition, carrying clam rakes and a bucket with holes punched in the bottom and sides; Stevie rolled an inflated black inner tube, and Nell danced ahead, thrilled by the whole thing. Stevie had told them to wear old sneakers, and they had, but Jack noted that hers really took the prize.

"When you said 'old sneakers,' you weren't messing around," he said, looking down at her feet. She wore an ancient pair of red Converse high-tops, with the tops cut down to a fraying edge. The rubber soles were separating from the canvas, and they squeaked as she walked.

"Be careful, don't insult my clam shoes," she said. "I've spent years breaking these in."

"You'd never know," he said.

"So," she said. "Tell me what you found at the castle." Jack had spent the morning going over every inch of the building—measuring, testing, surveying. "It's in a pretty bad state," he said. "And I'm glad your aunt spoke to you when she did. Another couple of bad winters, and I think the ceilings and floors would be beyond repair. As it is . . ."

"Is it fixable?"

"With substantial work. It won't be cheap, Stevie. Your aunt was working when I first got there, and then Henry and Doreen showed up, so I never got the chance to really ask her about her plans. Does she have the money to do this?"

"Uncle Van loved to live," Stevie said. "So much so, that I think he left her with more bills than funds. She's incredibly respected as an artist, though, and does very well."

"It would take a few good sales to earn enough to fund the trust and start to repair the castle," Jack said. "I'm doing what I can, to come up with some ideas, but the foundation she creates will really need to hire an architect and builder, someone who specializes in stonework, to do most of it."

"Dad—*you* specialize in stonework. Bridges, bridges, bridges made of stone," Nell said, skipping backward.

"I know, Nell, but—"

"He wants to do it," Nell said. "He really does. He wouldn't be going over there on his vacation if he didn't. And you should see the stone bridges he built in Maine! And the one in South Carolina, on the island where the wild ponies live!"

"He's done so much for us already," Stevie said. "I know my aunt is very thankful."

Jack just smiled, glad she was so pleased. He knew what Nell was doing: angling for him to stay here to work on the castle project. It was tempting, too. He had felt excited by the massive challenge, the idea of restoring such a magical place. But he held back from saying any more; Nell was already in serious denial about them leaving. After he'd brought up Scotland the other night, she had blocked her ears to any further conversation. As far as she was concerned, they were never leaving Hubbard's Point. For this afternoon, Jack was happy to pretend right along with her.

They walked east, along the shady, winding roads that led to a nearly hidden beach near the train tracks. Jack vaguely remembered coming here when he was a teenager—it was far from the main beach, a good place to build a fire and drink beer and feel the trains roar by.

Stevie had timed the tide perfectly: it was all the way out. The tidal flats gleamed like varnished mahogany in the late daylight. Stevie began to walk out; Nell ran to catch up to her, and Jack followed. Their sneakers slapped on the wet sand.

Jack was just fine, walking behind. He couldn't take his eyes off Stevie. Her hair was cut straight across, revealing the nape of her neck. She wore cutoff jeans and a paint-smeared black T-shirt that said TALKING HEADS. The sleeves were cut very short, showing the tops of her shoulders, which looked strong and delicate at the same time.

The flats gave way to shallow water. They waded in, which made the going a little slower. Stevie now set the inner tube down, letting it float. She tied a rope to it, letting Nell pull it along.

Jack had spent the morning with Stevie's aunt. She had told him about Stevie's childhood, how she had lost her mother at such a young age.

"Were they close?" Jack had asked.

"Yes, very. Stevie was almost destroyed by the news. She . . . literally pulled her hair out. Johnny, my brother, went into her room and found great hanks of hair on the pillow, in her fists; he had to pry them out. That night she went color-blind. It was a bizarre, trau-matic reaction. . . . She'd always been an artist, from a tiny child, and it was as if her psyche had just decided that life was over, and deprived itself of color."

"How long did it last?" Jack asked with shock.

"Six months. Johnny took her to neurologists, who were completely stumped. They'd never seen it before. They recommended therapy, even hospitalization. Johnny found a good doctor for her, but he kept her home, of course. Susan was a miracle worker . . . she helped Stevie to recover. A mixture of art and talking therapy . . ."

Jack remembered what Stevie had said about her meetings with Susan; her words had helped him feel better about Dr. Galford.

"Through Susan's guidance, Johnny bought some paints and encouraged Stevie to finger paint. She did it . . . without being able to see the colors. All her pic-tures were of birds. She told him . . ." Aunt Aida's voice broke. "That she wanted to grow wings, so she could fly to heaven and see her mother."

The sight of Stevie and Nell together filled Jack with a kind of momentary despair—the knowledge that life could change in an instant. But seeing them wading out, joking, also made him feel happy—to think that his daughter had found someone she liked so much, and to know that Stevie, of all people, knew exactly what Nell had been through. Jack had made up his mind, after Emma died, to do whatever he had to do for Nell. He wanted her to love her mother, as Stevie had loved hers. But protecting her memory came with such a high cost. He thought of his sister and trailed back.

"Why does your shirt say 'Talking Heads'?" Nell asked, her voice carrying back across the water.

"It's a band that went to my school."

"Did you know them?"

"No, they were ahead of me. But I like their music."

"What school was it?"

"RISD. Rhode Island School of Design."

"How come painters and musicians went to the same school?"

Stevie laughed. "Art isn't any one thing," she said. "It's big, bigger than anything. It's how you express what's inside."

"Who would want to know what's inside me?" Nell asked, giggling nervously.

"The whole world would," Stevie said.

"I don't get that," Nell said.

"I think you will someday," Stevie said, touching Nell's head, and the sight of it made Jack's heart turn over. "I'm pretty sure there's an artist in there."

Nell laughed again. The sandy bottom had suddenly turned mucky, and they stopped walking. Stevie hooked the bucket inside the inner tube, and she gave Jack and Nell the two clam rakes. They had long, curved iron "tines" and old wooden handles, splintery from getting wet with salt water and drying out again.

"Okay . . . you just drag the rakes through the mud till you feel something . . . then pull it up and flip it into the bucket."

"What'll it feel like?" Nell asked.

"It's hard to explain," Stevie said. "But when it happens, you'll know!"

"What'll you use?" Jack asked, because there wasn't a third rake.

Stevie beamed and lifted a sopping red sneaker out of the water. "My feet!" she said.

They went to it. Jack raked the mud, feeling a strange satisfaction and excitement. There was something about the uncertainty, never knowing which rakeful would yield treasure. He thought about how results-oriented and workmanlike he had become. When he drew lines and angles, plans and blueprints, bridges were inevitably built. He was into equations he could solve, formulas he could count on. He gravitated toward foregone conclusions.

That's what Scotland was to him. Quit Structural, pack up daughter, move as far from the truth as possible—happy, normal life. But it stuck in his mind—the pleasure of doing something for no reason at all, and the way his heart had flipped to hear Stevie talking to Nell about art.

"I got one!" Nell squealed.

Jack and Stevie leaned in, watched her bring up the rake. Gray muck dripped into the water as Nell dropped the whole thing into the bucket suspended in the inner tube. Water flowed through the holes, dispersing the mud, revealing a nice big cherrystone.

"Wow, good job!" Jack said.

"That is a great clam," Stevie said, holding it up, admiring it in the light.

"What will we do with it?" Nell asked.

"Well, if we catch more, we can have dinner," Jack said. "Maybe Stevie will join us."

"Thank you," Stevie said, her face glowing as much as Nell's.

They kept at it as the sun began to go down. They must have found a good spot, because suddenly they all began getting clams. Stevie seemed to feel them with her feet, then worked them to the surface, and picked them up. The light was clear and gray, tinged with purple and gold. It lay across the water, creating a flat pewter shine, and it hit the rock islands in the southeast, North and South Brother, turning their granite crags burnt orange.

The tide turned, and the water began flooding back in. Jack felt the surface rise from his knees to his thighs. Stevie was waist deep, and Nell was up to her chest. They both started to laugh, and at once ducked under. Coming up, their hair slick, shoulders dripping, the black shirt stuck to Stevie's body. She glanced at him, eyes sparkling with the fun she was having, and he forced a smile. She was beautiful and radiant, and Nell loved her, and she was about as far from a foregone conclusion as Jack could imagine, and he made himself look away.

THEY WENT to Stevie's house. Since her dad was so tall, his clothes hadn't gotten wet. So he went into the kitchen to wash the clams while Nell and Stevie rinsed off in the outside shower. Nell loved it—standing outside in the cool air, smelling honeysuckle and sassafras while hot water poured over her head.

They wrapped up in towels and ran barefoot up the side hill, into the kitchen.

"Don't look, Dad," Nell laughed, and her father pretended to hide his eyes. She and Stevie went upstairs; because Nell's clothes were soaking wet, Stevie rummaged through her drawers for something she could wear.

"How about these?" she asked, holding up a pair of pedal pushers and a sweatshirt.

"Sure," Nell said. She pulled them on. She liked the way the shirt felt so soft and smelled like Stevie. Stevie found a big safety pin, and she pinned the waistband of the pants, to keep them from falling down. The sun was down now, and the bird was asleep in its cage. Nell went over and stared at it while Stevie got dressed. The crow looked so alone, its head tucked under its wing. The sight made Nell's heart hurt. She wondered where its family was.

Downstairs, they all worked together to get dinner ready. Stevie showed Nell where the table-setting things were. She used cloth napkins, which seemed very, very special, and Tilly sat on the table, watching that Nell put them in the right places. Out in the kitchen, her father chopped garlic and shallots. He made a joke about the onion making him cry, but Nell and Stevie could see he was really laughing. That made Nell feel so happy.

"We've got pasta boiling, we've got shallots and garlic cooking in olive oil," her father said. "What else do we need for the sauce?"

"Fresh herbs!" Stevie said, grabbing both of their hands. She pulled them outside, to the small herb garden beside the house, with Tilly scooting into the trees. "Hubbard's Point herb gardens are magical," she said. "Almost every house has one."

"But not as magical as yours," Nell's father laughed. "We all know what the kids say about you."

"Dad!" Nell said, shocked that he would bring up the witch rumor.

"Oh, Nell . . . there's a little bit of truth in everything the kids say," Stevie said, standing knee-high among the fragrant herbs. "I do believe in magic."

"Really?" Nell asked, stepping in to stand beside her. The scents of rosemary, thyme, mint, and chervil swirled around them and made her feel almost dizzy.

"Yes. I believe that if you want something enough, and wish in the right way, then the right thing will happen."

"The right way?" Nell's father asked.

"Yes," Stevie said, pointing out which herbs to pick. "But how?"

"Well, you do your best to bring it about. And then you give up control of the results."

Nell reached down; it was dark, and she couldn't see what she was grabbing. There could be mice, or spiders, or snakes in there. But she trusted Stevie. And the herbs smelled so good, and the night felt enchanted. She picked handfuls of parsley and cilantro.

"Who do you give up the control to?" Jack asked.

Stevie didn't answer, and neither did Nell. She closed her eyes tight. She remembered being in Georgia, being so sad at every single thing, and how she had wished, wished with everything she had, that she and her father could be happy. And that very weekend, he'd told her that they were going to move to Boston to try something new. And that step had somehow led them to coming to Hubbard's Point for the summer, where she'd met Peggy . . . and Stevie. With her eyes still closed, she wished their time together would never end.

Just then they heard some music booming from down at the beach. Nell felt scared—it sounded so strange and eerie, like voices coming from the sky.

"What's that?" she asked.

"Beach movie," her father and Stevie said at the same time.

"Can we go?" she gasped, looking from one to the other.

"Dinner's almost ready," her father said.

"We could eat fast . . ." Stevie said.

"Let's do it," her father said.

They went inside; Stevie threw the herbs into the copper pot. It only took a few minutes for the clams to open. Nell's father made her some plain linguine with butter, just in case, and that was good, because Nell didn't want to eat the clams she'd just dug. But her father and Stevie ate them, and said they were the best they'd ever had.

When they finished eating, Stevie and her father quickly rinsed the plates, and Nell danced around the first floor with Tilly watching her from a hiding spot on the mantel. Nell felt as if this was her house, and she wished she could come back again and again. The wish made her stop dancing.

She thought of what Stevie had said in the herb garden. That you wish and do your best . . . and things happen.

Nell had wished that this day would never end, and now they were all going to the beach movie together. It made her feel strange and powerful. She hadn't had something to believe in in a long time. It was like raking the mud, finding a perfect clam. Or being in the dark, sticking your hand into a garden you couldn't even see, coming out with herbs for dinner.

Maybe Stevie *was* a witch, after all. . . .

STEVIE COULD hardly believe she was doing this. Although her house faced the beach, and the sound of the movies bounced up the rock ledge every Thursday night in the summer, she hadn't been down to a beach movie since she was a teenager. She and Nell bundled up in extra sweaters, and she gave Jack an old Trinity sweatshirt of her father's. The cartoons were just ending as the three of them crossed the footbridge.

Nell raced across the beach to look for a good spot to put their blanket. The projector was set up on the boardwalk, focused on a somewhat rippled screen hanging from what looked like a weather-beaten goalpost. The crowd was made up of a combination of families with young kids, teenage girls out for the night, and teenage couples taking advantage of the dark and a legitimate reason to be lying on a blanket together.

Peggy was there with Bay, Dan, Tara, and Annie. Billy was haunting the boardwalk with his pals. Everyone seemed to see Nell at once, and they all called and said they'd move their blankets over and make room. Stevie walked through the crowd to the spot, aware that people were noticing. Nell held her hand proudly while Jack spread out the blanket.

"Hi, everyone," Stevie said.

"Hi, Stevie, hi, Jack."

"Thanks for making room for us," he said. The night was dark, but the projector light on the blank screen illuminated everyone's face.

"Oh, we're thrilled to!" Bay said, grinning so madly, Stevie wondered what she was thinking. Tara seemed to be beaming with the same intensity. Peggy gave her a long, cautious stare; Stevie tried to reassure her with a smile.

"Where's Joe?" Jack asked.

"Oh, out keeping the world a safer place," Tara said. "And leaving me footloose and fancy free at the beach movies."

"Watch it—you're a betrothed woman," Bay warned.

"I know. Love has taken the sting out of this cruel, cruel world," Tara said. "Watch out, Stevie—once I say my 'I do's,' you'll officially be the designated Scarlet Woman of the Point."

"I wear it well," Stevie said, laughing.

Just then, the movie started. It was just as Stevie remembered from her youth—the old projector creaking along, the film ratcheting through the spools, the sound competing with the crash of the waves, and the picture distorted by folds in the windblown screen. In other words, the movie was beside the point. She laughed with the joy of being back.

Jack and Nell had dug a pit, patted the pile of sand into a sturdy backrest, and spread the blanket. The three of them settled into their seats, with Jack in the middle, so Nell could sit beside Peggy on one side. The movie was *Tiger Bay*, and Stevie was completely positive she had seen it—probably this very same ancient copy—with Emma and Madeleine.

"I don't think of you that way," Jack said, turning toward Stevie, his voice too low for the others to hear.

"What way?"

"As a scarlet woman. I'm sure Tara was just teasing you."

Stevie looked at him, surprised, then actually stunned—that he would come to her defense. "Thank you," she said. "But I am, sort of. Unintentionally."

"No . . ." He took her hand. Their hands were hidden between them on the blanket, and he laced his fingers with hers, and a shiver went all the way up Stevie's spine. No one could see them, and the secret felt both thrilling and safe. "You're not," he said.

"Thank you," she said again. The sea breeze picked up, blowing through her hair. He reached over to brush it out of her eyes, and their eyes locked. She had a hard time catching her breath, and she had to force herself to concentrate on the screen. The movie blared, showing Hayley Mills hiding in the staircase. Nell and Peggy were scared to look, so they asked for their ice cream money early and went tearing up to the Good Humor truck.

"I've seen this part before," he said, turning toward her. He let go of her hand and put his arm around her shoulder. She felt sixteen—no, even more excited than she remembered feeling at sixteen, with a boy at the movies. Her heart was pounding, as she felt his breath on her cheek.

"Me, too."

"Even if I hadn't, I'd rather talk to you."

She nodded. *Me, too*, she mouthed, smiling. He brushed her cheek with his lips. They watched the movie for a minute, and suddenly the film broke. Everyone moaned, but someone called out, saying it would be fixed in just a few minutes.

People surrounded them, but all Stevie could think of was kissing Jack. His arm tightened around her, and their hips pressed together. If they were younger, if Nell wasn't here, they'd go under the boardwalk . . .

The idea made her laugh, and he looked over. "What are you thinking?"

"Just that, once a scarlet woman . . ."

"I swear, I don't see it," he said stubbornly.

Stevie nodded. "I didn't grow up thinking, 'Oh, I want to be married three times before I'm forty.' I really didn't. I . . . did my best. I . . . fall in love easily."

"You do?" he asked, smiling broadly.

She tried to smile. "That didn't come out right. I . . . what I was trying to say is . . . I feel so much for the people that I . . . well, love. I can't turn it on and off. And I grew up believing in marriage, you know?"

He nodded. "Your aunt told me your parents had a great one."

"They did," she said. Talking about this was hard, in a way she hadn't expected. Suddenly she felt uneasy, having Jack hold her. Their pasts really rose up to swamp her, and she involuntarily pulled back. "They were in a world of just each other. No one else . . . Like you and Emma."

Why did he suddenly look away? Wasn't that the whole story? The great love he'd had for Emma? The reason he had left the south, Atlanta, their home? Wasn't it the reason he had stopped speaking to Maddie—because she had said something against his wife?

"It wasn't," Jack said.

"What?"

"My marriage. It wasn't great," he said quietly. "I thought it was. I really did. Emma seemed so happy. She stayed home with Nell, then started working at our church. St. Francis Xavier had a volunteer program—they went to nursing homes, a homeless shelter, the prison. Emma would read to prisoners. My sister's the one . . ."

Stevie waited. His face was creased with torment.

"She's the one who told me," Jack said. "I had felt something was wrong, but I was too dense to know what it was. Maddie had to tell me after Emma died."

"Oh, Jack."

"I want to tell you, but I'm not sure I can. It's been so amazing getting to know you, seeing how much Nell likes you. And realizing that you want to do the best for her. I have the feeling I can tell you anything. . . ."

"You can."

He shook his head resolutely. "Not this," he said. "I want to, but for Nell's sake—she's so young. She loved her mother so much, and I want to keep it that way."

"Of course. You want to safeguard Emma's memory," Stevie said, squeezing his hand. "I understand. But you should let it out to someone, Jack. It's already eaten away at you, destroyed a big part of your life. . . ."

"What do you mean?"

"Madeleine. It's kept you from your sister."

He stared up at the screen, as if he wished the movie would start, keep them from talking anymore. At the same time, he squeezed her hand hard, and she pressed back.

"What did she tell you?" Stevie asked.

The movie began again, the film shakily advancing, the sound fighting against the easterly wind. It was picking up, smelling of the sea—Stevie always felt a northeaster before it actually arrived. She felt the spray on her face, smelled the salt.

"Maddie told me Emma was going to leave us," Jack said. His voice cracked—or was he just being drowned out by the movie? Stevie looked at his dark eyes and held his hand tighter.

"Leave you?" Stevie whispered, but Jack didn't reply.

"She had a secret life," he said, not quite answering the question. "A real, true, secret life that I knew nothing about."

"But . . ." Stevie began.

"I don't want Nell to know, ever," he said. "I wish I never knew. I wish Madeleine had never told me."

"But she couldn't lie. . . ."

"I wish she had," Jack said with despair. "It's why I decided to take Nell to Scotland. I wanted her as far from here as possible—but now . . ."

Stevie waited, holding her breath.

Jack didn't say anything more and Stevie's heart turned over. He leaned forward, his lips brushing hers. The sea wind blew harder, drowning out the movie.

Nell was back. She raced to the blanket with Peggy, snuggled on the other side of her father. Jack squeezed Stevie's hand, then turned to Nell

The every-day, every-night being-a-father took over. Stevie felt him slip his hand out of hers, reach over to wipe the ice cream off Nell's face. Nell was riveted by the movie, the strange friendship between Hayley Mills and the sailor. She watched, openmouthed.

The movie continued, and when it ended, half the kids had fallen asleep. Nell was drowsy, but on her feet. Everyone packed up their blankets, and Bay and Tara called to Stevie and told her to stop by soon. She thanked them and said she would.

Nell walked a little ahead with Peggy, sleepily making

plans to get together the next day. Stevie took the opportunity to grab Jack's hand. She wished so much that she could give him the strength, the grace he'd need to face what was happening.

"I shouldn't tell you what I hope for," she said.

"But I want you to," he said.

"Stay here," she whispered. "Don't go to Scotland. Stay."

He touched her cheek, but he didn't seem to trust his voice. Stevie said goodbye for both of them. Nell ran over to give her a hug. And then she watched the Kilverts walk through the sandy parking lot toward their rented house, with their family's big secret shimmering between them.

chapter 19

MADELEINE TRIED TO STOP STARING at the phone, waiting for it to ring.

Her brother's silent calls had given her more hope than anything in an entire year. *Hope*: she hadn't even realized that that was what she had—that little glimmer of positive feeling, of faith, the thought that maybe the next time he called he'd actually talk, that maybe they could begin to straighten out what had happened between them.

But then the calls seemed to stop, and Madeleine plunged into a darkness she hadn't known existed. She barely had the energy to get out of bed in the morning. She had to force herself to do the smallest things. The sight of a woman with Emma's hair color made her burst into tears. Driving home one afternoon she heard a song on the radio that reminded her of Jack, and she had to pull over and weep.

Chris was worried, and wanted her to get help.

Although she had seen a therapist after the accident,

she didn't feel that it had helped at all. Talking about what had happened just seemed to stir up terrible feelings; instead of then flowing out, the emotions felt trapped in her body and mind, in her heart, under her skin. Her doctor's way of dealing with her torment was to put her on Denexor—which totally blocked her feelings and left her feeling alienated from herself. So she'd thrown out the medication—*and* the doctor.

One evening Chris gave Madeleine an article by a psychologist practicing in Providence, teaching at Brown. Her name was Dr. Susanna Mallory, and she specialized in the treatment of trauma. The title of her piece was "Waking the Dead," and it opened with accounts of accident victims, their bodies recovering but their lives on permanent hold. "Alive but hibernating," was how one of them put it.

Chris had left the article on Maddie's desk with a note: "This doctor seems to see things differently—do you think she would understand?" His tenderness and gentleness was so touching, it nearly did Madeleine in. She didn't have much confidence in "treatment" for what she'd been through—how could a doctor cure her relationship with Jack? But she decided to look at the story—more for Chris than for herself.

Chris was like a one-man hospital, giving her love, care, and almost endless patience. He didn't seem to mind that she sometimes drank too much, or that she cried in her sleep, or that she missed a lot of work. It was only when she stopped wanting to leave the house at all, and when he saw how much she was suffering, that he had really reacted.

"You love going out," he said. "I know you do. But you never want to eat out anymore. You don't want to take rides to Newport or Little Compton . . . you don't even want to go to the beach."

"No, that's not true," she'd said, trying to deflect him. "I'm just tired." Or, "I have a headache." Or, her personal favorite, trying to joke: "I'm in perimenopause. I'm having hot flashes and bone loss." "These are the calcium years," she'd say to him with a shaken smile. "I'm just not my old self. . . ."

He had gone along for as long as he could—letting her struggle through in her own way, understanding that she needed to cling to whatever control she had—but then he'd drawn the line. It was a month or so after her visit to Hubbard's Point, and another two weeks since Jack had stopped calling.

Periods of the day passed when she couldn't remember what she was doing. She felt stuck, emotionally paralyzed. At night, trapped in the horror, she relived the crash over and over. She heard Emma's scream. And she found herself imagining, almost all the time, how it would feel to walk up the Newport Bridge and dive off. . . .

Chris finally *made* her call Dr. Mallory.

The doctor's office was in a brick house at the Fox Point end of Benefit Street in Providence, with black-and-white photos of mountains and bare trees on the walls. She was in her mid-fifties, tall and slender, with great hair, compassionate eyes, and a deep capacity for listening.

Madeleine talked. She was an administrator, and she

knew the value of getting to the point. Without tears or any apparent emotion, she told the doctor why she was there: she felt frozen, that she was having a hard time doing things. She was grieving for her sister-in-law, who had died in a car accident. Madeleine had been driving. Although she, Madeleine, had been hurt, her injuries were far from life-threatening. A concussion, and her shoulder had been torn.

What sort of therapy had been required? The doctor wanted to know.

Several surgeries and occupational therapy, Madeleine reported.

The doctor watched her for a minute; Madeleine knew she was waiting for something. Her eyes were steady and kind, and even without speaking, her unasked question made Madeleine's throat ache, as if she were choking on tears.

"Occupational therapy . . . surgeries," the doctor said. "The injury must have been very serious."

Madeleine wondered whether Chris had told her— that Madeleine's arm had nearly been severed. She swallowed the story—she had talked about it with the other doctor, and it had made her crazy with grief. Because, how could she stand to complain about what the accident had done to her arm—when it had killed Emma?

Her husband had been wonderful through it all, she told the doctor instead. Her brother and she, though, were . . . well, estranged.

Then she started off giving the rest of the history, in as dispassionate a way as possible, to get to the point, and to show that she was capable, in control, and completely sane. Where she was born, who her parents were, her brother, Jack . . . a happy, close, well-adjusted family. She gave the rundown on her health—generally good. Not much exercise—she'd stopped playing tennis, which she used to love.

"Were you close, you and your brother?"

Madeleine nodded. "He was four years ahead of me," she said. "But he always walked me to school. He'd let me tag along with his friends, to Goodwin Park. The tennis courts didn't have lights then, but we'd play till dark anyway—sometimes long after! We'd play by sound—listening for the ball. And he used to take me downtown—sometimes we'd hitch a free ride on a bus— sitting on the back bumper!" She'd smiled to show the doctor that she hadn't been scared. Telling the story brought back a strong memory—the feeling of her brother bracing her with his arm, saying "Nothing's gonna happen to you, Maddie. I won't let it."

Maddie hadn't even replied—it hadn't even occurred to her that she could get hurt with Jack around. Telling Dr. Mallory brought back the powerful feelings of loving and trusting her brother that much, and it made her smile.

"Why am I telling you this?" she asked. "It doesn't have much to do with why I'm here."

The doctor smiled.

"Our family took summer vacations at a beach called Hubbard's Point. We didn't have much money, but our father always saved, and wanted to give us everything he could. We were teenagers then, but Jack still let me hang around. Before I met my own friends there—one would turn out to be Emma, and the other Stevie," she paused, looked at the doctor. "But before that, he took me under his wing. We didn't know anyone there."

"But you had each other."

She nodded. "He drove up to Hartford whenever he could—he had a girlfriend there. But we'd play tennis together, or he'd take me fishing. We'd race out to the raft. One day we just rode our bikes all around . . . we explored the roads. And we found this old water tower, up by the railroad tracks. I climbed up the ladder, to impress him . . ." Madeleine closed her eyes, remembering. "He called to me to come down, but I wanted to show him I could do it."

The doctor listened.

"It was a rickety old ladder. Made of some kind of silver metal—but very thin and rusty. I got all the way to the top—and made the mistake of looking at the ground."

"You were high up?"

Madeleine nodded. "Thirty feet or so. I just froze." Her body tensed, and her fingers involuntarily tightened, as if around the ladder rung. "I couldn't move—I couldn't move a muscle. I just clung to that ladder, sure that I was going to fall off and die. I was paralyzed."

"And your brother?"

Madeleine swallowed. Tears sprang into her eyes. "He climbed up to get me," she said.

The doctor was silent, watching Madeleine's face. Maddie let the memories come—the heat of the day, the way the ladder shook as Jack climbed up, the terror she felt.

" 'Hold on, Maddie,' he said. You're fine—just don't look down. I've got you.' He was down below me, and I felt him grab my ankle. I told him to let go—that if I crashed down, I didn't want to take him with me."

"And did he? Let go?"

Madeleine shook her head, tears freely flowing now. "No. He didn't. He told me that I wasn't going to fall—that I was strong, all I had to do was move one hand at a time. He stayed with me . . . talked me down . . . and never let go of my ankle. You know what I think?"

"What?"

"That if I had fallen, he was completely prepared to hold on—and not let me crash."

"It sounds that way," the doctor said gently.

The doctor sat in her chair across the small office while Maddie sobbed quietly. She reached for a tissue from a box on the table beside her. Madeleine's left ankle tingled, as if his fingers were still around it.

"I grew up thinking he'd save my life if he could," she cried.

Dr. Mallory's eyes were kind, filled with sadness—as if she was feeling Madeleine's pain right along with her.

"He got you safely down to solid ground when you felt paralyzed on the ladder."

Madeleine nodded, weeping.

The doctor was quiet, and Madeleine's thoughts moved slowly, tangled like a ball of yarn. She held a tissue to her nose, trying to stop crying. When she did, she saw Dr. Mallory watching her.

"You said at the beginning of the session," the doctor said, "that you felt 'frozen.' That sounds something like feeling paralyzed."

"Just the way I felt on the ladder," Madeleine said, her ankle prickling again.

"And this time your brother . . ."

"Isn't here to save me," Madeleine blurted out. "Doesn't even *want* to."

Dr. Mallory sat silently, letting Madeleine's words resonate. Maddie pressed the wadded-up tissue to her eyes, trying to stop the tears. "He thinks I killed his wife," she whispered. "And I did."

The horrible words rang in her ears, but the doctor's kind expression didn't change.

"I didn't mean to!" Madeleine cried.

"I know," the doctor said.

"Why won't he forgive me? How can I live, or why should I, if he really hates me that much . . . thinks I killed his wife, Nell's mother?" Madeleine turned her head, gasping for air. "Can you help me," Maddie begged, "so my brother will forgive me?"

The doctor was silent for a moment, but then she leaned forward—so far that her knees were almost touching Madeleine's. "I can't promise you that," Dr. Mallory said, her hazel eyes glinting with compassion. "But I can help you forgive yourself."

The words were too much for Madeleine to take in, so she just closed her eyes and let the sobs wrack her from the inside out.

chapter 20

THE NEXT THREE MORNINGS, WHILE Nell was at recreation, Jack went over to Lovecraft Hill. He got Jim Mangan, an engineer from the Boston office, to drive down and meet him. They walked the property with a site map; Jim was a licensed surveyor, so he shot lines and marked boundaries.

While they hiked, Jack thought about Stevie. "Don't go to Scotland. Stay," she had said. His patented way of dealing with pain was to walk away from it as cleanly as possible. He needed only to think of his sister to realize that that was true.

But Stevie had said *Stay,* and he was thinking about staying.

Deep in the woods, they found trails made by deer or other animals. They discovered caves hidden under rock ledges, streams, a pond, miraculously huge dawn redwood trees. Jack made notes as he walked along. He thought the widest stream called for a bridge, and he thought that placing large natural stepping stones in the flow would work the best.

"Thanks for coming down," he said to Jim.

"No problem," Jim said. "You really got me out of a jam on that Piscataqua River project. I'm just sorry to hear that you're leaving. Francesca's burning that you went over, or past her, to get to Ivan Romanov."

"He advertised the position," Jack said. "I applied."

"Hell hath no fury, and all that."

"I'm sorry she took it that way," Jack said, feeling like a heel. Talking about Francesca with Jim—as good a guy as he was, he was trying to pick up the office dirt—and leading her on in the first place. He hadn't meant to.

"Like my brother always says, 'Men are scum,' " Jim said.

"I hope that's not true. I've got a daughter."

"Yeah, well. We sure manage to screw up royally at the worst possible times. My wife'll be happy to tell you. She's living in my dream house, the one I designed and built, while I'm sleeping on my brother's couch."

"What'd you do?" Jack said. Their footsteps sounded loud, tromping through fallen leaves and underbrush.

"Fell in love online. Janice figured out my password and read my e-mails."

"That's bad," Jack said.

"Which part?"

"All of it," Jack said. E-mail was dangerous.

His mind took an unexpected turn back to a time in Atlanta, just before Emma's accident. He hadn't known it then, but looking back, he realized that he had started to feel restless—it wasn't just her. Being married had been like swimming. Sometimes it was smooth and cool and buoyant, and other times it was hitting cold patches that made him want to get out of the water.

During one of those cold patches, he had started e-mailing a woman in the Cleveland office. Had he sensed what was going on with Emma? She had gotten so involved with the church, and volunteering at the prison. That's what he told himself now—to excuse his own secret behavior.

The e-mails had started out completely innocently— all about a Cincinnati suspension bridge project they were both involved with. The woman was witty and warm. Jack was feeling cold and unappreciated. The business e-mails had led to more-personal sharing. He remembered mornings when he'd wake up before dawn, just to see whether she'd sent him something during the night.

"Did anything actually happen between you?" Jack asked Jim, stepping over a narrow brook. "Your e-mail friend."

"Yeah. That's what got me kicked out. I deserved it."

At least Jack hadn't acted on anything. He thought back to those weeks, though—feeling alienated from his own marriage, seduced by his online intimacy with a woman he barely knew. It sort of stunned him to remember; since Emma's death, he had put a lot of effort into idealizing his marriage. The calls to Madeleine, hearing her voice, had been like opening a Pandora's box of things he really didn't want to face or remember.

She had only been the messenger, Jack thought. The betrayal had been Emma's alone.

"The Internet is the devil's workshop," Jim said, stepping over a narrow brook. "That and the male mind. My crosses to bear—*but* now that I'm separated and you're no longer an item, maybe I'll ask Francesca out for dinner."

Jack didn't reply. He wanted to protect Francesca from Jim, but he figured she would be able to take care of herself. He continued through the woods with Jim, wondering at the thoughts raging through his head. Other memories of his marriage came up. He remembered how infrequently he and Emma made love. Why think about that now? What good could it do?

He and Jim measured the westernmost boundary line. While Jim looked through the scope, Jack rustled through dry leaves looking for the "granite boulder marked with 'X.' " Looking for the buried marker, he uncovered buried feelings. He had never really forgotten, but he'd sublimated the real reason Emma had gone off with Maddie on that vacation.

Although it had been Madeleine's birthday, that was only the occasion for Emma's trip—not the deeper reason. He remembered the fight he and Emma had had the week she decided to go. He had been spending more and more time at the office. She had been decorating their new house, but had now decided that the project was excessive, materialistic—her work at Dixon proved that.

"The prisoners have nothing," she said. "They've had

to look inside themselves—find inner resources. So many of them grew up in poverty and abuse."

"So they went out and inflicted it on other people?" Jack asked.

"You don't understand."

"I understand that some of them are in there for rape and murder."

"You never support me," she said. "What I believe in. I'm there trying to help people."

"I support you, Emma," his expression leaving his real feelings unspoken.

"No you don't," she said, shaking her head violently. "You supported me when I volunteered in nice places—the children's hospital, or the nursing homes. But Dixon—"

"I'm worried about it, okay?" he exploded. "I don't know who you're meeting there, whether they might track you home. How about that one who got your number? What if someone found out where you lived, what about Nell? I don't want them near us."

" 'Them,' " she spat back. " 'They.' As if they're so *other*. They're human beings who've had bad breaks. I'm helping Father Richard teach these men to read—doing important work, maybe for the first time in my life."

"I think raising Nell is important work, too."

"You're so sanctimonious, Jack."

"Look, when a convicted felon calls you at home, I'm going to get upset." He took a breath. "I'm sorry if it seems I'm belittling your work. I'm not. I know you're good at anything you do. But does it have to be the prison? Before Father Richard came to the parish—"

"I know what you're saying. But the volunteer program was so stagnant. I felt we were just being sent places . . . just to keep us busy."

Reading to kids in the pediatric oncology ward was just keeping busy? Jack didn't say it out loud. He held it inside, his chest exploding, thinking of how fascinated Emma had gotten with the terrible stories she heard from the prisoners, how terrible their lives had been, how badly they'd been treated.

Just six months earlier, she had decided she wanted different bathroom tiles. The "old" ones—less than two years old—were Mexican, painted with flowers. Then she wanted marble. Now she thought that tiles were beside the point. She was on fire—the first time Jack had ever seen her like this—passionate about her work.

Jack had said fine, whatever she wanted. But inside, something had come clanging down—he knew she was using her prison work as a way to avoid him. He actually wondered whether she'd developed a crush on one of the prisoners—the one who had called their house. Whenever he wanted to talk, or go out, she was involved in planning her reading lessons, or talking to her fellow volunteers about how they could effect meaningful change at Dixon.

"What's wrong?" he'd asked her.

"They don't have a library," she said. "Not a real library, anyway—just a few books donated by family members."

"Not what's wrong at Dixon Correctional—what's wrong with us?"

"You'd know better than I do. You're always at your

office. And when you're not, you're on the computer. Or watching TV."

She was right—except, if he believed what Madeleine had told him, she was lying then. Still, how could Jack tell her he did those things because she seemed so hostile—or, worse, indifferent to him? They had had so much fun when they were first married. She'd gone on every business trip with him. They had laughed about everything. Then Nell was born.

Jack had never thought he could love anyone as much as Emma. Ever. But then Nell had entered the picture. She had shown up, taken complete control. Instead of being jealous of the time Emma spent with the baby, Jack was jealous that she got more time with Nell than he did.

Nell changed everything. She made Jack a new man. She made the sun brighter, the ocean deeper, color, truer, the moon whiter, peaches sweeter. She got Jack up at two in the morning, she got him to love being spit up on, she made him go to work exhausted and count the minutes till he got to return home, she got him to love finger painting, and to replace his office art with her crayon drawings, to go to every nursery school recital, to hang a wreath made of a circle of her green handprints.

She got him on roller skates, and on the merry-go-round, and to matinees of the latest Disney cartoon, and to the ice cream stand, and the peach orchard, and PTA meetings, and church. Jack even went to church, because Nell sang in the children's choir.

And as close as he got to his daughter, he seemed to

veer that much farther from his wife. He didn't love her any less; he just noticed that they changed toward each other. They still talked, but they didn't laugh as much. There seemed to be so much planning, so much duty. They both preferred nights at home with Nell, so they didn't hire many babysitters; maybe if they had, they wouldn't have lost each other.

Jack worked a lot—he was ambitious, and he wanted to succeed. He wanted to provide for his family, have enough money so Nell could go to any college she wanted. Emma stayed home, but she had started talking about going to graduate school—getting a master's degree in social work.

Emma never used to be so involved in the church. She and Jack used to joke that they were "cellular Catholics"—they felt it in the cells of their bodies, in their bones, even though they weren't devout. Jack didn't go to church every Sunday, but Emma made sure he got to St. Francis Xavier on major holidays. Nell made her First Communion, and went to catechism on Wednesday afternoons.

As time went on, Jack began to notice that Emma seemed to yearn for something more. Their big house wasn't fulfilling her—and she seemed to almost feel embarrassed by it. She started doing weekend retreats at their church—sleeping home at night, but spending Saturday and Sunday in spiritual workshops. Her circle of women friends shifted, from the country club to Xavier. Even her dreams seemed to change. Everything Jack had thought she wanted, now began to turn on him.

She seemed enraptured by Father Richard, and the idea of public service. She was drawn to the edge—to help those who'd had hard lives, the men at the prison. Jack had failed to notice her depths, her great reservoir of compassion. He had categorized his own wife—he really had. He had thought of her as a woman made happy by Mexican tiles, a house in the right neighborhood, staying home with their daughter. He had missed the rest of her.

By the time he started to notice, she was completely involved in her volunteer work. It wasn't that they didn't have free time, it's just that they always seemed to use their free time for everything but each other.

Jack thought back to that last trip, when Emma went away with Madeleine. He knew his sister had meant to help—she and Chris had been down the prior Christmas, and she'd felt alarmed by the coolness she saw in Emma. The phone rang in the middle of dinner—until after her death, Jack hadn't known who it was from. But Emma took the call—while he carved and served the turkey—and she didn't come back till everyone was starting on seconds. Jack remembered how red and puffy her eyes looked, and how Nell had dropped her fork and asked, "Why are you crying, Mommy?"

Emma had said something about an eyelash in her eye. . . .

So when Madeleine began calling, a month or so later, to try to get Emma to go away with her for a "girls only" birthday trip that next June, Jack was all for it. He knew that if anyone could get Emma to talk about what was bothering her, Maddie could. He wanted to ask Maddie himself—what she knew, what Emma told her. But he held back.

Emma herself was unsure of whether she should go. She loved St. Simons Island, and she yearned for the beach—one of the drawbacks of being in Atlanta was how long it took to get to the Atlantic coast. But she hesitated about leaving Nell. Not Jack—Nell. He kept pressing her, encouraging her to go and have fun.

Selfishly, he thought that maybe the hot sand and blue water would loosen her up; maybe he would get his old Emma back. Maybe she'd touch him again, act like she wanted him; maybe she'd stop pretending to be asleep every time he reached for her. It was during those post-Christmas months that he started e-mailing Laurie in Cleveland; he felt so lonely in his own home, but he'd started hating himself for how much he looked forward to "you've got mail."

And then the week before Maddie had scheduled her trip, he and Emma had had the biggest fight of their marriage—supposedly about the time she was spending at Dixon. Really, though, about the long slide of their relationship, from love and partnership into some sort of hateful charade—neither of them happy, neither of them seeming able to change.

Jack surveyed the line with Jim, uncovering more boundary markers and posts. He hadn't thought this way for a long time. Birds flew overhead, flushed from the underbrush by the activity. Jim called out notations, and Jack wrote them down in the notebook.

Shadows and light fell across clearings and woods. Jack's mind spun with old memories.

He still couldn't think about the accident without cringing. But he was able to remember the aftermath—when Emma was in the hospital, before they had lost hope for her survival, when he had knelt by her bedside and prayed for her to live. He had begged God to make her whole and well again. And when God turned him down on that, Jack had prayed for Emma to haunt him—to love him the way she had at the beginning.

Maybe that was why he related to Aida—loved her on first meeting, actually. Because the woman wanted to preserve this place where she and her husband had known such great love. Jack's heart squeezed inside his chest. He heard Jim call out another number, and he wrote it down. His throat ached.

Because he knew he would do whatever he could to help this woman maintain her land and the castle her husband had loved so much. And because he seemed to be running as fast as he could, as far as he could, from any place that he and Emma had ever lived—from the lie their life had become.

Scotland was far away. And Jack was so tired of running.

He had made his plans, arranged for work permits, given his word that he would start work within the month. The problem was, he no longer wanted to go. Every night he dreamed of staying, dreamed of walking the beach, splashed by warm waves, going to old, almost unintelligible beach movies, holding hands with a kind, curious, open, beautiful woman. With a woman who had obviously won the heart of his brokenhearted daughter.

Stay, Stevie had said.

Romanov was counting on him. And Francesca and the people at Structural felt betrayed by his leaving, and would probably love to see him fail.

Penance came in unexpected places. This dilemma must be Jack's punishment, for loving badly the first time. If Emma hadn't been so unhappy with him, she wouldn't have had to go down the road she had chosen. He thought of what Madeleine had told him—in a medicated stupor, her hysteria subdued.

That while Madeleine drove down that rutted country road, Emma had slapped her in a fit of rage, sent the car out of control. Jack had refused to listen then, and he didn't want to listen now. He needed to keep Emma's memory safe. He'd force himself, if necessary, for Nell's sake.

But somehow now, emerging from the woods and seeing Stevie's Aunt Aida coming toward him with such kindness and wisdom in her violet eyes, Jack thought of Madeleine, Nell's aunt, and felt a sickness in his soul that told him that just maybe he'd been blaming the wrong person all this time.

"Hello, Jack," Aida said, giving him a hug. "Thank you so much for taking the time to do this. It's your vacation . . . I really have no business taking you away from the beach, and Nell . . ."

"That's okay, Aida," he said. "This is such a wonderful place, I'll do whatever I can to help save it."

"I'm going to load the equipment into the car," Jim

said. "I've got tickets for a Red Sox game tonight, and I've got to hurry back. Take care, Jack. Nice meeting you, Aida."

"And you, too, Jim—thank you *so* much," she said, shaking his hand. "Now, can I offer you some tea?" she asked Jack.

"Sure, thanks," he said, and followed her into her small house.

It was almost entirely an artist's studio, with a small daybed pushed against the wall behind the easel and table. She went out into the yard, to fill a copper kettle with water from the well, then set it on the narrow stove. They sat in straight-backed chairs at a scarred oak table, streaked with pigment. Her hands were elegant and capable, knuckles and fingernails rimmed with paint, like Stevie's.

"You have quite a daughter," she said, staring at Jack, as if taking his measure.

"Thank you. I know it."

"She knows her own mind. I still can't believe she went searching for Stevie—and found her. And was brave enough to knock on her door."

"She skinned her knees that day, badly," Jack said, remembering. "She came home with scrapes and Band-Aids. Stevie had bandaged her up. But it hit me, seeing Nell, that she must have really wanted something very badly, to take a fall like that and keep going."

"What do you think she wanted?" Aida asked. The kettle whistled, and she poured hot water into mugs.

Jack didn't answer. The question hung in the air, then drifted off. There was something dreamlike about the visit—everything seemed very vivid, and laden with meaning—or no meaning at all. He saw black-and-white photographs on the wall of Aida as a young woman—tall, lean, theatrical. Dressed in gowns, costumes, nude . . .

"Van took those," she said. "He was so talented. A great actor, but he could easily have been a photographer, as well. That's him—"

Jack followed her gaze to a series of photos of a large, rotund man with an aggressive nose and chin, and intense dark eyes. Dressed as Iago in some and Falstaff in others, he seemed equally at home in both roles—intense, expressive, larger than life. Jack saw the resemblance to Henry, and could well imagine such a man fathering a naval officer.

"Henry's father," Jack said.

"Yes. They adored each other, but had a hard time showing it. I'm convinced that every battle Henry ever fought was for his father."

"He's getting married now?"

"Yes. After all this time. His parents' marriage was quite difficult—his mother was very hurt, and always let him know. That was her prerogative, but oh, it damaged him terribly. He never trusted himself to love someone and not hurt them."

Jack closed his eyes, thinking of how painful and mixed up it all got.

"He's so . . ." Aida's eyes grew misty. "He's so the opposite of Stevie in that way—and yet exactly like her."

"What do you mean?"

"As I've told you, Stevie's parents had an idyllic marriage. One of the truly rare ones. My brother was a poet,

calm and gentle and insightful. My sister-in-law was an
artist and art historian. . . . They were, to use that terribly overused expression, 'soul mates.' They are Stevie's
model. She has such a strong belief in love, and she
wants to have what her parents had."

"Maybe it doesn't exist," Jack said, surprised by the
bitterness in his heart.

"Oh, I know it does," Aida said.

"Because of you and Van?"

She nodded. "It wasn't the first go-round for either
of us. Mistakes get made, and people get hurt. That's
tragic—lives are affected. But love is there—it's real. You
find it, or it finds you . . . that's all it takes."

"That's why you want to preserve this place, isn't it?"
Jack asked. "Because you loved Van here?"

Aida nodded. "I did, and do," she said. "I can never
thank you enough for helping me this way. I've called
my lawyer, and he is going to set up a land trust. I have
a major show scheduled for October, and I plan to use
all the proceeds to fund the trust. This will be 'the Van
Von Lichen Nature and Art Center.' The Black Hall art
types will love it. Van was a great supporter of the arts,
and he had many a wild party with the Connecticut Im-
pressionists here."

"That's not what you paint, though, is it? Impres-
sionism?" Jack asked, embarrassed not to know
enough about art to be sure of the difference.

"Please!" she said. "Darling, I'm in love with the *new*.
Although it's been rather a few decades since Abstract
Expressionism was considered new. . . . anyway . . ."

"Thanks, Aida," he said. "As soon as I get my notes together, I'll send you what I have. Before I leave for Scotland."

"Stevie mentioned that you're moving there. I must say. . . . I feel sad about it."

"Oh, I'll stay involved with your project, even from there. Your lawyer can call me, to discuss the plans, or talk over ideas . . ."

"Jack, that's not why I feel sad. It has nothing to do with my castle, or the hillside."

"Then what?"

Aida was silent. She sipped her tea, staring at Jack over the rim of her mug with eloquent dark-rimmed eyes. He felt as if she could see right into his heart.

"I don't know you very well," she said, "and yet I feel I do. Stevie has told me a bit. . . . It's a feeling that I have. Simply, that . . ."

"What? Please tell me."

"I think my niece will be very sorry if you go. You and Nell. I know Nell will be. And . . . I think you will be, too."

Jack wanted to tell her she had no idea. He cleared his throat. "There's the matter of the contracts I signed."

"The marvelous thing about contracts," she said, "is that there's always a way out. It might cost you more in money, but it will save you in the things that matter."

"What would they be?"

"Oh, come now, Mr. Kilvert," Aida said, her solemn eyes twinkling. "You wouldn't be here, walking these acres and saving my castle, if you didn't know exactly what they are."

Jack drank his tea and thought of Stevie's story about the magical castle and the wise aunt. He didn't reply to Aida's question, because he didn't want to hear himself say that he did know; he knew all too well.

chapter 21

MADELEINE SAT IN HER CAR, PARKED at Emerson's Market, just outside the train trestle that was the gateway to Hubbard's Point. She felt nervous but determined. While she sat there, two trains went by: one toward New York, one toward Boston. When she and her brother were young, they used to count the train cars.

After quite a while, she saw what she was looking for: Jack's station wagon came down the Shore Road and drove under the bridge, into Hubbard's Point. Madeleine had scouted it out two days earlier, on a dry run. She had driven down from Providence, cruised the cottages around the tennis courts, where Stevie had said he was staying, hoping to run into her brother. But when she'd seen him and Nell climb into their car and drive away, she'd lost her nerve and driven back home.

Today she was back, braver than ever. Was Nell with him? Madeleine craned her head to see—no, the passenger seat was empty.

Her heart was beating so fast, she felt as if she'd run a marathon. She was sure her face was bright red—and her lips felt so dry, and her hands were sticky on the steering wheel.

She hadn't told anyone of her plan—not Chris, not Dr. Mallory, not Stevie. Her therapy had been going well; she was starting to feel better after just a few sessions. She felt clearer about everything—if Jack would just give her a chance, she could talk to him. She could sit with him, face-to-face, rely upon their old love for each other to lead her into exactly what she needed to say. She purposely hadn't told Stevie that she was coming; although she knew that her friend would support her desire to set things right, she needed to do this all by herself.

As she pulled out quickly behind Jack's car, she nearly rear-ended him. She had to calm down—she hadn't expected to be this frantic. Talking in her therapist's office was one thing. It was safe there—free from the reality of confrontation. But here, at the beach, anything could happen.

She saw Jack catch sight of her in the rearview mirror. Their eyes met and held.

What was going to happen? Madeleine clutched the wheel and coasted into the driveway outside a beach cottage, directly behind her brother.

JACK COULDN'T MOVE. He parked the car in the sandy driveway and looked into the mirror, straight into his sister's eyes. The castle blueprints and plans lay on the seat beside him. He'd been thinking of Aida's words of wisdom, and of Stevie asking him to stay. He had planned to go straight over to Stevie's and tell her that he was calling Ivan Romanov in the morning—contract or no, he was bagging the Scotland plans. Swirling around in that decision was the need to work things out with his sister.

But actually seeing her was a shock to his system. Slowly, he reached for the door handle, pushed the door open. Madeleine was already out of her car. She stood back slightly, clutching her hands together.

"Jack," she said. Her eyes filled as she said his name. "Don't run away."

"I won't, Maddie," he said slowly.

He let himself really look at her. It had been a year since he'd seen her, and he saw the scars: dark red, from her neck to her shoulder, running under her dress. She had gained weight, and her face looked swollen. Her hair was neatly brushed, held back with tortoiseshell combs; she had put on fresh lipstick. Somehow the care she'd taken broke his heart. She looked so vulnerable, he didn't think he could stand it.

"How have you been?" he asked.

"I'm fine, getting better," she said bravely. "I know I look terrible—it's from the steroids, I had to take them after the surgery, they've made me gain weight. I hate having you see me fat."

"Maddie, you're not—"

"Please, don't say that," she said, shaking her head, as if she couldn't stand any dishonesty between them. Jack's heart was in his throat. He took a step forward, wanting to hug her. But she shook her head harder, stopping him in his tracks, burying her face in her hands.

"I tried calling you," he said.

"I knew," she sobbed. "I *knew* it was you. Why didn't you say anything?"

"I wasn't sure what to say, Maddie. It all seems so complicated. What Emma said to you, and what she did . . . and then, the accident . . ."

"I killed her," Madeleine said. "I wouldn't have hurt her for anything, but she slapped me, and I lost control—"

Jack's stomach clenched. He loved his sister—there was no doubt about that. But he couldn't stand to hear details of the crash. What Emma had confessed, how violent she'd been with Maddie—were too much for him to handle, even a year later.

She stopped, frozen by the stricken look on his face.

"I just want to explain it all to you," she said.

"Let's not go down that path right now," he said.

"It's the only way," she said. "To make you understand that I didn't mean to destroy everything."

"Stop, Maddie," he said, his heart searing. Sweat poured down his neck, and he felt sick. He wanted to be reasonable. This summer had healed him a little—meeting Stevie, spending time with her, seeing Nell getting better. Talking to Aida, seeing her with her own niece. Memories of Emma—and Maddie—good memories, had been everywhere here at Hubbard's Point.

"But you have to listen, Jack—you have to!"

"I can't!" he shouted.

The silence was deafening. All the happy Hubbard's Point activity seemed to stop—tennis balls and basketballs ceased bouncing, radios were turned down, people stopped talking. No one yelled here. Jack's voice echoed in his own ears. Madeleine stood in front of him, pale and paralyzed.

"I'm sorry," he said.

"I'll go," she said, her voice shaking.

"No, Maddie—" he said, his hands trembling. He moved toward her, but she was already climbing into her car. She fumbled with the seat belt, couldn't get it fastened. He wanted to reach in to her. But he didn't dare touch her. She seemed so breakable . . .

"Jack," she said. "I love you."

"Madeleine," he said. Their eyes met, and he felt the tears fall down his cheeks. He couldn't get the words out. He loved her too much to even say. Sometimes when he thought of the accident, he was so angry with her, he wanted to shake her. And other times, all of his considerable rage was directed at Emma—for nearly killing his sister. If Emma hadn't been having a crisis, Madeleine wouldn't have been driving her down that road.

"What?" she asked.

"Don't leave."

"I shouldn't have come."

The sight of her eyes was breaking Jack's heart. "Maddie," he said. He wanted everything to be different, the way it used to be, when loving his sister had been the easiest, most automatic thing in the world.

"I've got to go now," Maddie said.

"Don't," he said.

"Tell Nell how much I love her."

Her window was open, her hand on the wheel. Jack realized he hadn't even hugged her. He reached through the window, and his fingers brushed hers. She shook her head, and gulped a sob.

"You don't know how much she loves you—you have no idea, Maddie," he said. But she wouldn't stop—she just drove away.

Jack stood in the driveway. What had just happened? How badly had he blown it? The crazy thing was, none of it made sense. It wasn't logical—it was all just too soon. One year after the accident, and seeing his sister made him feel as raw as if it had happened yesterday. Maddie hadn't killed Emma. But she had killed his idea of her.

Death had taken Emma, but she'd been ready to leave all on her own. Seeing Madeleine brought that memory right to the surface. He needed to sort through all of it, come to terms with it, find solid ground somewhere where he could get his head straight and concentrate on being father and mother to his little girl. He had to do what was right for Nell. He had left her care one hundred percent to her mother, and look what had been about to happen there. Now he couldn't afford to make any mistakes. Nell was too fragile and needed him too much.

Everything happened for a reason—that's what the nuns used to tell him at school. It was a catch-all explanation for the worst things: for kids who flunked, who got kicked off the team, whose parents died. The strange thing was, those words floated back to him now, standing in his driveway. Madeleine's coming here had shown him one thing: he loved her as much as ever. But he just wasn't equipped to deal with everything that came with it—the truth about Emma, about what a lie their life together had become.

And his instinct had been right all along—to get away, as far and as fast as he could.

NELL AND PEGGY finished swimming with the others, then ran off to hop on the bicycle-built-for-two. They had gotten really good at it, and today was Nell's time to drive it. She immediately set off for the Point.

"I know where we're going," Peggy called from behind.

"No you don't!"

"*Heart of stone, house of blue . . .*"

"Her house isn't blue anymore. Besides, didn't you like being at the movie with her? It was so fun."

"I know . . ."

Since Peggy wasn't really protesting, Nell just grinned and rode up behind the tennis courts, around the corner, onto the shady Point road. When they got to Stevie's, they leaned the bike against her stone wall. Nell took Peggy's hand, to give her courage. They started up the stairs, passing the sign.

"Can't you read?" Peggy whispered.

"She doesn't mean me," Nell said, feeling certain.

When they got to the back door, Nell knocked loudly, wiping the sand off her bare feet. Peggy did the same. They were wearing their bathing suits, which were still fairly damp. Plus, the waves had been bigger than usual, churning up the bottom, so they had some sand in their suits. Nell considered the fact that they should have changed, and was frowning over the thought, when Stevie opened the door.

"What a great surprise!" she said. "Come on in!"

"Um, our bathing suits are wet," Nell said. "And kind of sandy. I'm sorry."

"Sorry, shmorry," Stevie said. "Beach girls are supposed to have wet, sandy bathing suits. I'm glad you came. Hi, Peggy."

"Hi," Peggy said, in the quietest voice Nell had ever heard her use.

"I liked seeing you at the movie the other night. How are your mom and Tara? Did Joe get home?"

"They're good, and yes—Joe's back," Peggy said, perking up. Nell saw her glancing around. Probably looking for Stevie's black hat, cape, and broomstick. Tilly sat in the corner, giving them stern looks. Nell giggled, crouched down, and held out her hand. For the first time, Tilly walked over to rub up against her.

"She knows me!" Nell said. "She helped me set the table the other night!"

"I can tell," Stevie said, "that she's glad you're here. Guess what I was just about to do?"

"Paint a picture for your book?" Nell asked. Then, because she felt so proprietary and happy, she turned to Peggy and said, "She wrote a book all for me and my dad. About a magical castle that we went to. My dad is there now, helping Aunt Aida save the hillside from the wicked bulldozers."

"Oh, he's there now?" Stevie asked, sounding a little funny.

Nell nodded. "He's been there every day. He showed me the drawings he did about how to keep the castle from crumbling anymore. Today he was going to look into the woods, to plan bridges and walkways. That's his specialty—bridges."

"Cool," Peggy said.

Stevie just smiled, but Nell thought she looked a little worried. That made Nell feel funny—as if she'd said the wrong thing. So she touched Stevie's elbow and asked, "What was it you were about to do?"

"Teach Ebby to fly," she said. "Come on upstairs."

"Ebby?" Peggy asked as they walked through the house.

"The bird your brother brought me. He's a crow, so I named him Ebony. Nicknamed Ebby."

Nell saw Peggy looking around the room, at the comfortable old wicker furniture, faded pillows, hooked rugs, baskets of shells and stones, and paintings on the wall. The house was so colorful and friendly, it was as far from witchdom as it could possibly be. Nell laughed, because Peggy looked so surprised.

Up in Stevie's room, the bird was already flying! She had left his cage door open, and he was sitting on the top, cawing. As Nell watched, he flew up to perch on the top of Aunt Aida's large canvas. Then he flew up to land on a rafter.

"This is where you paint?" Peggy asked, eyes wide.

"It is," Stevie said.

"Cool," Peggy said.

"Look at this," Stevie said, leading the girls to her side window. It gave onto her terrace, where the red flowers grew. As Nell looked down, she saw several hummingbirds, and she remembered that moment at Aunt Aida's with Stevie. The memory made her feel even closer to Stevie, and she leaned against her side. But Stevie wasn't pointing at the hummingbirds today.

"Can you see?" she asked. Nell peered out, at a cedar tree growing behind the blue stone terrace. Several crows were hidden in its branches.

"What are they doing there?" Peggy asked. She took a step back into the room, as if the sight of the birds scared her.

"I think they're waiting for Ebby," Stevie said.

"They're his family," Nell said, breathless.

"I think you're right, Nell," Stevie said. "The crow is the Native American totem for creation, spiritual strength, and loyalty."

"How do you know that?"

"Well, I study birds," she said. "For the books I write."

Peggy tugged Nell's arm and mouthed, "Maybe she *is* a witch."

Nell shook her head resolutely. She and Peggy stood back, as Stevie opened the window, removed the screen. A breeze blew in, moving the curtains. The crows didn't even flinch at the commotion—they just held their spots on the branches, waiting.

As the girls held their breath, Ebby flew off the rafter and began to circle around the room. He had grown a lot in the time since Billy had brought him to Stevie—he was no longer a soft fluffy baby, but a lean teenage crow. Nell grabbed Stevie's hand, without even thinking.

Ebby landed on the windowsill. He seemed to lift his head to the sky. The crows in the cedar tree all began to caw. Nell felt goose bumps on her arms. For some reason she thought of her own family: of her father, Aunt Madeleine, Uncle Chris, waiting for her.

"They're waiting for you," Stevie whispered.

And in a flash of black wings, Ebby flew. He faltered slightly, tumbling down toward the first floor, but then caught himself and rose, rose, toward the uppermost branches of the cedar tree. His relatives saw him coming, and all lifted off at once—a glossy black cloud of wings, bearing Ebby home.

Nell realized that she had let go of Stevie's hand, was gripping the windowsill to watch him go. She saw the crows fly over the beach, into the trees behind the marsh near Peggy's house—where Billy had found Ebby in the first place.

"He's with his family now," Nell said.

"I can't wait to tell Billy," Peggy said, her eyes shining.

Nell looked up at Stevie. Her hair was as black as the crows' backs. She wanted to reach up and touch, to see whether there were soft, shiny feathers. She could almost imagine that Stevie was part of her own family, her crow aunt. Or mother. The idea made Nell feel like crying and laughing, at the same time.

"When I go away, will you be waiting for me?" she asked.

"Always," Stevie said. "You can fly back here any-time."

Nell ducked her head, hiding a small smile. But where would she be flying back from? The summer was long and wonderful, with no end in sight: Nell didn't even want to think about it. It almost didn't matter, as long as she could return to Hubbard's Point.

"Are you excited about Scotland?" Stevie asked.

Nell tilted her head. Had her father told Stevie about the dumb trip they were maybe taking there? "Not really," she said.

"Really? You're not excited about going to live there?" Stevie said.

"Live in *Scotland*? Dad mentioned it, but I think he meant *visit*."

"Nell—that's so far away! You can't move to another country," Peggy said.

Stevie's face turned red. She exhaled, giving Nell the definite idea that she had said the wrong thing. Nell heard herself gasp. It couldn't be possible. Scotland was across the ocean. How could she get back here, to Stevie? And how would her aunt ever be able to find her—in a foreign land? She was moving to *Scotland*?

JACK WAS still in a sort of slow-motion shock when Nell came home. He had stood in the driveway for a ridicu-lously long time, hoping Maddie would come back. At some point a neighbor had walked past. "Everything okay?" she'd asked, seeing him stare into nothing.

"Fine," Jack said.

He had walked into the backyard, to sit on the picnic bench under the trees. Stevie and he had sat here the morning she'd brought coffee over. An hour passed, and then another. He didn't move. The sight of his sister sobbing had rocked him to the core.

"Scotland?" Nell called, tearing around the corner and pulling him back to the present. "We're going to live in Scotland?"

"Who told you that?" he asked, his stomach dropping.

"I'm not telling you, 'cause you'll just get mad at her. Dad, I am not going to live in Scotland," she cried. A dog walker paused to watch.

"Come inside," Jack said, jumping off the bench, walking over to open the screen door. Nell walked in, sand from her bathing suit raining down on the linoleum floor with every step.

"You weren't even going to ask me what I wanted?"

"Honey, I was. I am. I'm just trying to do what's best for us," Jack stammered. He was still shaken by Madeleine's visit, in shock at his reaction to seeing her, confused about everything.

"I don't want it," Nell said. "I want to stay here."

Jack had thought the same thing that morning—it seemed ten years away. Everything had looked so beautiful up at the castle; and Stevie's word, *stay*, had seemed just like a challenge or a promise he wanted to accept. But now . . .

"What's wrong with Atlanta, Dad? What's wrong with Boston?"

"I thought you didn't like Boston."

"I didn't like *Francesca*. That's all, and you know it!"

"You didn't seem very happy there."

"Dad—I liked the swan boats. I liked the Freedom Trail."

Jack's head began to ache. What did landmarks have to do with where a family made their home? Besides, *had* she liked the swan boats? He remembered her seeming sullen the day he'd taken her. And taking her to the Old North Church had been like dragging the statue of Paul Revere himself up the steps, down the aisle. Suddenly he had a premonition of what it would be like, taking her to Loch Ness, or Inverness Castle. What had he been thinking?

"The best part about Boston is, it's not very far from Hubbard's Point. So, please, Dad . . . Go back to work at Structural, and that'll be fine."

"I can't, Nell," he said, the truth of it all hitting him. "I gave my notice there. And my new boss, in Scotland, is waiting for me to start."

"No!" she sobbed.

"Nell," he said.

"Please, Dad. Please don't do this. I love it here."

"I do, too," he said. But even as he spoke, he knew: sometimes love wasn't enough. If it was, he would have been able to make things work with Emma. If it was, then he and Madeleine would have been able to make everything okay between them. Sometimes love was a driving force—but in opposite directions. And at that moment, however hard it was, he was sure that going to Scotland was the right thing. It would be new, fresh— they'd have time to get on their feet, both of them, he and Nell.

I've got to go now, Madeleine had said.

Well, so did Jack. He was an idiot to think he could stop running now.

"Sweetheart," he said, reaching for her.

"You're hurting me," she wailed, tearing at her own hair. "Can't you tell? You're hurting me, Dad! First you won't let me see Aunt Maddie, and now you're taking me away from Stevie. And Peggy! I don't want to go to Scotland. I don't want to, I don't . . ."

Sobbing, she tore up the stairs. Her wails came through the floorboards, as if her heart were being broken, and Jack sat in a chair down below, his own heart cracking at the same time.

THAT NIGHT, Stevie couldn't sleep. She lay in bed, listening to the waves build, pierced through at bringing everything crashing down on Nell. A storm was building out at sea, and the wind picked up a little more each hour. The moon was waning, but still over half full. Filtered through high clouds, its light shone through her window all night long, till finally she gave up, got out of bed, pulled on her bathing suit and a shirt and walked down to the beach.

The sky was dark blue, glowing with moonlight. Thin clouds were moving in, veiling the light. Stevie walked all the way to the end of the beach, feeling the hard sand under her feet. The waves came in and out, licking her ankles. She had had a lifetime of love and happiness here, dating all the way back to her summers with Emma . . . and then Madeleine.

Beach girls today, beach girls tomorrow, beach girls till the end of time . . .

What had gone wrong? And why did she have the feeling she had failed them both—her two dearest friends? She had tried to bring Madeleine back with Emma's family, and she'd tried to welcome Nell into the fold. Her heart felt heavy; she should have stayed a hermit. Walking along, the darkness was thick and heavy. She heard the waves, saw the white ripples, silver in the moonlight. A wet, salt breeze blew from the east, stinging her cheeks.

When she got near the footbridge, she dropped her shirt on the sand and stood there in her bathing suit. She needed to swim, to feel the salt water buoying her up—she just wanted to feel *held*, even by the sea. The tide was all the way out, as far as it would go. She hadn't skinny-dipped since that first morning when Jack was sitting on the boardwalk watching her. Remembering that, she turned around to look—and he was there.

Stevie froze, then began to walk up the beach. He came down to meet her.

"Hi," she said.

"Hi."

"Of all the beaches on all the oceans, you had to walk onto mine," she said. They stood together, toes touching, as she looked up and tried to see his eyes. His hair fell across his face, shadowed by the moon.

"I'm sorry for telling Nell about Scotland," she said. "I thought she knew."

"I've tried to broach the subject with her before," he said. "But she's stubborn about things she doesn't want to hear. So, don't worry. She had to find out somehow."

"Is she okay?"

He nodded. "Finally she is. It took half the night, but she eventually cried herself to sleep. I—the walls were closing in on me up there. I needed a walk. Are you going to swim?"

"Yes," she said.

"Me, too. Let's go in."

He dropped his shirt beside hers, and they dove into the next wave. The night air was cool, so the water felt warm. Stevie swam strong and fast, out toward the raft. She felt the tide start to turn—felt resistance as it started coming in. The moon hung low in the sky, casting a wide, gold path on the rising black water. She heard Jack swimming nearby, caught a glimpse of his sleek back.

Her lungs ached, but the exertion felt so good. She had the feeling that he was trying to wear himself out, too. Her muscles stretched as she sped up, picking up the pace. Jack got into the spirit, racing her to the raft. They hauled themselves out, laughing. She shook her hair and sat down beside him.

"Didn't your mother ever tell you not to swim after dark?" he asked.

"That was one thing she didn't tell me," Stevie said. "She had a serious appreciation for the beach, and she knew that night swimming, especially with a friend and a storm moon, is one of the high points."

"But you didn't know you'd have a friend tonight," he said. "Did you?"

"No," she said. "But neither did you. Did you?"

"I thought you might be there."

"Those other times, I swam at dawn. I don't know what time it is now—"

"Probably about four-thirty. I felt it anyway. I can't explain how. Maybe it's because I have to tell you something."

"What?"

"Maddie came to see me."

"Jack!" she said, thrilled.

"It was so good to see her," he said, but his eyes looked stricken. Her heart caught in her throat as she saw him shake his head.

"What, Jack?"

"Nell and I are leaving."

She turned slowly to look at him, her stomach dropping.

"Now that the reality has sunk in for her, the longer we stay, the harder it'll be. She's . . . she's really crazy about you. And about this place. I've screwed up something huge—but I can't undo it."

"But seeing Maddie—you said it was so good to see her."

"It's too hard, Stevie. It's too big—for both of us. She

drove away first—she couldn't handle it either. There's too big a hole in our family for anyone to fix."

"It doesn't have to happen all at once," she said.

"I wanted to stay," he said. "I did. You have no idea how much. When you said it that night, after the beach movie . . . *stay*. I've heard your voice ever since. And I've thought—really thought—what if we did? I tried—I wanted it to happen."

"Why can't you?" she asked.

"I've signed a contract. I changed our plane tickets— we're going to leave Hubbard's Point tomorrow, leave for Scotland this weekend."

"You can't," Stevie said.

"I wish I couldn't, but I have to."

She thought of Madeleine, how unfinished everything was. There had to be a way to heal it, to make everything right before Jack left—if he had to go at all. "Maddie loves you," she said. "And I know you love her."

"There's no doubt about that," he said. "There's a part you don't understand. And I can't talk about it. I'm not sure I'll ever be able to. It's easier to push it away when I'm not so close . . . to people who knew Emma."

"But think of Nell," she whispered into the chilly wind. "You're taking her away from people who really love her."

"Stevie, I'm doing it *for* Nell. I'm her father—I have to take care of her the best way I know. You know how much I wish things were different, don't you?"

She nodded, but he didn't give her a chance to reply. He threw his arms around her, kissed her with fierce intensity. His mouth was hot, and his salty skin was wet against hers. They kissed wildly as Stevie's thoughts raced, as she fought to hold back tears. They held each other for a long time, their bodies keeping each other warm in the chilly air, until Stevie gave up and let the tears come—she was covered with salt water anyway. Lying back, holding each other, they felt the raft moving beneath them on the waves.

Stevie held his arms, tingling from his touch, soothed by the movement of the sea. Why did he have to leave? The question would hit her, and she'd tense up again. But he kept holding her. The wind came up, drowning out the words he tried to say to her. They were on a ship, far from land; she told herself they were far from all their problems. The full moon had cast a spell when she had seen it rising from the castle tower, had brought them together out here, on this raft in the bay.

The wind swirled down, chilling their skin as they slid off their bathing suits. Jack's body gleamed in the tawny light, powerful shoulders and arms, strong thighs, poised over her. Stevie was strong, too, pale from working in her studio. She couldn't wait for him, arching up to kiss his neck, taste the salt, moan as he entered her. The wind-whipped waves moved underneath, and he thrust from on top, and she never wanted to let go.

Her heart was pounding, and her insides were throbbing. Jack was whispering in her ear, but she could barely hear the words. She gripped his back, holding on with everything she had. Their eyes met, and the truth was right there. They each had reasons for not wanting to say it out loud, but on a moonlit night when an offshore wind was blowing and the tide was flooding in, all bets were off.

"I've fallen in love with you," she whispered in a voice much too low for him to hear.

"I've fallen in love with you, too," he whispered back.

She felt him in the wind and the tide, and she knew she would feel him in every swim she ever took, and she felt him right then, inside her, his arms around her, holding her, just holding her.

Somewhere during their lovemaking, the moon set. They were alone in the dark, on a raft anchored fifty yards out from the beach. Waves beat against the rocks and raft, mysterious music singing from the deep. Stevie thought of Henry calling her Luocious, the siren with the dangerous song, and her eyes filled with tears again. She remembered him saying, "It's your boat that always gets wrecked."

Jack looked into her face, but it was too dark to see the tears. She held him inside her for as long as she could. She thought of all the mistakes she had made in love, all during her life, and she knew that this wasn't one of them.

They fell asleep in each other's arms. When they woke up, the sky was turning light in the east—the sun was getting ready to rise. Stevie watched Jack's face—long dark lashes on his lean cheeks, eyes flickering beneath the lids, alive with dreams. Would he dream of her after he left?

She kissed his lips, to wake him up.

"The sun's coming up," she said.

He stared moodily east, as if he wished he could send

the sun back below the horizon. Or maybe he was thinking of Scotland.

"You'd better get home to Nell," she said.

"I know."

They pulled on their suits and stood, hugging. Jack held her hand, looking at her as he got ready to dive in. She shook her head.

"You go," she said. "I'm staying here."

"It's windy—the waves are kicking up. Please, Stevie?"

"No," she said. "I need a little time . . . I'll be fine."

He held her hands for a long time. She watched the expressions cross his face, the worry lines in his forehead. If only they had met sooner, or later, or differently; if only they hadn't so much history. The waves splashed in, and Stevie thought, *If only, if only* . . .

"I don't want to leave you," he said.

"Please," she said. She had a lump in her throat, and this time she wouldn't have darkness to hide her tears.

"Stevie?"

"Please . . ." she said again. He nodded. He kissed her once, then dove into the water. She watched him swim the whole way back to shore, getting farther and farther away. Tears streamed down her cheeks, and she watched him climb out of the water and pick up his shirt. He turned and raised his hand briefly in a final wave and then turned and walked away, back to his sleeping daughter, to their future on another rocky coast an ocean away.

Stevie just sat down on the raft and watched him go.

chapter 22

NELL COULDN'T BELIEVE THAT THIS WAS really happening. The bags were packed, her father was sweeping the kitchen floor, the soda cans and water bottles were stacked by the door, ready to be thrown into the recycling bin, and the real estate lady was standing there saying "Oh, I hope you come back next year."

"I'll let you know," her father said, holding the broom.

"Well, you've paid through till the end of the month," the real estate lady said. She was tan and pretty, with curly brown hair and a pink flowered dress. "I'm sorry I can't refund your money, because I don't have other renters coming in this summer."

"That's okay," her father replied. He kept sweeping. He gave the strongest hints possible, but the real estate lady wasn't picking up on them.

"Was there something wrong with the cottage? Were you unhappy at Hubbard's Point?"

"We *loved* it here," Nell said, standing in the corner

in her yellow sundress, the most dressed up she'd been in weeks, since coming here, with her arms folded tight across her chest.

"Then—?"

"A change in plans," her father said. Then, as if he'd heard how clipped and rude he sounded, he leaned on his broom and said, "It's business."

"It's crummy!" Nell chimed in.

"Nell . . ."

"It's so unfair! I want to stay. You go to Scotland, and I'll stay here. We paid for it, Dad."

Her father threw a watered-down smile toward the real estate lady, who was looking half horrified, half starved for the gory details of the father-daughter showdown. "I don't think Mrs. Crosby would think that's such a great idea."

"No, dear, it's probably not," she said. "Besides, don't you want to go to Scotland with your daddy?"

"About as much as I want to have my eyes pecked out by seagulls," Nell said under her breath.

"Scotland's lovely!" the lady said, in a way that Nell knew was designed to please her father. "All that heather, and the lochs and castles . . . and great bargains on plaid and tweed. And scotch . . ." she laughed, "for your father . . ."

"Dad," Nell said, ignoring dumb Mrs. Crosby and her flirty ways. "We have a castle right here. I'm not going. I'm staying with Stevie."

"Nell . . ."

"She'll let me! She'd love it! I could help her with her painting. I could tell her what kids like to read. She told me that I inspired her a *lot* for the story she was writing about the hummingbirds . . . we could do *tons* more things."

"We're not going to bother Stevie about this."

"Stevie Moore?" Mrs. Crosby asked, cocking her eyebrow in a funny way.

"She's our friend," Nell said.

Mrs. Crosby seemed momentarily speechless. Nell's father just kept sweeping. And Nell knew she had to use this moment to escape, or she'd start to cry.

"I'm going out to say my goodbyes, Dad."

"We're leaving at two. I want us to be on the road at two sharp. You got that, Nell?"

She just scrunched up her nose and nodded her head—he was her dad, but even if she had to do what he said, she didn't have to like it. Then she raced outside. She kicked her shoes off in the yard, savoring the feeling of hot tar under her bare feet.

The salt wind blew through her brown hair and stung her green eyes. As if in honor of her dark mood, the day was overcast, threatening rain. A storm was whipping up at sea, driving big waves into the beach. She stopped on the boardwalk, flung her arms out to the sides, and leaned into the easterly wind.

It held her up. Blowing so hard, no matter how steeply she leaned forward, it pushed her back. She swallowed the wind, tasting the sea. She looked up and down the beach, trying to memorize every inch. Gone were the bright umbrellas and beach blankets. A few diehards were huddled in beach chairs, trying to read as their book pages fluttered wildly. Some kids bodysurfed the waves—Nell recognized Billy McCabe and his friends, as well as Eliza and Annie. She scoured the group for Peggy—then realized that she was waiting for Nell at home.

Nell left the beach, heading for the marsh path. Just twenty yards from the beach, the wind dropped. It was protected here, quiet and warmer. Her bare feet squished through the marsh mud. The tide was up, the creek overflowing its banks. She peered into the murky water, saw blue crabs clinging to the spartina. Their claws flashed azure blue in the dim sunlight, as they danced and moved in the flowing water.

When she came to the plank bridge, she thought of her father. He built bridges for his living. He was taking her to Scotland, so he could build some over there. The whole world would be filled with her father's bridges, but if he didn't use them himself—to cross them and get to the people who loved him—then what use were they?

Nell balanced on the silvered wood, step by step, thinking of the people she wanted to see on the other side: Peggy, Stevie, her aunt. Her father would probably build a span across the Atlantic Ocean, if he could, to get away from everyone.

Running now, Nell got to Peggy's house and knocked on the door. Peggy's mother and Tara were waiting inside, both looking sad. Peggy was sitting on a stool at the counter, and she couldn't even turn her head to greet her friend. The women hugged Nell in a sort of huddle; she wished she could hide there and stay.

"We're going to miss you so much," Peggy's mother said.

"I wish we could kidnap you and keep you here with us," Tara said. "But my fiancé would probably get in trouble with his bosses at the FBI."

"I wouldn't press charges," Nell said hopefully.

The women laughed, kissed the top of her head. Then she turned to Peggy, whose eyes were red. Nell stared at her, and felt a huge weight in her stomach. Neither one of them could talk. Nell gestured to the door, and Peggy shrugged and followed. A quick glance at the kitchen clock told Nell it was one-fifteen. Forty-five minutes till doom-hour.

The girls climbed on the blue bicycle, with Peggy in front. She set off along the marsh road, then down the dead end behind the seawall. Blustery wind whipped their hair into their eyes and mouth, but Nell didn't care. It was warm and strong, a tropical system heading up from the Georgia barrier islands she loved so well; she swore she could smell mangroves, Spanish moss, wild ponies.

They pedaled along, and without being asked or told, Peggy pedaled up toward the Point. At high tide, the parking lot flooded with water from the boat basin and a patch of marshland, so they splashed through the salt water, scattering minnows as they went. Up the hill behind the tennis court, and then onto the Point.

When they got to Stevie's house, Peggy pulled over.

"How did you know this is where I wanted to come?" Nell asked.

"I'm your best friend," Peggy said.

Nell nodded, the weight in her stomach even heavier. They headed up the hill, and when they got to the sign—it wasn't there! Nell saw a little hole in the ground, where the small post had gone. Maybe some kids had stolen it. She hurried up the hill, to knock on the door, but Stevie was right there, waiting—as she had been that first day, when Nell had come to call.

"Your sign's gone!" Nell said.

Stevie nodded. "I know. I took it down."

"Took it down? How come?"

Stevie smiled. Her eyes looked serious, through her dark bangs, but the smile was slow and warm, and Nell felt it imprinted on her heart. "That would take a long time to explain," Stevie said, "and I'd rather spend this time talking about you."

"Where's Tilly?" Nell asked, looking around. But then she looked down and saw the cat right by Stevie's side—pressed lightly against her leg—as if she somehow knew that Stevie needed protecting today.

"Come on in," Stevie said, and they all went into the living room. From here, they could see the beach, with the big storm waves rolling in. They were more like ocean breakers, not the calm little Long Island Sound waves Nell had known all summer. It was as if the weather knew her mood and was responding accordingly.

Nell and Peggy sat on the loveseat, and Stevie and Tilly sat in their wicker chair. Stevie had made sugar cookies, and they were on a flowered china plate on the table, but no one felt like eating them.

"Tara said we should kidnap Nell, and I think that's a good idea," Peggy said, gulping tears.

"I had some thoughts along those same lines myself," Stevie said, her eyes still warm and serious. "But I know . . ."

Nell blinked slowly, hanging on Stevie's words.

"I know her father knows what's best for her. And he has a good plan. And . . ."

"And what?" Nell asked, because she didn't believe the first part at all.

"And we'll both write her lots of letters—right, Peggy?"

Peggy nodded, red hair bobbing into her tearstained eyes. "My mom already got me some overseas airmail stamps. They're more expensive than the other kind. But she said she'd get me as many as I wanted."

"Oh, I remember . . ." Stevie began, then bit her lip. She tried to brush whatever she'd been about to say away by focusing on Tilly, who sat on the chair arm beside her. "Tilly, Tilly—will you write to Nell too?"

"What do you remember?" Nell asked. She leaned forward, and Stevie must have seen that she needed to hear.

"I remember being just like this when your mother and aunt would leave at the end of the summer," Stevie said. "We couldn't stand to go away from each other. Our goodbyes were endless. We'd say goodbye, and forget one thing we'd meant to say, and then our parents would have to drive us to each other's houses on the way out of Hubbard's Point, so we could say it."

"Like what kind of things would you forget?"

"Like, 'Remember when we rowed over to Rocky

Neck for a picnic?' Or, 'Don't forget how we convinced all the beach kids that the ice cream man was buying crabs for bait, and how all summer his line was filled with kids trying to sell him crabs and he couldn't figure out why!' "

"We should have tried that!" Peggy said, laughing and sniffling.

"My mom and aunt did that?"

Stevie nodded. "The three of us did—that first summer we met, when we were still young enough to get away with such things. The later summers, the things we wanted to say had more to do with boys."

"Oh, like kissing at the movies, right?" Peggy asked.

"Yes, like that."

"Kind of gross," Peggy said.

Stevie just smiled a little sadly, as if she knew things they didn't. Nell shivered—as if the wind had turned cold, which it hadn't. She looked out the window, saw crows in the sumac on Stevie's hill.

"Are they—?"

"Ebby's family," Stevie said. "I think he might think I'm his aunt or something. See? There he is—"

Nell pressed her face against the window. Sure enough, there was the young crow—smaller than the others, but just as glossy and proud. She thought of how important family was, so important that a baby crow would stay loyal to his adopted aunt.

"The one thing I want to tell you," Stevie said.

Nell turned to look at her.

"Both of you," Stevie continued, "is how much I wish I'd stayed in touch . . . with my dearest friends."

"My mom and aunt?"

Stevie nodded. "We meant so much to each other. And we swore we'd never grow apart. But life gets so busy, and before you know it, you forget who you used to be, those summer days with your best, best friends . . . and you stop writing to each other."

"Never," Peggy swore passionately. "My mother and Tara never stopped. . . ."

"They're smart, and they're lucky," Stevie said.

Nell was silent, clenching her fists. She knew what it was like to stop. To love someone so much you'd spend every Thanksgiving and Christmas together, to call each other every Sunday, to remember birthdays and anniversaries—and then to just *stop*. "If I feel this way about my friends, you," Nell said to Stevie and Peggy, her voice thick, "I can't imagine how I'd feel about a sister. How could a person just stop speaking to a sister?"

"I'd never stop speaking to Annie," Peggy said.

Stevie just sat there, gazing at Nell with grave eyes. Nell knew that she knew this was about Aunt Maddie. She remembered the scene upstairs, weeks ago, when her father had carried her out in a weeping mess. She felt that way again, but she held the tears inside.

"I don't have any sisters either, Nell," Stevie said. "But I asked my Aunt Aida about it."

"What did she say?"

"She said she understands . . . because brothers and sisters can grow up being so close, the hurt is just that much stronger. So when it comes, the hurt, there's sometimes no other way out, except to hide from it."

"But he's making me hide from it, too," Nell said,

feeling the tears spill over. "Hide from her, and now hide from you. I don't want to go to Scotland."

"I know, honey," Stevie said. She opened her arms, and Nell didn't even care that Peggy was right there watching her be a baby: she fell against Stevie and cried and cried. She cried for so long that she emptied herself out. She felt Tilly's whiskers tickling her face, and she felt Stevie's warm breath on her hair. She could have stayed there forever.

Finally, very gently, Stevie eased her right arm away, and reached for a portfolio—it reminded Nell of the ones her father sometimes carried his engineering drawings in. But this one was beautiful red leather, and small, just the size to fit under Nell's arm.

"This is for you," Stevie said, handing it to her.

Nell blinked away tears, untied the red grosgrain ribbons that held the case together. It fell open—and inside were loose pages that looked just like pages from one of the many books of Stevie's that had gotten her through the summer's sleepless nights.

"What is it?" Peggy asked.

"It's *Red Nectar*," Nell whispered. "Stevie's hummingbird book—right?"

"That's right," Stevie said. "These are the first set of page proofs. I wanted you to have them."

Nell saw beautiful, bright paintings of the pair of hummingbirds outside at Hubbard's Point, with the beach curving in the background and the blue cove and swimming raft . . . and on another page, another pair— feeding at the red flowers growing up the crumbling walls of Aunt Aida's castle.

Breathless, she turned the pages, seeing the birds flying high over the world, migrating across oceans. And then coming back to Black Hall . . . she saw that Stevie had shown the hummingbirds flying above two girls on a blue bicycle-built-for-two—one with brown hair and one with red.

"Me and Peggy!" Nell exclaimed, and Peggy gasped.

And then there were pictures of the castle, the pair returning from their migration to see Aunt Aida painting another canvas of the beach and sea . . . the vine growing up the gray stones, brilliant with red trumpet flowers . . . with Nell's father standing at the top of the tower with Nell, and with his brass scope.

"It's all of us!" Nell said. "Except you . . . where are you, Stevie?"

"Oh," she said, "I'm watching over you, painting what I see."

"Look, Nell," Peggy said, picking up a page without pictures that had fluttered to the floor. "It's the dedication!"

Nell read it out loud: "To Nell, who has the heart of a hummingbird."

She clasped the book to her chest and couldn't speak. The heart of a hummingbird . . . those beautiful, strong, brave birds that flew so high and far . . . She wanted to say thank you, she wanted to ask Stevie why she'd picked her to dedicate the book to. She had a million questions, but they all just jumbled together. Suddenly Tilly heard something alarming, because she sprang off the chair and hid under the loveseat.

A knock sounded at the door. Just then Nell looked

at Stevie's watch, and saw that it was after two. With Stevie's hand on her shoulder, they all walked into the kitchen.

Nell's father stood at the door.

"How did you know I'd be here?" she asked.

"Because I knew you were saying your goodbyes."

"Can you come in?" Stevie asked, through the screen door. Nell saw something cross her eyes that reminded her of the wind outside—warm, salty, troubled. But her father, of course, just shook his head.

"We'd better get going."

"He hates goodbyes," Nell explained.

"I've noticed that," Stevie said softly.

There were hugs that Nell would never forget. She held and rocked Peggy as if they were dancing. Peggy went on, almost blabbering, about writing every day, and Nell said the same things back to her. Then, Stevie. Nell reached up her arms, and Stevie bent down for a hug. It went on and on, and Nell didn't want it to end. She felt a lump in her throat, and she knew she would have it forever. Her cheeks were wet with tears—so were Stevie's.

"Thank you for the book," Nell said.

"You're welcome. Thank you for *everything*. All the inspiration."

"I inspired you?"

"More than you'll ever know."

"If you talk to Aunt Maddie," Nell said, "tell her about the book, okay? I want her to know."

"I will. I promise . . ."

"Say bye to Aunt Aida."

"Of course I will."

"I don't want to go," Nell said, clinging to Stevie's hand. She thought that if she held on hard enough, maybe Stevie would somehow keep her from going . . . would keep them both from leaving. . . .

Stevie crouched down till she was eye-level with Nell. Stevie's dark eyes were violet, calm, deep, full of such kindness and love that Nell felt a shiver from the top of her head down to her toes, at the idea of ever leaving her.

"Nell," Stevie said. "You . . . well . . . you *have* to go."

"No," Nell whispered. Couldn't Stevie at least pretend to fight to hold on to her, to show her father how much she didn't want them to go?

"It's a mission," Stevie whispered.

"A what?"

"A mission . . . you have important work to do. For the beach girls."

"For the beach girls . . . What kind of work?" Nell asked, feeling her hair tingle again, as if a breeze had just swept through the kitchen.

"Well, you have to check out the beaches in Scotland. To see what they're like."

"I already know they're not *half* as good as Hubbard's Point."

"Well, I can understand why you'd think that—but they might be. They could be even better."

"I know they won't be," Nell whispered hotly.

"Maybe 'better' isn't the point. Maybe you could just look them over, and report back on what you see."

"Like what?"

"Well, the different kinds of shells you find there. And whether the sand is white, or pink . . . whether it's smooth or rocky . . . whether the seaweed is the same as here . . ." Nell closed her eyes, picturing the springy brown weed of Hubbard's Point rock pools, the long tendrils of kelp that lay in heaps along the beach's tide line after storms, the delicate, lettuce-y green weed to which tiny, almost microscopic periwinkles attached themselves. She felt her insides melt with grief, just at the thought of leaving Hubbard's Point seaweed. . . .

"What the sea glass is like," Peggy added. "Whether the beaches have boardwalks, movies, crabbing places—right, Stevie?"

"Right," Stevie said. "Those are exactly the kinds of things we need to know."

"But why?" Nell heard herself ask, opening her eyes.

"Because maybe we'll go visit her in Scotland, right, Stevie?" Peggy asked, tears spilling over.

Nell saw the look in Stevie's eyes as she glanced up at Nell's father. Nell knew that parental code all too well—adults never wanted to get kids' hopes up or make promises they couldn't keep.

"Well," Stevie said, "I don't know about that, exactly. But whether we go or not isn't even the point. We just want to know, Nell. We want to know about the way the sand feels under your bare tootsies . . . and how salty the water tastes when you go swimming . . . and what the sunsets look like reflected in the bays . . . and how bright the stars burn over the sea—because we're beach girls. That's all. That's the only reason."

"It's a good reason," Peggy whispered.

"It's time to go now," Stevie said, squeezing Nell's hand a little tighter. Nell saw the tears rolling down Stevie's face, and suddenly she knew that Stevie had just made up the whole beach girl assignment—to make her feel better about leaving. Her feelings bucked inside her. She didn't know how she would live through this.

Her father had been standing outside the door. She thought he was just waiting for her, watching her say her goodbyes, but when she turned around, she saw that he was staring at Stevie. The look in her father's eyes was intense and mysterious, and it sent a fast, furious shiver down Nell's spine—she didn't know why. She hadn't seen him look at anyone like that before—maybe not even her mother. Or maybe she'd just been too young to notice. Or too happy and secure. But seeing his eyes do that for Stevie felt like magic, wildly filled with home. Those eyes were lightning bolts—and they told Nell he didn't want to go.

"I notice you took your sign down," her father said, the look in his eyes sharper than ever.

"I did," she said.

"What made you do that?"

She didn't reply. Nell grabbed Peggy's hand. They stepped aside, by the stove, holding on and never wanting to let go.

"Wish, wish," Nell whispered. "Wish that Stevie can bring us back, me and my father, from wherever he has to go. . . ."

"I'm wishing," Peggy said, her eyes closed tight.

"Me too," Nell said, feeling the magic of the summer

and the hummingbirds and the beach girls swirl li[k]e
gold dust, straight into her heart.

Then the screen door opened, and Nell felt her father's hand touch her head. Stevie was pushing her out
the door, portfolio in hand. Nell heard Peggy crying
softly, and she heard her father whispering, "Come on,
Nell."

And then she heard something quiet and fast—two
people kissing over her head. And then she heard her
father say again, softly, "Come on, Nell."

And then no one could speak, not even to say just
one more goodbye.

And Nell and her father went to Scotland.

Part Three

STEVIE TRIED TO PAINT. SHE TRIED TO garden. Neither seemed quite possible. It was mid-August, her favorite time of year, but she hardly noticed. She no longer got up before dawn. She found herself staying in bed as long as she could, pulling the covers over her head to block the light and stay asleep—to help the days along, so they wouldn't feel so interminable. Paradoxically, she felt very tired—for, although she never seemed to fall into a deep sleep, she also never quite felt that she was all the way awake.

"It's called depression, darling," Aunt Aida said to her on the telephone one day when Stevie had called to apologize for forgetting a meeting that her aunt had wanted her to attend with the lawyer, regarding the setting up of a foundation board.

"Really?" Stevie asked. "I've never been depressed before. I'm not the depressed type!"

"Be that as it may. What you are describing is classic. It's exactly what I felt after Van died."

"I'm okay," Stevie said.

"Darling, you're an artist, and an Irish artist at that. There's a certain amount of pain that comes with *that* territory, and once you throw love into the mix, forget it!"

"Love?"

"Let's not fool each other, shall we? We've been through too much together, dear girl. Jack and Nell. They're gone, and you're grieving."

"I'm also thinking about my whole life, all the mistakes I've made," Stevie said, her eyes flooding, "that led me to this point. Henry used to say I was a siren called Lulu, wrecking men's boats, wrecking my own. Aunt Aida, I really wanted this one to stay afloat," she said, choking on a held-back sob.

"I know, Stevie," her aunt said.

Stevie closed her eyes. Sunlight blazed on the bay's surface, filling the beach with pure white light. She couldn't look.

"You're having what Saint John of the Cross would call 'a dark night of the soul,' " Aunt Aida said. "Follow it through, darling. Try to abide with the feelings, and know that you're being shown something you've never seen before. Have faith that morning will come."

Stevie swayed as waves of despair washed over her. A dark night . . . on such a beautiful summer day. She loved and trusted her aunt too much to dispute anything she said. But she could hardly believe that the feelings would pass. Summer's colors seemed dim, gray, as they had when she went color-blind after her mother's death. She felt that at last, after so many illusory paths, she had found lasting love, happiness right on her doorstep . . . and that now it was gone forever.

Aunt Aida said a blessing in Gaelic, and then Stevie hung up and lay back down. Tilly lay on the bed beside her, stretched out against Stevie's right leg. Stevie petted her gently. She had had the cat for so long—truly, Tilly had been with her through it all. Stevie thought about what her aunt had said . . . to abide with the feelings. She looked across the room at her easel—and the blank paper. She knew she should work, but she couldn't. Her heart hurt so much.

She had received six postcards from Nell—one of Inverness Castle, on which she'd written, "The castle's nice, but not half as magical as Aunt Aida's!"—and one of Loch Ness. The rest had been from the Orkney Islands, where her father had taken her on business, and Nell's messages had duly reported on the sand, seaweed, and shells.

Last week she had received a note from Jack.

"We're settling in—sort of," he wrote. "How are things with Aida, and setting up the foundation? I've jumped right into the job—designing bridges to connect refineries to other outposts in the Orkneys, mainly occupied by people involved in North Sea oil development. Nell let me know how she feels about it by cutting a picture out of the paper of ducks killed in an oil spill—in the town to be served by my first bridge. The poor birds were covered in black crude, and Nell drew a balloon over their heads with the words, 'Stevie, write your next book about how oil kills ducks!' Nine years old, and she's already an activist. I know she misses you."

She had first focused on the photo—which he had enclosed in the letter. She had seen all too many pictures like this—waterfowl tarred by spilled oil, unable to fly or escape, sometimes held down in the water until they drowned. When she was a child, such pictures had made her sad—now they made her angry.

During other difficult periods of her life, she had used her work to get through. Each of her divorces had been so painful, and she'd survived each by doing another book—and by falling in love again. Even the breakups had been charged with a sort of raw energy— that had driven her to her easel. She hadn't succumbed to depression then—so why should she now?

Outside the window, the brilliant light of Hubbard's Point seemed to explode. It bounced off the water and white sand. The flowers in the backyard absorbed the light, gave it back. The light of Hubbard's Point was rare, incredible—especially from Stevie's house on the hill. It was as if her parents had chosen this location with the knowledge that their daughter would become an artist.

Through all her summers here, the wild light had inspired her to go forward—but today she turned away from it, her back to the window. The darkness inside was weighing her down, and she couldn't fight it—even the brilliant sunshine couldn't penetrate.

When the phone rang, Stevie almost didn't answer it. Who could it be, that she would want to talk to?

Tilly just lay there, inert and uninterested. Stevie listened to the ringing—five times, six—and then she reached over to pick up.

"Hello?" she said.

She swore she heard the whole Atlantic Ocean passing over the line, announcing the caller's great distance . . . a time lag, and then a madly exuberant voice: "Stevie! It's *me*!"

"Nell!" Stevie said, sitting bolt upright.

"Did you get my postcards?"

"I did—I love them."

"I've been on beach patrol . . . every chance I get, I make my dad drive me to a new one. There are lots of them here."

"Well, Scotland has a lot of coastline," Stevie said.

"Did you like what I reported, on the weird shells and the eelgrass?"

"Yes—excellent reporting, Ms. Kilvert."

Nell giggled, and the sound was so tender and familiar, Stevie felt it in her ribs, her collarbones, her heart.

"The Isle of Harris is supposed to have pink sand and palm trees—we're going there soon. Not for business, but for a fun weekend," Nell said, sounding so excited that Stevie actually felt her heart fall. *Come on—pull yourself together for her,* she told herself.

"My father's been working himself to death," Nell continued. "He does nothing but toil at his drafting table! I have to remind him to eat. It's a nightmare."

Stevie smiled at the expression, then asked, "And what about you? Have you seen your school yet? Met your teacher?"

"Uh-huh, Dad's going to have to travel all the time, so he found me a tutor. She's nice. Miss Robertson. I showed her your book."

"You did?"

"She saw the dedication and said that you and I must be really good friends."

"We are," Stevie said. "Maybe you can tell her about the real-life hummingbirds. . . ."

"I will," Nell said. "I miss you."

"Oh, I miss you, too, Nell."

They were silent for a few seconds. Stevie wondered whether Jack was standing there.

"I wish I were back there, at Hubbard's Point," Nell said.

"The beach will always be here, Nell. Whenever you come back," Stevie said, welling up with tears.

"I know," Nell said.

"Keep up the beach girl reports," Stevie said. "They're really great."

"I will," Nell said. "Are they really helping?"

"They really are," Stevie assured her. Another long minute of silence stretched out, and then Nell said a soft goodbye and hung up.

Stevie lay back on her pillow, holding the phone. The dial tone rang in her ears. If she closed her eyes, she could almost see Nell: her green eyes, short brown hair, big smile. She could almost see Jack walking up the hill behind her, on the way to visit. She could almost hear their voices . . .

But it was just the dial tone. The strange thing about a phone call like the one she'd just had was that it made her loneliness even deeper. She thought of her aunt's words: *Abide with the feelings as long as you can.* It seemed almost unbearable.

Tilly lay motionless, lost in a dream. Closing her eyes, Stevie tried to hold on to the sound of Nell's voice, that she'd heard just a few minutes earlier, and the sound of Jack's, that she'd heard weeks before. But the voices were already gone. . . .

JACK WAS swept up in the whirl of moving to a foreign country, getting Nell settled, and starting a new job. The relocation department at IR—the engineering firm was named for its founder, Ivan Romanov—had found Jack and Nell a house on the outskirts of Inverness, in the shadow of the Western Highlands. It was an old vicarage, built of river stone, dating back to the 1600s.

Nell's first impression had imprinted itself on his memory—she'd been overtired from the flight, hungry because she hadn't liked the food on the plane, sullen because she had set the alarm on her watch to beep at exactly three o'clock every day—the precise moment she had said goodbye to Stevie and Peggy—and it had just beeped.

They had climbed out of the airport taxi, stood on the sidewalk in front of the bleak, imposing gray manor. Although Georgian, elegant in design, something about it seemed institutional.

"What is this?" Nell asked quietly.

"It's our house," he said.

They were met at the door by Ms. Dancy Diarmud,

the IR relocation liaison. She was about thirty-five, very pretty, trim in a cherry red wool suit. Bright and friendly, she greeted them warmly.

"Welcome to Scotland," she said, shaking hands. "Mr. Kilvert."

"Jack," he said. "And this is Nell."

Dancy smiled, and led them through the first floor—a living room, dining room, parlor, chapel, kitchen, pantry, and what she called "the flower-arranging room—the vicar's wife often prepared the funeral arrangements." Nell gave Jack a brooding look. Although numerous, the rooms were small, the ceilings low. There were front stairs, curving up from a narrow hall, and back stairs, proceeding up, steep and vertical, in what Dancy called "the stair closet," from the kitchen.

She walked them through the bedrooms—six of them. There was a sameness to rental property, Jack thought. No matter how expensive looking the sofas or beds or paintings were, they had a soullessness to them—as if they were never meant to be lived with for long. They were like the one-night stands of furniture. He thought of Stevie's lived-in house, with so much of her present in every inch, and his chest hurt.

JACK GOT SETTLED at work. IR had planned a series of cocktail parties, to introduce him to the other engineers and the clients—oil executives based in London, Moscow, and Houston.

The production schedule was intense—he had to

visit the Orkney Islands, to see the sites where his bridges would be built—stone spans pleasing to the islanders, yet rugged enough to accommodate the refinery traffic currently handled by ferry boats. Luckily there was no shortage of extraordinary beaches for Nell to visit.

The chain of seventy islands stretched north from the northernmost point of mainland Scotland. A short flight from Inverness landed them on Ladapool, one of only seventeen inhabited islands. The landscape was wild and mystical, all sea and sky, with sites of ancient cairns and standing stones, reminding him of the Scottish trip he'd taken with his family, of how Madeleine had been so intrigued by the power and magic of standing stones.

Unfortunately, just around the corner from some of the most spectacular bays were Brooks Oil refineries, tankers waiting to offload—offshore at anchor, supply ships clogging docks, and parking lots lined with oil trucks. Jack couldn't help thinking of the photo Nell had cut out of the newspaper . . . and of the book she wanted Stevie to write about birds affected by the oil spills.

Nell came along on the trips. While Jack walked the road, talked with other engineers, viewed the site plans, she did her schoolwork with Miss Robertson. During free time, she scurried down the roadside to the beach—a long stretch of pebbly sand along a glassy-smooth protected cove. The shape reminded Jack of Hubbard's Point—a half-moon bay, embraced by headlands. He could almost see where the raft should be, the raft where he and Stevie had made love . . .

He forced his attention back to the other IR engineers while Nell collected shells. When she was finished, she came up to stand beside him—with eyes steady and grave.

"What's wrong?" he asked her when he had a break.

"Nothing," she said.

"You look upset."

"I'm just thinking," she said. "Trying to memorize everything about the beach. So I can report to the beach girls."

"Ahh," Jack said. He reached into his pocket, gave her a small notepad and his fountain pen. He didn't have to tell her how precious the pen was—it had been his college graduation present from his sister.

"What're these for?" Nell asked.

"For taking notes. So you don't forget anything that you might want to tell the beach girls."

She'd solemnly nodded her thanks. Then, while the other engineers resumed conferring about the bridge, she'd scrambled back down to the beach.

"So," said Victor Buchanan, a senior IR engineer. He was tall and burly, red-cheeked, with shaggy gray hair. Jack knew that he was one of Ivan Romanov's top people—he had signed off on hiring Jack. "Do you always bring your daughter on-site?"

"Yes," Jack said.

"A good nanny would help you with that."

"We have a tutor. And I want Nell with me."

Victor and two of the others laughed—Leo Derr, a

young, clean-cut Englishman, and April Maguire, a smart American woman, an MIT and Structural alum, just like Jack. He had worked with her many times—she had been instrumental in setting up interviews directly with Romanov himself. The laughter seemed good-natured; so Jack smiled.

"She doesn't get in the way of my work," Jack said to the others, standing on the road in Ladapool.

"We were just thinking of your social life!" April said.

"She basically is my social life," Jack said, smiling wryly.

"Well, we have a good old time," Victor said. "To-night we'll be heading off to the Golden Peat—it's a place for tasting scotch from all the distilleries around here. Single malts . . . not a place for a wee one!"

Jack shrugged, trying to look disappointed. The truth was, he wanted as much of his free time as possible to be Nell-centered. She'd been shaky ever since arriving in Scotland. Her nightmares were back—Dr. Galford had given him a name in Inverness, and he knew he had to call. Now she wasn't just crying for Emma—she was crying for Stevie, Peggy, and Madeleine, too. How could he have taken what had already felt awful and made it this much worse?

"You'll want to find yourself some good child care before next month," April said quietly, when the others resumed looking at plans. Jack wondered about the twinkle in her eyes.

"Why?" he asked.

"Well, because we're getting another team member."

Jack had heard rumors that Ivan himself was planning

to oversee this project. The Brooks Oil Company was one of the firm's biggest clients, and he wanted to make sure the bridge was built on time and under budget.

"Ivan?" he said.

April waved her hand, laughing. "No. If it were Ivan, you'd be so busy, we probably wouldn't be heading off to the Golden Peat. Someone else. A 'hired gun,' just like you used to be . . . we're subcontracting part of this job back to your old company."

"Structural?" Jack asked, his heart kicking over.

April nodded, smiling wider as if she'd heard company rumors. "Exactly. Francesca is coming on board."

As everyone went back to work, he glanced over at Nell, combing the beach. One hand cupped, she filled it with shells and pebbles. Occasionally she'd transfer them into her pocket and sit down to take notes, intense and focused.

His daughter was taking Stevie's assignment very seriously. He could almost picture Madeleine at the same age, walking on other Scottish coastlines, collecting impressions to share with her best friends. Jack remembered seeing her at a desk in the hotel, bent over postcards, writing ferociously.

He had felt strangely envious—he'd realized that he'd never had friends he felt that passionately about, to interrupt his holiday and to sit down and write anything. Yet Maddie had done it . . . and Nell was doing it now, her posture an uncanny echo of her aunt's. The funny thing was, they'd both written to the same woman: Stevie.

He stared at his Nell, huddled over the notepad,

scribbling furiously. Was she reporting about the rock-iness of the beach, the dark gray color of the clouds, the chill in the salt air, the wind blowing straight off the sea? As it happened, they were on the west side of an isthmus, connecting two parts of a narrow island halfway up the archipelago. To the east, he could see the North Sea. But if he looked west, he could see the North Atlantic—a straight shot to North America.

Hubbard's Point was out there somewhere, Jack thought. If Stevie was walking on her beach, they could almost see each other. Almost.

If there weren't three thousand miles of ocean be-tween them.

He looked at Nell again, wondered what she was writing. Would Stevie share Nell's thoughts with that other loyal beach girl?

Would Stevie send Nell's cards on to Maddie?

What are you doing here? he asked himself, not for the first time—not even for the hundredth time—since ar-riving in Scotland. Meeting Stevie had done something to him: it had stopped him in his tracks, unhooked him from the cycle he'd invented, of running and hat-ing and hiding—from his sister, from their tragedy.

From the truth.

The wind blew into Jack's eyes, making them sting and water. He turned away, back to his colleagues, back to the comparatively simple chore of building a four-lane bridge to replace the old cart path inclined to flood at high tide.

chapter 24

NELL FINISHED HER SCHOOLWORK, then ran down to sit on a driftwood log.

Her father and the other engineers were trying to figure out how to build a bridge pretty enough for the islanders and practical enough for the oil company to get their trucks back and forth from the refinery. Nell knew her father didn't think she paid attention to his work, but she did. She cared about the bridges he built. She cared about every single thing he did.

Her notebook was getting filled with lots of things. She took notes about the cold water, silvery driftwood, channeled whelks, and tiny clam shells. She took off her shoes to feel the water temperature and wrote: *cold!* When birds flew overhead, she shielded her eyes from the sun and viewed their shapes. Then she tried to draw outlines on the page.

This beach, like others she and her father had visited in the islands, was covered with large smooth stones and small pebbles. Some of the stones were black, and looked gnarled—like walnuts. The first time she picked one up, her fingers got all greasy. When she tried to wash them, the grease just got stickier.

Her father had been standing with Mr. Buchanan and Mrs. Maguire. When Nell had run up, to show her father, Mr. Buchanan had grimaced and rolled his eyes. "The downside of this particular project," he said, offering Nell his handkerchief. Nell was confused, especially when Mrs. Maguire told him to put his nice linen hanky away and pulled out a small foil-wrapped square instead. She said to Nell's father, "You'll need to lay in a stock of these if she's going to roam the beach."

Nell's father took the square, tore it open, and wiped Nell's fingers clean. Their eyes met, and her father smiled his reassurance.

"What is it?" Nell asked.

"Oil," Mr. Buchanan said. "Brooks has very sophisticated cleanup measures, but some always manages to slip through the booms."

"Oil? Like the kind that killed the birds?" Nell asked, squinting at her father. He nodded, but with a look in his eyes that told her to drop it. The other adults were saying something about scientists washing the birds with special soap so they could fly safely away, but all Nell could picture was their slick, black, dead bodies in that newspaper photo, and she knew that the adults were just telling a story to make everyone feel better.

Nell felt worse. How could they think that special soap could make everything okay? Her fingers still smelled like gas. Her eyes teared up to think of birds having such a gross film on their feathers.

Now, casting a look back over her shoulder, she set off down the beach. Cool, clear sunlight sparked on the cove. The rocky beach was hard to walk on, but she made her way slowly, looking down at her feet for shells. Up ahead were a flock of gulls, pecking at something that had washed up. As Nell approached, the birds wheeled away—her ears rang with their mournful cries.

Nell could see that whatever they'd been feeding on was dead, lying inert in the rocks. When she got close, she saw that it was a duck, sticky with tar, its side freshly torn open by the gulls. She raised her eyes, saw other ducks with similar markings swimming in the cove. The duck's family, she thought, thinking of Ebby—of how his fellow crows had gathered outside Stevie's house. Not even thinking, she jumped to her feet and began to madly wave her arms—to drive the ducks away.

"Leave here," she cried out. "Go away . . . fly!"

She wanted them to be safe, not get stuck in the oil that had killed the duck that lay at her feet. And as she watched them dance across the water's surface, striving toward flight, their webbed feet slapping the waves, she imagined them lifting her up with them, flying her away—to safety, to love, to Hubbard's Point. Surely her father would have to follow her if she left . . . he would understand how much she needed to go home, back to America, back to her real life.

"I'll be like you," she wept to the dead bird. She felt

choked, as if she had swallowed a ball of tar, as if her feathers were all stuck together by a substance that wanted to kill her. She felt almost the way she had back in Georgia, right after her mother's death; as if life was unreal, as if she didn't belong with the living anymore.

She had felt that way until Hubbard's Point, until Stevie. The strange thing was, she knew her father had felt it, too. . . . She wouldn't want her father to know this, but since leaving Stevie and Hubbard's Point, her nightmares had changed.

This time, it wasn't her mother who was dead: it was her father. He was giving up on all the things he loved— his homeland, his sister, his memories. Even, in Nell's dreams, Stevie. Flying away from Stevie, her father had left something that had made him seem alive again. . . .

She glanced down the beach—her father was still standing with the others, half-watching her.

He couldn't imagine, looking at her, that inside she felt as horrible as this oil-blackened bird. Just then, her attention was drawn to some other things caught in the clump of seaweed. A snippet of fishing net, covered with the same oil. A tangle of kelp, a small colony of mussels torn from some rocks, still held together by their silken threads. And a bottle . . .

Nell reached for it. It was clear plastic, had once held soda. Although most of the label had come off, she recognized the brand. It was American . . . maybe it had floated across the ocean, riding the currents. . . .

And suddenly, Nell had an idea. She unscrewed the cap, wiped her hands on her jeans, reached for her notebook, and pulled the top of her father's fountain pen off. The gulls were circling overhead. Ignoring them, Nell began to write.

"Stevie," she wrote. "We need you. My dad and I. We need you. . . ."

Tearing the paper from the pad, she rolled it up and edged it into the neck of the bottle. She didn't actually believe that the bottle would make it to Hubbard's Point—or even out of this cove. She couldn't let herself imagine the miracles it would take to get her message all the way from Scotland to Stevie.

But she thought back to those last minutes with Peggy, when they'd wished, wished, with all their might. . . . A message in a bottle was really just a wish . . . a wish pulled from the air, or from a girl's heart, and written down and set upon the sea. It's just a wish, Nell told herself. That's all it is: *just a wish*.

Just a wish . . . if it came true, Nell knew that she and her father would go back to Hubbard's Point; her father would work on Aunt Aida's castle; Stevie would be in their lives; and Stevie would make sure Aunt Madeleine was, too. . . .

"It's just a wish," Nell whispered out loud.

Even so, her heart was pounding—in a way that told her the wish was about to become a hope, which was one step closer to becoming real. Stevie, the non-witch, would understand, and so would Tilly. Nell wound up, stepped into the throw, and with a cry let the plastic bottle sail into the air. The glaring sunlight blinded her, so she couldn't even see where it landed.

There it was—shielding her eyes with one hand, she saw the bottle bobbing out where the birds had been swimming. Was it heading for America, or back onto the beach? Nell stared at it for a long time, feeling her heart beat in her throat. It seemed to be drifting out . . . she watched it go.

The gulls screeched louder, trying to drive her away from the ravaged duck. Intent and driven, she found a spot above the tide line and dug a hole in the rocky sand as deep as her arms could reach. Then she walked back and picked up the bird. Putting its body in the hole, she felt a terrible tug in her chest. She slowly rubbed her tarry hands in the sand, trying to get them clean. Burying the bird made her think of how beautiful things died. Her mother. And her father's spirit, her own heart.

They died, and there was nothing Nell could do about it.

Except send a message in a bottle, and wish and wish, and ask Stevie for help.

NELL'S WISH flew like an arrow.

Stevie woke with a start and a spark, fresh from a dream. In it, the room was filled with blinding light, so bright she could hardly see. Through the glare, a black bird sang in a cage. Somehow, the way mysteries in dreams take on strange, crystal-clear meanings, Stevie knew that she had to open the cage door. When she did, the bird flew out. It landed on the windowsill, and Stevie heard it talking, like a parrot. It said, "If you let me go, you may never see me again. But that depends on you . . . because you have wings, too. You can find me and fight for me." And then it had flown away.

Stevie had opened her eyes. She didn't really analyze the dream; she wasn't good at such things. But it had created a powerful feeling inside that she wanted to hold on to. The black bird, the cage, the flying away . . . It might have seemed oppressive, hopeless, but instead, the dream spurred Stevie to get out of bed and go for an early swim.

The sun was up above the trees, but the day was September-chilly. She dove in, swam out to the raft. Resting there, she placed her hand flat on the surface—where she and Jack had lain. The memory came back to her. She closed her eyes and could almost feel his arms around her. As a young woman, that was all she had ever wanted: to have someone hold her and never let go, to be as much a part of her as her own breath.

Of course such loves were impossible, could never last. She had proved that to herself three times. It was as if some primal, preverbal Stevie had taken command of her adult heart, demanded the closeness she had only ever really known from her parents.

But now she was a grown-up. She had fallen in love again, and why bother telling herself it didn't matter? It did. She'd been in despair because they had flown away, and she'd felt powerless to do anything except let them go. The dream was still with her, churning inside like crazy.

By the time she swam back to the beach, walked up the hill, and rinsed off at the outside shower, she felt the fire inside. The scent of late-summer roses filled the air. She toweled off, ran barefoot into the house. She filled Tilly's bowl, didn't even stop to make herself coffee, and hurried up to her studio.

When she entered the room, it was like reentering her dream: the room was blazing with sunlight. The light of Hubbard's Point . . . undimmed, luminous, radiant, gleaming, glistening, glittering, scintillating, shimmering, glowing . . . surrounding her with its brilliance, almost blinding her as she approached her easel.

Stevie had thrown all Nell's postcards in her bedside drawer. She now got them out, thumbtacked them to the wall beside her easel. There were postcards of Inverness Castle, Loch Ness, a puffin in the Orkney Islands, low mountains ringing a sea loch, a baby seal on a rock in Ladapool, and a flock of geese silhouetted by orange sunset on a bay in the Western Highlands—and the newspaper photo from Jack's letter, of the waterfowl killed by the oil spill.

Stevie stood by her easel now, pulling on clothes. She dressed in jeans and the Trinity College sweatshirt Jack had worn to the beach movie. Tilly lay on the bed's rumpled white sheets, soaking up the sun, watching her mistress. Staring at the gallery of cards and picture, through the incredible brightness, Stevie felt the stirrings of a new book—and so much more.

Her house was filled with light. She suddenly saw herself—on a journey her whole life, a circuitous and sometimes even tormented route in search of love that could make her whole. . . . All that time, and just this morning, she had finally realized that the journey led to the light inside. Where she *was* whole: she had her house, her painting, her stories, and her dreams. She had let Jack and Nell go, because they had had to. But she had wings, too.

She thought of her dream and knew that this was worth fighting for, worth flying after. Mixing paints, she peered at the photo Jack had sent her, of dead and dying oil-soaked birds. Nell's words glimmered above them. Stevie already had a title in mind: *The Day the Sea Turned Black*.

She thought of the black bird in her dream, saw the crude-soaked creatures in the news photo. She thought of all the seabirds she could paint: kittiwakes, black guillemots, puffins, razorbills, storm petrels, Manx shearwaters, mallards, teals, widgeons, goldeneyes, oystercatchers, curlews, sandpipers, arctic skuas, gannets, red-breasted mergansers, eider ducks, and great northern divers.

But, because Nell had asked that the book be about ducks, Stevie decided on mallards. She checked a field guide to confirm their range—yes, they inhabited the Scottish highlands. And then, with swift brushstrokes, Stevie created a pair of waterfowl. Their story was already unfolding in her mind. The book would be set in Scotland—on a small island halfway up the Orkney archipelago. She envisioned the clear northern light, the boreal fire, the dark reflective sea. She saw the mallards—their green neck feathers iridescent. There would be a young girl who walked the beach . . .

That was all Stevie knew, for now. The story would unfold from her paintbrush and Nell's postcards. She wet her brush, and got to work.

chapter 25

MADELEINE'S WORK WITH DR. MAL-
lory was arduous, enlightening, exhausting,
and illuminating. She was forty-four years
old, and she really felt that she was getting to know herself for the first time. She had been stuck in the emotional horror of the accident, living it over and over in
nightmares and flashbacks. Facing Jack had broken
something open inside, given her so much strength
and hope, a desire to get better quickly.

Gently, Dr. Mallory introduced Maddie to the idea
that she was suffering from PTSD—post-traumatic
stress disorder. It was a paradox: she was completely
gripped by memories and sensations of the accident,
and she also completely blanked it out. Both states
were equally real and true to her.

"I can't feel my body," Maddie said quietly one day,
admitting that it had been months since she and Chris
had made love.

"Tell me about that," the doctor said.

"I'm just not there," she said. "There are days when the only thing I can feel is my scar—throbbing pain. It's as if that's the only part of me that exists. I love my husband, but I can't let him touch me." She wished she could describe how numb and terrified she always felt.

She had missed so much work at the Brown Development Office that her boss had suggested she take a leave of absence—or lose her job entirely. So she took the leave.

After several talk sessions, during which Madeleine found it impossible to access memories—and, in any case, too painful to describe the accident—Dr. Mallory had suggested they try EMDR—Eye Movement Desensitization and Reprocessing. It was a treatment so simple, Madeleine couldn't believe it would work.

But she knew how much her life had changed since the accident. She had become so withdrawn, like a recluse. Chris was patient, but she knew that he wanted his old Madeleine back—and so did she. Maddie missed herself.

She'd sit on the sofa in the doctor's office, and Dr. Mallory would sit opposite her, in her chair. The lights were dim. The doctor would hold up her hand, two fingers extended, telling Madeleine to focus. And then Dr. Mallory would start to move her hand rapidly, back and forth, while Madeleine stared at her fingers.

Somehow the rapid eye movement replicated REM sleep. The doctor reminded Madeleine to breathe steadily, pay attention to sensations in her body. Almost immediately, Maddie felt pain in her shoulder, twinges in the side of her head, a sensation of fire in her chest, and the sense of sand draining through her torso. The feelings grew stronger, dissipated, left Madeleine feeling drained—and then, suddenly, revived.

When she left the office the first time, she felt more alert and alive than she had in longer than she could remember. The second time, she felt the same mysterious twinges and roaring pains, and she ended the session with sobs—and the memory of holding Emma with one arm while her other arm hung by a thread.

Dr. Mallory told her that trauma is stored in the body's cells and in the deepest regions of the brain, deep, deep inside—beyond thinking and understanding—the more primitive regions.

EMDR unlocked those places, and enabled Madeleine to bring the memories up and out . . . and in doing so, she began to have new insights into what had happened. As Dr. Mallory's articles said, humans—like all animals—have strongly developed "fight or flight" responses. Their cells are programmed to react—to run, fight, or freeze—when confronted with threats to life or safety.

When those responses were blocked—with Madeleine unable to stop her own car accident or save Emma's life—the thwarted defensive reactions got stuck inside her nervous system. All this time she'd been physically trapped, paralyzed in a state of physiological readiness to fight or flee from the accident that had happened over a years ago—unable to handle her own life.

The sessions brought up shocking memories—of the blood, the pain, Emma's screams. They released pent-up rage—at the ambulance crew, for being unable to free Emma for so long, while her blood gushed out—

and at Emma herself, for having confessed her secret to Madeleine, and then leaving her behind to deal with it.

"I'm taking the blame for what she did," Madeleine said. "She left me to tell my brother, and now he blames me—as if I did it instead of Emma!"

"And how does that make you feel?" Dr. Mallory asked, as she so often did.

"Angry . . . at him for blaming me . . . and for keeping me from Nell—over a year has passed without my seeing her! She's moved away. She's grown taller, she's a whole grade ahead in school, she's had a birthday, there's been a holiday season without her . . . she likes music I don't know about . . . books I'm not aware of . . . she has friends I'll never meet . . ."

"Never?" the doctor asked.

"I went to see him," Madeleine said. "And we couldn't even talk to each other."

"Well," the doctor said, her eyes lit from within, as if she knew something wonderful. "It was a start. And that is something to work with."

"None of this was my fault," Madeleine said.

"No—it wasn't," Dr. Mallory said.

"I don't want to blame Emma . . ."

"Perhaps you don't have to," Dr. Mallory said gently. "Perhaps the point of all this could be understanding— just that. Instead of the placement of blame."

"But my brother . . ." Maddie began.

"You can't change the way he feels," the doctor said. "But you can change the way you react to what he says and does. You have power over that, Madeleine. His emotions don't have to dictate your responses."

"But isn't it true—that it only takes one person in a family to bring about an estrangement?"

The doctor tilted her head and, after a moment, seemed to smile. "On the other hand," she said, "It only takes one person to reach out and try to bring the estrangement to an end. And you've already started to do that."

The statement was so true, and simple, and pure, that all Madeleine could do was take it in and start to smile back.

STEVIE'S NEW BOOK was coming out in a white heat. The story, of mallards living in a pristine environment threatened by oil pollution, flowed out—the necessary passion and emotion were there. She'd had a few false starts—should it be one catastrophic spill, like the Exxon *Valdez*, or just the slow destruction of wildlife due to a series of smaller, less publicized mishaps? Talking to her editor, she decided on the latter. Her readers, although young, loved nature and had always responded to how she dealt with difficult realities, the balancing act between human beings and fragile ecosystems.

So she painted a series of pages depicting bays and tidal pools, the mallards, a girl combing the beach, an oil refinery in the distance. She had Nell and the ducks down pat, but when it came to the setting, she felt she was coming up short. The landscape looked like Hubbard's Point. The inhabitants of the tidal pools were Hubbard's Point crabs, eels, starfish, and mussels.

In mid-September, she wrote a letter to Nell, saying,

"Now I *really* need the beach girl reports! I've taken your suggestion to heart, and have started writing a book called *The Day the Sea Turned Black,* inspired by the news clipping you gave your father. Your notes have been great, but I need them even more than ever, as precise as you can be . . . what exact varieties of shells, shorebirds, seaweed, etc., are there?"

One afternoon about a week after she'd sent the letter, she went over to Aunt Aida's to check on the progress. Her aunt was working madly, trying to finish up her last *Beach Series* canvas for the show in October. Aida-with-a-Purpose was formidable indeed. A contractor had estimated repair costs to the castle would run about eight hundred thousand dollars, and Aida figured that if she sold every painting, she could donate almost half of the needed amount.

"I've never thought of you as painting for money," Stevie said, smiling as she watched her aunt work. Outside, the castle grounds were filled with pickup trucks, electricians' and glaziers' vans, and a backhoe. The staccato of power tools filled the air. Aida grinned ferociously.

"Just watch me," she said. "If this is what it takes to keep Van's dream intact, I'll do it."

"Really?"

"Yes. More than ever—I *have* to establish this place as a nature center in his memory. I want children to visit and know the beauty of the Connecticut shoreline that he so loved. I'm just so afraid I won't be able to pay for it."

"What does your lawyer say?"

"He set up the foundation—so we can raise money.

But I don't have the first idea of how to do that—all I know how to do is paint. He says we need someone who understands nonprofits, who can call on people with lots of money to donate."

"The kind of thing artists hate to do."

Aida nodded, focusing on her canvas. The dimensions were as large as ever—fifty-four by fifty-four inches, broad horizontal bands of color suggesting sea, sand, and sky. In that way, it was absolutely familiar. But as Stevie watched, she saw that her aunt was doing something very different: by stroking one translucent film of color over the next, she was actually mixing the paints on the canvas instead of on the palette.

"What are you doing?" Stevie asked, watching as she layered yellow over blue—sunlight on water—resulting in a passage of mysterious green.

"I'm letting the colors mix in the eyes of the viewer, instead of on the canvas."

"Have you ever done that before?"

"Never," she said, eyes narrowing with intensity. "It's a first. Complete shock to me. Innovation so thrilling even I'm stunned. . . ."

"Then why? How—now? Just when you're . . ."

"Selling out? Painting for commerce?" Aida laughed. "Dear girl, you of all people should know there's no such thing! Motivation is a gift, whatever it is. If it feeds your talent, then so be it. In my case, the motivation is love—for Van. In your case, it's love for . . ."

Stevie was silent, staring at her aunt's simple composition, the bands of thin, luminous color, listening to the saws whine and hum.

"I know about the letter you sent Nell."

"What letter?"

"The one asking about shore species in Scotland. For your new book. Jack told me that Nell is very excited about it."

Stevie listened, her heart thudding as she considered the fact that Jack and Aida had spoken again.

"You know why you set it in Scotland, don't you?"

Stevie did know, but she couldn't answer.

"Because you have to go there. You knew that you would have to travel to Scotland, to research your material. Just as you went to the polar ice, to research emperor penguins."

"I went to Antarctica with Linus," Stevie said. "My research trips have been a travelogue of marital failures."

"Sweet girl, why must you be so hard on yourself?"

"Love is too hard," Stevie said. The thought of flying to Scotland, getting Nell's hopes up about something, and then having things not work out with Jack was too devastating to contemplate.

"No," Aida said calmly, still painting. "Love is not hard. It's the easiest thing there is. It's the layers of doubt and fear and expectation that we layer on that makes it complicated. Just look at Henry and Doreen."

"I know." Stevie had gotten their wedding invitation—the ceremony would be held next Saturday in Newport, where they had met, where Henry had gone through Officer's Candidate School, and where they would live.

"Henry layered so much fear onto that situation that he almost lost her," Aida said. "You know, those weeks when he was staying in my guesthouse here, we had some good long talks. It just about broke my heart to see my big, strapping, fifty-something naval commander stepson sitting at my table with tears rolling down his cheeks . . . realizing that he was about to lose Doreen, just because he'd been so chicken."

"I never think of Henry as chicken," Stevie said, picturing him in his uniform.

"No, one wouldn't. But that was the case, nonetheless."

Stevie listened, thinking of how afraid she felt—much more of a coward than Henry could ever be. She called it self-protective, but it was the same thing. Or she told herself she was thinking of them—Jack and Nell. That she'd made so many mistakes, she didn't want to inflict her messy life on them.

"Love is not hard," Stevie said, echoing her aunt's words.

"No, it's not," Aida said. "It just takes care of itself, if you'll let it. We'll see the proof of that on Saturday, with Henry and Doreen at St. Mary's Church. If you believe in that kind of love, it can move heaven and earth."

"Like what you're doing with Uncle Van's castle," Stevie said, as the sounds of the backhoe moving earth and men reroofing the tower in the sky blasted through the cottage.

"Yes. Love," Aida said. "And, God willing, the help of a really, really good fund-raiser."

chapter 26

THE LADAPOOL TEAM WAS ALL geared up, trying to beat projections and get the project into the realm of the builders as soon as possible. They had taken a block of rooms at the Highlands Inn, one of the business hotels that had come to the Orkneys to serve the oil business.

Jack and Nell had a suite on the fourth floor, overlooking the site. Jack knew that his soul was in serious trouble—he knew it by the fact that he could look at the view from his window, over glassy bays, rock islands, distant mountains, and call it "the site." Nell did her schoolwork there; Miss Robertson came up for a few days every week.

During her free time, Nell pored over the field guides he had bought her, matching up shells, feathers, crustaceans, egg cases with names in the books. She wrote to Stevie as soon as she'd identified something new—which was every day.

Propped up on the bureau were two invitations that

had arrived in the mail—both from Aida. One was for the opening of her art show—a glossy card showing one of her translucent, meditative *Beach Series* paintings. The other was for her stepson Henry's wedding, which was going to be in Newport, Rhode Island, that Saturday.

"I want to go, Dad," Nell said one morning after they'd had breakfast. She sat at the desk by the room's window, drawing a picture of ducks she'd seen at dawn.

"Go where?"

"To the wedding."

"Nell, they only sent us an invitation to be polite."

"No they didn't! They want us there!"

"Nell—we hardly know Henry. I have the feeling that it's a small family wedding, and Aida just sent us the invitation to let us know about it."

"Aunt Aida wouldn't do that," Nell said. "Sending out invitations and hoping we don't come. Just so we'll send a present."

"That's not what I meant, honey—it's just that we're here in Scotland—three thousand miles away."

"We could get on a plane, couldn't we?"

"Nell, she doesn't expect us to fly all the way home for the wedding."

"You said it, Dad," Nell said, jumping up from the table. "You said 'home.'"

"I meant—"

"The United States is our home—not here. I miss it so much! I miss Peggy, and the beach, and Aunt Aida, and Tilly—and Dad, I miss Stevie!"

"I know . . ."

"And now Francesca is here. Right in our hotel, staying right across the hall!"

"We don't have to see her very much."

"You do. At work. She's a big intruder!"

"Sssh, Nell," Jack said quickly, wanting to calm her down before she got worked up into a full-blown attack. He reached for her, to hug her, but she wrenched herself away. Grabbing the invitation, she held it to her chest.

"We're invited—I want to go."

"It's too far. You know the kind of pressure I'm under to get this job done. Maybe when it's finished, we could talk about a visit home. Thanksgiving, or Christmas, maybe. Or even Aida's art show in October . . ."

"That's different," Nell said, her voice quavering. "That's something anyone can go to. Henry's wedding is special. Like you said, only family are invited. I want family, Dad!"

"You have me, honey."

"But I want other people, too," she said. "Don't you? We used to have so much. I had you and Mommy, and I had Aunt Maddie and Uncle Chris. . . . We had Stevie. . . . They're all gone!"

"Nell—" he said, grabbing for her, but she ran over to the window, leaned her head against the glass, and sobbed. Jack walked up behind her, his hands shaking. She seemed so wounded, he couldn't even bring himself to touch her shoulders.

"I'm not going anywhere," he said.

"But you might," she wept. "You leave when things get good. We had a place to live at Hubbard's Point, and we could have stayed longer . . . we went clamming and to the beach movies with Stevie . . . we were happy . . ."

"I know," he said, stunned by the truth of her words.

"I have an aunt who loves me, loves you, and you won't even talk to her. What if I did that to you, Dad? What if I got so mad at you that I never spoke to you again?"

"Nell, you're my daughter."

"She's your sister! That's what you do to the people who love you the most—you just leave them."

"I would never leave you, though—"

Nell sobbed and shook her head. "That's what you say now," she said. "But what if I do the one wrong thing that makes you so mad you hate me as much as you hate Aunt Maddie?"

"I *never* could hate you. And I don't hate her—I love her." The words' truth rang through him as he saw his sister standing by her car in the driveway at Hubbard's Point—the ten feet between them as hard to cross as a canyon.

He stared at the back of Nell's head. She wouldn't turn to look at him, even when he touched her hair.

THE PHONE RANG; April had heard Nell crying through the walls.

"I'm a mother," she said. "In-room movies work wonders as a bribe."

"I think we're past that," Jack said, frowning, watching Nell stand by the window, shuddering with silent, restrained sobs.

Leaving her there was excruciating, but he didn't have much choice. He, April, Victor, and the other engineers converged on the road. Some were surveying the lines, others observing as geologists took more tests of the bedrock, as oceanographers measured up from mean low tide. Jack walked down to the edge of the water, to sit on a rock, compile all his data, and try to compose himself. As soon as he went back to the room, he'd find the number Dr. Galford had given him.

Francesca, seeing him there, made her way down the sand. She swore, and Jack looked up. She wore high black boots, and the heels were sinking. Glancing at him, she gave a wry smile. It was their first private face-to-face meeting since she'd arrived the day before.

"I'm tempted to call you 'Benedict,' as in 'Arnold,' you defector."

"Well, you know how it is when an opportunity presents itself," Jack said. "You have to take it, or you lose it." The words rang in his ears, in a very different context.

"Ivan wanted you—that's for sure. He liked the work you did in Maine. Guess he thought you'd be more familiar with this rocky back-of-beyond backwater."

Jack chuckled, looking at her boots. Francesca was always more comfortable on city streets, strolling Boston's Newbury Street with her hair swinging and everyone's eyes on her.

"Okay, okay," she said, laughing. "I'd have been a disaster over here. My God, where do you get a good latte around here?"

"I guess you have to like tea," Jack said, thinking of the tea Stevie had served, and Aida . . .

Francesca rolled her eyes. She took a step closer to Jack and let her hand brush against his cheek. Their eyes met—her hair was long, dark blonde, swinging in front of her face, making her expression even more seductive.

"Have you noticed—aside from the fact that you've moved across the ocean—that things have changed?" she said.

"What things have changed?"

"Jack, we don't work for the same company anymore. We don't have the same . . . prohibitions."

Jack stared into her sultry eyes—expertly made up, along with the rest of her face. Her lips were so full, lined with subtle color. Jack thought of Stevie, the fact that he couldn't even imagine her in makeup, and looked away.

"There are different kinds of prohibitions," Jack said.

"None that matter," she said. "We had a good working relationship . . . and I know we could have more than that. Everyone here sees it—why do you think April put our rooms across the hall from each other?"

April might have been trying to help, Jack thought. But she didn't know the real story about any of it.

"It's romantic here," Francesca said. "Once you get past the lack of civilization. I mean, aside from the fact that the place is latte-challenged. I've heard you can see the Northern Lights . . . we could take a walk later, tonight."

"I have Nell," he said.

"I'll bet Nell would love to play some video games," Francesca said. "Or read one of her Stevie Moore books. . . ."

Jack's stomach flipped, just hearing her name.

"Nell's actually helping Stevie write one," Jack said. "About the birds here. And how they're threatened by oil spills."

"You're joking, right?"

"No, I'm not. Nell's upstairs, writing to her right now."

"About oil pollution?"

Jack gestured down at the tide line, where balls of black, oily tar had washed up with the seaweed. Francesca stared, then looked away quickly.

"Don't let Ivan hear you talking like this," Francesca warned. "He'll see it as subversive to the relationship he's built up with Brooks. Environmentalism is all well and good, if it doesn't interfere with his bottom line."

"Certain things are more important than bottom lines," Jack said.

Francesca laughed. "Coming from the man who left his job to work for IR—knowing they specialize in Scottish oil refinery sites—isn't that a little hypocritical?"

Jack felt stung by the words—reflecting on what Nell had said. He stared at a raft of birds, swimming in the bay. They were silhouetted by bright sun, with its low northern declination, painting the scenery with light. Light both illuminated and disguised, he thought— who knew what was happening beneath the surface?

"I don't know," he said. "Maybe it is."

"So quit, and I'll take your position!"

Jack didn't reply, just watched the birds. He turned around to look up at the hotel. The sun was hitting the front windows, but as he counted up from the ground, he saw his room, spotted Nell still standing there—watching him with Francesca.

"Look," Francesca said, pointing at the tidal pools. "Oil isn't the only pollutant. There's all sorts of other trash. Pieces of wood . . ."

"It's called driftwood," Jack said.

She shrugged. "Okay. So it's picturesque trash. But what about those Styrofoam cups, that Coke bottle?"

"They probably came from our team, standing up there on the road," Jack said, wading in to get them out of the seaweed. He tossed the garbage onto the sand, by the rock where he'd been sitting, and heard Francesca squeal.

"Look!" she said. "In the bottle—it's a message!"

Jack peered down at the beach—she was right. There was a piece of lined paper, all rolled up and stuck inside.

"We have to read it," Francesca said.

Jack unscrewed the cap, turned the bottle upside down, tapped the opening against his palm. The rolled-up paper came out easily. With Francesca watching, he read the message.

"What does it say?" Francesca asked. "Come on—you have to tell me! Is it from some shipwrecked sailor, waiting to be rescued?"

Jack didn't, or couldn't, speak. Francesca was half right—the message was from someone waiting to be rescued. His hands were trembling as he folded the message in half, stuck it into his breast pocket. Francesca was protesting, asking to see it, but he hardly heard her.

He was too busy staring up at his hotel window. The sun's glare was harsh, but through it he saw Nell leaning against the plate glass, hands held up against the huge pane. He couldn't see clearly, but he knew she was crying. He knew, because he'd read her message, and he felt like crying, too.

STEVIE TOOK it all in—every word her aunt had said, the sight of all that industry on Lovecraft Hill, her aunt's miraculous new painting style, and her words about fear. She held the conversation close, as something precious, as she decided what to do next. The September light poured into her studio, brighter than she'd ever seen it. Her mind was wild with ideas—so much so, she couldn't sleep or sit still. Some moments she felt she'd never see Jack or Nell again, filling her with despair. But then she'd start to work, enveloped by the golden beach light, and her heart would even out.

The next morning, Stevie had just gotten back home from her swim when the phone rang. Wrapped in a towel, and shivering in the autumn air, she ran to answer.

"Hello?" she said.

"Hi, Stevie—it's me."

"Maddie!"

"How are you?"

"I'm fine—how are you?"

"Better and better. Especially since getting your message about coming to Rhode Island."

Stevie had held back from calling her. Her feelings about the Kilvert family were very raw. She understood how hard the meeting between Jack and Maddie must have been, but she couldn't help feeling sad about it— because it seemed to have been the thing that had pushed him into leaving for Scotland. Not that Stevie blamed Maddie in any way—just that she missed Jack and Nell so much.

"It's a family wedding, this Saturday," Stevie said. "I'll be staying in Newport Friday and Saturday nights, and I was thinking maybe you could drive down and we could have either Friday dinner or Sunday brunch."

"How about Friday—I have so much to tell you, and the sooner the better. . . . But won't there be a rehearsal dinner you have to go to?"

"They've been rehearsing for this the last fifteen years," Stevie said with great fondness for Henry. "No, everything is very informal. I'll be completely free. Where should we meet? Someplace on the beach?"

"I was thinking the same thing," Madeleine said. "There's nothing like that in Newport proper, but just down Memorial Boulevard, there's a little place on Easton's Beach. It's called Lilly Jane's, right on the boardwalk. She serves the freshest fish in town, and the key lime pie is great."

"As long as we can take a walk on the sand together," Stevie said.

"Yes," Maddie said.

"And hear the waves . . ."

Even now, after all that had happened, she knew they could rely upon the beach to make things all right.

"When you put it that way," Madeleine said, "who cares about food?"

"I know," Stevie said softly. "The important thing is to see you. That's what matters."

chapter 27

EVEN IN SEPTEMBER, NEWPORT WAS a bustling town. Boats preparing to go south for the winter lined the docks or rocked on moorings, white hulls flashing in the sunlight. The harbor hotels were all booked with people wanting one more weekend, one last Saturday night dining out under the summer stars.

Aunt Aida had taken a block of rooms at Maplehurst Manor, an old Victorian house at the foot of Dresser Street. It had wide, graceful porches, many chimneys, and ten venerable Chinese maple trees shading the yard, in homage to the sea captain who had plied the China trade and built the house in the nineteenth century.

The blue clapboard inn stood at the beginning of Cliff Walk, the spectacular ten-mile path high above the sea that skirted Newport's cliffs and mansions. Easton's Beach curved out on the left, its silver sands glistening as long, white-topped waves rolled in from the ocean. Sitting in rocking chairs on the front porch, Stevie and Henry listened to the soothing sound of the waves, keeping each other company. According to Aida, Henry had been up most of the night before, throwing up.

"Are you feeling better?" Stevie asked, giving him an amused, but concerned, look.

"I am, Lulu. Thanks for asking. Don't know what got into me."

"Could it have been a few too many bourbons?"

"Ha-ha—very funny. My bachelor party was that in name only—a bunch of long-married, retired sailors, half of them in AA. We went to the Officer's Club and tried to reminisce about the wild times we'd had in Phuket and Hong Kong, but wound up talking about grandchildren and the thrills of paying off mortgages. It was pathetic."

"So what made you so sick?" Stevie asked.

Henry rocked in his rocking chair. He gazed out to sea with stern eyes and weathered cheeks. This was a man who had steered a frigate through battle, who had once dived into the shark-infested waters of the Persian Gulf to rescue a sailor who'd been knocked unconscious and fallen overboard. Stevie loved him as if he were her own brother.

"Don't tell anyone this, okay?" he asked.

"I promise."

"I've sailed a lot of seas. You know that."

"I do."

"This is the part no one knows: whenever we'd leave port, steaming away from whatever dock we were at, through the harbor, past all the small craft . . . everything would be fine. I'd be right as rain."

"Commander Von Lichen," Stevie said.

"Damn straight. But as soon as we'd hit the sea buoys—"

"What are they?"

"Well, basically, the sea buoy lets you know you're leaving inland waters and saying hello to the open ocean. It's where the sea starts getting rough, where the ship starts rocking and rolling."

"Okay."

"Anyway, we'd hit the sea buoys—I'd get fucking horribly, apocalyptically seasick. That's just not supposed to happen, you know? I'm career Navy. I've got my sea legs. The ship's mine—and I'm downwind or in the head booting."

"Well, it happens," Stevie said, smiling.

"No, Lulu—it doesn't. Not to me. It's embarrassing. The seasickness didn't last or anything—it wasn't a cruise-long phenomenon. It would come on like a typhoon, I'd get it over with, and the feeling would pass. But even so, there's a ship code—the officers don't get seasick. I mean, I'm a commander. The crew takes orders from me. They see me meeting Ralph when the sailing gets rough, my authority goes down the drain. So I made sure no one saw. Over twenty years, not one person ever knew."

"I guess that was the manly way, Henry," Stevie said. "Being so brave and stoic. What would you have done if some poor deckhand had seen you?"

"I'd have had to kill him," Henry said without smiling.

"And here I am, asking you about getting sick last night. Am I in danger of being offed?"

"Nah, Lulu. We're beyond secrets. Here we are, a couple of old hands—we've been through a lot together. So I know I can tell you—last night I felt as seasick as I've ever been, and I wasn't even on a ship. My knees went all rubber, my insides were flipping out. It was bad."

"Well, what did you expect?"

"Huh?"

"You hit the sea buoys," Stevie said, with the sure knowledge of a veteran. "The sea buoys of love. You're getting married tomorrow."

"Blow me down," Henry said. "You think that's it?"

"Hell, yes. Your body knows that everything is about to change. You're sailing into the high seas, my boy."

"You've been through it," he said. "Three times."

Stevie cringed. She was about to say "Don't remind me," but instead, she stopped to think. Yes, she had been through it three times. Sitting here on the porch with Henry, she felt his excitement, anticipation, and trepidation. Tonight was his wedding eve. Stevie closed her eyes, remembered how on each of her wedding eves, she had believed so completely, wholeheartedly, in what she'd been about to do, in the voyage she was about to embark upon. Had she been wrong—just because they hadn't worked out? Even now, she wasn't sure . . .

"What can you tell me about it?" Henry asked.

Stevie reached between their rocking chairs. She

took his hand and squeezed it. "That your fear is real . . . and it's not unfounded."

"Shit. Thanks, Lulu."

She held his hand a little tighter. "It's there for a reason, Henry," she said. "The reason you got seasick, I'll bet, was that your instincts were kicking in, your body telling you something. Before you became a big, decorated naval commander, you were a person, a man, a little boy. Deep inside, beneath the bravery, is a desire for self-preservation. . . . You probably felt the waves getting bigger, and part of you wanted to fight against the possibility of being swallowed up."

"You're telling me marriage swallows you up?"

Stevie tilted her head, thinking back. The funny thing was, her memories of the past were being washed out by her feelings about Jack and Nell. "In a way, it does," she said. "It consumes you with desire, concern, love. . . . As close as you start to feel to the person, you long for even more closeness. At least, I did. Suddenly you're thinking about someone else's wants and needs . . . and if you're not careful, you forget that you have your own."

"What if it's the opposite?" Henry asked. "And I'm just a big selfish jerk who always wants to watch football and forgets our anniversary?"

"Doreen will take care to not let that happen," Stevie said, smiling. "She's got your number."

"I'm worried about last night. Getting sick like that. What if it means I'm not suited for marriage, and—like you said—my body knows it? Rejecting the whole thing, just like a body spitting out a transplant heart? One big physical revolt?"

"I think it's just like your first day at sea. Seasickness hits you once, and then it's all over. You panic a little, and then you remember that you're in the Navy, you've got your sea legs, you've ridden through hurricanes and come back to tell the story. That's all—one moment of fear, and then a great voyage."

"I nearly lost her," Henry said.

Stevie nodded. She looked into his eyes and saw regret, sorrow, relief.

"But you didn't lose her," Stevie said. "When you think about it, you found her."

"I want that for you, Lulu. I think you've finally found—"

Stevie put up her hand. It hurt too much to hear him say anything about Jack. She knew that Aunt Aida had sent Jack and Nell an invitation—along with sheaves of information about the castle project, the foundation incorporation, the construction report. Of course he had declined—Aida had reported this to Stevie with such somber disappointment, Stevie had wound up comforting *her*.

"This is your wedding," Stevie said, patting Henry's arm. "Let's just focus on you, okay? I'm so happy for you."

"I couldn't have gotten here without you," he said.

"Well, that's nice to hear, but I think you could. Doreen would have seen to it. Now . . . I'd better get ready for dinner. I'm meeting my friend right down there—in an hour." She stood and pointed down at the beach pavilion. People were already starting to gather on the terrace.

"Have fun," Henry said. "Aida told me your friend is the sister of—"

"Yes, but mainly she's my friend. One of my best, oldest friends," Stevie said hurriedly, to cut him off.

"That's love, too," Henry said, and Stevie had to smile.

"You really *have* changed," she said. "You're a renaissance commander."

"You've changed, too," he said. "No more Luocious."

"I don't know about that," Stevie said, facing east over the sea as she slipped her arm around his neck and kissed the top of his head. She was looking toward Scotland; amazing that it was a whole ocean away, and her boat was lying wrecked on Scottish rocks, on an island she'd never even visited.

On the shores where her heart had gone. Stevie hid her eyes, so Henry couldn't see them welling up.

"Press on regardless," he said, holding her hand.

"Aye-aye, Commander."

MADELEINE AND STEVIE were given the best table at Lilly Jane's, at the edge of the terrace. Waves broke on the beach at their feet, and a light breeze misted their faces with salt spray. A waitress handed them menus with a page of cocktails with names like "White Shark Martini" and "Sex on Easton's Beach."

"I hate to let Lilly Jane down," Stevie said. "But I'm just going to have sparkling water."

"So am I," Madeleine said, registering the pleased surprise in Stevie's eyes. "I'm, um, not drinking."

"Really?"

"Yes. I was a little out of control when I visited you at Hubbard's Point. I've been a little out of control for a year." The waitress brought them a big blue bottle of seltzer, and they toasted each other.

"This is wonderful," Stevie said, smiling.

"It is," Madeleine said. They perused the menu, and both ordered grilled tuna. A band played reggae in the bar. Maddie felt so relaxed, filled with a sense of well-being here at the beach with her old friend. They talked in a general way about the summer, carefully skirting around difficult topics. Stevie told about her painting and about her stepcousin's wedding; Madeleine talked about Chris and how he'd started taking piano lessons for the first time. They ate dinner, listening to the music and the waves. The sun began to set, splashing gold and violet on the sea. A pair of young women sat at the table beside them, and one ordered a Sex on the Beach. Madeleine felt a pang, remembering Emma.

"That last vacation we took," she said, "Emma ordered one of those. She said to me, 'Remember when 'sex on the beach' was a way of life, not just a drink?' "

"That sounds like Emma," Stevie said.

"She laughed, said that we'd all lost our virginities on the beach at Hubbard's Point the same summer—when we were seventeen."

Stevie tilted her head. "But I was actually eighteen. And it happened with Kevin, my first husband, at college."

"And I was twenty-one," Madeleine said. "A good

Catholic girl—I waited till I was at least engaged. Even though I never married him."

"I wonder why Emma thought that . . ."

"Well, it was like that full-moon circle ceremony—she liked to think of us as bonded for life. Joined at the hip . . . if not in reality, then at least in a legend of the beach girls," Madeleine said as the waitress came to clear their plates. They ordered coffee and a crème brûlée to share. The music got a little louder, and the breeze picked up.

"Isn't it funny that you, Emma, and I never discovered Newport as teenagers? It's not all that far away . . . but on the other hand, why would we ever want to leave Hubbard's Point?" Madeleine asked.

"That's what . . ." Stevie said, stopping herself short.

"Go ahead—what were you going to say?"

"Well, that's what Nell says. She sounds just like her aunt," Stevie said.

"Are you in touch with her much?"

"I am, actually," Stevie said, and then went on to describe her new book, *The Day the Sea Turned Black*, and how Nell was helping her by sending lots of information about the beaches on Scotland's Orkney Islands. Her forehead was wrinkled, as if she thought Madeleine might be upset that she was in contact with Nell.

"I'm so glad about that. Without her mother, she needs one of us," Madeleine said.

"She needs you," Stevie said quietly.

Madeleine nodded. "I think so, too."

"Jack told me a little about what happened between you and him," Stevie said. "After Emma died."

Madeleine nodded. She breathed deeply, feeling the sea air cool on her skin. She sat tall, gazing into her friend's eyes.

"He thinks that the truth about Emma will ruin everything," Madeleine said. "He wants to keep it sealed up and hidden. It's our family's Pandora's Box."

Stevie brushed the hair out of her eyes, took a sip of coffee. Madeleine knew she was going to ask the question . . . and Madeleine felt almost ready for it.

"What *is* the truth?" Stevie asked.

"She was planning to leave."

Stevie frowned, brushed hair from her eyes. "He told me that, but I don't quite get it—his need to run away and protect Nell. It's sad, but people do leave—marriages do break up."

"This wasn't just the marriage. Emma was going to leave everything. Leave her whole life. Nell, too."

"She couldn't do that—"

"That's what I said, what I thought," Madeleine said, thinking back to the trip, to all those hours on the beach, listening to Emma spill the truth and her feelings.

"She must have meant something very temporary—a week, or even a month—you said she'd never even been away from Nell overnight before that trip."

"No. It wasn't going to be temporary." Madeleine's heart started pounding.

"Jack said she had a secret life."

Madeleine nodded. "She did. He's right."

"Was she having an affair?"

"Not exactly."

"How can you 'not exactly' have an affair?"

"They hadn't slept together," Madeleine said.

"I don't get it," Stevie said. "Who was it?"

"Her priest."

Stevie just stared.

"I know," Madeleine said, seeing the disbelief in Stevie's eyes. "Father Richard Kearsage. He was new to their parish—was very active in getting people involved in the community. He opened Emma's eyes, she said, got her interested in social change. He started a literacy program at the local prison, and Emma claims that helping him completely changed her life—and the way she saw the world."

"But what did that have to do with her leaving Jack?"

"They fell in love."

Stevie looked out to sea. The sun was down now, the waves topped with dark silver as they rolled in toward the beach.

"How could a priest do that to a family?"

"Emma said that priests are human, too. That they had desires just like other men. She seemed to feel almost more guilty about the fact that he was leaving the church to be with her than she was about leaving her family."

"How could she?"

"She was head over heels, Stevie."

"I don't get it!" Stevie said. "Okay—so she was married, and she fell in love with someone else. That's not good, but it happens. Your brother is wonderful, but say, for whatever reason, she couldn't stay with him. What about Nell?"

The questions, and Stevie's vehemence, brought

back memories of Madeleine's own reaction, and of the drive back from the beach to Atlanta. Her hands began to shake, so she clasped them in her lap.

"That's what I said. I couldn't understand it—couldn't believe she'd even consider leaving Nell," Madeleine said. "She was obviously lost in passion for him. She told me that no one had ever known her the way he did. She said he loved and accepted all her faults, her wounds, the things that she hated in herself."

"Give me a break—he's a priest. That's his job! How did he even hear about 'her wounds'? Probably after she went to him for help. You know? I used to do it myself. After I had the miscarriage, I would go to church and cry. One of the priests was so kind. He would sit with me for a whole hour, listening to me talk. I told him such intimate details—but I could never imagine anything more!"

Madeleine nodded. "She and Jack were having troubles. She confided in Father Richard, and he got her involved in his projects. She told me that the world came alive in a new way. Her eyes were glittering, and she seemed . . . as if she might levitate. But it was crazy—she also seemed so grounded. As if she had prayed it through, and had God on her side. As if she and Father Richard had a mission."

"What was their mission?"

"Working to bring literacy to poor areas—but not in Georgia. It couldn't be near Atlanta, because after he left the order, he would be denigrated in the community."

"He should be! For seducing a married woman, getting her to leave her family! I was raised Catholic—we all were. We all know there are good priests and bad priests. I'm sorry, but this guy is horrible."

Madeleine let Stevie rant. It felt good to have someone sharing her outrage. *If only Emma were still alive*, she thought. *Stevie and I could gossip our heads off, full of moral indignation, have a great bitch session, then go kidnap her and deprogram her and convince her to return home.*

"Jack didn't know anything?" Stevie asked.

"He knew that something was wrong. Emma told me that he actually encouraged her to see Father Richard. I guess he thought the priest would help their marriage."

"And instead he abused their trust."

"Yeah—that's how I see it. Emma defended him, though."

"Well, she would," Stevie said. "So would I. Falling in love is like magic. It gets you under its spell, and you're a goner. I know—I've made more mistakes than you can imagine in that condition. But I didn't have a child. . . ."

"That's the part that drove me crazy," Madeleine said. "Thinking of Nell . . ." She wanted to tell Stevie about the last minutes, in the car, when she'd driven off the road. But instead, buying time, she spun back a little.

"There we were, sitting on the beach at St. Simons Island, the way we'd done so many times before. And Emma was looking around, picking apart the resort for being too luxurious, and our bathing suits, for being too expensive. She began talking about poverty in rural Georgia—said that Father Richard had opened her eyes to things she had never seen or thought about before. Families who don't have enough money to make ends meet. Mothers who have to struggle to feed their children. Overcrowding in the prisons, the inhumanity with which the inmates were treated."

"Those are important issues," Stevie said.

"I know. And I was surprised and—at first—pleased to hear Emma talking that way. I mean, Jack would never call her spoiled, but that's what I thought—the way she always needed the biggest car on the block, or wanted to join the most exclusive clubs. She didn't even want us to read your books to Nell because they were too realistic, showed some ugly things about life!"

"I know," Stevie said.

"She stared at her diamond ring glinting in the sun and said, 'People die in diamond mines so rich women like us can wear these.' I told her, 'They're symbols of love—Jack's and Chris's.' And she said, 'If love is true, it doesn't need jewels to prove it.' When she said that, I knew something big was going on. Because for a long time before that, she'd measured how good a birthday or Christmas was by how fancy the jewelry Jack gave her was."

"It sounds as if she was having a transformation," Stevie said.

"I know. And at first I thought it was all positive."

"But it wasn't. . . ."

"She told me she and Father Richard weren't having sex. They had kissed and held each other, but they didn't want to do more till they figured out what they were going to do. He told her that he needed to have a period of 'discernment.' Where he would pray, ask what he should do. He went up into the hills where he'd grown up, all alone for . . . I don't know . . . she made it sound like forty days in the desert. At the end of his time there, he came back and told her he wanted to leave the priesthood to be with her."

"And all she had to do was leave her marriage."

"Yes."

"And Nell."

"It made me crazy, Stevie," Madeleine said. "We were driving home from the beach."

"The day of the accident?"

Madeleine nodded. She heard the waves hitting the beach. Telling this story was so hard, so terrible. But she needed to get it out, needed to have her friend understand. Stevie had known and loved Emma; she obviously adored Nell and Jack.

"I want to tell you," Madeleine said, her voice breaking. "Because I love and trust you. And I need an ally."

"An ally?"

"To help me move forward, to figure out what I have to do to heal things with my brother. And to help him heal, too. He's hurting so badly."

"I know he is," Stevie said, leaning forward to hold Madeleine's hand. She gazed into her eyes, warm and steady. Madeleine left her hand right there, feeling the pressure of Stevie's fingers.

"We were driving back to Atlanta. Emma wanted to show me where Richard had grown up. It was a small country town, in the Georgia hills. Very poor . . . Emma told me that he had taken her there on a drive, to show her the roots of poverty. He'd told her that some of his neighbors had wound up in prison for terrible things.

His own father had gone to jail just for forging a check, and he'd died there—stabbed by another inmate. Richard said that his own family had suffered, and that he'd known that he wanted to do something to help."

"So he became a priest?"

Madeleine nodded. "He must have been the family's pride and joy. He got a scholarship to Loyola University. From there, he went into the priesthood. Went to graduate school at Georgetown, their Program for Justice and Peace. Emma said he was passionate about social justice."

Stevie stared at the candle flame and seemed to shiver.

"What is it?"

"Oh, I was just remembering something my father said to me. When I was little . . . and I'd hide in the reeds, to watch sandpipers build their nests. Or I'd stay out on freezing cold nights to catch sight of an owl flying out of the woods. . . . He told me that I was passionate about birds, and that meant I would be passionate about everything. He told me that I had a fire inside. . . ."

"Which you do."

"He told me I had to learn how to use it—to temper it. I had no idea what he meant then. He told me that studying Irish literature had taught him that passion could destroy as much as it could enliven. He told me he envied what I had, but that it also made him worry about me. . . ." She paused, still staring at the flame as if seeing her own private demons. "Sounds as if Richard had the same fire inside."

"Yes," Maddie said. "But *I* destroyed Emma."

"Don't say that," Stevie said, looking up.

"I did, though. I drove her into a tree."

"Tell me, Maddie," Stevie said. "If you can."

Madeleine nodded. She took a deep breath, remembering all the sessions with Dr. Mallory, all the waves of shock and terror that had passed through her body, at last passed out of it.

"She told me that she had important work to do," Madeleine said. "That she and Richard had a mission too important to ignore. She said that Jack could take care of Nell. That when Nell was old enough, she would understand. Here we were, driving down this rutted dirt road way out in the middle of nowhere . . . past houses with tin roofs, tar-paper walls . . . with broken-down cars and old refrigerators out in the yards . . ."

"Past the house where Richard had grown up poor," Stevie murmured.

Madeleine nodded. "And I was just driving along, feeling that it was all so surreal—and how could Emma not see? So I said to her, 'You're in love with a man whose childhood pain haunts him still, every day.' I wanted her to see, to hear what she was about to do to Nell, to remember that raising her daughter was the most important work in the world."

"She couldn't see," Stevie said. "She was too lost in love."

"Yes, she was. So I told her—that if she left Nell, it would be like killing a part of her. The part that trusted, and loved, and believed. . . . I told her that she and Richard wanted to do something wonderful to help the world, but that they would be destroying one beautiful, trusting little girl."

Stevie's eyes filled, and so did Madeleine's, and for a few seconds Madeleine thought of Nell's pain, and the rift in her family, and how it had started with Emma falling in love, and she had to squeeze her eyes tight to keep from sobbing.

"Emma was furious with me. She told me that she and Richard had prayed about it, were praying about it every day . . . and it wasn't that she was abandoning her daughter—she was going away temporarily . . . that Nell would understand. That she could visit—it would be shared custody, she was sure Jack wouldn't give her any trouble."

"Maybe she didn't know Jack all that well," Stevie said.

"I know. I just turned to her and said I thought he'd give her more trouble than she could ever imagine. And I told her I'd help him—I'd testify for him in divorce court. I told her that she was being selfish, throwing Nell away. And that if she did that, she'd deserve to lose her daughter."

"Throwing Nell away," Stevie whispered hotly, staring at the dark water.

"She went crazy. I guess she thought we'd spent this sisterly time together, bonding about it all—she'd mistaken my quietness, my attempts to be understanding, as acceptance. I think she thought I'd be her ally."

"You were just trying to listen," Stevie said.

"Yes. But that was over—she told me she planned to tell Jack and Nell that night. And that she was moving out the next day. I told her I'd help my brother get sole custody and see that she didn't get a penny in alimony. And the funny thing was, that's what made her go insane. She told me she deserved money after all those years of marriage, and that she needed it to help support what she and Richard were going to do."

"That's ridiculous."

"I know. I was so angry, I must have hit the gas. We were going fast. . . . She yelled at me, that I was just Nell's aunt, didn't have the right to get involved . . . she made it all about Nell, but I know the thing that really pulled the pin was the idea of losing alimony. She said, 'You think you care about her more than I do? She's my daughter!' And then she slapped me so hard—"

"Oh, Maddie," Stevie said, taking her hand.

"Across the face—I saw stars." Madeleine closed her eyes, still feeling the shocking sting of Emma's hand across her cheek and eye. "The next thing I remember, we were upside down—we'd hit a tree and flipped over. My arm . . ."

Stevie squeezed her hand. Madeleine felt the searing sensations in her shoulder, as if it had been sliced, severed with a hot knife. She trembled, but calmed herself by looking into Stevie's eyes.

"My arm was hanging off. The blood was pumping out—my artery was cut through. Emma lay there, against my body. Her eyes were open . . . she was trying to talk, and blood was gurgling in her throat." Madeleine began to cry as she remembered. "I wanted to help her, save her."

"It wasn't your fault, Maddie."

"She just stared up at me—she wanted to live so

badly! I could see the panic in her eyes. She kept saying, 'Tell him I'm sorry . . .' " Madeleine sobbed.

"Who, tell who?"

"That's what I don't know!" Madeleine cried. "Did she mean tell Jack she was sorry for what she was going to do? Or tell Richard she was sorry for getting hurt and ruining their plans?"

"Oh, Maddie . . ."

"And then I passed out. When I woke up, I was in the hospital. Jack was with me . . . Chris was on the way. I was medicated, I'd just been through three surgeries to save my arm—and all I could think of was Emma. I wanted to know if she was all right. And I had to tell Jack about the crisis she was in—so he could stop her, get her back. I wanted him to prevent Father Richard from visiting her. I just thought, if he knew what he was dealing with, he could stop it. He could work to save their marriage, keep Emma from leaving Nell."

"You had to tell him," Stevie said.

"Really? Do you really think so? Because what did it matter, in the end? Emma died! I could have kept her secret and saved my family!" Madeleine sobbed.

"Maddie—it would have torn you up. You didn't know that Emma would die . . . you wanted to help."

"But if I had waited—waited till after the shock of the accident. He refused to believe me. He thought I was making it up. He was just so grief stricken about Emma, so afraid of losing her. He couldn't bear to see her in that terrible light—about to leave him and Nell."

"He was in shock," Stevie said.

"Total shock that's lasted more than a year. Taken

him from Atlanta to Boston to Scotland—he had to leave the country to get away from me!"

"Not from you," Stevie said. "From his own pain."

"If only I had kept Emma's story a secret," Madeleine said. "Then Jack wouldn't have had to face it, carry it."

"It was the truth," Stevie said. "His truth, and Nell's—not just Emma's. Maddie, don't you know that you acted out of love? Love for your brother?"

Madeleine bowed her head, wracked by sobs. The sound of her own blood rushing through her head merged with the crash of the waves on the beach. The tide was advancing, the waves slipping higher over the sands. The reggae band played easy, happy melodies. The sounds came together, surging in such a way that Madeleine barely heard his voice.

"Her idiot brother," he said.

There, not a foot away from their table, stood Jack, tears welling in his eyes too.

"You're here," Stevie gasped.

Madeleine jumped up and threw herself into her brother's arms. She couldn't believe that Jack was here, that he was really here. He held her, rocking her, saying, "I'm sorry, Maddie, I made a mistake, it wasn't your fault." It was the voice she'd grown up with, the voice of her big brother; something in her heart let go, and she cried harder, with relief now.

"Jack," she sobbed.

"Oh, Maddie," he said. "I went to Scotland with Nell because you loved it. But you're not there, and I can't go on without you in our lives."

Madeleine kissed his cheek, but couldn't quite speak. She let go of him, sitting down in her chair and closing her eyes for just a second. In that moment, she heard his voice again.

"You either, Stevie. We can't do this without you," Jack said.

When Madeleine looked up, she saw Stevie and Jack locked in a kiss, arms around each other and hair ruffled in the sea wind. The waves broke on the beach one after another, the steadiest sound in the world. Madeleine listened, feeling her heart beat harder than the waves, knowing that her brother had come home to stay.

chapter 28

ALTHOUGH THE INN WAS FULL, AUNT
Aida found a way to cram everyone in. Since
there was no way Madeleine was driving
home to Providence on the night when she and her
brother were reuniting, she called Chris and told him
she was staying—and for him to come down the next
day dressed for Henry's wedding. She and Nell would
be staying in Stevie's room—an upstairs parlor with
two beds and a Victorian chaise. Henry gave his room
to Jack.

"I don't want to put you out," Jack said.

"I'm going to stay with Doreen," Henry said. "I'd
planned on sneaking over there anyway. No way am I
spending one more night without her, starting now."

"That sounds like a very good idea," Jack said.

Stevie happened to look up as Jack said those words,
and she saw that he was staring straight at her. The
sight sent a quick shiver down her spine. She smiled at
him, and when he smiled back, the tremor started right

up at the top and shot down again. Madeleine's story was reverberating in her mind, but the shock and joy of seeing Jack and Nell momentarily pushed it aside.

Nell had slept on the plane and was now wide awake and raring to go. She clung to her aunt's hand. Stevie saw the rapture in both their faces—and Jack's. Aida sat in the background, smiling with barely contained satisfaction, as if she knew love—all sorts of love—was in the air, and that she had done something to bring it about.

"Were you surprised to see us?" Nell asked, looking up at Maddie.

"More surprised than I've ever been in my life!"

Stevie gazed at Madeleine. She had almost certainly aged since Nell had last seen her. She had been through a sort of war—and it showed in the lines around her eyes, a streak of gray in her brown hair, some extra weight around her hips. But Stevie thought she had never seen her friend more beautiful. She was a veteran who had made it through, surviving on love and faith.

"How about you, Stevie?"

"Me, too," Stevie said. "I still can't believe you're here."

"How did this come to be?" Aunt Aida asked.

"I put a message in a bottle and sent it to Stevie," Nell said, laughing. "But Dad found it."

"Is that true?" Stevie asked.

"It is," Jack said.

Stevie wondered what the message had said. She wondered whether Nell had really thought it would make it all the way across the Atlantic Ocean, through storms and currents, against the tide. Could Nell possibly have believed that could happen? But then Stevie thought of the birds she painted, the heart-stopping courage and tenacity of hummingbirds—birds no larger than a flower, migrating from one continent to another—and she thought, of course! Yes, Nell had expected the message to reach its destination.

And it had. It was right here, in the presence of Jack and Nell herself.

"That's my Nell," Madeleine said.

"She makes things happen, that's for sure," Jack said.

Everyone was tired, and tomorrow would be here before they knew it. So Henry kissed Stevie and Aida, told them he'd see them in the morning. Standing at the foot of the stairs, Jack kissed Nell and his sister goodnight. Stevie saw Madeleine and Nell bubbling over with happiness, and she told herself she wanted to give them a minute.

"I'll be right up," she said.

"Okay," Madeleine said, throwing her a look of total happiness.

When everyone else had gone upstairs, Stevie turned to Jack. They were alone in the lobby—the night clerk had gone home at nine. The room was warmly lit—lamps with fringed peach-silk shades, brass wall sconces, and a shaft of moonlight.

"Let's go outside," Jack said, "and take a walk."

"That sounds good," Stevie said. She was still reeling with Madeleine's story, and with the shock of seeing Jack and Nell. She needed to clear her mind and get her heart into some sort of normal rhythm.

They headed out the door, ran across the wide green lawn. A sturdy fence reached across the property, and they unlatched the gate to step out onto the Cliff Walk. Shining with moonlight, the wave-tossed bay was rough silver. They hadn't gone five steps before Jack grabbed Stevie's hand.

"Why did you really come?" Stevie asked.

"Nell's message," he said.

"What did it say?" she asked.

"I'll tell you," he said. "Only not right now." Instead, he wrapped her in his arms, pulled her hard against his chest, and kissed her. It was a kiss to end all kisses. His mouth was hot and filled her with passion. Her hands gripped his arms—she needed to feel his skin. His body felt hard and strong, and she wanted to press against it all night.

When they broke apart, they continued on in silence, keeping the moonlit bay on their left. The tide was in, the waves crashing on the rocks below. Stevie felt a sense of vertigo that had nothing to do with the cliff's steepness. Jack was holding tight to her hand, but she felt herself falling—she actually had to catch her breath.

"Are you okay?" he asked.

"I am," she said. It was a soaring feeling, as if she had spread her wings, was gliding over the bay. She had always studied birds for her work—their anatomies, their wingspans, the way the air held them aloft—and right now she felt like one of them. This wasn't like other times when she had fallen in love—where she had felt she needed to hold back, when she knew she wanted more than the other person was capable of giving. In flying home from Scotland, Jack had met her more than halfway.

"You're smiling," he said. "I can feel it, even though it's dark."

"I was just thinking about flying," she said.

"What about flying?"

"You don't know how many times I thought about traveling to Scotland, to do research for the book."

"Do you think Nell didn't plan on that?"

"Did she?"

"And do you think I didn't know she was planning it, when I bought her art supplies to send you drawings?"

"But what is it all about?" she asked. She needed to know. "Why are you there? And why am I writing a book about there?"

"It has to do with distance," he said solemnly, as if the statement was completely profound instead of just obvious. With a rush, Stevie realized it was both.

"Is part of it . . . what happened to Emma? Maddie told me the story."

"About the accident?"

"Well, more about what happened before the accident. About Father Kearsage."

"It's been really hard to believe," he said. "She went to him for help—counseling, I guess. I've hated looking at myself in all this. She always told me I needed to communicate better—wanted us to go to a therapist. I always thought people who went to a marriage counselor were one step away from breaking up."

"She wanted you to go see him together?"

"Initially. But I always put her off. I was working hard—traveling for my job, building bridges all over the Northeast. I thought, 'As soon as things settle down, I'll be more available. She'll be happier.' You know?"

Stevie nodded, thinking of the many ways she had stayed in ruts, ignored the real problems in her marriages until it was too late.

"But then he invited her to join this volunteer program he ran. She loved it—and suddenly she was saying she really felt she had a purpose."

"Emma was always such an enthusiastic person," Stevie said. "I can completely see her joining right in."

"I was hurt," he said. "Offended . . . I mean, I thought she already had a purpose—being my wife and Nell's mom."

"She was those things," Stevie said quietly. "But she was also her own person. That must have been the part she needed to bring out."

"Well, Father Richard did that for her," Jack said. "He got her so involved in the world . . ."

"She did that herself," Stevie said. "He can't take credit for it."

"He tried, though," Jack said.

"What do you mean? You talked to him about it?"

"I didn't just talk to him. I went after him—nearly killed him."

Stevie just walked beside him, listening to him open up to her.

"He attended her funeral. I saw him there, but I was still in so much shock, and I wasn't at all ready to believe Madeleine, so I didn't say anything. He didn't officiate or anything—just sat in the back. He gave me this stare, on my way out of the church. I wanted to throw him down—a priest, right there in church, in his collar."

"Why didn't you?" Stevie asked, her own pulse jumping at the idea of that stare.

"Nell," Jack said.

"She was right beside you," Stevie said, picturing herself as a child, walking out of her mother's funeral with her father.

"Yes. So it had to wait. The next few weeks were taken up with . . . God, you can't imagine. Getting Nell through. Easing her back into school, picking her up, sitting with her while she cried. All that."

"I know . . ." Stevie murmured.

"Madeleine was in the hospital, having surgeries on her arm. Chris stayed with us, but as soon as she could be moved, he took her home.

"I heard through the grapevine that Kearsage left the parish. Then I heard that he left the church. I was glad. If he disappeared, I wouldn't have to face anything about Emma."

"It doesn't work that way," Stevie said.

Jack shook his head. "One day I came home from work and found him waiting in his car outside my house."

"Why?"

"He said it was because he loved Emma. He felt guilty, he said—about 'sending' her off on a weekend with Madeleine. She hadn't wanted to go, he said. She'd wanted to tell me she was leaving, and then she was going to meet him."

"What was his purpose in telling you?"

"He went on about 'luminous mysteries.' He wanted to purge his conscience, and he wanted to—see Nell—wanted to know her, because she was half Emma."

"Oh, God."

"I went crazy. I told him he was a pathetic narcissist. That it wasn't enough that he wanted to break up my family, take my daughter's mother away from her—but that now he had the fucking nerve to show up at our house and want to see Nell. I . . . well, I knocked him down. I was in a blind rage—I don't even remember doing it. I just felt my fist in his face, and next thing, I was beating the shit out of him."

"Even he had to know he had it coming," Stevie said, their feet crunching over pebbles on the path, the waves breaking down on the rocks.

"It was pretty bad," Jack said. "Not just because he was a priest, but because I didn't know I had such violence in me. I told him to get in his car, drive away, and never come back. I'm lucky he didn't call the cops on me. The next day, I put in for a transfer to Boston. That was no problem—moving within Structural was always easy. And since most of my projects were based in New England, it made a lot of sense."

"But Maddie," Stevie said quietly. "If Kearsage admitted that what she'd said was true, then why did you have to shut her out?"

They walked in silence for a while. The mansions on the right were getting bigger; Italianate palaces of marble, their tile roofs glowed blood-red in the moonlight. Stevie could feel Jack struggling with her question. She reached for his hand.

"I shut her out because she loved me so much," he said when he could talk. "Because she knew the whole story, and was so completely on my side. I couldn't bear how angry she was at Emma, on my behalf. I wanted to shut it *all* out—to close off everything but Nell. The truth was too devastating—I couldn't take any chance at all that Nell might find it out. She's smart—you know how quick she is. She'd have picked up on Madeleine's bad feelings about Emma in two seconds. I didn't want her losing her memory of her mother."

"I think you underestimate them both," Stevie said.

Jack didn't respond, as they approached Marble House and entered the tunnel beneath Mrs. Vander Gilt's Chinese teahouse. Inside, the darkness was total. They had to walk slowly, holding each other's hand.

"Madeleine would never hurt Nell—she completely honors her love for Emma. And even if that wasn't so, there is nothing, nothing, anyone could ever do to change the way Nell feels about her mother."

"How do you know?" Jack asked.

"Remember how she first found me?" Stevie asked. "She was on a quest—looking for a woman who lived in a blue house. Because that's where her mother's best friend lived. She wasn't really looking for me . . ."

"She was missing her mother," Jack said.

"Yes."

"It may have started out that way," Jack said. "But she's fallen in love with you."

"The feeling's mutual."

They emerged from the tunnel, into almost blinding moonlight. As they strolled along, Stevie thought about how people have to find their own ways to the light. People take as long as they take, and there wasn't any use trying to rush them. As much as she had wanted to push Jack back to his sister, he had to find his way in his own time.

"What are you thinking?" he asked.

"That right now I feel very grown up. Terrible things happen in life, and they're not fair, and we don't ask for them. But once we've stopped reeling from it all, we realize we've grown from it."

"Life shapes us," he said.

"Yes. One little bit at a time."

"What has it shaped you to be?" he asked.

She had to think. They paused to lean on a wall, look out at the great silver expanse of ocean stretching all the way to Scotland. "A woman who trusts herself. Who's getting to know her own heart. And who loves the people in her life very much. How about you?"

"A man who was running as fast as he could from where he most needed to be. And who's making his way back."

Stevie put her arms around his neck and kissed him long and hard. He held her tight, so their hearts were right up against each other. In the mysterious chemistry of love, much of these transformations had happened from a great distance. Her fear had disappeared. His fear was draining away.

Love changes things, she thought. Nell had come to

visit her, and two whole families were transformed. For so long, Stevie had looked to birds—the smallest of creatures—for lessons worth learning, worth painting, worth passing on. Why shouldn't a child, the newest beach girl, turn out to be the wisest of all?

"Should we go back to the inn?" he asked.

"Yes."

"Henry's staying with Doreen. I have my room to myself . . ."

"I was thinking the same thing."

"We can't have all night," he said, his mouth hot against her neck. "Nell will be waiting up for you."

"I can handle that," she whispered, feeling the shiver go down her spine again. They walked along, looking out at the sea. When they got to the tunnel again, it didn't seem as dark as it was before. Stevie thought of how much easier it all was, once you knew that you really *were* coming back out into the light. It was easier to have faith when someone was holding her hand in the darkness, and she knew that he wasn't going to let go.

And neither was she.

WHEN THEY GOT back to the inn, it was nearly midnight. From outside, Jack could see that all the upstairs windows were dark; maybe Nell had fallen asleep after all. Only the porch and lobby lights were still lit. He and Stevie slipped inside, and went quietly upstairs, laughing when the stairs creaked beneath their feet.

Stevie went into her room, to check on Nell. Jack

waited, leaning against his door, all the way at the other end of the hall. He watched her, coming toward him smiling. Shadows played on her face, softening her fine cheekbones, the sharp cut of her hair.

"She's asleep," Stevie whispered. "They both are."

"Good," Jack said, opening his door. "Then they won't notice you're gone."

He put his arms around her, just holding her for a few moments. They rocked back and forth together, and he thought about how he had flown all the way from Scotland, just for this chance. White moonlight slanted through the windows, illuminating the room. He pulled back, to see Stevie's face.

He smoothed her bangs back so that he could look into her eyes. They were violet, mysterious, but glowing with a warmth that cracked his heart. The feeling scared him. He wouldn't admit it out loud, but his heart had been under attack these last few years. He had screwed up so badly, he'd driven his wife into the arms of their priest. How could Jack have loved her so badly? How could he have made such mistakes?

"It's okay," she whispered to him.

"How do you know?" he whispered back.

"I can just tell. Can't you feel it?"

"I feel it so much—that's what worries me."

She laughed. He kissed her. She was so small—her head only came up to the middle of his chest. He always expected her to feel fragile, but she didn't. She felt strong and sexy, full of tensile strength. He kissed her mouth, wanting all of her.

They went to the bed and eased each other down. He

unbuttoned her shirt, kissing her collarbones, feeling the pulse between them, and touching her side, rubbing his hand down her ribs, seeing her nipples harden and darken, and then lowering his mouth to them.

She moaned, and he was crazy with desire. He wanted her body—he'd wanted that ever since he'd seen her on that first morning, diving into the waves when she'd thought she was alone. Perhaps it had been that—her aloneness—that had touched him most, had drawn him to her, made him know that he had to find out, had to know her better, had to see whether she had the answers he needed.

She reached down, unbuttoned his jeans, laughed a little with embarrassment because she couldn't do it with one hand. He helped her, his eyes open—hers, too—thinking how much he wanted this, how wild his desire for her was. Not just for her body, which was beautiful and so sexy it made him dizzy, but for every other bit, for the hidden parts, for whatever it was in her that made him know that she'd been alone, too—in spite of other marriages, other men, in spite of Emma, in spite of their whole histories and dramas and tragedies—that they were somehow here together, alone together, starting from scratch.

Her hand was small, hot where she touched him. She pushed his boxers down his hips, made him harder than he'd ever been. He reached down, the heel of his hand curving up on her hip bones as he slid her black panties down her legs. The last time they had made love was on a raft. They'd been too shipwrecked to figure out how to swim to shore together. But here they were now, on dry land.

She was wet. He entered her, her thighs hot around him. His heart was pumping hard, like water rushing through a channel. She gripped his back, lifting her head from the pillow to kiss his lips. She held on so tight, he'd never felt this close, this physically one, never that he could remember, but he was past thinking, he was just joined with her now, steel on steel, they weren't going anywhere, they were right here, right here . . .

She held on so tight, he felt her chest rise into his, her back arching, spine curved like a bow, pushing her upward, right into him. They came together, crashing into something new. Moonlight spinning, reflecting off the sea down below, her violet eyes luminous under thick black lashes.

"I don't want to let this go," he said, smoothing her bangs off her damp forehead.

"Do you think we could, even if we tried?" she asked.

"What do you mean?"

"This feels bigger than we are. We both tried as hard as we could to push it away and make it not happen."

"Like your sign," he said. "Please Go Away."

"You had one of those, too," she said. "It was bigger than mine. It was a billboard—in neon. I could see it flashing, all the way from Scotland."

"I've made a mess of things in my life."

"So have I," she said.

"I've read all your books," he said. "Night after night, to Nell. They're wonderful. But you know, they upset me. Every last one of them. Because even the god-damn birds are smarter than I am about their lives."

"Me, too," she said. "My characters always know so much more than I do. Even the avian ones. Which tells me . . . since I actually wrote them . . . I must know more than I think."

"That makes sense. I must, too. Considering I'm here right now—instead of three thousand miles away."

"As Aunt Aida would say, we've got a lot of Louis Vuitton between us," Stevie said.

Jack shook his head, not getting it.

"Baggage," she said.

"Yes," he said. "That we do have."

"I guess what really counts," she said, touching his face, "is that we also have something else."

"What?" he asked, really wanting and needing to know.

"Well, each other," she said. "And Nell."

And since that was just so true, there didn't seem to be anything else, for the moment, to say. So they didn't talk at all.

chapter 29

THE WEDDING WAS AT ST. MARY'S, ON
Spring Street. The imposing second-period
Gothic church spire rose above the seaside
town. A vine of red trumpet flowers grew up beside the
front door, as if announcing tidings of hope and joy.

John F. Kennedy and Jacqueline Bouvier had married in the church on September 12, 1953. Doreen
Donnelly had been baptized there, had made her first
communion and confirmation there, and her parents
had had their funerals there.

Henry could barely hold himself together.

"I'm going to lose it, Lulu," he said to Stevie, standing outside on the steps. She and Nell had walked up
from the inn to be with Henry while Aida helped
Doreen get dressed. "You know how much it means to
her to get married here? She's only been waiting for it
her whole life. Doreen and Jackie Kennedy, married at
the same church. I'm going to take one look at her

standing up there with her veil and flowers, and I'm going to turn into a total blubbering fool."

Nell giggled.

"What's so funny, young lady?" he asked.

"Just that you look a certain way in your white uniform, and it seems funny to think of you blubbering."

"You do make a really dashing bridegroom, Commander," Stevie said. She felt incredibly light and happy—standing with Nell, knowing Jack was down at the inn talking to Madeleine, ready to come meet her. They had stayed together almost all the night before, till the sun had started coming up. They'd made love again, and then Stevie had sneaked into her room, to pretend to fall asleep on the sofa.

"What are all those ribbons on your chest?" Nell asked.

"Oh, just a few mementos of life in the Navy," he said.

"He's a highly decorated naval officer," Stevie said, putting her arm around Nell. "He's sailed all around the world, fighting battles."

"That's an ironic way to put it," Henry grumbled, raising one eyebrow at Stevie. "You should talk."

"What's that one?" Nell asked, standing on her tiptoes to point.

Stevie didn't know, so she waited for Henry to say. He seemed to blush—something she was not accustomed to seeing him do. After a few seconds, he said, "It's the Purple Heart," he said.

"What's it for?" Nell asked.

"It's for people wounded in combat," he said.

Stevie stared at him with shock. She had been feeling so ebullient, excited about the wedding, that the words hit her hard.

"What do you mean?" Stevie asked.

"It was off Bahrain, in the last war. I got hit with shrapnel."

"You got shot?" Stevie asked. "Why didn't I know?"

"I didn't tell Aida, because I didn't want to upset her. It was hard enough for her, knowing I was over there. Besides, it wasn't that serious."

"Since when is getting hit with shrapnel not serious?"

"When buddies of mine got killed at the same time."

Stevie was quiet, thinking. She glanced down at Nell, not wanting her to be upset by the conversation. But to her surprise, Nell's gaze was riveted on Henry's face. She stepped forward, getting very close to him.

"Your friends died?"

"They did," he said.

"And you just got hurt, so you thought it didn't really matter?" she asked.

He nodded.

"That's like my mother and my aunt," Nell said. "My aunt just didn't know how to be . . . after my mother died. And we didn't know how to be, either—my father and I. Everyone hurt, but we didn't think we should complain about it . . . or even say anything. Because my mother . . ."

"Because compared to your mother dying, it didn't feel like very much," Henry said.

Nell nodded. Stevie watched them, two of the people she loved most in the world—the seasoned naval officer and the nine-year-old girl, standing on the church steps.

"But it is," Stevie said. "Missing people we love is as bad as it gets."

Just then, Stevie saw Henry undoing a pin on the front of his uniform; she realized that he was unfastening the small bar representing the Purple Heart. Bending down, he pinned it on Nell's dress.

"You're giving it to me? Why?" Nell asked.

"Because you earned it. You're a brave sailor, Nell Kilvert."

"Thank you," she said, touching the bar.

"I wish I had another one to give you," Henry said, raising one eyebrow at Stevie.

"Me?" she asked.

He nodded. "All those shipwrecks over the years, Luocious. You deserve a Purple Heart for surviving them all."

She laughed and blinked away sudden tears, looking up at the church steeple. He was right, in so many ways. Her heart had hurt so badly, she had closed herself off from the world. She had barricaded herself in her beloved cottage, painting and writing love stories about birds. But then the Kilverts had come along.

"The truth is," Henry said. "I don't think you need one. Your heart is in fine shape."

"I know," she said, standing beside Nell. "I think you're right."

"One thing: watch carefully today. I know you've had a few walks down the aisle, but today Doreen and I are going to show you how it's done right. Good things come to those who wait."

"Are you talking about you or me?"

"Both of us, kid," Henry said. "You've got to admit, we've had one hell of a rocky ride. It's about time we found some calm water in a safe harbor."

Jack and Madeleine had let everyone else leave the inn in their cars.

The church was just about twenty minutes away, past Bellevue Avenue and down Memorial Boulevard. They set off quickly, not wanting to be late. The day was brilliant, clear and fine. Jack remembered other September days when he'd walked his sister places—to school, to Goodwin Park, to the tennis courts. The memory of all those years got clearer with every step.

"What do you think it means . . ." he began, just as she said, "How did you come to fly here . . ."

They laughed, and then Madeleine said, "You go first."

"Okay," Jack said. "What do you think it means, that you were right there, sitting with Stevie, just when Nell and I arrived?"

"I have my theories," she said. "But tell me what you think."

He shook his head. "I don't know. I knew I needed to see you both. Henry's wedding was my excuse for flying over now, this weekend—Nell wasn't going to let us not come. We got to the inn, and Aida told us that Stevie was having dinner right on the beach, down below the Cliff Walk. She pointed out the restaurant, and I headed down."

"And we were right there."

Jack nodded. "There you both were."

"When I saw your face, all I could think of was, 'He hates me—he's going to turn around and leave.' " Her voice broke.

"Oh, I don't hate you, Maddie . . . the opposite . . ."

"It's seemed that way," she said. "And for so much of the last year, I've hated myself."

"Why would you feel that way?"

"You're my big brother, Jack. For you to turn against me the way you did, I knew I'd done something terrible. For you not to forgive me means that what happened was unforgivable."

"Couldn't it mean that I was a fool and made a huge mistake?"

"You're my big brother," she repeated, the words so simple and innocent that they pierced Jack straight through.

"I kept thinking over and over—I shouldn't have taken Emma on that trip, I shouldn't have told Jack what she said, no one had to know. . . . I wasn't sure whether you'd stopped speaking to me because Emma told me what she did—or because she died."

"I didn't know myself," Jack said. The uphill climb got a little steeper. Madeleine seemed winded. She'd always been a tender, emotional girl; her heart was huge. And she'd always adored her big brother. He felt that now, and slowed his pace.

"I only wanted to help," Madeleine said. "And look what I did—"

"You did help, Maddie," he said. "You knew Emma

was unhappy, and you wanted to be there for her, give her a chance to talk."

"I took her to the beach," Madeleine said. "Because that's where she was always happiest. I thought, if we could sit on the sand, go for long swims, walk with our feet in salt water . . . I thought that the sea would wash her pain away, and she could get back to how much she loved you."

"That should have been my job," he said.

"You're not excusing her," Madeleine said.

"I don't know," Jack said. "It seems like I might be."

"You can't," Madeleine said. "Because you're forgetting—Nell."

As they got close to the hill's crest, traffic flowed by in both directions. A cool breeze swept up from the harbor. The sidewalk was dappled with shadows from graceful trees overhead. Jack glanced over at Maddie, saw that her breath was coming even faster. He felt her love—for him, for Emma, but especially for Nell. He wished he could take all that had happened back right now, in this instant.

"I'm not forgetting Nell," he said.

"Emma was going to leave . . ."

"You know something?" Jack asked. "She wouldn't have."

Madeleine's eyes widened.

"She might have told you that. She'd gotten swept away with something. But Emma could never have left Nell—not for good. I know that, Maddie. You do, too."

"I thought you had left me for good," Maddie said. A stiff, warm breeze was blowing, rustling the leaves overhead. It was still officially summer, but fall was just around the corner. Jack could hardly hear her voice over the traffic and the wind, so he took a step closer to her and clasped her hand.

"I could never have done that," he said. "You're my sister."

They walked in silence, over the top of the hill. Jack thought of all the walks they'd taken together. There'd been the time she'd gotten her first "C" on a test at school. And the time she'd tripped on the playground, in front of her whole class. The day she'd lost her kitten. The morning of their mother's funeral, going into the church.

"I'm just so glad you're back," she said. "However it happened. Was it . . ."

He waited for her to finish the sentence.

"Was it Stevie?" she asked.

"Stevie made it happen faster," he said. "But it was coming all on its own."

"Stevie really loves Nell," Madeleine said. "And I think . . ."

Jack waited, his heart kicking over for some unknown reason. "What?" he asked.

"She loves you, too."

"That sounds right," he said. "Considering it's mutual."

"So what are you doing in Scotland?" she asked.

"Trying to figure out how quickly I can come back."

"Back?"

He nodded. "I've given my notice at IR. Structural can't rehire me—there's a no-compete clause in the contract I signed. So I'll have some free time, and I thought I'd over-see Aida's castle project."

"Wow, Jack," Madeleine said. "Stevie said her aunt is already eternally grateful to you."

"There's one big problem," Jack said. "Construction is expensive. Even if I donate my services, she'll still have to figure out a way for the foundation to pay all its bills."

Madeleine's gaze sparked, and a smile sprang to her face.

"I know a really good fund-raiser," Jack said. "She's a whiz at development."

"I'm on hiatus from the university," she said.

"So, you're available?"

"Depends on who's asking. For my brother, defi-nitely."

"Then I'm asking."

"Then, definitely!"

The steeple of St. Mary's came into sight. It was dark and graceful against Newport's blue, blue sky. Jack stared at it pointing up to heaven. He thought of the steeple as an arrow, showing him the way to go. Up-ward, toward his dreams. He saw it as a message from Emma—telling him that she was looking down over Nell, that she'd be there whenever their daughter needed her. Jack knew it, as clearly as if she'd whispered in his ear.

STANDING ON the sidewalk outside St. Mary's, Stevie and Nell had kept Henry calm. The scent of flowers wafted from the trumpet vine and planters of late-season petunias—aromatherapy for the nervous groom. When the time came, he'd gone inside to stand by the altar and await his bride. Then the cars bearing Doreen, her matron of honor, and her bridesmaid arrived. Aunt Aida pulled up moments later.

The time had come. Organ music, Bach, wafted through the church doors. Where were Jack and Madeleine? Stevie knew that Nell was getting very nervous. She paced the sidewalk, craning her neck in the direction of the inn. Stevie tried to engage her, discussing the story so far of *The Day the Sea Turned Black*. But Nell couldn't concentrate.

Stevie knew that the child was thinking that perhaps Jack and Maddie had had a fight, or exchanged harsh words, or unleashed all their anger at each other. Nell looked paler by the minute. Her hands clenched and unclenched, and her bottom lip was raw from chewing it.

"Everything's okay, Nell," Stevie said gently.

"But how do you know?" she asked.

"I just know it is," Stevie said. "They're ready to do this."

"But what makes you so sure?" Nell asked with such vehemence that it stopped Stevie short and made her think. She wanted to be very sure before she answered.

Stevie thought about her own life. She had been a hermit, with only Tilly and her work for company. She had poured all her love and passion and delight and adoration of life into the birds she painted, the stories she told. That sign had been by her steps, in her front yard for so long, that vines had entwined around its base. Finches had perched on top. It had been as much a part of her home as her front door, as Tilly's bed, as her easel.

But then one day—seemingly out of the blue—Stevie had been ready to take it down. She couldn't have rushed that action one bit—not by one day, not by one minute.

"Do you know about tulips?" she asked.

"They're pretty flowers," Nell said.

"Yes, they are. And they grow from bulbs."

"I know. I helped my mother plant them in our garden."

"Then you know that you plant them in the fall," Stevie said. "You dig deep holes in the ground, put the bulbs in, and press dirt down tight. They're down in the earth, dormant through the whole winter. Snow falls, and the ground is frozen, covered with fallen leaves. The migratory birds have all gone south."

"The hummingbirds . . ."

"The hummingbirds are far away, where it's warm, and the sun is shining. But that garden, where you've planted the bulbs, is ice cold. The sky is gray, and it seems as if the snow, or cold rain, will never stop falling."

"Winter lasts forever," Nell whispered.

"But that's where we forget," Stevie said. "Winter only seems to last forever. Because just when we've forgotten where we've planted the bulbs, one day the first shoots come up. Right through the dirt, that just a few weeks ago might have been frozen solid."

Nell nodded, listening.

"That's what it's like with your father and aunt," Stevie said.

But even with Bach getting louder, and Doreen and Aida about to go inside the church, Stevie felt her stomach flip. What if she was wrong? What if Jack's anger had been too deep, or Madeleine's hurt too profound?

And just then, Stevie saw them come around the corner, hurrying down Spring Street. As they reached the foot of the stairs, the bridal party entered the church.

Madeleine kissed Nell's head, threw Stevie a brilliant smile, and put Jack's hand into hers.

"From one beach girl to another—take care of my brother," she said, running up the steps.

Stevie stood there with Jack. Nell hovered on the step above them, dancing with excitement. Jack stared into Stevie's eyes—she couldn't look away. That's the thing about faith, she thought. It's so hard to have it when the bulbs are in the ground, when a person hasn't yet come around the corner, when a small hand-painted sign is keeping all visitors at bay.

"Come on, we're going to miss the wedding!" Nell said.

"We wouldn't want to do that," Stevie said.

"Okay, then," Jack said.

They started up the steps. Stevie felt the breeze at her back, coming off Newport harbor, blowing with it swirls of wind from Hubbard's Point, St. Simons beach, and the Orkney Islands. Everything was connected. She knew Emma was right there with Nell, and always had been. Her heart seized with a promise: *I'll take care of them and love them, Emma. . . .* The words were clear as the church bells ringing.

And so was Emma's response.

"Look!" Nell gasped.

Right there, at the trumpet vine of beautiful, plentiful red flowers, each a trumpet blasting out its own mysterious song, were a pair of hummingbirds. They darted in and out of the flowers, drinking the nectar.

Stevie knew they were just birds—they had always been just birds, in spite of all the human traits she gave them in her books. But what did "just birds" mean, except for the heart to stay together, to fly thousands of miles year after year, to keep coming back, to inspire Stevie to go on? A trumpet vine that had grown up around the base of the stone angel on her mother's grave, attracting hummingbirds to keep her company. Stevie remembered Emma telling her to write about it.

"Thank you," Stevie whispered.

"Why are you thanking them?" Nell asked.

Stevie glanced up at Jack. He was smiling, as if he already knew.

"I'll tell you after the wedding," Stevie said.

They took hands—all three of them. Nell was in the middle, gripping as hard as she could, as if she could hold them together for the rest of their lives. Jack gave Stevie a look over the top of Nell's head as he pulled open the heavy door.

And the three of them walked inside.

About the Author

LUANNE RICE is the author of *Beach Girls, Dance with Me, The Perfect Summer, The Secret Hour, True Blue, Safe Harbor, Summer Light, Firefly Beach, Dream Country, Follow the Stars Home*, a *Hallmark Hall of Fame* feature, *Cloud Nine, Home Fires, Secrets of Paris, Stone Heart, Angels All Over Town, Crazy in Love*, which was made into a TNT Network feature movie, and *Blue Moon*, which was made into a CBS television movie. She lives in New York City and Old Lyme, Connecticut. Visit the author's official website at www.luannerice.com.

LUANNE
RICE

THE *NEW YORK TIMES* BESTSELLING AUTHOR OF
BEACH GIRLS

SILVER
BELLS

A Holiday Tale

The enchantment of the holidays meets
with the pure storytelling genius of
Luanne Rice,
as one of our most beloved authors
presents readers with a special gift for
the season and a Christmas classic
in the making:

SILVER BELLS

LUANNE RICE

Watch for it in hardcover in
Fall 2004
wherever books are sold

Please turn the page for a special advance preview

ALL SUMMER LONG THE TREES HAD GROWN TALL and full, roots deep in the rich island soil, branches yearning toward the golden sun. The salt wind had blown in from the east, gilding the pine needles silver. Everyone knew that the best Christmas trees came from the north, with the best of all coming from Nova Scotia, where the stars hung low in the sky. It was said that starlight lodged in the branches, the northern lights charged the needles with magic. Nova Scotia trees were made hardy by the sea and luminous by the stars.

On Cape Breton's Pleasant Bay, in the remote north of Nova Scotia, was a tree farm owned by Christopher Byrne. His family had immigrated to Canada from Ireland when he was a child; they'd answered an ad to work on a Christmas tree farm. It was brutally hard work, and they were very poor, and Christy remembered going to sleep with a gnawing hunger in his belly.

By the time he was twelve, he was six feet tall, growing too fast for the family to afford—and his mother had often sacrificed her own food so her oldest child would have enough to eat. He'd need it to withstand the elements. For the north wind would roar, and Arctic snows would fly, and summer heat would blaze into flash fires, and Christy would work through it all. His mother would ring the dinner bell, to call them home from the field. He loved that sound, for no matter how little they had, his mother would do her best to make sure Christy had more than enough love and almost enough food.

His hunger had made Christy Byrne a fierce worker, and it had given him a wicked drive for success. He saved every penny he made, buying land of his own, using the skills and instincts he'd learned from his father to plant his trees and survive the brutal elements. His mother's love and generosity had made Christy a fine man, and that had made him a good father. He knew he was a good father. It couldn't be in doubt; he had a fire in his heart for his children. So that was why this year, cutting the trees on the mountainside in preparation for going south to sell them, he felt such a storm of hope and confusion.

Every year on the first day of December, Christy drove south to New York City. Hordes of tree salespeople would descend upon the glittering island of Manhattan, from the flatlands of Winnipeg, the snowy forests north of Toronto and east of Quebec, the green woodlands of Vermont and Maine, the lakes of Wisconsin, the lonely peninsulas of Michigan. Their trees would be cut and tied, hauled by flatbed trucks over the brilliant garland bridges spanning the East and Hudson Rivers, offloaded on street corners from Little Italy to Gramercy Park, from Tribeca to Morningside Heights, in the hopes of making a year's worth of income from one month's worth of selling.

A scruffy bunch, the tree salespeople were. Dungarees and Carhartt jackets were their uniform. Some arrived in caravans, like Gypsies, parked their trailers by the curb, and lived out December in the vans' cramped chill. Some would stick a huge illuminated Santa or snowman on the van roof.

When it came to vending Christmas trees, Christy had no peer. He used to travel alone—set up his stand on the corner in Chelsea, string up white lights to show off his trees with their salt-sparkle, and use his silver Irish tongue to sell every last one at top dollar in time to get home on

Christmas Eve—laden with sugarplums, walnuts, fine chocolates, and cheeses from the best Manhattan markets; golden-haired dolls, tin soldiers, silver skates, and Flexible Flyer sleds for Bridget and Danny; soft red wool sweaters and fine cream silk nightgowns for Mary. Why not spend some of the profits on his family? He'd made plenty off the glamorous people of New York City.

He'd go home and tell everyone about it, tell Danny what he had to look forward to. "We'll be partners, you and I," Christy had said. "When you get old enough, you're going to own half this farm. Study up in school, son."

"You're saying it takes book knowledge? To be a farmer?" Mary had asked, laughing. Christy had held in his hurt—she'd never appreciated the skills it took. Her father had done two years of college in Halifax, worked in the front office of a lobster company, and Christy knew she had similar designs for their son.

"That, and instincts," Christy had replied, aware that Danny was listening, wanting him to be proud of his tree-farming heritage. "Running the land takes the best we have—all of it! It's magical work, it is, to make Christmas trees grow out of nothing much more than sun and dirt."

But after Mary's death four years ago, he had had to take the children with him to New York. Danny had been twelve then, and Bridget eight. The school always gave them permission, along with a month's worth of lessons and homework to do while their father hustled the trees. Danny's eyes had just about sprung out of his head, the first time he saw the city: the towers, bridges, fancy stores.

"This is New York City?" he'd asked that first year, mesmerized. "It's so—big, Pa! Like a forest of buildings, all lit up."

"Just don't lose sight of the farm," Christy had warned.

"Never, Pa," Danny had said.

So Christy would rent two rooms at Mrs. Quinn's boardinghouse right there on Ninth Avenue, where he could keep an eye on the trees. A big room for him and Danny, a smaller one for Bridget—he could afford it, because his blue and white spruces, Douglas firs, and Scotch pines were the best, and he could always get the rich New Yorkers to pay half again as much as they would for the trees on other street corners.

Mary used to chide him for his cynical attitude about the wealthy denizens of Manhattan. "Christy, they're paying our way the year round. They've been meeting the mortgage on our land, and they're going to pay for college—if you'll ever let Danny off the farm long enough to go. So don't go putting your mouth on them!"

"Ah, they've got so much money, they don't even notice the air they breathe," Christy said, ignoring her dig. "They don't notice the snow, except to complain that it ruins their expensive shoes. They're so busy rushing to get out of the wind, they forget to feel the sting on their faces, letting them know they're alive."

"Well, you're happy enough to take their dollars," she'd say.

"That I am," Christy would laugh. "Believe me, they've enough so they won't miss it. If I doubled my prices, I'd probably sell out twice as fast—the rich people love to spend their money, and if something costs them a lot, it gives them a reason to swagger."

"You're a scandal, Christy Byrne," Mary would say, shaking her head. "Selling Christmas trees with that kind of a mentality is some kind of a sin, it is. It's going to get you in trouble—mark my words."

Mary's family had been comfortable, and she'd never gone to bed hungry. What did she know? he'd ask himself in the tree fields wet with rain, the short, enchanted Nova

Scotia summers when he'd walk along the crystal-cool streams, feeling the rapture of summer's breeze as he pruned the spruces' golden growth into Christmas tree shapes, calculating the handsome dividends they'd bring.

This year, with the power saws roaring like demons, spitting out wood chips in their vicious, hellish destruction of nature's best, Christy knew that Mary had been right. Last winter, Manhattan—for all the money it had given him over the years, had exacted the greatest price imaginable, interest on all his profits, on what Mary had called his greed, compounded beyond comprehension: New York City had taken his only son.

Three years of city lights had proven too much temptation for the teenage boy. And last Christmas Eve, after a banner season of tree selling, Danny had informed his father he wasn't returning home. He was going to stay in New York—find a job, make his way.

"What do you mean?" Christy had asked.

"Let me go, Pa—I can't talk about it anymore! You don't get it!"

"Staying in New York? Are you mad, Danny?"

Christy grabbed his sleeve, felt Danny pulling away. And that made Christy hold on tighter.

"There's no talking about this," Danny said. "There never was. It's just your way, Pa—the farm. I have something I want to do right now. It's my dream, Pa. And I have to follow it! You've taught me not to waste time talking, when work needs to be done."

Danny was serious, and he was right: Christy had taught him that very thing. Talking took up too much time, where there was a whole farm that needed tending to. Of course, what Danny didn't know was that Christy was afraid of talking. He feared his children asking him questions he didn't know the answers to, telling him things that would stir up his emotions. He loved his kids with passion beyond words.

Now Danny was staring at his father with the resolute, not-to-be-deterred eyes of a dreamer. How could his son have a dream, something that would keep him here, in New York, that Christy knew nothing about? Deep down he knew enough to blame himself—he hadn't exactly been an open listener. But how could he leave Danny alone in this place? It couldn't happen. Christy tightened his grip. Danny broke free.

They'd had a fistfight, right there on the street corner—Christy had scuffled with his own son, and scrambling to hold on to him had torn his jacket—the new down parka he'd bought for Danny at the start of the season. Feathers flying, Danny's elbow accidentally cracking Christy's nose, blood flowing as Christy tried to hold Danny still—if he could only talk to the boy, keep him from running—he could get him to see reason. There they were, struggling on the snowy sidewalk, Bridget screaming for them to stop.

The police were called. Squad cars had converged, sirens blaring. Christy's white lights lay tangled on the sidewalk, illuminating the bloody snow. One cop had grabbed Christy, handcuffed his hands behind his back—and Danny had used that opportunity to escape.

Christy's last glimpse of his boy had been of him illuminated by blue police strobes, dodging through the crowd of gawkers, white goose down spewing from his ripped jacket like a snow squall.

"It's frigid out," Christy had said to the officer booking him at the station. "He's going to be hungry and cold, with his parka ruined."

"That's the Christmas spirit. Maybe you should have thought of that before you beat him up," the cop said. His name was Officer Rip Collins.

Christy was too proud to protest, to spill his true feelings of grief and terror, to a New York police officer. What did the cop know? What did anyone from this brutal, blazing, glittering city know? With all its false light, its temples to greed, its foolish people so easily tricked into paying small fortunes for simple pine trees?

ROR—released on his own recognizance—Christy returned to the boardinghouse. His blood was roaring through his veins—he was hoping against hope that his son would be there. But all he'd found was Bridget, sitting on the bed, her face streaked with tears.

Christy had packed up his daughter and, with the heaviest heart imaginable, gone home to Canada. There was a hearing scheduled for March, but Officer Collins spoke to the ADA in charge, telling him what had really happened. And with Danny nowhere to be found—in spite of Collins and other city cops looking for him—the charge against Christy had been thrown out. Where he should have been relieved, Christy was instead soul-sick; to the New York police and court system, his family had become just another statistic of domestic trouble, and his son had become just one more street kid.

Now, one year later, the pickup was packed and ready for him and his daughter to return to New York. They'd had just one postcard from Danny; of the Brooklyn Bridge, with not a clue in the message about where he was living or how he was really faring. Just the brash words: "I'm doing grand—don't worry about me."

Not a word about missing Christy or Bridget or their thirty acres of fir trees on the edge of the world. The boy had come from magical northern land, inhabited by bald eagles, black bears, red and silver foxes, and great horned owls. He had left it for the urban caverns of New York, populated by players and hustlers. Christy hated the place with a passion, never wanted never to set foot in the city again.

But he knew he had to. Had to set up his trees on the same Chelsea corner, had to string up his lights so they'd set the salt crystals on the trees' needles gleaming and entice the customers, had to cock his smile and throw the charm, had to sell out his evergreens and put money in the bank. But most of all, had to be in the same place he always was, so Danny would know where to find him.

"Come on, Bridget," he shouted up the stairs. She appeared at the top, dragging another huge suitcase behind her.

"What's that?" he asked.

"It's my things, Pa," she said.

"Your things are in the truck, Bridget! We're only going for twenty-four days. What've you got in there?"

"Party clothes, Pa." Her green eyes were shimmering.

Christy stared up at her. She was twelve now, a young lady. She'd curled her pretty brown hair by herself, tied it with a burgundy velvet ribbon she'd found somewhere. What the hell did she think she'd be needing with party clothes? Christy worked all day every day until his trees were sold.

"Bridget," he started.

"Danny's coming back to us, and we're going to take him somewhere special to celebrate."

"Leave the case here. Be a good girl, and let's get going."

"I've seen it on TV, a program about New York City, Pa," she said, the words spilling out as she started to bump the huge suitcase down the stairs. "Fancy places we've never gone to yet. Places Danny would love—palaces, Pa! All with crystal and gold, and with Christmas trees bigger than the oldest ones on our mountain, all covered with garlands and tiny lights. Like a fairyland, honest! Girls having tea with their fathers in places like that, and boys all dressed up with ties, everyone so happy and celebrating the holiday together, Pa."

"That's not how you celebrate a holiday," Christy said gruffly.

"But we have to do something wonderful, when Danny comes back to us!"

"Get in the truck now, Bridget," he said, pointing with force at the front door. She scowled, limping past him under the weight of her case. Reluctantly he lifted it for her, into the compartment behind the seat. They climbed in and slammed the doors.

Christy had warmed up the cab for her, but he didn't suppose she noticed. That's okay, he told himself. One of the ways he measured that he'd been a good provider was that his kids never commented when they were warm enough, or when their stomachs weren't hurting from hunger; they took their comfort for granted, which was just what children should do. Christy wouldn't even try to force Danny come home—he swore it to himself.

He just had to make sure his boy wasn't hungry. And to hear if he'd gotten any closer to his "dream." Looking down the farm's hillside toward the sea, he wondered how any dream could be better than this—this was all Danny's and Bridget's. If he could harness the wind, capture the sunlight, he would. And he would give it to his kids.

THE HOLIDAY SEASON STARTED earlier and earlier every year. Once it had been the day after Thanksgiving—the unofficial day that Manhattan would start to put up decorations. Now, Catherine Tierney thought, it seemed to happen in October—even as the greenmarkets were overflowing with pumpkins and grocery shelves were laden with Halloween candy. The city began to dress in its winter finery, weighting Catherine's soul a little more each day.

All through November Catherine had watched tiny, twinkling white lights appearing in midtown shop windows. Bell-ringing Santas would clang away, standing in front of Lord & Taylor and Macy's as passersby stuffed their cast iron kettles with dollar bills. Salvation Army bands would start playing "Silent Night" and "God Rest Ye Merry, Gentlemen" outside Saks Fifth Avenue to the captive audience of people lined up to see the famous holiday windows. Squeezing past the crowd, Catherine kept her face stoic, so no one could what the carols were doing to her heart.

By the first of December, the city was in full holiday swing. Hotels were filled with shoppers and people in town to see City Ballet's *Nutcracker*, Radio City's Christmas show, Handel's *Messiah*, and, of course, the Rockefeller Center tree. The avenues crept with yellow cabs, and on her way to the subway, Catherine would be jostled by wall-to-wall people inching along in their thick coats.

Catherine Tierney worked as a librarian in a private library owned by the Rheinbeck Corporation. The Rheinbecks had made their fortune in banking, and now real estate; they were philanthropists who supported education and the arts. The library occupied the fifty-fourth floor of the Rheinbeck Building at Fifth Avenue and Fifty-ninth Street, just across the Grand Army Plaza from Central Park.

The Rheinbeck Tower was fantastically gothic, with arched windows, pinnacles, flying buttresses, finials, and gargoyles, rising sixty stories to an ornate green cast stone point. The offices, and Catherine's library, had astonishing views of the park—the eight-hundred-and-forty-three-acre green haven in the city's midst.

The building's façade was lit year round, Paris style, with gold light. For the holidays, the illumination changed to red and green. The spectacular four-story barrel-vaulted lobby accommodated an enormous tree, covered with colored balls and lights. The Byzantine-style mosaics glistened like real gold, and evergreen roping garlanded the frescoed second-floor balconies.

Choirs sang carols in the lobby at lunchtime, a different city school group every day. That afternoon Catherine returned to work with her sandwich, and she paused to listen. The children's voices joined together, sweet and pure.

One little girl in the back row was off-key. Catherine watched her, head thrown back with brown braids hanging down, mouth open wide, singing her heart out. The choir director shot the girl an ice-cold look and a hand signal, and suddenly the girl stopped—her eyes wide with dismay as they flooded with tears. Catherine's stomach churned at the sight. She had to walk away, hurry upstairs, to keep from getting involved—telling the girl to keep singing, berating the director for squashing her spirit. That's what Brian would have done.

The look in that girl's eyes was with Catherine all day. From "Joy to the World" to the shock of being silenced. She felt the child's shame in her own heart, and for the rest of the day found it almost impossible to concentrate on her project—pulling up material from the archives on stone angels and gargoyles on buildings in Manhattan. She couldn't wait to get home and put this day behind her.

At five-thirty Catherine locked up and headed for the subway. She lived in Chelsea. Situated west of Sixth Avenue, roughly between Fourteenth and Twenty-third Streets, that part of town had its own personality. Eighth Avenue was playful, shop and restaurant windows decorated with wreaths of red peppers, Santa in a sleigh drawn by eight flamingos, candles shaped like the Grinch and Betty Lou Who.

The side streets had a nineteenth-century feel, with many Italianate and Greek Revival brownstones set back from the sidewalk, their yards enclosed by ornate wrought iron gates and lit by reproduction gas lamps.

Some residents decorated for the holidays as if Chelsea were still part of the estate of Clement Clark Moore—the author of "A Visit from St. Nicholas"—with English holly, laurel and evergreen roping, Della Robia wreaths, red ribbons, and gold and silver balls. It was so understated that if you didn't want to notice, you didn't have to.

The minute Catherine stepped off the E train at Twenty-third and Eighth, she breathed a sigh of relief. The buildings were low, and she could see the sky. The air was frigid, crystal clear, and so dry that it hurt to draw a breath. She wore stylish boots and a short black wool coat; her knees and toes were cold as she hurried across West Twenty-second Street, on her way home.

At Ninth Avenue she turned south. The Christmas tree man had arrived again—she stopped short when she saw him there; her pulse felt like galloping horses. For a second, she considered crossing the street to avoid having to look him in the eye.

She had witnessed the scene with his son last year—and she had doubted that he would come back. But here he was, just setting up his display of spruce and pine, making the sidewalk smell like a mountain forest. The trees stretched a quarter of the way down the block of small stores—an antiquarian book dealer, two avant-garde clothes designers, a new bakery, a florist, and Chez Liz.

In a brilliant fit of quirkiness possible only in Chelsea,

Lizzie sold hats, which she made, along with hard-to-find poetry books and antique tea sets. When she was in the mood, she would set the mahogany table inside with her Spode and Wedgwood china and serve tea to whoever walked in. Catherine felt so nervous, seeing the man, she dove at Lizzie's door to duck inside. The shop was warmly lit by silk-shaded lamps, but the door was locked—Lizzie and Rose had already left.

"She closed early tonight—left with the little one," the tree man said, leaning against the makeshift rack of raw pine boards, holding numerous wreathes, sprays, and garlands. "I asked her, beautiful as she looked in that black velvet hat with the one peacock feather sticking up, was she going to the theater or opera?"

"Hmm," Catherine said, her palms damp inside her gloves, wanting to get away.

"She told me that she was going to 'the banquet.'"

Catherine hid a smile. Lizzie would say that.

"What I think she'd say to you, if she was here," he said, stamping his feet to keep them warm, his Irish brogue coming out in clouds, "is that you should buy a nice fresh Nova Scotia Christmas tree from me. And a wreath, for your front door. I see you walk by every day, and you look to me like someone who would fancy white spruce . . ."

The man was tall, with broad shoulders under a rugged canvas jacket. His hair was light brown, but even in the dark she could see it was grayer than it had been the year before. He had been warming his hands by a kerosene heater; he stepped closer to Catherine, and after what had happened last year, she leaned sharply back.

"I don't want a white spruce," Catherine said.

"No? Then maybe a hardy blue—"

"Or any other tree," she said. She had had a headache

ever since the carol incident in the lobby, and she just wanted to get home.

"Just look at these needles," he said, brushing a branch with one bare hand. "They're as fresh as they day the trees were cut—they'll never fall. And see how they glisten? That's the Cape Breton salt spray . . . you know, it's said that starlight gets caught in the branches, and . . ."

He paused in the midst of the sentence, trailing off as if he'd forgotten what he was saying or lost the heart for his spiel. Catherine had noticed his blue eyes sparkling during hard sells in the past, but tonight they were as dull as last week's snow. They held her gaze for a moment, then looked down at the ground. She felt her heart pounding as she kept her face neutral so he couldn't read her thoughts.

"Thank you anyway," Catherine said, edging away.

As she walked home, she felt doubly uncomfortable. She was still upset about the little girl, and now she had to face the fact that the tree man would be in her neighborhood till Christmas Eve, and she'd probably have to change her route. She wondered whether his daughter had come with him this year. She hoped his son was somewhere warm. Her nose and fingertips stung with the cold. A December wind blew off the Hudson River, and when she turned right onto West Twentieth Street, she saw little clouds of vapor around the gaslights of Cushman Row.

In spite of the brutal chill, she paused to stare at the penumbra around one flickering lamp. The globe of light might have been due to moisture blowing off the river, forecasting a storm like a ring around the moon. It reminded Catherine of a ghost. It's a harbinger, she thought and hoped as she clenched her freezing hands and walked on.

Chelsea was haunted at Christmas. Or at least one room in one townhouse, in the very middle of Cushman Row.

Like its neighbors—other brick Greek Revivals with tall brownstone steps, pocket-sized yards, and ornate cast-iron railings—the house where Catherine lived had been built in 1840 by Don Alonzo Cushman, a friend of Clement Clark Moore.

Catherine paused, holding onto the iron railing and gazing at the brick house, four stories up to the small attic windows. Leaded glass, encircled by plaster wreathes of laurel leaves, they were one of the house's prettiest, most charming features. The tiny panes of glass gave onto the sky. Strangers walking by often stopped to peer upward at those mysterious little windows.

People always made assumptions about other people's lives. Catherine thought of passing strangers imagining happiness inside. Perhaps they gazed at the pretty townhouse and pictured elegant dinner parties going on inside. They would probably assume it belonged to a loving couple with brilliant children—perhaps their playroom was up in the attic, behind those small wreathed windows.

Why shouldn't they imagine such things? Catherine had herself, at one time. Her eyes on those windows, she felt a cold tingle down her spine. It gripped her as if she were being electrocuted, wouldn't let her move or look away. There were ghosts in the street tonight; she closed her eyes tight, trying to feel the one she loved, beg it to visit her tonight in the attic.

The season was here again. December, once such a source of joy and delight, had become a time of sorrow and pain—Catherine didn't celebrate at all. It brought nothing but sad memories—she wanted to rush through the pre-holiday craziness.

Shaking herself free of the shiver and such thoughts, she ran up the front stairs to close the door behind her and pull the covers over her head.